The Bachelor List

Jane Feather

BANTAM BOOKS

THE BACHELOR LIST
A Bantam Book / February 2004

Published by Bantam Dell
A Division of Random House, Inc.
New York, New York

ISBN 0-553-58618-1

Manufactured in the United States of America
Published simultaneously in Canada

OPM   10 9 8 7 6 5 4 3 2 1

Chapter 1

Constance Duncan nodded at the doorman as he held open the glass doors to Fortnum and Mason. The buzz of voices greeted her from the wide marble expanse of the tearoom, all but drowning the brave strains of the string quartet on the little dais at the rear of the polished dance floor.

She stood for a moment at the threshold of the tearoom until she saw her two sisters sitting at a coveted table beside one of the long windows looking onto Piccadilly. The windows were streaked with rain, however, and offered little view of the street beyond or Burlington House opposite.

Her sister Prudence saw her at the same moment. Constance raised a hand in acknowledgment and hurried between the tables towards them.

"You look like a drowned rat," observed Chastity, the youngest of the three, when Constance reached them.

"Thank you, sweetheart," Constance said, raising an ironic eyebrow. She shook rain off her umbrella and handed it to the morning-coated attendant who had appeared as if by magic. "It's raining cats and dogs."

She unpinned her hat and examined it ruefully. "I think the ostrich feather is ruined . . . At the very least it's going to drip all over everywhere." She handed the hat to the attendant. "You had better take this too. Perhaps it'll dry off in the cloakroom."

"Certainly, Miss Duncan." The attendant received the dripping hat, bowed, and glided away.

Constance pulled out a spindly gilt chair and sat down, spreading out the folds of her damp taffeta skirts. She drew off her kid gloves, smoothed them, and laid them on the table beside her. Her sisters waited patiently until she was comfortably settled.

"Tea, Con?" Prudence lifted the silver teapot.

"No, I think I'll have a shooting sherry," Constance said, turning to the waitress who now stood at the table. "I'm so cold and damp I might just as well be on a grouse moor, even though it is only July. Oh, and toasted tea cakes, please."

The waitress bobbed a curtsy and hurried away.

"Prue and I didn't get caught in the rain at all," Chastity said. "It started just as we arrived." She licked her finger and chased pastry crumbs around her plate. "Do you think we can afford it if I have another one of those delicious millefeuilles, Prue?"

Prudence sighed. "I don't think we'll go bankrupt on your sweet tooth, Chas. It's the least of our worries."

Constance regarded her sister sharply. "What now, Prue? Something new?"

Prudence took off her spectacles and wiped the lenses on her napkin. She held them up to the light, peering shortsightedly. Deciding the smudge had gone she replaced them on the bridge of her long nose. "Jenkins came to me this morning looking even more mournful than usual. Apparently Father has instructed Harpers of Gracechurch Street to lay down a pipe of port for him and replenish his cellar with a dozen cases of a very special Margaux. Mr. Harper sent a very large and very overdue bill to Father with a polite request that it be settled before he filled the new order . . ."

She broke off as the waitress appeared with a silver-lidded salver and a glass of rich dark sherry. The waitress placed them before Constance and lifted the lid on the salver to reveal a fragrantly steaming stack of toasted tea cakes studded with plump raisins and oozing golden butter.

"Those look delicious." Chastity stretched a hand and took one of the tea cakes. "You don't mind, Con?"

"No, be my guest. But I thought you wanted another millefeuille."

"No, I'll just share these, it'll be cheaper." Chastity took a buttery bite and wiped her mouth delicately with a fine linen napkin. "So how did Father react to Mr. Harper's bill, Prue?"

"Guess . . . I'll have a slice of that decadent chocolate cake, please." Prudence leaned back in her chair and pointed to the confection on the cake trolley. "He started thundering around, threatening to take his business away from Harpers . . . *This family's been customers of Harpers of Gracechurch Street for nearly a hundred years* . . ." She took a forkful of cake and carried it to her lips. "The usual diatribe . . . oh, this is *very* good."

"Perhaps I'll have a slice too." Chastity nodded to the waitress. "What about you, Con?"

Constance shook her head and sipped sherry. "This is all the sweetness I need."

"I don't know how you can resist all these luscious goodies," Chastity observed. "But I suppose that's how you stay so slim." She glanced down somewhat complacently at her rounded bosom contained beneath the bodice of a white lace blouse. "Of course, you're a lot taller than I am. That gives you an advantage."

Constance laughed and shook her head. "To revert to the previous topic of money . . . I took some copies of *The Mayfair Lady* to a few newsagents this afternoon and asked if they would display them. Just one or two to start with to see if they would sell."

"This edition?" Prudence reached beneath the table for her capacious handbag and drew out a broadsheet, which she laid on the table.

"If that's the new one." Constance leaned forward to look. "Yes, that's the issue with the article about the new pub licensing laws." She smeared a piece of tea cake in a puddle of butter on her plate and ate it with relish. "I pointed it out to the newsagents as something that their customers might find interesting. You know . . . how they can't drink themselves silly at any hour of the day or night anymore; whether it'll reduce drunkenness and increase productivity and stop men beating their wives. People must have *some* opinions on the subject, wouldn't you think? It's something that will affect your average Londoner."

"Did you get any interest?" Prudence inquired, leafing through the three printed sheets.

"Well, two of them agreed to carry it for a week and display it with the other magazines. We're only charging twopence, after all."

"Twopence a copy won't tow us out of the River Tick," Chastity observed.

"Well, that's just for the man on the street," Prudence pointed out. "We're charging sixpence a copy for Mayfair folk." She gestured eloquently to the elegant, chattering throng of tea drinkers and cake eaters around them. "I managed to persuade half a dozen hairdressers on Regent Street and in Piccadilly to display it on the counter by the till and Chastity laid siege to the modistes and milliners on Bond Street and Oxford Street."

"With some success, I might add." Chastity sat back in her chair and regarded her empty plate somewhat regretfully. "I rather fancy myself as a saleswoman. I was very persuasive from beneath my veil."

"Well, it's a start," Constance said. "But I think we need to offer more...more in the way of services...if we're going to charge for it." She leaned forward over the table, dropping her voice. "I have an idea that might turn out to be really lucrative."

Her sisters leaned forward, elbows on the table, copper-colored heads close together. "You know those cards people put in shop windows," began Constance. "Well, I saw—" She broke off at a pointed cough just behind her.

"Oh, Lord Lucan!" Prudence said, sitting up straight and smiling without too much warmth at the young man who had approached the table. "Good afternoon. We didn't hear you creep up on us."

The visitor blushed crimson. "I...I...Forgive me. I didn't mean to creep up...or interrupt...I just wondered if Miss Chastity would give me this dance." He gestured rather weakly towards the dance floor, where couples were moving to the strains of a leisurely waltz.

"I should be delighted, David." Chastity gave him a radiant smile. "How kind of you to ask me." She stood up as he drew back her chair, then she raised an eyebrow at her sisters. "I won't be long." She went off on Lord Lucan's arm, the emerald green wool of her skirt flowing gracefully with her step.

"Chas is so patient with these poor young men," Prudence said. "They hover around her like wasps at the honey jar and she never shows the slightest irritation. It would drive me insane."

"Our baby sister has a very sweet nature," Constance declared with a half smile. "Unlike us, Prue dear."

"No," Prue agreed. "Positive ogresses, we are. We'd eat 'em alive given half a chance."

"But remember how Mother always used to say that Chas, for all her seemingly amenable disposition, is no one's fool," Constance pointed out.

Prudence made no immediate response and for a moment the two sat in silence, both occupied with their own memories of their mother, who had died three years earlier.

"Do you think she'd turn in her grave at the idea of our making money off of *The Mayfair Lady*?" Constance asked after a while as the strains of the waltz came to an end.

"No . . . she'd applaud it," Prudence said stoutly. "We have to do something to keep this family afloat, and Father's not going to help."

After a little while, Chastity returned to the table on the arm of her partner, whom she dismissed with a sweet smile that was nevertheless firm.

She took her chair again. "So, where were we?"

"Moneymaking plans," Constance said. "I was asking

Prue if she thought Mother would be horrified at the idea of selling *The Mayfair Lady*."

"No, of course she wouldn't be. She'd have done it herself if there'd been any need."

"Not that there would have been. If she was still alive Father wouldn't have thrown his money away on an impulsive gamble." Prudence shook her head in some disgust. "What could have possessed him to invest every sou in some chimerical venture? Who ever heard of a railway line across the Sahara?"

"The Trans-Sahara Railway," said Constance with an involuntary chuckle. "If our situation wasn't so dire, it would be funny."

Prudence was betrayed into a choke of laughter as reluctant as her elder sister's and Chastity tried not to smile but failed miserably. Their mother, Lady Duncan, had instilled in all three of her daughters a frequently inconvenient and always irrepressible sense of humor.

"Don't look now, but my ears are burning," Chastity said casually, picking a fat currant off the salver. "I'd lay any odds we're being earnestly if not salaciously discussed at this moment."

"Who by?" Prudence leaned back in her chair and swept her myopic gaze around the salon.

"Elizabeth Armitage has just sat down with a man I've never seen before."

"Interesting," Constance said. "A stranger on this scene is certainly a rare sighting. Where are they?"

"Behind you, but don't turn around, it'll be too obvious. I know she's talking about us, I can almost read her lips."

"She's such a gossip," Prudence declared.

"There's nothing wrong with gossip," Constance responded. "I write it all the time." She gestured to the broadsheet still lying on the table. "Look at the column I wrote on Page 2 about Patsy Maguire's wedding."

"That's not real gossip," Chastity said. "That's just Society chitchat. Everyone loves that. It's not malicious."

"I could imagine writing something malicious if I thought it would serve a useful purpose," Constance said thoughtfully. "Mother was all in favor of exposing people's hypocrisy if she believed it would do some good."

"Then it wouldn't be simply malicious gossip," Chastity stated. "But I wish I knew what Elizabeth is saying about us. I must say, that man is an attractive specimen. Far too attractive to be gossiping with Lady Armitage. Let me see if I can disconcert them." She propped her elbow on the table, rested her chin on her palm, and gazed steadily and serenely across the room at the table where an angular lady in her middle years was discoursing with a tall man whose hair waved luxuriantly across a broad forehead.

"Chas, you're so bad," Prudence said even as she imitated her sister's elbow-propped pose and steady stare. Constance, whose back was to Lady Armitage and her companion, could only hide a grin and wait for a report.

"Ah, that got to her. She's looking through her handbag," Chastity said with satisfaction. "And he's gazing around the room everywhere but here. He seems to be taking an inordinate interest in the dance floor. Perhaps he likes to tango."

Constance could resist it no longer. She dropped her napkin to the floor, bent to pick it up, and as she did so, turned as casually as she could to look over her shoulder.

"Oh, you're right. A very handsome specimen," she said. "Distinguished-looking, I would have said."

"Bit arrogant, *I* would have said," added Prudence. "I suppose we should stop by the table on our way out?"

Constance nodded solemnly. "It would only be polite. Elizabeth is a family friend, after all." She raised a hand towards the waitress and signaled for the bill.

"But you haven't told us what your other idea is," Prudence reminded her.

"Oh, I'll tell you while we dress for dinner." Constance picked up the copy of *The Mayfair Lady,* smoothing the sheets with her flat palm, while Prudence counted coins onto the table.

The three women rose as one, gathering gloves, scarves, and handbags, then they strolled together through the tables, greeting occupants with a smile or a bow, pausing to exchange a word here and there. In this manner they arrived at the table occupied by Lady Elizabeth Armitage and her mysterious companion.

"Elizabeth, how are you?" Constance bowed politely. "Terrible weather for the middle of summer, isn't it?"

"Yes, indeed, terrible. How are you all, my dears? You look charming." Lady Armitage had recovered her poise and greeted the younger women with a dowager's smile. "You're out of half mourning now."

"Lavender and dove gray grew a little boring," Constance said. "And Mother was never a stickler."

"No, indeed. Poor woman." Lady Armitage allowed a small sympathetic sigh to escape her, then remembering her companion, turned in her chair.

"My dears, allow me to introduce Max Ensor. He just won the by-election for Southwold and is newly arrived to take his seat in Parliament. His sister is a dear friend of mine. Lady Graham...so charming. I'm sure you're all acquainted with her. Mr. Ensor, may I present the Honorable Misses Duncan." She waved a hand between the gentleman, who had risen to his feet, and the ladies.

He was taller than she had expected, Constance thought, and his rather powerful frame was set off to great advantage by the formality of his black frock coat, black waistcoat, and gray striped trousers. She found the contrast between his silver-threaded black hair and his vivid blue eyes set beneath arched black eyebrows most striking. "Constance Duncan, Mr. Ensor," she said. "My sisters, Prudence and Chastity." She smiled. "We are certainly acquainted with Lady Graham. Do you stay with her at present?"

Max Ensor bowed in both greeting and assent. "Until I can find a suitable house in Westminster, within hearing of the division bell, Miss Duncan." His voice was surprisingly soft, very rich and dark, emerging from such a powerful body.

"Of course, very important," Constance agreed with a knowledgeable nod. "You couldn't risk missing an important vote."

"Quite so." His eyes sharpened as he wondered if he had heard a slight hint of mockery behind the apparently solemn agreement. Was she making fun of him? He decided he had to have been mistaken; a man's devotion to duty was hardly cause for ridicule.

"Do sit down again, Mr. Ensor," Chastity said. "We only stopped for a minute to greet Elizabeth. We have to be on our way."

The gentleman smiled, but remained on his feet, his gaze still sharp.

"Have you ever seen this publication, Elizabeth?"

Constance laid the copy of *The Mayfair Lady* on the table.

"Oh, it's a dreadful thing!" Lady Armitage exclaimed. "Lord Armitage won't let it in the house. Where did you get it?" She reached a hand towards it with an eagerness she couldn't disguise, although her mouth remained in a moue of distaste.

"In Elise's Salon on Regent Street," Chastity responded promptly. "She had three copies on sale."

"And I saw several in Helene's," Prudence put in. "She had the most delicious straw bonnet in the window. I couldn't resist going in to try it. Quite impractical in this rain, of course. But there were copies of the broadsheet right there."

"For sale?" exclaimed Lady Armitage. "It was never for sale before."

"No, but I think there's more in it now," Constance said thoughtfully. "Some of the articles are really quite interesting. There's something in here about the Maguire wedding that you might enjoy."

"Oh, really, well, I . . ." Lady Armitage's hand hovered over the sheets. "Perhaps I could just take a peek."

"Keep it," Constance said with an airy gesture. "I've read it already."

"Oh, how charming of you, my dear, but I couldn't possibly take it home. Ambrose would have a fit." She folded the sheets carefully during this protestation.

"Leave it in the retiring room when you've finished with it," Prudence suggested casually. "No one need know you'd read it."

"Oh, I shall tear it up and throw it away," Elizabeth declared, deftly tucking the sheets into her handbag. "Such a scandalous rag, it is."

"Quite so," murmured Chastity with a tiny smile. "The Maguire article is on Page 2. We'll see you at the Beekmans' soirée this evening. They have an opera singer, I understand. From Milan, I believe."

"Oh, yes, I shall be there. It's not dear Armitage's cup of tea, but I do so adore singing. So charming." Elizabeth patted her throat as if preparing to break into an aria.

The sisters smiled, murmured their farewells to the Member of Parliament for Southwold, bowed again in unison, and left the salon, their heels clicking on the marble floors.

"How are we going to make any money if you give the broadsheet away?" Prudence demanded as they waited for Constance's hat and umbrella.

"It's one way to create demand," Constance pointed out, regarding her somewhat sad-looking hat with a grimace. "I knew the feather would be ruined." She peered into the mirror as she adjusted the pins. "Perhaps I can replace the feather and keep the hat. What d'you think, Prue?"

Prudence was diverted by the question that appealed to her highly developed fashion sense. "Silk flowers," she said. "Helene has some lovely ones. We'll go there tomorrow. Then we can see if she's sold any *Mayfair Lady*s."

"So what did you think of the Right Honorable Gentleman, then?" Constance inquired as they went out onto Piccadilly. She laid gentle stress on Max Ensor's official title as a Member of Parliament. It had stopped raining and the pavements glistened under the feeble rays of the late-afternoon sun.

"Certainly distinguished, and quite possibly pompous," Chastity pronounced. "We're bound to meet him if he's Letitia Graham's brother."

"Mmm," murmured Constance, looking up and down the street for a hackney cab. She raised her umbrella and a carriage clattered to the roadside beside them, the horses' wet flanks steaming in the now muggy summer air. "Ten Manchester Square, cabby," she instructed the coachman as she climbed in, her sisters following.

If Prudence and Chastity noticed their sister's reluctance to impart her own impressions of Max Ensor, they said nothing.

Max Ensor gazed thoughtfully after the three sisters as they left Fortnum and Mason. He was convinced now that not only he but also Elizabeth Armitage had been exposed to a degree of gentle mockery. He wondered if Elizabeth had noticed it. Somehow he doubted it. It had been so subtle, he'd almost missed it himself. Just a hint in the voice, a gleam in the eye.

They were a good-looking trio. Redheads, all three of them, but with subtle variations in the shade that moved from the russet of autumn leaves to cinnamon, and in the case of the one he guessed was the youngest, a most decisive red. All green-eyed too, but again of different shades. He thought the eldest one, Constance, with her russet hair and darkest green eyes was the most striking of the three, but perhaps that was because she was the tallest. Either way, there was something about all three of them that piqued his interest.

"Are they Lord Duncan's daughters?" he inquired.

"Yes, their mother died about three years ago." Elizabeth gave a sympathetic sigh. "So hard for them, poor girls. You'd think they'd all be married by now.

Constance must be all of twenty-eight, and I know she's had more than one offer."

Tiny frown lines appeared between her well-plucked brows. "In fact, I seem to remember a young man a few years ago...some dreadful tragedy. I believe he was killed in the war...at Mafeking or one of those unpronounceable places." She shook her head, briskly dismissing the entire African continent and all its confusions.

"As for Chastity," she continued, happy to return to more solid ground. "Well, she must be twenty-six, and she has more suitors than one can count."

Elizabeth leaned forward, her voice at a conspiratorial volume. "But they took their mother's death very hard, poor girls." She tutted sorrowfully. "It was very sudden. All over in a matter of weeks. Cancer," she added. "She just faded away." She shook her head again and took a cream-laden bite of hazelnut gâteau.

Max Ensor sipped his tea. "I'm slightly acquainted with the baron. He takes his seat most days in the House of Lords."

"Oh, Lord Duncan's most conscientious, I'm sure. Charming man, quite charming. But I can't help feeling he's not doing a father's duty." Elizabeth dabbed delicately at her rouged mouth with her napkin. "He should insist they marry—well, Constance and Chastity certainly. He can't have three old maids in the family. Prudence is a little different. I'm sure she would be content to stay and look after her father. Such a sensible girl...such a pity about the spectacles. They do make a woman look so dull."

Dull was not a word Max Ensor, on first acquaintance, would have applied to any one of the three Duncan sisters. And behind her thick lenses he seemed to recall that Miss Prudence had a pair of extremely light and lively green eyes.

He gave a noncommittal nod and asked, "May I see that broadsheet, ma'am?"

"It's quite scandalous." Elizabeth opened her bag again. She lowered her voice. "Of course, everyone's reading it, but no one admits it. I'm sure even Letitia reads it sometimes." She pushed the folded sheets across the table surreptitiously beneath her flattened palm.

Max Ensor doubted that his sister, Letitia, read anything other than the handwritten menu sheets presented to her each morning by her cook, but he kept the observation to himself and unfolded the papers.

The broadsheet was competently printed although he doubted it had been through a major press. The paper was cheap and flimsy and the layout without artistry. He glanced at the table of contents listed at the left-hand side of the top page. His eyebrows lifted. There were two political articles listed, one on the new public house licensing laws and the other on the new twenty-mile-an-hour speed limit for motorcars. Hardly topics to appeal to Mayfair ladies of the Elizabeth Armitage or Letitia Graham ilk, and yet judging by its bold title, the broadsheet was addressing just such a readership.

His eye was caught by a boxed headline in black type, bolder than any other on the front page. It was a headline in the form of a statement and a question and stood alone in its box, jumping out at the reader with an urgent immediacy. WOMEN TAXPAYERS DEMAND THE VOTE. WILL THE LIBERAL GOVERNMENT GIVE WOMEN TAXPAYERS THE VOTE?

"It seems this paper has more on its mind than gossip

and fashion," he observed, tapping a finger against the headline.

"Oh, that, yes. They're always writing about this suffrage business," Elizabeth said. "So boring. But every edition has something just like that in a box on the front page. I don't take any notice. Most of us don't."

Max frowned. *Just who was responsible for this paper?* Was it a forum for the women troublemakers who were growing daily more intransigent as they pestered the government with their demand for the vote? The rest of the topics in the paper were more to be expected: an article about the American illustrator Charles Dana Gibson and his idealized drawings of the perfect woman, the Gibson girl; a description of a Society wedding and who attended; a list of coming social events. He glanced idly at the Gibson article, blinked, and began to read. He had expected to see earnest advice to follow the prevailing fashion in order to achieve Gibson-girl perfection, instead he found himself reading an intelligent criticism of women's slavish following of fashions that were almost always dictated by men.

He looked up. "Who writes this?"

"Oh, no one knows," Elizabeth said, reaching out eagerly to take back her prize. "That's what makes it so interesting, of course. It's been around for at least ten years, then there was a short period when it didn't appear, but now it's back and it has a lot more in it."

She folded the sheets again. "Such a nuisance that one has to buy it now. Before, there were always copies just lying around in the cloakrooms and on hall tables. But it didn't have quite so many interesting things in it then. It was mostly just the boring political stuff. Women voting and that Property Act business. I don't understand any of it. Dear Ambrose takes care of such things." She gave a little trill of laughter as she tucked the sheets back into her handbag. "Not a suitable subject for ladies."

"No, indeed," Max Ensor agreed with a firm nod. "There's trouble enough in the world without women involving themselves in issues that don't concern them."

"Just what dear Ambrose says." Elizabeth's smile was complacent as she put her hands to her head to check the set of her black taffeta hat from which descended a cascade of white plumes.

She glanced at the little enameled fob watch pinned to her lapel and exclaimed, "Oh, my goodness me, is that the time? I really must be going. Such a charming tea. Thank you so much, Mr. Ensor."

"The pleasure was all mine, Lady Armitage. I trust I shall see you this evening at the Beekmans' soirée. Letitia has commandeered my escort." He rose and bowed, handing her her gloves.

"It will be a charming evening, I'm sure," Elizabeth declared, smoothing her gloves over her fingers. "Everything is so very charming in London at the moment. Don't you find it so?"

"Uh . . . charming," he agreed. He remained on his feet until she had billowed away, then called for the bill, reflecting that *charming* had to be the most overworked adjective in a Mayfair lady's vocabulary. Letitia used it to describe everything from her young daughter's hair ribbons to the coals in the fireplace and he'd lost count of the number of times it had dropped from Elizabeth Armitage's lips in the last hour.

However, he would swear that not one of the Honorable Misses Duncan had used it.

Women taxpayers demand the vote.

It would be both interesting and enlightening to discover who was behind that newspaper, he reflected, collecting his hat. The government was doing everything in its power to minimize the influence of the fanatical group of headstrong women, and a few foolish men, who were pressing for women's suffrage. But it was hard to control a movement when it went underground, and the true subversives were notoriously difficult to uncover. Unless he was much mistaken, this newspaper directed at the women of Mayfair was as subversive in its intended influence as any publication he'd seen. It would definitely be in the government's interest to draw its teeth. There were a variety of ways of doing that once its editors and writers were identified. And how difficult could it be to uncover them?

Max Ensor went out into the muggy afternoon, whistling thoughtfully between his teeth as he made his way to Westminster.

Chapter 2

"So what was this plan of yours, Con?" Prudence poured sherry from the cut-glass decanter on her dressing table into three glasses and handed two of them to her sisters before sitting down in front of the mirror. Her bedroom windows stood open to let in a slight breeze that refreshed the damp air of the long summer evening, and the shouts of children and the thud of cricket ball on bat drifted up from the square garden.

Constance was repairing the torn lace edging to her evening gloves, setting tiny stitches into the cream silk. She didn't reply until she'd tied the end of the thread and bitten it off. "That'll have to do," she observed, holding the glove up to the light. "I'm afraid these have seen better days."

"You could borrow my spare pair," Chastity offered from her perch on the worn velvet cushion of a window seat. "They were Mother's, so they really belong to all of us."

Constance shook her head. "No, these have a few more evenings left in them." She laid them down beside her on the bed coverlet. "Do you remember, I was talking about those cards you see in newsagents' windows? People advertising things to sell, puppies or chests of drawers . . . those kinds of thing."

Prudence swiveled on the dresser stool, a powder puff in her hand. "And?" she prompted.

"Well, I went into two newsagents on Baker Street this morning and they each had cards on their doors. Not the usual advertisements but people wanting people."

Chastity wrinkled her forehead. "I don't follow."

"The first one had a card from a man wanting to find a woman. A widow preferably, he said, around forty with or without children, who wanted to find companionship and security in her later years and would be willing to keep house and see to his creature comforts in exchange . . . I'm not quite sure what the latter would embrace," she added with a grin.

"Anyway," she continued, seeing her sisters' continued puzzlement, "the second one, in the next newsagent's, was—"

"Oh, I see it!" Chastity interrupted. "A woman who fit the bill, asking for her own companion."

"Precisely." Constance sipped her sherry. "Well, I couldn't resist, of course. There were these two separate cards in two separate windows and never the twain would meet unless someone did something about it."

"What *did* you do?" Prudence dabbed the powder puff on the bridge of her nose where her glasses had pinched the skin.

"Copied each one of them and paired 'em up, so both newsagents now carry both cards. When the advertisers go to check on their cards, that's what they'll see." She chuckled. "They can take it from there, I think."

"I agree you've done your good deed for the day," Prudence said. "But I don't see the relevance to our own somewhat dismal affairs."

"Don't you think people might pay for a service that puts them in touch with the right mate?" Constance's dark green eyes darted between her sisters, assessing their reactions.

"You mean like a *matchmaker*?" Chastity crossed and uncrossed her neat ankles, a habit she had when she was thinking.

Constance shrugged. "I suppose so. But I thought more like a go-between. Someone who facilitates meetings, carries messages, that sort of thing. Like what I did this morning."

"And we'd charge for this service?" Prudence caught up her long russet hair and twisted it into a knot on top of her head.

"Yes. I thought we could advertise in *The Mayfair Lady*, have a poste restante address to preserve privacy—"

"Not to mention our anonymity," Chastity put in, going over to help Prudence with her hair.

"Yes, of course."

"It's certainly an original idea," Prudence said thoughtfully, holding up tortoiseshell hairpins for her sister. "I vote we give it a try."

"Me too," Chastity agreed. "I'm going to take the next issue to the printer tomorrow. I'll add the advertisement to the back page. Do you think that's the right spot?" She teased a long ringlet out of her sister's elaborately piled hair and stood gazing intently at her handiwork in the mirror.

"I think it should go on the front page," Constance

stated. "At least for the first couple of times. Just to draw the most attention. What should we call the service? Something eye-catching." She frowned in thought, tapping her lips with a fingertip.

"What's wrong with 'Go-Between'?" asked Chastity. "Since that's what we're offering."

"Nothing wrong with it at all. What d'you think, Prue?"

"I like it." Prudence turned her head this way and that to get the full effect of her sister's hairdressing efforts. "You're so good with hair, Chas."

"Perhaps I should open a salon." Chastity grinned. "Where's the curling iron? You need to touch up your side ringlets."

"Oh, I have it." Constance stood up. "In my room. I'll fetch it." She paused on her way out to examine her own reflection in the long swing mirror by the door. Her evening gown of cream silk chiffon fell in rich folds, the hemline brushing her bronze kid shoes. Her bare shoulders rose from the low neckline edged in coffee lace and a broad satin ribbon of the same color spanned an enviably small waist that owed nothing to the restrictions of whalebone.

"I think the coffee ribbon and lace really do transform this gown," she said. "I almost don't recognize it myself and this is its third season."

"It doesn't seem to matter what you wear, you always look so elegant," Chastity observed. "You could be in rags and heads would still turn."

"Flattery will get you everywhere." Constance whisked out of the room in search of the curling iron.

"It's true," Chastity said.

"Yes, but part of Con's charm is that she doesn't seem

to notice it. Once she's dressed and checked herself she never looks in a mirror again for the entire evening." Prudence put on her glasses and peered at her own reflection. She licked her finger and dampened her eyebrows. "I wonder if Max Ensor will be at the Beekmans' this evening."

"Why would you wonder that?" Chastity was curious; her sister rarely made purposeless remarks.

"No reason, really." Prudence shrugged. "But Con is looking particularly lovely this evening."

"You don't think she was attracted to him, surely?"

"He *is* an attractive man with that silvery dark hair and those blue eyes. You must admit he commands attention."

"Well, yes, but Con hasn't been seriously interested in any man since Douglas died. She amuses herself a little but her heart's not in it." A frown crossed Chastity's countenance, a shadow of sorrow that was mirrored in her sister's eyes.

"Surely she can't grieve forever," Prudence said after a minute. "She doesn't show her grief at all, not anymore, but it's still there deep down. It's as if she believes no other man could measure up to Douglas."

"When I look around at who's on offer, I tend to agree with her," Chastity observed with unusual tartness.

Prudence laughed slightly. "You have a point. But I just felt some stirring in the air this afternoon around Mr. Ensor."

"Oh, that was just because Con loves teasing Elizabeth Armitage."

"Yes, probably," Prudence agreed, although the tiny frown remained in her eyes. "Dear Elizabeth, such a *charming* woman."

Chastity laughed at this remarkably accurate imitation of the lady's fulsomeness and let the subject of Max Ensor drop. "Is Father dining in this evening?" she inquired. "I'm sure we won't see him at the Beekmans'. Opera singers are not quite in his style."

"The ones who go to Mayfair soirées, you mean," Prudence responded with a judicious nod of her head. "I'm sure the more euphemistic opera singers are very much in his style."

Chastity raised an eyebrow at this caustic comment. "He is what he is," she said pacifically.

"Who is?" This from Constance, who had just returned with the curling iron. "Oh, you mean Father."

"Prue was accusing him of dancing attendance on opera singers."

"I'm sure he does. Mother wouldn't begrudge it, he's been a widower for three years." She set the curling iron onto the trivet over the small fire in the grate, lit for just this purpose, although it also helped to keep at bay the residual dampness in the air from the afternoon's downpour.

"I don't begrudge him anything but what it costs," Prudence said with the same acidity. "We go without new gowns while some opera singer or whatever she is wears the latest fashions and is all hung about with jewelry."

"Oh, come on, Prue. You don't know that," Chastity chided.

"Oh, don't I?" her sister said darkly. "There was a bill from Penhaligon's the other morning for a bottle of perfume from the House of Worth, and I don't smell it on any of us."

"Ask him about it at dinner, if he's in," Constance suggested. "See what he says."

"Oh, no, not I." Prudence shook her head vigorously. "I'm not risking one of his tantrums. You know how he resents any suggestion that I might be looking over his bills."

"I don't mind the shouting so much." Chastity took up the now hot iron and twisted her sister's ringlets around it. The smell of singeing hair rose momentarily. "I can't bear it when he looks sad and reproachful, and starts talking about *your dear mother,* and how she never would have dreamed of questioning his actions let alone his expenses." She set down the curling iron.

"Quite," Prudence agreed. "You can ask him if you like, Con, but don't expect me to back you up. It's all right for me to manage the household accounts, but to pry into his own personal business? Oh, no!"

"I shall be silent as the grave," Constance assured. "Are we ready?" She went to the door.

As they descended the wide curving staircase to the marble-floored hall the stately figure of Jenkins the butler emerged from the shadows as if he'd been waiting for them. "Miss Prue, may I have a word?" He stepped back into the gloom beneath the curve of the stairs.

"Yes, of course." They moved towards him into the shadows. "Trouble, Jenkins?" asked Constance.

"His lordship, miss. It's the wine for tonight."

Jenkins pulled at his long, pointed chin. He was a tall, very thin man with a rather spectral appearance enhanced by his pale face, his black garments, and the shadows in which he stood. "Lord Duncan ordered two bottles of the '94 Saint-Estèphe to be brought up for dinner tonight."

"And of course there's none in the cellar," Constance said with a sigh.

"Exactly, Miss Con. We ran out some months ago and Lord Duncan instructed me to order replacements..." He spread out his hands palms up in a gesture of helplessness. "The price of a case is astronomical now, miss. When Lord Duncan bought the original to lay down it was quite inexpensive, but now that it's drinkable it's quite another matter." He shook his head mournfully. "I didn't even attempt to put in an order to Harpers. I hoped his lordship would forget about it."

"A fond hope," Constance said. "Father has the memory of an elephant."

"Couldn't you substitute another wine? Decant it so he can't see the label," Chastity suggested, and then answered her own question. "No, of course not. He'd recognize it right away."

"Why don't we tell him that Harpers didn't have any more of that vintage but you forgot to mention it earlier?" Prudence suggested. "What could you substitute for tonight that would console him?"

"I brought up two bottles of a '98 claret that would go particularly well with Mrs. Hudson's chicken fricassee," Jenkins said. "But I didn't want to mention it to his lordship until I'd discussed it with you."

"Forewarned is forearmed," Constance said with a grimace. "We'll tell him ourselves. We can say that you mentioned it to us."

"Thank you, Miss Con." Jenkins looked visibly relieved. "I believe his lordship is already in the drawing room. I'll bring in the sherry."

The sisters moved out of the shadows and crossed the hall to the great double doors that led into the drawing room at the rear of the house. It was a delightful room, its elegance only faintly diminished by the worn carpets on the oak floor, the shabby chintz of the furniture, and the shiny patches on the heavy velvet curtains.

The long windows stood open onto a wide terrace with a low stone parapet that ran the width of the house and looked over a small, neat flower garden, glistening now with the afternoon's raindrops. The redbrick wall that enclosed the garden glowed rosy and warm beneath the last rays of the evening sun. Beyond the wall the hum of the city buzzed gently.

Lord Duncan stood before the marble-pillared fireplace, his hands clasped at his back. His evening dress was as always immaculate, his white waistcoat gleaming, the edges of his stiffened shirtfront exquisitely pleated, the high starched collar lifting his rather heavy chin over the white tie. He greeted his daughters with a smile and a courteous bow of his head.

"Good evening, my dears. I thought I would dine in tonight. Shall we take our sherry on the terrace? It's a lovely evening after the rain this afternoon."

"Yes, I got caught in it," Constance said, kissing her father's cheek before stepping aside so that her sisters could perform the same greeting. "I was drenched when I got to Fortnum's."

"Did you have tea?" Arthur Duncan inquired with another benign smile. "Cream cakes, I'm sure."

"Oh, Chas had the cream cakes," Constance said.

"And Prue," Chastity exclaimed. "I wasn't alone in indulgence."

"Well, you all look quite handsome tonight," their father observed, moving towards the open windows just as the butler entered the room. Jenkins raised an inquiring eyebrow at Constance.

"Oh, we ran into Jenkins in the hall," she said swiftly. "He was concerned because he'd forgotten to mention that Harpers has no more supplies of the wine you wanted him to bring up for tonight."

Prudence stepped out onto the terrace beside her father. "He's suggesting a '98 claret," she said to him. "Mrs. Hudson's chicken fricassee will go very well with it."

A pained look crossed Lord Duncan's well-bred countenance. "What a nuisance. It was a particularly fine St. Estephe." He turned to Jenkins, who was following him with a silver tray bearing decanter and glasses. "I hope you told Harpers to let us have whatever they can lay hands on as soon as possible, Jenkins."

"Indeed, my lord, but they were doubtful of finding another supply. It was a small vintage, as I understand it."

Lord Duncan took a glass from the tray. He frowned down into a stone urn on the parapet planted with brightly colored petunias. There was a short silence in which everyone but his lordship held their breath. Then he raised his glass to his lips, muttered, "Ah, well, these things are sent to try us, no doubt. So what are you girls planning for this evening?"

The crisis had been averted. Jenkins moved back into the house and Lord Duncan's daughters breathed again. "We're going to the Beekmans' musical evening," Chastity informed him. "There's to be an opera singer."

"I don't imagine you'll want to escort us, Father?" Constance asked with a touch of mischief.

"Good God, no! Not my kind of thing at all!" Lord Duncan drained his glass. "No, no, I shall go to my club as usual. Play some bridge..." He regarded his daughters with a suddenly irritated frown that indicated he was still put out by the loss of his St.-Estèphe. "Can't think why none of you is married yet," he said. "Nothing wrong with you that I can see."

"Perhaps the problem lies with potential suitors," Constance said with a sweet smile. "Perhaps there is something wrong with *them*."

There was something in that smile and her tone that caused her father's frown to deepen. He remembered Lord Douglas Spender's untimely death. He didn't care to be reminded of unpleasant things, and Constance had rarely exhibited an excess of emotion over the loss of her fiancé... at least not in front of him. But he was astute enough to realize that with this oblique reminder she was taking him to task for his thoughtless comment.

He cleared his throat. "I'm sure it's only your business," he said gruffly. "Let us go in to dinner."

Dinner passed without further incident. Lord Duncan drank his claret without complaint and made only a fleeting reference to the rather limited selection of cheeses presented before dessert.

"Jenkins, would you ask Cobham to bring the carriage around in half an hour?" Constance asked as she rose with her sisters to withdraw from the dining room and leave their father to his port and cigar.

"Certainly, Miss Constance." Jenkins poured port for his lordship.

"Ah, I meant to tell you. I have it in mind to purchase a motorcar," Lord Duncan announced. "No more of this horse-and-carriage business. We can be at Romsey Manor from the city in less than four hours with a motorcar. Just think of that."

"A motor!" exclaimed Prue. "Father, you can't be serious."

"And why can't I?" he demanded. "Keep up with the times, my dear Prudence. Everyone will have one in a few years."

"But the cost..." Her voice faded as she saw a dull flush creep over her father's countenance.

"What is that to you, miss?"

"Why, nothing at all," Prudence said with an airy wave. "How should it be?" She brushed past her sisters as she left the dining room, her mouth set.

"He is impossible!" she said in a fierce undertone once they were in the hall. "He knows there's no money."

"I don't know whether he really does know," Chastity said. "He's denied every fact of life since Mother's death."

"Well, there's nothing we can do about it at present," Constance said. "It always takes him a long time actually to do something, so let's wait and see." She hurried to the stairs. "Come on, we don't want to miss the opera singer."

Prudence followed her upstairs with a glum expression that did not lighten while they collected their evening cloaks and returned downstairs, where Jenkins waited by the open front door. A barouche stood at the bottom of the shallow flight of steps that led down to the pavement. An elderly coachman stood on the pavement beside the carriage, whistling idly through his teeth.

"Evening, Cobham." Chastity smiled at him as he handed her up into the carriage. "We're going to the Beekmans' on Grosvenor Square."

"Right you are, Miss Chas. Evening, ladies." He touched his cap to Constance and Prudence as they climbed in beside Chastity.

"Did you hear that Lord Duncan is talking of getting a motorcar?" Constance asked him when he had climbed somewhat creakily onto the driver's box.

"Aye, miss, he said something to me the other morning when I was taking him to his club. Reckon I'd make a poor chauffeur. I'm too old to learn new tricks . . . no time for those newfangled machines. What's going to happen to all the horses if there's no call for 'em? Are we going to put 'em all out to grass? Put me out to pasture, that's for sure," he added in a low grumble.

"Well, if he mentions it again try to persuade him that it's a very bad idea," Prudence said.

Cobham nodded his head as he flicked the whip across the horses' flanks. "Expensive business, motors."

The Beekmans' house on Grosvenor Square was brilliantly lit both within and without. A footman stood on the pavement directing the traffic and a trio of underfootmen held up lanterns to light the guests' way up the steps and into the house.

"Ah, if it isn't the Honorable Misses Duncan," a familiar smooth voice declared from the steps behind them as they went up. "How pleasant to meet you again."

Constance was the first to turn and the first to realize that she had responded to the greeting with more than ordinary alacrity. She disguised this beneath a cool smile and offered a small bow of her head. "Mr. Ensor. A pleasure." She turned unusually enthusiastic attention to his sister beside him. "Letitia, you look wonderful. Such an elegant gown; is it Paquin? The gold trimming has her look. We haven't seen you for several weeks. Were you in the country?"

"Oh, yes, Bertie insisted we fetch Pamela from Kent ourselves. She spent a few weeks in the country but she gets bored so quickly. Children do." Lady Graham smiled fondly. "Her governess gets quite distracted trying to keep her occupied."

Constance inclined her head in acknowledgment but she couldn't help the slightly disparaging lift of her mobile eyebrows that frequently betrayed her true responses. It was an involuntary reaction she thought she had inherited from her mother. She smiled in an effort to counteract the effect of the eyebrows and continued up the steps.

"May I help you with your cloak, Miss Duncan?" Max Ensor moved behind her when they reached the majestic pillared hall and with a calm and seemingly innate confidence reached around her neck to unclasp her silk cloak.

"Thank you." She was taken aback. Men did not in general presume to offer her such attentions unasked. She saw that Letitia was in animated conversation with Prudence and Chastity and clearly no longer in need of her brother's escort.

Max smiled and folded the cloak over his arm, turning to find a servant to take it from him. "I have a feeling you disapproved of my niece's inattention to her governess," he observed once he'd divested himself of his own black silk opera cloak, its crimson silk lining a jaunty flash of color against the black and white of his evening attire.

"My wretched eyebrows," she said with a mock sigh, and he laughed.

"They do seem rather eloquent."

Constance shrugged. "I have very strong feelings on the education of women. I see no reason why girls should not be expected to learn as well as boys." She noticed a twinkle in Max Ensor's blue eyes as she spoke that disconcerted her. Was he laughing at her? Mocking her opinion?

She felt her hackles rise and continued with an edge to her voice, "I can only assume your niece has a poor governess. Either she's incapable of making her lessons interesting, or she's incapable of making her charge pay attention."

"The fault I fear lies with Pamela's mother," Max said, and while his eyes still contained that glint of humor his tone was now all seriousness. He offered Constance his arm to ascend the wide sweep of stairs leading to the gallery above, from whence the strains of a Chopin waltz drifted down. "She will not have the child subjected to any form of structure or discipline. What Pammy doesn't like, Pammy doesn't do."

Constance looked up at him. His mouth had now acquired a rather severe twist and the amusement in his eyes had been replaced by a distinctly critical expression. "You don't care for your niece?"

"Oh, yes, I care for her a great deal. It's not her fault that she's so spoiled. But she's only six, so I have hopes she'll grow out of it."

He was speaking with the level certainty of experience. Her antagonism died under a surge of curiosity. "Do you have children of your own, Mr. Ensor?"

He shook his head vigorously as if the question was absurd. "No, I don't even have a wife, Miss Duncan."

"I see." How old was he? Constance wondered. She cast him a quick upward glance as they stood together in the doorway to the large and brightly lit salon waiting for the butler to announce them.

He looked to be in his late thirties, perhaps early forties. Either way, a little old to be beginning a parliamentary career, and certainly of an age where one would expect a wife by the fireside and a nursery full of children. Perhaps he had had a wife once. Or some grand illicit passion that had ended in disaster and disappointment. She dismissed the thought as pure romantic nonsense. Not something she indulged in as a rule.

"The Honorable Miss Duncan . . . the Right Honorable Mr. Max Ensor," the butler intoned.

They stepped forward to greet their hostess, who regarded Max Ensor with sharp, assessing eyes. She had two marriageable daughters and every single male newcomer was possible husband material. To Constance, whose own unmarried status made her a possible rival, she merely nodded. She then began to question Max Ensor with artful ease.

Constance, who knew Arabella Beekman's tactics all too well, smiled politely and moved on to greet other friends and acquaintances. She took a glass of champagne from a passing tray, then found herself watching Max Ensor. To her amazement, he managed to extricate himself within five minutes from his hostess's formidable investigative curiosity. Something of a record in these circumstances.

He paused, looked around, and made a beeline for Constance. Constance, embarrassed that he had probably sensed her own interested gaze, turned away, and began to address a lanky youth whose spotty complexion and hesitant manner generally kept him on the social sidelines at such functions.

"I feel as if I've been subjected to the third degree," Max Ensor declared as he came up to her. "Oh, you've finished your champagne." He took the glass from her suddenly inert fingers and handed it with a firm smile to the young man. "You should always make sure that your companion has everything she needs, you know. Fetch Miss Duncan another glass of champagne."

Constance was about to protest but the youth stammered an apology and almost ran away with her glass. "I have no need of another glass," she said, not troubling to hide her annoyance.

"Oh, nonsense," he said carelessly. "Of course you do. Anyway, how else was I to relieve you of your companion?"

"It didn't occur to you that perhaps I didn't wish to be relieved?" she said tartly.

He raised his arched black eyebrows in incredulity. "Oh, come now, Miss Duncan."

And despite her very real annoyance, Constance could not help but laugh. "The poor boy is so shy it's only charitable to engage him in conversation. Did you realize that Arabella Beekman was sizing you up for one of her daughters?"

"I thought it might be something like that."

"And are you in the market for a wife?" she queried before she could stop herself.

He took two glasses of champagne from a tray proffered by a footman and handed one to Constance. He caught sight of the lanky youth out of the corner of his eye. The boy had halted a few yards off with a refilled glass and a nonplussed air.

"I've never given it much thought," Max answered finally. "Are you in the market for a husband, Miss Duncan?"

"I suppose one impertinent question deserves another," she responded after a second's hesitation.

"And one honest answer deserves the same." He regarded her over the lip of his champagne glass.

Constance could not deny the truth of this. She had foolishly started the conversation and she had to finish it. She could not bear to continue such a potentially painful topic. She said carelessly with an air of dismissal, "Let's put it this way, Mr. Ensor. I am not *looking* for a husband, but I'm not actively against the idea."

"Ah." He nodded slowly. "And are your sisters of the same opinion?"

"I wouldn't presume to speak for them," she retorted.

"No... well, perhaps that's laudable. It strikes me as unusual, though, to find three attractive sisters..." He let the sentence fade as if aware that he was about to say something offensive. It had occurred to him that this particular reader of *The Mayfair Lady* might well share that paper's political opinions.

Constance took a sip of champagne. "Three sisters happily facing the prospect of a husbandless future, you mean." Her voice was perfectly calm and even, but her spirit was dancing at the prospect of a battle. This was much safer ground.

"Spinsterhood is not generally a sought-after goal among women of your age." He shrugged with seeming carelessness, although he was very curious now to see what he could flush out about Constance Duncan's views. "Women are not equipped to manage their own affairs. Indeed, I would say it's most unsuitable for them to do so."

For a moment Constance, despite her delight in the

challenge, was breathless. Of all the presumptuous, pompous, arrogant male statements. Utterly unequivocal, without entertaining the slightest possibility of there being another opinion on the issue. She stared at him. "Unsuitable?" she demanded, no longer able to pretend nonchalance.

"Well, yes." He didn't seem to notice her outrage. "Women are not educated to handle financial matters or business affairs. And that's how it should be. There should be a division of labor. Men take care of the business side of life and women are best suited to household management, nursery matters, and . . ." Here he laughed. "Amusing themselves, of course."

"And cosseting their husbands . . . waiting upon them hand and foot, of course," Constance said, a dangerous light in her eye.

"It's only reasonable for a man to expect a little pampering in exchange for providing security and all the little comforts women find so necessary to their wellbeing."

The man was beyond the pale. He wasn't worth doing battle with. "I think it's time for the music to begin," Constance declared. "I see your sister gesturing to you. I imagine she would like your protection during the arias."

Max saw the glitter in the dark green eyes and he had the uneasy sensation of being in a cage with a tiger. Perhaps he had gone too far. "I can see we don't share the same opinion," he said with a placatory smile.

"How perspicacious of you, Mr. Ensor. Excuse me, I must find my sisters." She walked off in a swirl of cream silk chiffon, and her dark red hair that had struck him as richly colored but scarcely fiery now seemed to Max to be suddenly aflame.

Definitely a woman to be handled with care. He pursed his mouth thoughtfully, then went to obey his sister's summons.

Chapter 3

Constance seethed throughout the opera singer's performance, oblivious of the soaring perfection as the soprano's glorious voice hit every high note. Her sisters, sitting on either side of her, were acutely aware of her distraction. Prudence gave her a quick sideways glance and saw how tightly Constance's hands were clasped in her lap.

At the end of the performance Constance remained seated on the little gilt chair, until Chastity nudged her. "Con? Con, it's over."

"Oh." Constance blinked and looked around as if she were awaking from a deep sleep. "It was wonderful, wasn't it?"

"How would you know?" Prudence asked. "You didn't hear a note."

"I most certainly did." Constance gathered up her evening bag and rose to her feet. "But I've had enough for one evening. Let's make our farewells."

"Are you quite well, Con?" Prudence asked with concern.

"Just a headache," Constance replied. "Nothing much but I'll be glad of my bed. There's Arabella by the door. We'll catch her before the crowd." She moved forward swiftly, aiming to reach her hostess before the rest of the guests took their farewells.

Prudence exchanged a knowing glance with Chastity and followed on her elder sister's heels.

"Are you leaving so soon, my dear Constance?" Arabella exclaimed. "There's supper in the yellow salon."

"I have a slight headache." Constance touched her brow with a fingertip in emphasis and offered a smile that she hoped was convincingly wan, although she felt remarkably robust. Anger was a great energizer. "But it was a delightful evening, Arabella."

"Isn't the singer wonderful, utterly charming? A sublime voice . . . just sublime. I was so fortunate to be able to catch her." For all the world like a butterfly in a net, Constance thought, but she smilingly agreed.

They moved away towards the doors to the gallery and the stairs leading to fresh air and escape.

"Miss Duncan, Miss Prudence, Miss Chastity . . . leaving so soon?" Max Ensor pushed through the crowd towards them. "Allow me to call for your carriage."

"There's no need, Mr. Ensor. One of the footmen will call him." Constance gave him her gloved hand. "I bid you good night."

"At least allow me to collect your cloaks, ladies," he protested, tightening his hold slightly on the silken fingers. He dropped them immediately when their owner gave a sharp tug.

"There's not the slightest need, I assure you," Constance said firmly. "I know you're looking forward to your supper."

"If you know that, you know more than I do," he said. "I've never felt less like supper."

"Oh." Constance was silenced, then repeated firmly, "Well, I bid you good night." And turned away towards the head of the stairs.

"I trust I may call upon you ladies?" Max said, addressing himself to Prudence since he didn't feel inclined to talk to Constance's rapidly retreating back.

"Of course," Prudence said. "We are At Home on Wednesdays from three o'clock. We should be delighted to see you." She gave him her hand and a somewhat speculative stare, before following her sisters.

"So what was all that about?" Prudence asked as she and her sisters stood on the steps outside waiting for Cobham.

"All what?" Constance scanned the street intently.

"You know perfectly well. Why were you giving Max Ensor the frozen treatment?"

"I wasn't. I don't know him so I'm hardly going to treat him like a bosom friend." She glanced at her sisters and read their skeptical looks. "If you must know, he's the most arrogant, pompous, stuffed shirt of a man it's been my misfortune to talk to."

"Oh, sounds interesting!" Chastity said. "Whatever did he say?"

Constance didn't reply until they were in the carriage, and then she treated her sisters to a succinct account of her conversation with the Right Honorable Max Ensor.

"Mother would have made short work of him," Chastity observed with a chuckle.

"We'll have some fun with him if he comes to an At Home," Prudence said, her eyes gleaming under the streetlamps. "We'll ambush him."

"You didn't invite him, did you?" Constance asked.

"He asked if he could call."

Constance grimaced, then said, "Well, if he comes, he can expect a less than enthusiastic welcome."

"Oh, I think we should try to convert him," Chastity said. "Mother would have done."

"I don't think he's worth the effort," Constance responded. "Not even Mother wasted her time on lost causes."

"He *is* a Member of Parliament," Prudence pointed out. "Just think how useful a convert he could be."

Constance regarded her sisters, a light dawning in her eyes. "How right you are," she said slowly. "The Right Honorable Member for Southwold is about to discover that there are some women in London society who don't quite fit his stereotypes. Perhaps he'll come this Wednesday."

"You don't really have a headache, do you?" Chastity asked.

"It was a headache called Max Ensor," Constance responded. "And curiously it has quite gone away."

"Good," Chastity said. "Because we need to draft the advertisement for the Go-Between, and check the final layout for next month's issue. I have to take it to the printer tomorrow morning."

"We'll do it before we go to bed."

The barouche drew up outside the house on Manchester Square and Jenkins had opened the door before Constance could get out her key. "You must have seen us coming," she said.

"I was watching out for you, Miss Con."

"Is Lord Duncan in?" Prudence drew off her gloves as she stepped into the hall.

"No, Miss Prue. He went to his club. He said there was no need to wait up for him."

The sisters nodded. It was not unusual for their father to return to the house in the early hours of the morning, and sometimes not until dawn. Where he spent the night was not a question they cared to examine.

"You had a pleasant evening?" Jenkins closed the heavy front door.

"Very, thank you," Prudence replied with a quick grin directed at her sisters. "At least Chas and I did. Not so sure about Con. Good night, Jenkins."

"Good night, Miss Prue." He watched them up the stairs and then extinguished all but one small lamp on a console table before taking himself off to his pantry in the basement.

The small square sitting room at the front of the house on the second floor had been Lady Duncan's private parlor and was now used exclusively by the sisters. It had a pleasantly faded, lived-in air. The furniture was worn, the colors of the upholstery and curtains bleached by years of sunlight and laundering. But there were bowls of fresh flowers on every surface amid a cheerful clutter of books, magazines, and sewing materials. As usual, a pan of milk stood on the sideboard ready to be heated over a small spirit stove.

"Ham sandwiches tonight, and Mrs. Hudson has made her luscious macaroons again," Chastity announced with satisfaction, peering beneath a linen cloth on a tray beside the milk. She struck a match and lit the flame beneath the milk. "While that's heating we'll look at the draft pages. I think I put them on the secretaire." She rummaged among a stack of papers on the overcrowded desk. "Ah, here they are."

Constance tossed her cloak over the back of the chesterfield and perched on one of the broad arms. She took the sheets her sister handed her and glanced through them. "You know what might be fun..."

"No," Prudence supplied the required answer.

"Why don't we write a review of tonight's performance? There were... what? Less than a hundred people there. Not a grand crush but everyone who is anyone in these circles was there, and the only newcomer that I could see was Max Ensor. And as Letitia's brother and an MP he's hardly an unknown quantity." She chuckled. "It'll really set the cat among the pigeons. It will have to have been written by a guest. Can you imagine the speculation about who could possibly have written it?"

"Great publicity," Prudence said, turning the heat down under the milk. "The details of a private party are much harder to get hold of than those of a Society wedding or... or, say, a grand ball. There are always gate-crashers and newspeople at those do's anyway. But tonight was very different."

"People will be desperate to get their hands on a copy," Chastity said. "We should double the print order, I think. Who's going to write it?"

"I will," Constance stated. She had a tiny smile on her lips that hinted of secrets. "I have it roughed out in my head already."

"I'm not sure you can be totally accurate when it comes to the arias," Prudence observed. "You weren't listening."

Constance waved a dismissive hand. "I'm only going to touch on that anyway. That's not what's going to interest people. It'll be the intimate details, the kinds of things only an insider could have gathered."

Chastity regarded her thoughtfully. "You've got something up your sleeve."

"Maybe," her eldest sister agreed with another little smile. "Let's get on with this Go-Between advertisement."

"Do you want chocolate in your milk, Chas?" Prudence broke a square off a bar of chocolate.

"Yes, please."

"How can you two drink that sickly stuff?" Constance said. "I shall have some cognac instead."

"Each to his own." Prudence dropped two squares of chocolate into the saucepan, stirring it with a wooden spoon. A few minutes later she brought two wide-mouthed cups filled with dark, fragrant liquid over to the sofa, where Chastity was laying out the sheets of closely written paper.

Constance poured a small measure of cognac into a glass, took a ham sandwich, and then carried the plate over, holding the sandwich in her mouth. She set the plate down on the low table in front of the sofa and reflectively chewed her sandwich. "Why don't we have a banner headline for the advertisement? Just under the title. It'll draw the most attention."

Chastity took a clean sheet of paper and a sharpened pencil. "What shall we say?"

"*Are you lonely? Craving companionship? Do you spend long evenings with your own thoughts?*" Prudence began, helping herself to a sandwich. "*Can't find the right match...*"

"*You need a Go-Between.*" Constance chimed in. "*The Go-Between service will help you find your match. We guarantee discretion; we guarantee security. All inquiries personally vetted and personally answered. Send us your—*"

"Not so fast," Chastity protested. "I'm trying to write

this down." She paused to drink some of her hot chocolate.

Her sisters waited patiently until she took up the pencil again. "All right. *Send us your . . .*" She looked up inquiringly. "Your what? *Requirements*. No, that sounds a bit clinical."

"Desires?" suggested Prudence, settling her glasses more securely on her nose.

Constance choked on her sandwich. "We're not advertising a brothel, Prue."

Prudence grinned. "I suppose it might sound a little suspect."

"How about something really straightforward? *Send us a brief account of yourself and a description of the person you would like to meet. We will do the rest.*" Chastity scribbled fiercely as she spoke.

"Bravo, Chas. That's perfect." Constance applauded. "Now we need an address."

"Why don't we ask Jenkins if his sister would mind getting this mail? She has a corner shop in Kensington and I know she acts as a poste restante for people in the neighborhood who don't have a proper address for whatever reason. It would be easy enough to fetch it from her." Prudence brought over the basket of macaroons. "Jenkins is on our side in all of this, after all."

"Just as he was on Mother's." Chastity took a macaroon and bit into its gooey depths with a little murmur of pleasure. "He used to run her errands for *The Mayfair Lady* if one of us couldn't do it."

"I'll just run down and ask him. He won't be in bed yet." Constance went to the door. "That way we can get this finished tonight."

Jenkins, ensconced in the butler's pantry with a

tankard of ale, listened to the request with his customary imperturbability. "I'm sure my sister will be agreeable, Miss Con," he said, when she'd finished her explanation. "I'll be seeing her on Sunday evening, as usual. I'll explain the situation to her then. You'll be wanting the address." He took a sheet of paper from the dresser and wrote in his meticulous hand.

"That's wonderful, Jenkins," Constance said warmly as she took the paper. "Thank you so much."

"No trouble at all, Miss Con."

Constance smiled, bade him good night, and hurried back upstairs to the parlor. "That's all settled," she said as she closed the door behind her.

"Did he think it was a strange request?" Chastity asked.

"Not particularly. He's used to the eccentricities of this family," Constance replied with a grin. "Here's the address." She handed them a scrap of paper. "Now, I'm going to write my piece about this evening while you two finalize the layout." She sat down at the secretaire, pushed aside a toppling pile of papers, and took up her pen.

Her sisters settled companionably to their task while their sister scribbled behind them. It was the usual division of labor, since Constance, as the most fluent writer of the three, penned the majority of the longer articles.

"I've had another idea," Chastity said suddenly. "Rather on the same lines. Why don't we provide a personal column . . . you know, if someone has a problem they write in and ask for advice. Then we publish the letters and give advice."

Constance looked up from her work. "I don't see myself giving advice," she said. "I have enough trouble organizing my own life."

"That's because it takes you forever to make up your mind," Prudence said. "You always see both sides of every question, and then a few extraneous aspects as well."

"'Tis true," Constance agreed with a mock sigh. "At least until I do finally make a decision. Then I'm constant as the evening star."

"That is also true," Prudence conceded. "I'm not good at dispensing advice either, most of the time I can't see what people are worrying about. I think Chas should do that column, she's so intuitive."

"I'd like to," Chastity said. "And to get the ball rolling I'll make up a problem letter. We'll only use initials to identify the writers so people will feel secure about making their problems public." She sucked the tip of her pencil. "What kind of problem?"

"Love's always a good bet," Constance suggested. "Torn between two lovers, how about that?"

She blotted her paper and reread the three paragraphs she had written. "There, I think that'll do. What d'you think?" She carried the paper to the sofa and took up her glass again, taking a sip as she watched her sisters' reactions.

Chastity gave a little choke of laughter. "Con, this is scandalous." She began to read aloud. "'This evening, the Right Honorable Max Ensor, newly minted Member of Parliament for the county of Southwold in Essex, made his social debut at the delightful musical soirée given by Lady Arabella Beekman in her charming mansion on Grosvenor Square. Mr. Ensor is the brother of Lady Graham of 7 Albermarle Street. The Right Honorable Gentleman turned quite a few heads as an eligible newcomer to Society, and several anxious mamas were

seen jockeying for a chance to introduce him to their
daughters. It is unknown whether Mr. Ensor is a fan of
the opera, but he certainly made fans of his own this
evening.' "

Prudence whistled softly. "Declaration of war, Con?"

Constance grinned. "Could be."

"Well, it's outrageous," Prudence said, chuckling.
"It's not really about the soirée at all."

"Oh, it goes on," Chastity said. "Descriptions, lavish
praise for the singer, some faint disapproval of the Gluck
aria . . . so you were listening, Con . . . and a nice little tidbit about Glynis Fanshaw and her new escort." She
looked up. "Was Glynis really escorted by that old roué
Jack Davidson? She's really scraping the barrel."

"I didn't say that," Constance said piously.

"No, and I suppose you didn't imply it either."
Chastity shook her head. "People are certainly going to
have some fun with it."

"That is the idea, after all. Where shall we insert
this?"

"Inside the back page. We'll save the fluffy stuff for
that page and hope that readers will be distracted by
Con's serious pieces on their way to the cream."

"On the nursery principle of bread and butter before
cake," Prudence mused. "How's the problem letter coming along?"

"I've kept it very simple," Chastity replied, "but who
should they be writing to? Dear *who*?"

"Someone grandmotherly," Prudence said. "Smelling
of gingerbread and starched aprons."

"Aunt Mabel," Constance said promptly. "No, don't
laugh," she protested. "It's a very fine name denoting
stability and wisdom and all the coziness of a favorite

aunt. You couldn't imagine ever being led astray by an Aunt Mabel."

"Aunt Mabel, it is," Chastity said. "I'll read the letter to you. 'Dear Aunt Mabel—'" She broke off at a knock on the door. Lord Duncan called, "Are you still up, girls?"

Constance swept the papers off the table and stuffed them behind a cushion. "Yes, we're still up," she called. "Come in, Father."

Lord Duncan came into the parlor. He carried his black silk hat in his hand and his tie was crooked. His gaze was benign but bleary. "I saw the light under the door as I was passing," he said. He leaned against the door, his eyes wandering around the parlor. "Your mother loved this room." He frowned. "It seems very shabby. Why don't you replace the curtains, and surely some new cushion covers would improve the look of it."

"We like to keep it as Mother had it," Constance said, her tone soothing and reasonable.

He nodded and coughed into his hand. "Oh, yes, I see. Of course . . . of course. A nice sentiment. Did you enjoy your evening?"

"Yes, it was delightful. The singer was magnificent," Prudence said. "We were just chatting about it over our hot chocolate before going up to bed."

"Good God! You don't want to be maudling your insides with that pap," he declared. His eye fell on the cognac glass that Constance still held. He said with a nod of approbation, "At least one of you has an appreciation for the finer things of life."

"I consider chocolate to be among the finest things in life," Chastity said, smiling at him.

He shook his head. "I suppose such solecisms are only to be expected with a house full of females." His gaze fell suddenly on a sheet of newsprint that had fallen to the floor. "Good God! What's that disgraceful rag doing in here?" He stepped forward and bent to pick up the fallen copy of *The Mayfair Lady*. "There was a copy of this in the club this evening. No one could imagine how it got through the door." He held it by finger and thumb as if it might be infected.

"I wouldn't expect to find it in an all-male establishment," Constance observed serenely. "But it's a more substantial newspaper than it used to be."

"Your mother used to read it," Lord Duncan said with a grimace. "I tried to forbid it . . . all that nonsense about women's rights." He shrugged. "Forbidding your mother anything she'd set her heart on was a futile operation at best. I don't imagine it would do much good with you three either. Oh, well . . ." He shrugged again as if the recognition didn't much disturb him. "I'll bid you good night. Don't stay up too late: you need your beauty sleep if you're to—" The door closed on the silent end to the sentence.

"Catch husbands," the three chimed in unison.

"You'd think he'd get tired of singing that song," Constance observed. "Well, beauty sleep or not, I'm ready for bed." She retrieved the papers from behind the cushion. "Thank heavens he knocked. I didn't hear him come up the stairs."

Prudence yawned. "I think we've done enough for one evening. I'm for bed too." She took the sheets from her sister and locked them in the secretaire. "I confess to being intrigued as to how people are going to receive this edition. I think it might well bump up our circulation considerably."

"Just as a matter of interest, how did a copy get into

Brooks?" Chastity inquired, taking the dirty cups to the tray. "Any guesses?"

"Oh, I think it's possible that your Lord Lucan accidentally discovered a copy in his overcoat pocket," Constance said airily. "He was on his way to Brooks yesterday morning when I bumped into him inside Hatchards. We chatted for a while. His coat was just hanging over his shoulders and he was very animated, flinging his arms around, and the coat fell to the floor so I picked it up—*et voilà*. I expect he abandoned it in the cloakroom at Brooks without even knowing what it was. He's not the brightest bulb in the chandelier."

"Poor soul. He's very good-natured," Chastity said kindly.

"Yes, sweetheart. And so are you." Constance kissed her cheek as she held the door for her sisters. "Prue and I should take a leaf out of your book."

"I can be nasty," Chastity said with a touch of indignation. "As nasty as anyone, in the right circumstances."

Her sisters laughed, linked arms with her, and went up to bed.

Chapter 4

"What are we to do about these suffragists?" demanded the Prime Minister, seating himself heavily in a large leather armchair in the Members' Lounge in the House of Commons. Sir Henry Campbell-Bannerman had a perpetually preoccupied, worried air that was not diminished by the large goblet of post-luncheon cognac in front of him and the fat cigar he drew on with obvious satisfaction.

"The Pankhurst woman has started up her Women's Social and Political Union in London now. At least while they stayed in Manchester we could ignore them for the most part." He examined the ashy tip of his cigar critically. "Now we can expect petitions and delegations and excitable meetings right on our own doorstep."

"Appeasement," one of his companions suggested. "We'll get nowhere by provoking them. Promise them a steering committee; it doesn't have to come to anything."

Max Ensor leaned across the glossy surface of the low table in the square formed by the armchairs of the four men who were digesting a particularly substantial lunch with an equally fine cognac. He pushed a copy of *The Mayfair Lady* towards the Prime Minister, and indicated the black boxed headline: WILL THE LIBERAL GOVERNMENT GIVE VOTES TO WOMEN TAXPAYERS?

"This seems to be a particularly sensitive issue. We could announce that we're establishing a committee to discover how many women taxpayers and ratepayers there are in the country. That would quieten them down, at least for the moment."

Sir Henry picked up the newspaper. "A copy of this found its way into the Cabinet Office," he said. "How the devil did it get in there? I've asked all the staff but no one will admit to it."

"You see it everywhere...they'll be wrapping fish and chips in it next." One of the four gave a sardonic laugh as he reached for his goblet on the table.

"Does anyone have any idea who writes it?" the Prime Minister asked.

"Not a clue." Two of his three companions shrugged in agreement. "Perhaps it's the Pankhurst women."

"No, they're too busy organizing meetings and protests. Besides, it has its lighter side. I don't see Mrs. Pankhurst indulging herself in society gossip and fashion news. And in the latest edition they're offering some marriage broker service. The Go-Between, they call it. What with that and this Aunt Mabel, who'll wrestle with your love problems, I doubt the Pankhursts would sully their eyes or their hands with it."

"But it's a clever strategy," Max said. "Most ladies wouldn't be in the least interested in a political tract, but they are interested in the other stories on offer—"

"I notice you're mentioned in this one," one of his fellows interrupted with a deep chuckle. "Quite complimentary, really."

Max looked less than gratified. "It's arrant nonsense," he said shortly. "But my point still stands. Women who wouldn't ordinarily think about these issues will have their attention drawn to them the minute they leaf through the paper."

"If we're not careful, we'll have our wives and daughters waving placards on the steps of every town hall in the city," muttered Herbert Asquith from the depths of his armchair.

"Whoever wrote it had to have been present at the Beekmans' soirée," the Chancellor of the Exchequer continued. "No one could have written this commentary on Ensor without having been present. What d'you think, Ensor?"

"I think that's obvious, Asquith." Max tried to keep the irritation from his voice but barely succeeded. He had been stung by the underlying mockery of the piece. As a politician he thought he had developed a thick skin, and yet those little darts had somehow managed to penetrate. "At least we know the paper's written by a woman . . . or women."

"How so?" The Prime Minister held a long curl of gray ash over a deep marble ashtray, waiting reflectively for it to drop from the cigar tip of its own accord.

"It's obvious," Max said with a dismissive wave at the newspaper. "Only women would write of trivialities in that mischievous way. Gossip is not a man's forte. Neither is idle chitchat, not to mention this matchmaking service. It's a women's newspaper."

"A Society women's newspaper," Asquith stressed. "So who could be responsible?"

Max was silent and his companions regarded him with interest. "Max, you have some idea?"

"Perhaps," he said with a careless shrug. "Just a hunch. But I wouldn't bet the farm on it."

"Well, I certainly wouldn't mind knowing who's behind it." The Prime Minister yawned. "What is it that's so soporific about steak and kidney pie?"

It was a rhetorical question. Max stood up. "If you'll excuse me, Prime Minister . . . gentlemen . . . I have an engagement at three o'clock."

He left them dozing peacefully amid the soft snores and discreet conversational buzz of the Members' Lounge and made his way to Albermarle Street to collect his sister. He was looking forward to the rest of the afternoon. A little cat and mouse with Miss Constance Duncan.

"I can't think where Constance is. Did she say when she would be back?" Chastity asked her sister as Prudence came into the drawing room with a large crystal bowl brimming with heavy-headed, deep red roses.

"No, but since she was only going to Swan and Edgar's for some ribbon, I assumed she'd have been home long since." Prudence set the roses on a round cherry wood table and wiped a drop of water from the tabletop with her sleeve.

A worried frown crossed Chastity's face. "Surely she would have said if she wasn't going to be back for three o'clock?"

"Normally she would have said if she wasn't going to be back for lunch," Prudence declared, trying to dissipate her sister's concern with a briskly cheerful mien.

It worked to a certain extent, diverting Chastity's

anxiety for a minute. "Well, she didn't miss much," Chastity responded, plumping up cushions on the sofa. "Last night's warmed-over fish pie." She wrinkled her nose. "There's something about second-day fish, particularly cod, that's more than ordinarily unappetizing."

She caught her elder sister's expression and said, "Oh, don't look so disapproving, Prue. I can make a comment, surely. I know perfectly well we can't waste food, heaven forbid, but I don't have to like old cod, do I?"

Prudence shook her head ruefully, wondering why she so often felt responsible for the shifts they had to make to manage some degree of solvency. It was true she made these sometimes disagreeable choices for them all, but someone had to. "No, you don't," she agreed. "And neither do I. But we can only eat up leftovers when Father's not at the table."

"So we must take the opportunity when it arises," Chastity responded with a wry grimace. She glanced up at the handsome Italianate gilt clock on the marble mantelpiece. "Look at the time. Where *is* Con? It's almost half past two. People will start ringing the bell at three." The worry was back in her voice.

Prudence tried another diversion. Once Chastity started fretting, she would soon be imagining every kind of disaster. "I wonder if Max Ensor will beat a path to our door this afternoon?" She went to the French doors that opened onto the terrace. "Should we open these?"

Chastity forced herself to concentrate on the issue. "Why not?" she said. "It's a lovely afternoon, people might like to stroll on the terrace." She repositioned a group of chairs into a conversation circle. "If he does come I'm sure it'll be in pursuit of Con. You could tell how interested he was that night at the Beekmans'. Tactless but interested," she added with a chuckle, forgetting her concern for a moment. "He can't have any idea what devil he's aroused in Con. I can't wait to see her demolish him, or rather, his pompous arrogance." Then she demanded again, "Where *is* she?"

Prudence stepped back from the now opened doors. She said soothingly, "She can't have had an accident, Chas, we would have heard. A policeman would have been here by now . . . Oh, Jenkins . . ." She glanced at the butler, who entered with a tray of cups and saucers. "No sign of Con yet?"

"No, Miss Prue." He set the tray on a console table. "Mrs. Hudson has prepared two kinds of sandwiches, cucumber and egg and cress. She could make tomato as well if you want more variety, but she was hoping to use the tomatoes for the soup this evening."

"Keep them for our soup, by all means," a voice chimed in from the door. "We could always give our guests potted meat paste or jam."

"Con, where have you been?" Prudence demanded, ignoring her sister's joking suggestion. "We were getting really worried. Or at least Chas was," she added.

"I wasn't really," Chastity said a mite defensively. "But you might have sent a message, Con."

Constance removed the pins from her wide-brimmed felt hat. "I'm sorry," she said, instantly penitent. She knew how quickly Chastity became anxious. "I didn't mean to worry you. I would have sent a message, only I couldn't. I have had the most invigorating day." Her cheeks were flushed, her dark green eyes asparkle; energy seemed to flow from her with every long-legged stride as she crossed the room. "I'm sorry," she said again. "I've left you with all the work."

"There's not much to do," Chastity reassured. She was now smiling, her relief at her sister's reappearance visible in her eyes and in the relaxation of her mouth. "Mostly you were fortunate to miss the old cod pie."

"Last night's?"

"Mmm."

"Oh, and I had a Cornish pasty and a glass of sherry," Constance said with a stricken expression. "But mostly it was food for the mind."

"Well, what were you doing?" Prudence regarded her with curiosity.

"Do you remember Emmeline Pankhurst, Mother's friend?"

"Oh, yes, Mother worked with her on the Women's Suffrage Committee, and the Married Women's Property Committee. I thought she was in Manchester."

"No, I knew she had moved to London but I haven't had a chance to visit her. But I bumped into her this morning. She and her daughter Christabel have formed a London branch of the Women's Social and Political Union. They're lobbying for votes for women, but of course you know that." Constance was rummaging in her handbag as she spoke. "I went to a meeting this morning and joined the Union afterwards...See?" She held up a purple, white, and green badge. "My official emblem in the colors of the WSPU."

"So you go out for ribbon and come back with a political badge," Chastity said. "How did that happen?"

"I didn't even get through the door of Swan and Edgar's. I bumped into Emmeline on the pavement outside and she invited me to this meeting. She was speaking at Kensington Town Hall. It was electrifying. You can't imagine what it was like."

Her words tumbled over themselves as her mind still raced with the details of the meeting she had attended. The excitement and enthusiasm of the audience still rang in her ears. She had grown up with the sentiments that had been expressed and the issues that had been aired at the Women's Social and Political Union but she had never participated in a group discussion before. Her mother had been convincing when she'd talked to her daughters about women's suffrage, but the surge of jubilation, the sense of a group of women in harmony, prepared to fight for a just cause, had been a new experience for Constance.

"I can't say it surprises me," Prudence said. "You've always been passionate about women's suffrage. Not that Chas and I aren't too, but I'm not a great one for soapboxes and joining associations."

Constance shook her head. "I didn't think I was either, but something happened there. I felt...well... inhabited by something suddenly." She shrugged, helpless to describe the overwhelming sensation any more clearly.

"Well, whatever you do, don't flaunt the badge," Prudence said seriously. "If it becomes common knowledge that you've joined the Union, it won't be long before someone puts two and two together with the political views of *The Mayfair Lady*. And the cat really would be among the pigeons then."

"You have a point," Constance agreed. "I'll be as discreet as I can. I'm sure I can attend meetings and even speak at them in parts of London where no one we know would be seen dead.

"Anyway," she continued in the same breath. "Since I was in Kensington, I stopped afterwards at your sister's shop, Jenkins, and picked up the mail. Four letters for *The Mayfair Lady*." She took white envelopes from her bag and flourished them gleefully.

"You haven't opened them?"

"No, I thought we should open the first ones together. But that's not all," she said with a significant little nod. "Before I went to Swan and Edgar's I visited all the shops on Bond Street and Oxford Street that had agreed to carry *The Mayfair Lady*. And guess what?" She paused expectantly, then when her sisters declined to guess, continued, "They had all sold out. Every last copy in every shop. And they all told me they would order three times the quantity next month."

"Well, something's working, then," Prudence said. "Is it Aunt Mabel, or the Go-Between, or your wicked gossip, Con?"

"It could be the politics," Constance suggested, then shook her head ruefully. "No, of course it's not. Not yet. But I live in hope. Chas will have to don her heavy veil and widow's weeds and go and collect the proceeds of all those sales. Shall we open these letters? Just quickly to see if they're for the Go-Between or Aunt Mabel."

"We don't have any time now," Prudence, ever practical, said reluctantly. "You need to change, Con, the doorbell will ring any minute now. You may be dressed for a political meeting but it's a bit severe for an At Home."

"Do you really think so?" She looked down doubtfully at the soft gray skirt and black, buttoned boots.

"Yes," Prudence said definitely.

Constance yielded as always to her sister's infallible

sense of what was appropriate dress for any occasion. "I'll be back before the first guest."

"We were thinking that Max Ensor might be ringing the doorbell," Chastity said with a mischievous glimmer.

"And it's for him that I should change my dress?" Constance asked, arched eyebrows lifting in ironic punctuation.

Her sisters made no response. Constance, aware of Jenkins's suddenly rather interested glance, brought the topic to a close. "I'll be no more than ten minutes." She whisked from the room and hurried upstairs to find a suitable afternoon gown for the sisters' weekly At Home. Not, however, that she intended to make any special effort on the off chance that the Right Honorable Member for Southwold might decide he was in need of a cucumber sandwich and a slice of Mrs. Hudson's Victoria sponge.

She examined the contents of the wardrobe as she pulled free the narrow tie she wore with her gray and white striped shirt and gray serge skirt. A very businesslike outfit that had, serendipitously, been exactly suitable for her unexpected activities of the morning. She selected a crêpe de chine blouse in pale green and a green and white striped silk skirt with a wide band that accentuated her tiny waist.

She sat on the dressing stool to fasten the buckles on her heeled green kid shoes and then turned to the mirror. The heavy chignon had loosened and wisps of dark red hair clustered on her forehead. She debated the need to undo the whole elaborate construction and start again, but decided she didn't have the time, instead placing a pair of tortoiseshell combs strategically in the mass piled on top of her head.

Her face struck her as a trifle flushed so she dusted her cheeks with powder. Her hand hovered over the tube of lipstick, a birthday present from a friend whose natural coloring was rarely seen beneath rouge, powder, and lipstick. The new cosmetics were wonderfully convenient; they could even be carried in a handbag for running repairs. Or could if Constance ever bothered with them. She despised lipstick; it was more trouble than it was worth, leaving smudgy mouth-shaped imprints on glasses and white table napkins. So why was she considering it now? She wasn't trying to impress anyone this afternoon. She snatched her hand away from the lipstick as if the tube was red-hot. She simply intended to put Max Ensor firmly in his place if he darkened her door this afternoon and she could very well do that without artificially reddened lips.

The doorbell pealed through the quiet house and she jumped to her feet, smoothing down her skirt, checking that the tiny pearl buttons at the high neck of her blouse were all fastened. She hurried to the door and headed for the staircase as Jenkins's dignified tones drifted up from the hall below.

"Lady Bainbridge, good afternoon," she said as she corrected her speed and descended the stairs with rather more decorum. She held out her hand to the rigidly corseted dowager in the hall and greeted the two younger women who accompanied her. They both wore spotted veils that they lifted in response to Constance's greeting. Two identical pairs of pale eyes were demurely lowered to the hems of their stiff bombazine gowns, bodices as firmly underpinned as their mother's.

Lady Bainbridge raised her pince-nez to her nose and subjected Constance to a critical stare. "You look a trifle flushed," she declared. "I trust there's no fever in the house."

"It's a warm afternoon," Constance said, maintaining her smile with some difficulty. The woman was a distant cousin of Lady Duncan and had been the bane of her life with her constant carping criticism. Her twin daughters were pinched and pale as if they lived in the shadows and rarely saw the light of the day. Their mama considered sunlight ruinous to the complexion.

Lady Bainbridge sniffed and sailed ahead of Constance into the drawing room, where she scrutinized Prudence and Chastity with the same stare that clearly searched for something wanting. Apparently she failed to find it in either of the sisters' smiling countenances and very correct afternoon attire, because she gave another audible sniff and inclined her head in a stiff bow before turning her attention to the drawing room.

"You've allowed this room to become sadly shabby, Constance," she declared. "Your mother always took such pride in her house."

Since the sisters could well remember diatribes on the lack of beeswax and silver polish directed at their mother, they allowed this remark to pass over them. Lady Bainbridge seated herself on a sofa, then frowned and began to pick at what Prudence realized was a very faint coffee stain on the upholstered arm.

"Sit down, girls. Sit down. No need to stand there like gabies." Her ladyship waved her fan at her daughters and Mary and Martha obediently perched on the edge of the opposing sofa.

"Tea, Lady Bainbridge?" Chastity brought a cup to their visitor while Jenkins proffered the plate of sandwiches.

Her ladyship peered at the offering on the platter and waved it away. She accepted the tea, however. Her daughters dutifully declined sandwiches and held their own teacups on their laps.

"So what's this I hear about Letitia Graham's brother coming to town?" Lady Bainbridge demanded. "I wasn't at Arabella Beekman's soirée last week, but I hear that he was there, causing quite a stir."

"We met him briefly," Chastity said. "Just an exchange of civilities. I didn't notice him causing a stir, did you, Con?"

"No," Constance responded with a delicate little frown. "As I recall, he seemed perfectly insignificant, madam."

"That's not what I read," her ladyship declared, sipping her tea.

"Oh? Did someone write about him?" Prudence leaned forward, her lively green eyes wide behind her spectacles.

"Did you receive a letter, Lady Bainbridge?" Chastity asked, her own eyes, more hazel than the pure green of her sisters, fixed with rapt attention upon the visitor.

"Oh, Mama found a copy of that newspaper," whispered Mary. "In the ladies' cloakroom in Swan and Edgar's, of all places."

"That will do, Mary," Lady Bainbridge declared. "You're always chattering."

The three Duncan sisters exchanged a glance. Mary spoke so rarely, the sound of her voice was a novelty.

"What newspaper?" inquired Prudence with an innocent smile.

"Oh, you must have seen it. A disgraceful thing." Lady Bainbridge set down her cup on the small table beside her. "It's called *The Mayfair Lady*. A dreadful misnomer if ever I heard one. There's nothing ladylike about it at all."

"Lady Letitia Graham and the Right Honorable Mr. Ensor, Miss Duncan."

Jenkins's voice from the drawing room door startled them all. No one had heard the front doorbell.

"Oh, Lady Bainbridge, I do so agree with you," trilled Letitia, wafting into the drawing room on a cloud of lavender water and a rustle of silk and lace. "It's quite shocking. My poor brother was quite dumbfounded to be the subject of such an article. So embarrassing, don't you agree? When one is but newly come to town, it's no way to be introduced to Society."

"Curiously, Letitia, I consider it quite flattering to have attracted such notice." Max Ensor's voice was as mellow as Constance remembered it, but she could detect an edge to it and guessed with satisfaction that he was not quite as sanguine about his appearance in the pages of *The Mayfair Lady* as he made out.

"Mr. Ensor, how nice of you to honor us with your company." Constance came forward with outstretched hand. Her smile, though polite, was cool, disguising the prickle of anticipation, the slight thrill in her blood at the prospect of engaging in battle with him.

"The honor is mine, Miss Duncan." He bowed over her hand.

"Not attending the Prime Minister's Question Time this afternoon, Mr. Ensor?" Chastity asked brightly.

"Apparently not, Miss Chastity," he replied, taking a cup of tea from Jenkins.

"Oh, but surely as a responsible Member of Parliament, Mr. Ensor, Question Time must be very important," Constance said. "Will you have a sandwich? Egg and cress or cucumber?" She extended the platter in invitation.

Max found three pairs of eyes of varying shades of green fixed upon him with smiling attention. But there was more than pleasantry in that attention. He felt a little like a mouse under the intently malicious gaze of a trio of felines. "If there are any questions of earth-shattering importance, you may rest assured that I shall be informed," he said, to his annoyance hearing a defensive note in the statement. "As it happens I lunched with the Prime Minister and left him in the Members' Lounge less than an hour ago." He took an egg sandwich.

"Oh, I see." Constance's smile remained constant. "You have a direct route to Sir Henry's ear. An unusual honor for a new MP, is it not?"

Max said nothing. If she intended to make him sound like a boastful coxcomb he wasn't going to play a duet.

Constance regarded him quizzically. "So I gather you were the focus of a piece in *The Mayfair Lady*. You found it complimentary?"

Max looked at the overstuffed sandwich in his hand and regretted his choice. Cucumber was a much tidier filling than mashed egg and strands of cress. "I barely glanced at it, Miss Duncan."

"Really? But of course you would have little interest in a women's newspaper. Women are rightly concerned only with trivialities. That is your view, Mr. Ensor, as I recall." The smile didn't falter; the dark green eyes never left his face.

He became aware that her sisters had rejoined their other guests on the far side of the drawing room and he was at an acute disadvantage facing this woman who was all armor while he stood there holding two soggy pieces of white bread from which white and yellow interspersed with green strands threatened to tumble to the carpet. He looked for somewhere to put it since he couldn't eat it and conduct any reasonable conversation—or rather, respond credibly and confidently to what was undeniably an attack. He had come prepared to play his own little game but now he realized Miss Duncan had her own basket of tricks. He must have touched a nerve the other evening.

"Ah, I see you need a plate, Mr. Ensor." Constance moved to the sideboard and took a bread and butter plate from the stack. "How remiss of me."

He suspected it had been an intentional lapse but accepted the plate with relief. "I know nothing of the newspaper, Miss Duncan. You gave Lady Armitage a copy the other week. As you say, it seemed mere uninformed babble to me. The kind of flippant insubstantial discourse that women like." He watched her face and noted the clear flash of chagrin that crossed her eyes. His point, he decided. That made them even.

"There was an article in there about the new licensing laws," Constance said with a casual smile. "You consider that to be the subject of insubstantial discourse, Mr. Ensor? I would have thought a Member of Parliament would have an opinion of his own and be interested in the opinions of others."

"Informed opinions, Miss Duncan, yes." He was enjoying himself now and sensed that Constance was too. Her eyes were flashing and dancing like fireflies.

"And women's opinions are not informed?"

"I didn't say that, Miss Duncan. There are many areas

where women's opinions are both informed and vitally important."

"Those involved with hearth and home, kitchen and nursery. Yes, you made that clear the other evening."

"And it offended you?" He raised a quizzical eyebrow. "Indeed, it was never my intention. I have only respect and admiration for your sex."

"And my sex is suitably complimented, Mr. Ensor. Allow me to introduce you to Lady Bainbridge and her daughters, Lady Martha and Lady Mary." She turned and the battle was over, for the moment. He was not entirely sure which of them had won that round.

Jenkins announced a trio of guests and the buzz of conversation filled the drawing room. Constance and her sisters were kept too busy taking care of their visitors to linger in any particular conversation, but Constance was aware of Max Ensor's hooded gaze following her as she moved around the room. He looked bored, she thought. He was standing behind his sister's chair, having abandoned both teacup and sandwich, taking no notice of the conversation around him. In fact he seemed oblivious of everyone but Constance.

Constance cut a slice of Victoria sponge and carried it over to him. "Mr. Ensor, our cook is renowned for the lightness of her sponge cakes." She handed him the plate before he could refuse. "Is there anyone I can introduce you to?"

"No, thank you," he said. "I came here to talk to you, Miss Duncan. No one else interests me."

The sheer effrontery of this took her breath away. "You're saying you find no one in this room worthy of your attention?"

"That was not what I said, Miss Duncan." He looked

at her, both challenge and question in his steady gaze. Constance felt a warmth creep over her cheeks and with an effort dragged her eyes from his. She searched for a swift comeback and for once was at a loss. A satisfied smile lingered at the corners of his mouth. He knew he had nonplussed her.

Max broke off a small piece of cake with his fingers. Constance couldn't help but notice that he had unusually long and slender hands for a man. She said coldly, "A person with such restricted interests can hardly expect to be considered interesting to others." She felt the snub barely began to express her true feelings but for once she was at a loss in the face of this supremely indifferent arrogance.

He pursed his lips on a soundless whistle. "Touché, Miss Duncan." His smile broadened. "I'm sure every one of your guests is most worthy," he said. "I daresay my lack of interest reflects poorly upon my own social skills." He gave an offhand shrug.

"I would have to agree with you," she retorted.

"I tell you, my dear Lady Bainbridge, I am seriously considering giving the woman her notice." Letitia's voice rose suddenly above the generalized buzz.

"I most strongly advise you to do so, Lady Graham. Waste not a moment." Lady Bainbridge snapped her fan against her hand. "One cannot entrust one's precious children to such women. They will corrupt those young and unformed minds. I wouldn't permit Martha or Mary to listen to such sacrilege."

"What sacrilege is this, Letitia?" Constance inquired, grateful for the opportunity to withdraw from battle and regroup.

"Oh, my dear, you won't believe it. But I was going

through Miss Westcott's bedroom this morning—Miss Westcott is Pammy's governess, you know. One must keep an eye on things. I consider it my maternal duty to inspect her room periodically." Letitia nodded her head virtuously. "But what should I find?" She paused for dramatic effect and now had the attention of all within earshot.

"I can't guess," Prudence said.

"One of those pamphlets from that organization, the Women's Union, or something."

"The Women's Social and Political Union," Constance said without expression.

"Whatever it's called. She'd hidden it away in a drawer. Of course she knows perfectly well that I won't have such scandalous nonsense in my house. I mean, what is the world coming to when you can't trust your own daughter's governess."

"What indeed?" Constance murmured. "Your vigilance does you credit, Letitia. I'm sure that the right to privacy is well sacrificed on its altar." She glanced at Max Ensor, and the light in her eye would have given a sensible man pause. "Are you of your sister's opinion, Mr. Ensor?"

It hadn't taken her long to renew the attack, he thought. But since he was extremely interested in what she might be persuaded or provoked to reveal about her own views of the WSPU he chose to disregard the warning flash in her eyes. "I haven't given it much thought," he said, then added deliberately, "There's some logic, of course, in saying that women who pay taxes should have a vote." He thought he detected a flicker of surprise cross her countenance. Watching her carefully, he continued with a dismissive gesture, "But it's such a small share of the female population that it hardly matters."

He had hoped to provoke a response but he was disappointed. Constance turned aside to pick up the teapot, offering it to Martha.

"Men can vote perfectly well for us," Letitia said. "I'm sure dear Bertie knows exactly the right things to vote for. But I don't know what to do about Miss Westcott... Pammy is so fond of her, and we've had so many difficulties with governesses. They so often don't suit Pammy."

"I doubt Miss Westcott's political opinions could mean much to a six-year-old, Letitia," Prudence pointed out.

"Oh, you'd be surprised, Prudence. The tricks these females use to corrupt the young," Lady Bainbridge said with a direful nod.

"No, well, I'm sure I don't know what to do," Letitia said. "I can't talk to her about it because then she'd know I'd searched her room." Letitia pouted in a manner that Constance thought would look more appropriate on her daughter.

"Yes, that is inconvenient," she murmured, catching sight of Chastity's outraged expression. Chastity's views on snooping and prying were akin to her views on theft and murder.

"I would think," Chastity said, "that you might remember the adage: *What the eye don't see the heart don't grieve over,* Letitia. How much more comfortable you would be if you hadn't discovered Miss Westcott's political interests."

"I have my daughter's welfare to consider," Letitia announced a shade stiffly, setting down her teacup. "Well, I must be on my way. I promised to take Pammy to call upon her great-aunt Cecily." She rose from her chair. "There's no need for you to escort me, Max, if you'd prefer to stay. Johnson is in the square with the barouche. He can very well convey me home."

Max gave the matter barely a second's consideration. He had come to see Constance Duncan and test the waters a little. It had been for the most part an amusing and enlightening engagement, once he'd recovered from the initial ambush, but he sensed that nothing further would be gained this afternoon. It was time to retreat and regroup.

"My dear Letitia, I escorted you here, I will escort you home," he said with a smooth smile. "Miss Duncan, ladies . . ." He bowed to the sisters in turn. "Delightful afternoon."

Constance gave him her hand. "I was afraid you were bored, Mr. Ensor. I'm so glad I was wrong."

"I cannot imagine how I gave such an unfortunate impression," he returned. His hand closed over hers, applying a faint but definite pressure. If she noticed it she gave no sign, merely offering him a purely social smile.

"Perhaps I may call upon you again and correct any wrong impressions," he continued, increasing the pressure of his fingers infinitesimally.

Constance, to her chagrin, was disarmed by this sudden change . . . the frank smile, the glow in the blue eyes, and the humorous tilt to his mouth. There was nothing bored, indifferent, or arrogant about Max Ensor at this moment. "If you think it's possible," she found herself saying.

"Oh, I think it is," he responded, his confident smile growing. "I think I deserve the chance at least." He raised her hand to his lips with old-fashioned courtesy, then offered his sister his arm as he escorted her from the drawing room.

Chastity and Prudence exchanged significant glances and Constance felt herself blushing slightly, something she never did. She shot her sisters what she hoped was a dampening look.

"Personable enough gentleman," pronounced Lady Bainbridge, rising to her feet with a creaking of whalebone. "Nothing to cause a stir about, though. Can't think what that dreadful paper could have meant."

"Harmless gossip, Lady Bainbridge," Chastity said with a soothing smile. "It was lovely to see you . . . and, of course, Martha and Mary." She smiled warmly at them as they gathered up gloves and fans. "We must walk in the park one afternoon."

"I trust you'll walk with me one day, Miss Chastity." Lord Lucan, a late arrival, hovered beside her, reluctant to take his leave with everyone else.

"We're going into the country this weekend. We would love it if you would join us. Just a small house party," Chastity said. "We're going to have a tennis tournament and I know how good you are at the game."

Lucan blushed and stammered his thanks, murmuring something about having to ask his mother since she made all such arrangements and he didn't know if she had made other plans for him.

Chastity mercifully interrupted his stumblings. "Well, let us know. We should like to see you if you can make it."

"It's to be a Friday to Monday," Prudence said. "If Lady Lucan would care to accompany you, we should be happy to see her." The invitation was pure form since the Dowager Lady Lucan rarely left her bedchamber, although she kept a fearsome eye on her only son's activities and allowed only those of which she approved.

Lord Lucan made his farewells in some disarray. Finally Jenkins closed the front door and the sisters were alone again.

"That went well," Constance said, piling dirty plates and cups on the tray.

"The ambush of the Right Honorable Member for Southwold or the party in general?" Chastity inquired through a mouthful of sponge cake.

"Both," Constance said, handing the tray to Jenkins. "I would like to think we'd seen the last of the gentleman."

"Oh, that I doubt," Prudence said with a shrewd glance at Constance. "I think he's picked up your glove."

"We *all* ambushed him," Constance said, catching the glance and not liking it.

"Only to get things started. You carried on solo," Prudence pointed out.

"And I can tell you that you definitely piqued his interest. I could feel it from across the room," Chastity said with a chuckle. "I'm very good at sensing such things."

Constance shrugged with apparent carelessness. "If I did, then I shall put it to good use. If he really has the Prime Minister's ear, then who knows what little whispers can be planted."

"You might find it an amusing exercise," Prudence observed with an exaggerated wink.

Constance gave up the battle. She could never fool her sisters. "I might at that." She walked to the open doors to the terrace. "Let's walk outside for a little and read our letters."

"Oh, did you bring them down?" Chastity set down the teapot she had been carrying to the sideboard.

"In my pocket." Constance drew the envelopes from the deep pocket of her skirt and flourished them.

They went outside into the tranquil garden where the early evening air was perfumed with the heavy scent of roses. The clatter of iron wheels and the clop of horses' hooves reached them from over the wall. They sat on the low parapet and Constance slit the first envelope with her fingernail.

Chapter 5

To the Go-Between:
The Mayfair Lady, July 14, 1906

I am interested in using the above named service advertised in the June edition of your newspaper. My situation is both delicate and complicated and I am reluctant to set down the details in writing since I suspect that my employer is in the habit of searching my room and personal papers. If it would be possible to meet with whoever provides the above service I would explain the full nature of my requirements at that time.

I am presently employed as a governess in Mayfair and am able to take time from my duties on Thursday afternoons between the hours of three and six, when my charge pays calls with her mother. If a meeting could be arranged at that time it would be most convenient. I must stress the urgency of my situation and of course I rely upon your utmost discretion. Please send the favor of a reply to Miss Amelia Westcott, care of the Park Lane Post Office. I am able to collect my post most mornings when I walk in the park after breakfast with my pupil. You didn't mention in the advertisement what charge you levy for this service. I should state at this point that that would be a consideration for me, but I am of course prepared to pay an initial consultation fee. I trust this will be satisfactory and I look forward to our meeting.

Amelia Westcott," Constance murmured, regarding the sloping signature from every angle. "It's too much of a coincidence, surely?"

"Not necessarily," Prudence said. "May I see?" She took the letter from Constance and read it again silently before handing it to Chastity. "It has to be the Grahams' governess. Her employer searches her room; she has these niggardly hours off. It fits to a tee."

"Well, I feel a great need to help that poor put-upon woman," Chastity declared, folding the letter.

"Her situation is hardly unusual," Constance pointed out. "You might even say she's fortunate. Think of the cook-generals, the maids-of-all-work, who rise at six and don't see their beds until midnight. Ill-fed, overworked, underpaid, with two hours off a week . . ."

"Con, get off your hobbyhorse," Prudence protested. "We know the facts as well as you do, and you know we sympathize, so we don't need a lecture."

"Sorry," Constance said with a ready smile. "It's just that after this morning's meeting I'm full of fire and brimstone."

Her sisters laughed tolerantly. "Save it for Max Ensor," Chastity advised.

"I feel a bit guilty actually," Constance said with a

frown. "I was rather acerbic about Miss Westcott, before I knew how grim her situation is, of course. And actually Max . . . Mr. Ensor . . . defended her."

"How so?"

"I made a rather hasty judgment when Letitia was saying how her daughter was always bored and her governess was at her wits' end to keep her amused." Constance shrugged. "I commented to Max Ensor that the governess obviously didn't know her job. Either she didn't know how to interest a child in her lessons, or she had no influence over the girl. He said it was Letitia's fault. She wouldn't allow anyone to impose discipline or structure on her dearest Pammy."

"Well, that's a promising piece of insight," Prudence observed. "Perhaps he's not as black as he paints himself."

"Then why would he give that impression?"

"Perhaps he has some ulterior motive," Chastity suggested thoughtfully. "I mean, you have one in cultivating him, so why shouldn't he have?"

Sometimes Chastity's intuitive observations only served to complicate matters, Constance reflected. Although her sister was frequently and uncannily on the ball. "I'll think about that later," she said, and hauled the subject back on course. "Let's see what the other letters are about. You open the next one, Prue."

Prudence took the envelope and slit it, then removed the sheet of paper and unfolded it. "Oh, look at this. Our first finder's fee." She held up a crisp banknote that had been enclosed in the fold of the letter.

"Another Go-Between letter?" Chastity leaned forward to look over her sister's shoulder.

"Yes, from a gentleman who prefers to remain anonymous," Prudence said. "He writes that he's looking for a young lady of good family but not necessarily possessed of an inheritance...or even of beauty." She looked up from the letter and raised her eyebrows questioningly.

"Interesting. What does he want her for?" Constance inquired.

"Marriage, of course."

"Then what's wrong with him?"

"You're such a cynic, Con," Chastity declared. "Why shouldn't he simply want to find a soul mate without fussing about money and looks?"

"No reason, really. But he's a very unusual man, in that case."

Prudence impatiently waved her sisters into silence. "He says here that he's a bachelor of reasonable fortune, doesn't like living in Town, so he's looking for a quiet young lady who likes country pursuits."

"But he wants to remain anonymous?" Constance frowned. "I wouldn't like to recommend some unsuspecting young woman to someone we haven't had a chance to vet in person."

"We'll suggest he meet us somewhere. At Jenkins's sister's post office, for instance. It makes sense to meet at the poste restante address. We'll be veiled just in case he might know us," Prudence suggested.

"I think just one of us should go in this instance," Constance said. "Chastity. She has the ability to analyze people. She'll know at once if there's anything suspect about him."

"I think you two should be there, even if you stay out of sight," Chastity said. "I'll be more comfortable."

"Yes, of course," Constance agreed instantly. "We'll

make an appointment for . . . oh, it'll have to be after the weekend. Wednesday morning, let's say. We can fit it in easily before the At Home. We need to meet with Amelia Westcott tomorrow since that's her afternoon off and we don't want to wait another week, and Friday we have to go into the country."

Her sisters nodded their agreement and Chastity opened the third envelope. "It's for Aunt Mabel," she said with a chuckle. "Oh, this lady really liked my response to the woman with two lovers. We have to publish this letter. Listen . . ." She adopted a tone of syrupy flattery. " *'Such an intelligent understanding response. Such wisdom and sagacity . . .'* " She looked up. "I thought they were the same thing."

"They are," Constance said. "Go on."

"Well, she says she had a similar problem and if only someone had been able to advise her in such fashion she wouldn't be in the situation she's in now."

"Which is?"

"Stuck with the wrong one," Chastity said succinctly. "I'd better write a response and we'll publish it underneath her letter."

"This one's another Aunt Mabel." Constance waved the fourth letter. "A married lady is having terrible problems with her mother-in-law, who dictates her every move, controls her son by keeping a close hand on the purse strings, and is now threatening to move from the dower house back up to London because the daughter-in-law doesn't seem to be managing the household adequately."

"Any signature?"

Constance shook her head. "It just says, 'Desperate in Knightsbridge.'"

"Well, I can think of several women that might apply to," Prudence observed.

Chastity leaned forward and took the letter from Constance. "I'll think of some creative solution, but I think it's probably best if we don't speculate over any of the letters. We'll soon be looking at all our acquaintances suspiciously."

Constance laughed. "You're right, Chas. But it seems that Aunt Mabel is a definite draw." She became serious again. "But how shall we respond to our first client?"

"Oh, yes, first things first. Amelia Westcott is top priority," Prudence stated. "We must write an answer at once. Jenkins will take it to the post when he has his evening constitutional."

"Down the pub," Chastity said in a passable cockney accent. "Very partial to his pint of mild-and-bitter is Mr. Jenkins."

"So we'll say we'll meet her tomorrow afternoon." Prudence was already moving back into the house. "The letter will go by the first post tomorrow morning and be at her post office by breakfast time. Where should we rendezvous?"

"Not Fortnum's. She'd be uncomfortable there," Chastity said swiftly, following her sister.

"Yes, of course she would." Constance nodded. "Oh, I know, what about the Lyons Corner House at Marble Arch? No one we know would be seen dead there. But it's perfectly respectable, very middle-class."

"With the added advantage of being relatively inexpensive," Prudence added. "I don't know what the etiquette is when it comes to having tea with clients, but if she's going to pay her way it's considerate to keep it reasonable, and if we're paying for clients then the same thing applies."

"Don't tell me a cream tea at Fortnum's would break the bank. Don't forget we're getting paid for this service," Constance pointed out.

"Something we haven't discussed at all," Prudence said over her shoulder. "Should it be a sliding scale? The rich pay more to subsidize the less well off?"

"Definitely," Constance said with emphasis, following them up the stairs. "Of course, it's easier when someone sends in his fee with his request, but they're not all going to do that."

"Also," Prudence said, opening the door to their parlor, "the nature of the services themselves could require different payments. Expenses, for instance ... supposing we have to take trains, or hackney cabs?"

"Since we have no idea exactly what kinds of services are going to be required, I don't see how we can anticipate." Constance went over to the secretaire. "I think we have to charge a sliding scale hourly rate with expenses on top, and have a provision for extra cost if the job needs something extraspecial." She took a sheet of writing paper from a pigeonhole. "This has Father's crest on it. We need plain paper." She rummaged at the back of the secretaire.

Prudence considered. "I think we can all meet with Miss Westcott. We know who she is and she has no idea who we are, and even if she did she has to be as interested in discretion as we are."

"With other clients we're going to have to do this cloak-and-dagger business," Constance said. "Heavy veils and disguised voices." She sat down at the secretaire and dipped her pen in the inkwell. "Stop laughing and concentrate. I'm being very serious. Now, what shall I write?"

They had just tucked the letter into its addressed envelope when a knock brought in Jenkins with a letter of his own. "This was just brought for you, Miss Con. The boy's waiting for an answer."

Constance turned in her chair, hand extended. "Thank you, Jenkins. And we have a letter that needs to go to the post this evening. Would you be able to take it?"

"Of course." They exchanged envelopes.

Constance looked at the handwriting on hers. It was unfamiliar but definitely masculine. Dark ink, strong downward strokes, no curls or flourishes. She knew immediately, instinctively, who it was from. The handwriting proclaimed the man as clearly as did his voice. Out of the blue she felt a jolt in the pit of her belly. She tried to ignore it and with an assumption of calm slit the envelope with the silver paper knife on the desktop and unfolded the single sheet. The bold signature was as she had expected.

"Well?" her sisters demanded.

"It's from Max Ensor. An invitation for dinner tonight." Constance reread the short letter, relieved to find that her voice was as steady as ever and that novel sensation in her belly had disappeared. "If I have no other pressing engagements . . ."

"Which you don't."

"No, I don't." She tapped the sheet against her mouth. "To go or not to go."

"That is indeed the question." Prudence took a fresh sheet of paper, this one engraved with Lord Duncan's crest, and laid it in front of Constance. "The boy's waiting for an answer."

"Why would he want to have dinner with me?" Constance questioned. "An intimate tête-à-tête so soon is rushing things rather, don't you think? Particularly after we did our level best to make him uncomfortable this afternoon."

"If you don't go you won't find out," Prudence pointed out, in her practical fashion.

"I suppose so. And it might be useful to prod him a little about the governess," Constance said with the same considering frown. "He must know something about her."

Prudence regarded her sister with a half smile. "It will be very useful," she agreed. "So write your acceptance and then we'll go upstairs and dress you."

"I wonder if he'll take you to the Savoy Grill or the Café Royal?" mused Chastity.

"Café Royal," Prudence stated, shaking the ink dry on Constance's message as she took it from her before she could change her mind. "I'll lay odds. Although," she added thoughtfully, "he is a Savoy kind of a man. Something about his dress and the way he carries himself just shouts it out. But then, the Café Royal is more suited to a quiet, intimate dinner. The Grill, on the other hand, is best for lunch."

Her sisters allowed her to consider the issue without interruption. Prudence was always right about such things.

Prudence made up her mind. "We'll dress you for the Café." She folded the sheet and handed it to Jenkins, patiently waiting for the second letter. "There, Jenkins. Make sure the right one goes to the messenger."

"Miss Prue!" he protested in dignified indignation.

"I jest, Jenkins." She gave him a quick kiss that produced a dull flush and a hasty exit.

Max Ensor inserted diamond studs into the high wing collar of his evening shirt. They matched his glittering cuff links. His valet hovered near the door with his crimson-lined opera cloak and black silk hat.

"That will do, I believe." Max gave a quick tug to the tails of his coat and held up one black-shod foot to the light. It gleamed with Marcel's champagne polish. "Another triumph, Marcel." Max was willing to admit to himself and his valet that he possessed a streak of vanity but he was also capable of making mock of both himself and Marcel's obsessive regard for the niceties of dress.

"Yes, sir." The man bowed, admiring as only a valet could the set of the coat across his master's broad shoulders. Reverently, he draped the cloak over the shoulders, smoothing the line with a fussy little pat. "Should I summon a hackney cab, sir?"

"No, it's a lovely evening. I'll walk to Manchester Square and hail a cab there." He took up his white gloves. "I doubt I'll be later than one o'clock."

"Very good, sir." The valet bowed his master from the bedchamber.

Max strode down the broad hallway of the Graham mansion towards the main staircase. As he passed the foot of the narrower flight of stairs that led to the nursery floor above, the sound of a large crash followed by a high-pitched wail of fury gave him pause. A tired voice said, "If you don't want it, Pamela, I'll take it away. There's nothing to cry about."

The wailing continued unabated, then ceased abruptly.

The silence in its wake had a curious suspended quality. Then again the wearily patient voice. "Please, Pammy, don't do that."

Max had never really noticed Miss Westcott. He supposed he'd passed her several times a day, and certainly run into her when she brought her charge to the drawing room to visit with Lady Graham every afternoon, but he was hard-pressed to picture her features. That weary resignation in her voice, however, caught his attention. After what he'd heard this afternoon about Letitia's treatment of the governess, and from what he knew of his sister's indulgent attitude towards her child, he could guess at the hell that was the life of the governess in this house.

It was no wonder, he thought as he climbed the stairs to the nursery floor, that educated women like Miss Westcott should find appealing the agenda of the Women's Social and Political Union. Downtrodden as they were, powerless to change their lives in any meaningful fashion, the idea of a vote could offer a smidgeon of hope, some possibility of influencing their working conditions. It was a novel thought, and one that until this afternoon in the Duncan sisters' drawing room had never disturbed the peaceful surface of his view of the social structures of his world. A wry little smile touched his mouth as he thought that Constance Duncan was entirely responsible for his present trek up the nursery stairs.

The door to the day nursery stood open, giving him a perfect view of its inhabitants. A small girl, with pigtails sticking out from either side of her head, stood beside an upturned chair in the middle of the brightly painted room, her face purple to the point of apoplexy, her eyes bulging. She was clearly holding her breath. A slightly worn woman in her early thirties stood regarding the child with an air of resigned exasperation. The young nursemaid who assisted the elderly Nanny Baxter, the grande dame of the nursery who had cared for both Max and his sister and was now past the age for the more active aspects of child care, stood wringing her hands, murmuring, "Oh, do breathe, Miss Pammy, do!"

Max lifted the child off the floor and held her high between his hands. In surprise, she took a gasping sob of a breath and her eyes returned to their sockets. He noticed that she didn't seem to have shed a single tear. He held her until her face had taken on a more normal hue and then set her down again.

"It seems something's not right with your world, Pammy," he observed amiably. His niece remained for the moment bereft of speech. She gazed up at him, her thumb finding its way into her mouth.

"I'm so sorry if you were disturbed, Mr. Ensor," the governess apologized. She brushed a limp strand of hair from her forehead where it had escaped the pins. "There was no need for the tantrum. She didn't want her buttered toast so I took it away immediately, but she still . . ." She shrugged, expressing a world of helpless frustration in the gesture.

Max regarded the child. "It must be so unsatisfying when opposition just crumbles at the first objection," he observed. "There's nothing like a well-justified tantrum for testing limits, but in the absence of limits, what's a small person to do?"

A glimmer of appreciation appeared in Amelia Westcott's gray eyes. "Lady Graham, sir, does not encourage limits."

"No," he said. "So I understand. Poor child..." He smiled at Miss Westcott. "And poor governess. You have my sympathies, ma'am."

"Thank you, sir." Color touched her rather faded cheek. "I think it's over for this evening. In general, once a night is all she can manage."

He shook his head. "I'll have a word with my brother-in-law."

She took a sudden urgent step towards him. "Oh, no, Mr. Ensor. That's very kind of you, but I wouldn't like Lady Graham to think I'm complaining about Pammy."

He slapped his gloves into the palm of one hand. Letitia might for the sake of convenience and her daughter's good humor put up with a governess with suspect political opinions, but she would never tolerate even the hint of disapproval about the child from anyone, let alone someone in her employ. Besides, privately he didn't think it would do any good to talk to Bertie. Lord Graham hated disharmony and kept his eyes firmly closed to anything that might cause it.

"Very well." He nodded and turned to go.

"Uncle Max." Pamela finally spoke. She tugged at the tail of his coat. "Where are you going? Can I come?"

"I'm going out to dinner," he said. "With another lady. I don't think I should put her off at the last minute, do you? It would be most dreadfully rude."

Pamela considered this. Her one protest of the evening over, she was perfectly prepared to be reasonable. "She might think I was...I was a rival for your affections," she declared with a triumphant clap of her still-dimpled hands.

Max stared at the governess over the child's head. "Where on earth...?"

"Nanny Baxter is very fond of romances, Mr. Ensor," she said, her face as straight as a die.

"Oh, I see."

"Lady Graham and Nanny Baxter are in the habit of discussing the love stories when her ladyship visits the nursery."

"Oh," Max said again. "Oh, I see." He gave his niece's pigtails a gentle tug, said, "I bid you good night, Miss Westcott," and left the now peaceful domestic scene with a swift step.

He encountered his brother-in-law in the hall. "Ah, Max, going to the House?" Bertie asked jovially, the words wafting on a whisky breeze. "Just came from the Lords...some cursed boring discussion about agriculture. Can't be bothered with it m'self. As long as the tenant farmers pay their tithes, let 'em alone, say I. What?"

"I represent a rather more urban constituency, Bertie," Max said. "As it happens, nothing that affects my constituents is on the agenda this evening. I'm taking Miss Duncan to dinner."

"Oh?" Lord Graham's bleary eyes struggled to focus. "The oldest one. Deuced attractive girl, reminds me of her mother, but she'll soon be on the shelf if she don't take some man...plenty after her. Shame about that chappie she was engaged to, can't remember his name now...killed in the war. Mafeking...or some other godforsaken part of the veldt. In the dragoons, I believe."

"That was what, five or six years ago?" Max mused. Constance Duncan would not have struck him as a tragic figure pining for a lost love.

"Something like that." Bertie waved a dismissive hand. "Caused the devil of an upset in the family. Mother took the girls to Italy for six months, hoping

Constance would get over it. Expect she has by now. Girl that age . . . can't weep forever."

Max absorbed this in silence, then headed once more for the door. "Well, have a good evening, Bertie."

"Oh, meant to ask you . . ." Lord Graham laid a hand on his brother-in-law's sleeve. "You think there's a cabinet post for you in the Prime Minister's reshuffle? Heard you were very tight with Campbell-Bannerman."

"No," Max said with a laugh. "I'm too new at the business for such an honor, Bertie."

"Pity." Bertie sighed. "Cabinet Minister in the family could be useful."

Max shook his head and left his brother-in-law to the whisky decanter and his reflections. It was a beautiful evening and he walked briskly through the Mayfair streets towards Manchester Square. His brother-in-law's question had not come totally out of the blue, although he had laughed it off. He was very much in the Prime Minister's confidence, but he was still too new a member of the House of Commons to achieve such a promotion. If he played his cards right it would come at some point sooner rather than later during the Liberal Party's reign. And he had every intention of playing his cards right. He had found the issue that would keep him in the forefront of the Prime Minister's mind. Campbell-Bannerman and his Cabinet were not in favor of women's suffrage but they could not afford to alienate those members of the Liberal Party who were. Finding a suitable compromise was going to be Max Ensor's route to the Cabinet. There were many covert ways to draw the teeth of the Women's Social and Political Union without angering its more influential supporters. And what better way to start than by cultivating the acquaintance of an active and passionate member of the Union.

He didn't know that Constance Duncan was a member, but she made no secret of her strong views on women's equal rights. He didn't *know* that she had something to do with *The Mayfair Lady,* but he suspected it. Either she was actively involved or she knew who was. If that newspaper was going to cause trouble, then it would be very useful to know exactly who was behind it. So he was very happy to combine business with pleasure in the cultivation of Miss Duncan.

He had thought hard about issuing tonight's invitation, wondering if it was too soon to suggest an intimate evening, but he'd decided that a full-frontal attack could well surprise her into an acceptance that a more measured approach might not achieve. He would be charming, a little seductive, disarm her. And then, he thought, he would pull back, leave her alone for a few days, and let her wonder about his intentions. It was a tactic that had worked for him before.

But he had to admit that he wasn't totally confident of success in this instance. Constance puzzled him. She didn't seem to fit into any category of woman known to him. She had all the bristly attributes of the bluestocking, the sharpness of the shrew, the face and form of the beauty, the savoir faire and dress sense of the Society woman. And yet she defied all categorization. She and her sisters. And now there was a dead fiancé to throw into the mix. Some bright and heroic scion of a noble family, killed while fighting for his country. If she still carried a torch for him, a pedestrian politician would find it hard to match up in the hero stakes, he reflected as he mounted the steps to the house.

The door opened at the peal of the bell and the butler he remembered from the afternoon bowed him within. "Will you wait in the drawing room, sir? I'll inform Miss Duncan that you're here."

"Thank you. And would you send someone to summon a hackney, please?" Max followed Jenkins into the drawing room and was taken aback when the butler announced him. "Mr. Ensor, my lord. He's waiting for Miss Con."

Lord Duncan turned from the open doors to the terrace. "Ah, I didn't know my daughter was going out this evening." He came towards his visitor, hand outstretched in greeting. "No one tells me anything in this house," he said. "Sherry . . . or would you prefer whisky?"

"Sherry, thank you."

"Daughters never tell you anything," Lord Duncan reiterated. "Rather like wives." He laughed and handed Max a glass. "So, where are you taking her? Don't mean to pry, nothing too paternal about the question . . . Con's more than capable of taking care of herself." He sipped his sherry.

"The Café Royal, I thought," Max replied.

"Oh, splendid choice. I took her mother there the night after our wedding . . . must be thirty years ago now." A shadow passed across Lord Duncan's countenance and vanished as swiftly. "You're the political chappie, aren't you? One of Campbell-Bannerman's protégés?"

"Hardly a protégé, sir."

"Up-and-coming . . . up-and-coming," declared his lordship with a conspiratorial wink. "Cigarette?" He flipped the lid on an engraved silver box.

"Thank you, no."

Lord Duncan lit his own and inhaled deeply. "So where did you meet my daughters? I assume that if you met one you met 'em all."

"Yes, indeed, Lord Duncan." Max looked restlessly towards the door. "I met them at Fortnum's, when I was having tea with Lady Armitage. She's a friend of my sister's, Lady Graham," he added in case his host needed further enlightenment.

"Oh, yes, I know that, dear boy. Well, you must come down to the country this weekend. We're having a small house party. The girls want to play tennis . . . not a game I care for. Give me croquet any day, much more vicious . . . just when you think you've—"

"Oh, Father, you'll bore Mr. Ensor to death with your croquet obsession." Constance made her entrance with a carefully executed swish of her black taffeta skirt. "Mr. Ensor, I hope I didn't keep you waiting long."

"Not at all, ma'am." He couldn't take his eyes off her. The black taffeta skirt had a bodice of a deep red that almost exactly matched the color of her hair. The neckline curved low to reveal just a hint of creamy breast, accentuated by the stunning jet collar that circled her neck. Her collarbone stood out in a way that lured his mouth and his tongue, so that he found himself curling his toes in his shoes. She was wearing heels that added at least an inch to her already noticeably tall and willowy frame. Her hair was piled high, dressed over pads, adorned with tiny jet black butterflies, and it begged to be loosened, each pin withdrawn, each lock and strand gently teased from restraint to fall to those perfect sloping shoulders.

He could not take his eyes off her.

"Con does look particularly beautiful tonight, Mr.

Ensor." Prudence spoke from behind her sister and Max mentally shook himself free of enchantment. He saw that both of Miss Duncan's sisters were regarding him over her shoulder with knowing smiles. They had read his reactions to their sister as if he'd shouted them aloud.

"Miss Duncan is lovely as always," he said with a slight bow. "As, indeed, are her sisters."

"Oh, prettily spoken, Mr. Ensor." Chastity smiled and although he looked sharply he could detect no hint of mockery. "So, where are you taking Con?"

Max thought that of the three of them, Chastity was probably the most benevolent. A man needed to be a little wary of the other two, they both had a wicked edge. As it happened, he found that edge, particularly in Constance, both challenging and perversely compelling. "The Café Royal, I thought. If that pleases you, Miss Duncan?"

"Greatly," she said. "Did I hear Father invite you to Romsey Manor for the weekend?"

Max bowed his acknowledgment and demurred, "But I'm not sure that I . . ." He let the sentence fade, watching her carefully for a flicker of hesitation. She would be duty bound to second her father's invitation, but he'd made one bold move and had not intended making another one. He was not prepared to risk his mission by accepting an invitation to which she showed the slightest hint of aversion. Better to go slow now and get there in the end than rush matters and scare her off.

Constance considered for only an instant. She could handle Max Ensor and he wouldn't even know he was being handled. A three-day country weekend would give her plenty of time to work upon him. By Monday she'd have him wearing the colors of the WSPU.

She bit back the chuckle that bubbled in her throat and said warmly, "Oh, I do so hope you can join us. I know it's short notice but we would all enjoy your company." She turned to her sisters for confirmation and they both acquiesced with the same enthusiasm.

They sounded convincing, but Max nevertheless felt a certain wariness. He could not, however, identify its cause, so he said simply, "Thank you. I should love to."

"Good, then we'll talk about it over dinner. You do play tennis?"

"Indifferently."

Constance regarded him through narrowed eyes. "False modesty, Mr. Ensor," she accused.

He laughed. "I'm not coxcomb enough to praise my game when I don't know the standard of the competition." He turned as Jenkins announced the arrival of the hackney. "Shall we go, Miss Duncan?" He offered her his arm.

"Enjoy yourselves," Chastity said.

"We'll see you in the country at the weekend, Mr. Ensor," Prudence called after them.

"You don't keep a carriage in town?" Constance inquired as he handed her into the cab.

"I have a motor," he said. "But I don't drive it in town."

"A motor, how dashing." Constance was genuinely impressed. "I've never ridden in one."

"Perhaps you'd allow me to drive you down to the country at the weekend."

Constance made no immediate response and he looked at her expectantly. "Did I say something wrong?"

"No, not at all." She sighed. "It's a little awkward."

He waited for her to explain and when she didn't, he let the subject drop.

Chapter 6

The hackney drew up outside the restaurant and Max escorted her inside, handing their cloaks to an attendant. They followed the maître d'hôtel up the wide flight of gilded stairs and were seated in a quiet alcove, from where Constance had an excellent view of the dining room and its occupants.

Max ordered champagne and opened his menu. He regarded his companion quizzically. "Do you like oysters, Miss Duncan? I see they have Breton oysters tonight."

"I do," Constance said. "But I'm not sure I feel like them this evening."

"Ah, then perhaps the quail eggs in aspic," he murmured, almost to himself. "And then the turbot in hollandaise, followed by the pigeon breast aux truffes." He looked up with an air of decision.

Constance laced her fingers. If there was one thing she detested it was a man presuming to order for her. And this man barely knew her. She opened her own menu, glancing up with a smile as the waiter poured champagne into her glass. "You make up your mind quickly,

Mr. Ensor," she said. "I for one like to linger over the menu. It always takes me at least fifteen minutes to decide what I want to eat."

Max heard the tincture of acid in her voice and hid his chagrin. He was accustomed to women allowing him to make choices for them; indeed, it had always been an infallible arrow in his seduction armory. Now it seemed if he was to preserve his dignity he had to pretend it was his own selection. He particularly detested turbot, was not overly fond of pigeon, and had been looking forward to the saddle of lamb, for which the Café Royal was justly famed.

He turned his attention to the wine list, determined that there she should have no input.

Constance sipped her champagne and watched him. "I always think a Sancerre goes well with turbot," she suggested. "And then a good burgundy with the pigeon, to bring out the truffles."

Max closed the leather-bound volume. He took up his champagne glass. "Perhaps, Miss Duncan, when you can tell me what you intend to eat, I can make some more informed choices."

"Oh, yes," she said, turning her attention back to the menu. There was an undeniable sparkle in her eyes, a distinct rosy tinge to her cheeks.

Max turned his champagne glass around between his long fingers. She was radiating smug satisfaction at having bested him. Should he yield the point? Disarm her with a frank apology for being overbearing? Or simply ignore her complacency and eat his turbot and pigeon even if they stuck in his craw?

The former, he decided. It would catch her off guard and he had the feeling that if he was going to get anywhere with Constance Duncan he needed to keep the advantage of the unexpected. He laughed ruefully. "I hate turbot," he said. "And I'm going to have the saddle of lamb."

She looked up, surprise clear in her eyes, and then she laughed with him. A warm, open chuckle that for once seemed to carry no underlying mockery. "I didn't mean to snub you."

"Yes, you did."

"Well, forgive me. It was very rude when I'm sure you were only being kind."

"Kind," he exclaimed in disgust. "I was not. I was being charming."

"Oh," she said. "Was that what it was? It always surprises me that men seem to think women find it appealing to have their decisions made for them."

"You are an unusual member of your sex," he said dryly.

"Perhaps not as unusual as you think," she responded. "I think there are probably quite a few of us around."

"Let us call a truce, Miss Duncan." He stretched a hand across the table.

Constance could see no reason to refuse the offer. At least for the duration of the evening. She shook his hand in a businesslike fashion. "Let us also dispense with formalities, Max. My name is Constance."

"Constance," he said, holding her hand for a moment longer than a simple handshake warranted.

She became aware of a sensation in her fingertips akin to pins and needles and caught herself contemplating his hands, thinking that she liked them, had liked them from the first moment of their acquaintance. Firmly she took back her own hand, dismissing the irrelevant and distracting reflection.

"What are you going to eat?" he asked into the moment of silence that threatened to become awkward.

"The lamb," she said. "Smoked salmon, lobster soufflé, and the lamb."

He nodded gravely and returned to the wine list. "Sancerre, you think?"

She raised her hands, palms towards him. "Please, I would not presume to guide my host."

"Oh, wouldn't you just?" He grinned and his vivid blue eyes crinkled at the corners. It gave him an almost boyish air and Constance was once more surprised. She was willing to acknowledge that he was an attractive man, but until now she had not found his appearance particularly appealing. Perhaps she hadn't given it a chance.

Another distracting thought. She sat back and allowed her gaze to roam around the dining room while he talked with the sommelier.

Constance was aware that they were drawing some interested glances. A new tidbit for the gossipmongers. It occurred to her that she could write a little squib for the next edition describing the dinner enjoyed by Max Ensor and Miss Duncan. An involuntary choke of laughter escaped her and Max turned back from the sommelier.

"Something amusing?"

"Oh, just a stray thought," she said carelessly, waving her fingertips at an acquaintance across the room.

Max proved a deft conversationalist and Constance was content to follow his lead as he discussed Bernard Shaw's latest play, *Man and Superman,* the recent death of the artist Camille Pissarro, and the design for the new Liverpool Cathedral. The range of subjects that seemed to interest him struck her as unusual. The depths of his interests went way beyond the ordinary social demands of skillful small talk.

"Let me guess," he said, as the waiter removed their plates with the remnants of saddle of lamb. "You're a cheese-before-dessert person."

"You're close but not quite close enough," she said, regarding him over the rim of her wineglass.

"Ah." He nodded his comprehension. "Cheese, no dessert."

"On the nose."

"Well, I can see the virtue, but I can't resist the crème brûlée here."

"My sister Chastity would tell you that the napoleon is the best in town. She is something of an expert."

"It's unusual to find a woman who has no sweet tooth," he observed.

Constance raised an eyebrow. "Another stereotype, Max?"

"An observation from experience," he retorted.

Constance turned in her chair towards the cheese trolley. It was her turn to be placatory, she decided. "As it happens, I think it *is* unusual. I inherit the lack from my mother . . . Some of the Epoisses, please." She pointed to a round cheese that was in the process of fleeing its board. "And a little of the Bleu d'Auvergne."

"A glass of port?" suggested Max, as he pointed to the wheel of Stilton. "In lieu of dessert."

"Lovely." An involuntary little sigh of pleasure escaped her as the waiter snipped off a bunch of green grapes and laid them on the plate beside her cheese.

"Port, cheese, and grapes... a ménage à trois made in heaven. Who could possibly want cake when one can have that?"

Max consulted once more with the sommelier and then leaned his elbows on the table, his hands loosely clasped. "So, will you permit me to drive you to the country on Friday?"

Constance shook her head. "No, I'm afraid I can't."

He looked disconcerted. "I'm a very safe driver, I assure you."

"I don't doubt it." She considered for a minute, then said in the low tone of one sharing a confidence, "My father, however, is not. His eyesight is not what it was but he's dead set on getting a motorcar. We're doing everything in our power to dissuade him, and if he sees me merrily aboard one our arguments are going to look somewhat hypocritical."

"Oh, I see." He nodded. "He could have a chauffeur."

"Yes, but he'd say that would be pointless—a case of keeping a dog and barking oneself. Besides, Cobham, our coachman, has already said he couldn't get used to these newfangled machines and he's been with us far too long to be put out to grass... to use his own expression." She shrugged and gave him a what-can-one-do? smile.

"Awkward," Max agreed. "Perhaps I should take the train myself."

"I hardly think such a sacrifice is necessary."

"Perhaps I'd choose to make it," he said, taking the scent of his port. He nodded at her glass. "Tell me if you approve."

Constance did so. "Why would you choose to forgo your drive? I hear it's very exhilarating," she added, unable to hide a wistful note.

"It is. But I would readily exchange it for your company on the train."

Did he really think she was so naïve as to be disarmed by such a piece of naked flattery? "You are a very smooth talker, Mr. Ensor," she observed, disappointed by such an unsubtle approach, although she supposed that a man who saw women in terms of generalizations would probably see nothing wrong with tried-and-true seduction maneuvers, however hackneyed.

"That implies insincerity, Miss Duncan," he said as he cut into his Stilton.

"If the shoe fits," she responded, then changed the subject before the exchange could become any sharper. "We usually take the noon train from Waterloo. It gets to Southampton at three, and connects with the branch line to Romsey, arriving at half-past. Someone will meet us with the trap."

"May I take that as an invitation to meet you at Waterloo?" He sipped his port, determined to persevere even though Miss Constance Duncan was the most prickly dinner companion he'd ever encountered.

"Please do." She raised her own glass and smiled at him across the ruby contents. Antagonism wasn't going to advance her cause at all and she could see how put out he was. She needed to blunt her tongue a little.

"I felt guilty this afternoon about what I'd said about your niece's governess," she said, peeling a grape with her knife.

"Oh?" He was instantly alert. "Why so? What has Miss Westcott to do with you?"

Constance began to peel another grape. It gave her an excuse for not meeting his eye. "Nothing, of course. And that's why I feel bad about what I said at the

Beekmans' soirée. I had no idea of the woman's situation when I presumed to pass judgment on her skills."

"Since she's unaware of your lapse in judgment I think you can safely lay your guilt to rest," he said aridly, still as sharply watchful as before. It seemed wise to assume that she had just delivered an opening salvo designed to distract him before the main attack.

Constance raised her eyes and gave him a disarming smile. "It's a little awkward. By apologizing for casting aspersions on the governess I am indirectly criticizing your sister."

"Yes," he agreed. "I confess myself fascinated to know why you're digging yourself into this particular hole." He had no faith in that disarming smile at all.

Constance met his steady gaze and dropped the pretence. "You were the one who defended the governess. I'm merely saying that after your sister's comments this afternoon I take your point."

He pursed his lips slightly but asked only, "Coffee?"

"When you've had your crème brûlée."

"I think the port has spoiled me for pudding." He nodded to the ever-hovering waiter. "So you feel a mother should not concern herself with the political and social opinions of those in charge of her children?"

"I think she has no right to invade her employees' privacy," Constance retorted. "If they keep their opinions private, then surely they are no one's business but their own. Is Miss Westcott able to stand up for herself?"

"Probably not," Max said, his expression carefully neutral.

"How long has she been with your sister?"

"Oh, I believe she's lasted almost ten months," he said. "At least six months longer than any of the others."

Constance suspected that he was trying to provoke her with his light insouciance. She refused to be provoked. "Is she very young?" She poured coffee into two cups from the delicate china pot set reverently at her elbow. The waiter took one cup and placed it in front of Max.

"Well above the age of discretion," Max said, taking a sugar lump from the bowl with silver tongs. "Why does she interest you so much?" He dropped the lump into his cup.

"She doesn't really," Constance said.

He looked at her askance. "Oh? I was assuming that as a downtrodden member of the exploited female classes Miss Westcott held a most particular interest for you."

Constance drank her coffee. "I won't deny that. My sisters and I were educated by a woman who felt very strongly about such issues."

He leaned across the table, his gaze intent. "And you would deny that children are influenced by the views of those who are responsible for forming their minds?"

"No, of course I wouldn't. I never said any such thing. I simply said that a woman is entitled to keep her opinions private if she's made it clear she wishes to do so. Is there any evidence that this Miss Westcott has attempted to press her own political views on the six-year-old?"

"I doubt Pammy has the concentration span to take in anything so complex," Max said. "Like most—" He broke off.

"Like most women," she finished for him. "Was that what you were about to say?"

He sighed. "Must you put words into my mouth?"

"You've made your views quite clear."

He leaned forward, resting his forearms on the table. "I do not understand why women should need the vote. They wield a powerful influence on their menfolk at home. Why, I know more powerful women than men, I can tell you. Their husbands and brothers do exactly what they're told."

Constance stared at him. "I can't believe you'd trot out that old saw," she said in disgust. "*Women are the power behind the throne.* And even if I concede that some lucky women do have influence over the men who make decisions for them, what about all the women who have no such power? Who's going to make decisions that would improve their lives? Who's even interested in them?" She shook her head, her eyes glittering with angry conviction, her cheeks flushed.

Max toyed with the idea of commenting that she looked beautiful when she was angry but decided that he'd provoked her enough for one evening. He was fairly certain now that she was a card-carrying member of the WSPU and would serve his purposes very well. It was time to retreat, offer a sop, and plan the next step. If he played his cards right she would spill all the information he needed.

"Maybe the WSPU has some merit," he said calmly. "But these women need to consider the far-reaching effects of such a social change. It must be considered from every angle."

Constance's angry flush died down. She couldn't argue that point. When she spoke, it was as calmly as he. "But we need some assurances from the government that they would consider the issue." The candle on the table flared in the breeze created by a waiter's coattails as he hurried past and Max saw golden light flash against the intent dark green of her eyes. He also heard the inadvertent *we*. She was showing her true colors.

"As I understand it, the issue is on the table in Cabinet," he replied.

Constance examined his countenance and could read no dissembling there. Presumably he would know if he lunched regularly with the Prime Minister and the Cabinet. "That's something," she said neutrally.

He inclined his head in acknowledgment and firmly closed the subject. "Would you like a cognac?"

"No, thank you. I need a clear head for tomorrow. But don't let me stop you."

"I too need a clear head." He caught the hovering waiter's eye and when he brought the bill asked him to summon a hackney. "Perhaps next time, if you'll do me the honor of dining with me again, we can take a drive in the motor. I could pick you up out of sight of Manchester Square and we could drive out along the river. There's a very pleasant spot near Windsor, good food, pretty view . . . ?"

"It sounds delightful," Constance said in the same neutral tone. She gathered up her evening bag. "If you'll excuse me . . ."

Max rose to his feet as the waiter pulled back her chair and she extricated herself with a graceful twitch of her skirts. Max watched her as she moved through the dining room towards the ladies' retiring room, pausing at a number of tables en route. He couldn't decide whether the evening had been a success or not. He'd discovered what he wanted to know, but he didn't think he'd succeeded too well in disarming the lady. She showed no inclination to respond to either flattery or overt seduction. And for his part, while she was a lovely woman and a stimulating companion, he found her passionate wrong-headedness and her constant sparring utterly exasperating. But perhaps it was a way to hold him at bay. If it was, it succeeded all too well.

And now his interest was truly piqued. He would topple the castle one way or another. There had to be a woman beneath the intellectual shell. It was all very well to be possessed by the passions of the mind, and he was more than happy to pay all due respect to her mental prowess, but there were other passions that even such a single-minded woman could learn to respect and enjoy.

Constance emerged from the retiring room, having discreetly left a copy of *The Mayfair Lady* in the basket of linen towels, out of sight of the attendant. She wasn't sure what she'd accomplished this evening. A few details about Miss Westcott, but nothing significant, and the possibility that the government was at least examining the women's suffrage issue. It wasn't much to take away. And she didn't think she'd made a dent in Max Ensor's Neanderthal views on a woman's place. *Power behind the throne, indeed*. But she had an entire weekend ahead of her. A weekend under her own roof. If she couldn't make some headway with the man, she wasn't the woman she believed herself to be.

Max was on his feet as she approached the table. She wore a little half smile, a secretive and rather complacent Mona Lisa smile, and a certain gleam in her eye that fascinated him even as it put him on his guard. *What had she been up to in the ordinarily innocuous confines of the ladies' retiring room?* He said only, "The cab's waiting."

Constance became aware of her smile as she caught his slightly speculative look. She realized that she had been smiling for the entire walk across the dining room and now hastily composed her features and murmured the correct pleasantries.

They sat in silence in the darkened interior of the hackney, but it was a suspenseful silence. Constance wondered if he would make a move, and wondered how, if he did, she should respond. It wouldn't be unusual at the end of such an evening for her escort to offer a discreet if not hesitant kiss. She waited, but not for long. Max laid a hand gently on her knee. She did not react. She let the warm pressure soak through the thin silk. He turned on the leather bench and with his other hand cupped her chin, turning her face towards his. She could see his eyes in the gloom, glowing and yet dark, the shape of his nose, the full sensual curve of his mouth. She remained still and silent, still unsure as to how she wanted to react.

Max ran a finger over her lips, wondering how to interpret her silence, her immobility that was neither rejection nor resistance. Then she parted her lips and lightly touched his finger with the tip of her tongue. The bold assurance of her gesture surprised him even as he realized that it was time he ceased to be surprised by Constance Duncan. He bent his head and kissed her. Her response told him clearly that she was no tyro in these matters. So much the better, he thought. Her mouth opened beneath his, her hands moved to encircle his neck, and as his tongue moved deep within her mouth she met him thrust for thrust. He had thought to offer nothing more than a chaste peck, but she had taken matters into her own hands. Perversely, he wasn't entirely sure that it pleased him.

The coach drew to a halt. "Manchester Square, guv." The cabby's lilting call broke the silence and they drew apart. Constance brushed her lips with her fingertips, smoothed her hair. "Thank you for a lovely evening, Max."

"The pleasure was all mine, Constance." His teeth gleamed white as he returned her formal farewell and the very polite smile. He stepped out to the pavement and gave her his hand to help her alight. He walked her to the top of the steps, pulled the bell rope, and raised her hand to his lips. *"À bientôt."*

"Friday, Waterloo, at noon," Constance responded.

"I look forward to it."

Constance raised a hand in a gesture of farewell and turned away as Jenkins opened the door for her. "You had a pleasant dinner, miss?" he inquired.

"I'm not entirely sure," she responded. "Are my sisters in bed?"

"I hardly think so, Miss Con," Jenkins said with a knowing smile. "I believe you'll find them in the parlor upstairs."

"Then I'll bid you good night." Constance gave him a wave and hurried up the stairs, holding her skirts clear of her feet. She couldn't avoid this tête-à-tête with her sisters, who would be eagerly awaiting her return, and she wouldn't want to anyway, but she wasn't sure how much she was prepared to reveal about the carriage ride home. She had intended to offer a light and playful good night kiss that would merely tease him. Somehow that was not what had happened. Not at all what had happened. She opened the parlor door.

Prue and Chastity were playing backgammon but they jumped up as she came in. "So, tell us all," Chastity demanded. "Did you squabble all evening, or did it become wonderfully romantic?"

"Oh, you are impossible, Chas." Constance drew off her gloves. "As it happens we squabbled almost nonstop and the only romantic moment was when he kissed me good night in the cab."

"A good kiss?" Prudence asked with raised eyebrows.

"I'm still trying to decide." She flung herself inelegantly into the depths of the chesterfield and kicked off her shoes. Her sisters were gazing at her with all the fixed attention of lions waiting to be thrown their food.

"On a scale of one to ten," Prudence demanded.

Constance pretended to consider the matter. She stretched out her hands and examined her nails. "Bold," she said thoughtfully. "Strong...warm...lips and tongue well plied...Since I don't think it's possible to give a ten because you never know what else you might experience, I'll say an eight."

"Pretty high praise," Prudence judged.

"Sounds a little forward for a first kiss," Chastity observed, beginning to gather up the backgammon pieces.

"I suppose it was," Constance agreed. "But it wasn't entirely his fault."

"Oh, really?" Her sisters regarded her intently. Then Chastity asked simply, "Was it at all like with Douglas?"

Constance didn't immediately reply. "I don't know," she said after a minute. "It's awful, but I can't really remember anymore what it was like with Douglas. It's hard enough to see his features clearly in my mind. But when I think of him buried under some South African kopje I want to tear my hair out, scream and hiss and spit at the whole damned injustice of it all." She stared down at the carpet, but her eyes were unfocused. "I'm over it, of course I am, but I'm in no hurry to bury his memory in some new passion."

"So Max Ensor isn't getting under your skin," Prudence stated.

"No," Constance said definitely. "His opinions are. He's positively Neanderthal. But I very much like the idea of working on him." She looked up, her expression once more relaxed, the shadows gone from her eyes. "I intend to give Max Ensor a radical education, and before I'm done with him he'll be wearing the colors of the WSPU."

"And he's definitely coming to Romsey for the weekend?"

Constance nodded. "Yes. He'll meet us at Waterloo."

"And you've already made some plans for him?"

"They're in embryo at present but they're coming together." A grin flashed across her countenance. "I'll tell you when I've sorted them out properly. Oh, by the way, he wanted us to drive down but I managed to dissuade him. I told him father's eyesight was bad but he still wanted to get a motor and we didn't want to encourage him."

"Nicely saved." Prudence yawned involuntarily. "Anything useful about Miss Westcott?"

"Not really. She's not some ingenue, that much I did discover. Past the age of discretion is how Max put it. She's managed to stick it out at the Grahams for longer than any other governess, so the child likes her. That's about it."

"Oh, well, it's something. I wonder what it is that's so delicate about her situation." Chastity went to the door.

"No doubt we shall find out." Constance extinguished the lights and followed her sisters up to bed.

* * *

Amelia Westcott hurried across Park Lane from Hyde Park, clutching the hand of her protesting charge, and entered the Park Lane Post Office just as a shower of rain gusted across the street.

"My hat is wet," Pammy complained. "It's my new straw hat. Mama just bought it, and now it's wet and spoiled."

"It will dry, Pammy," Amelia said. "See, we're out of the rain now." She let the door bang behind her. "Let's have a race with the raindrops on the window." She encouraged the girl over to the glass and pointed out two drops trickling slowly from the top. "The one on the left is mine." She indicated with her finger.

"I want that one."

"Very well. Then I'll have the one on the right." Suppressing a sigh, Amelia went to the counter, where the clerk gave her a sympathetic smile.

"Mornin', Miss Westcott. Got a letter for you ... arrived in the morning post." He turned to the wall of pigeonholes behind him and took out a long envelope.

"Mine won! Mine won!" Pamela danced over to the counter. "See, Miss Westcott. Mine won!" She grabbed her governess's hand, tugging her back to the window. Amelia pocketed her letter, smiled her thanks to the clerk, and allowed herself to be dragged to view the triumph of the anonymous raindrop.

"See!" Pamela jabbed at the bottom of the window. "That was mine. Let's do it again. I want to do it again." Her voice rose slightly as if she was anticipating argument.

"Which one is yours?" Amelia said quickly.

"That one!" The child pointed. "And that one's yours." Amelia reconciled herself to a tedious quarter hour playing this game. The letter itched in her pocket but nothing would be gained by rousing the devil in Pamela. She thought wearily that she had always liked children. She had told herself that becoming a governess wasn't the worst fate to befall an educated woman without means. Now, regarding this spoiled and rather sad child, she thought that a life on the streets might be considerably more congenial.

Finally, however, Pamela tired of the game and the rain stopped. They walked back to Albermarle Street, the child in great good humor, having secured herself a win in every raindrop contest. She prattled nonstop, skipping through puddles, heedless of the splashes to her smocked pinafore and white stockings. Nanny Baxter would grumble from the comfort of her armchair all afternoon, Amelia reflected. But this afternoon it wouldn't trouble her. She had a few short hours of liberty and a letter in her pocket.

In the day nursery she installed her charge at the lunch table under the supervision of the nursery maid, and went to her own bedroom conveniently situated next to the night nursery, in case Miss Pammy awoke with a nightmare. She withdrew the envelope from her coat pocket and slit it with a fingernail. She took out the single sheet and sat slowly on the narrow bed. The handwriting was feminine and the core of the message made her heart leap. *Lyons Corner House. Marble Arch, at four o'clock this afternoon.* Whoever or whatever constituted the Go-Between, she or they were prepared to help if they could.

Amelia lay back on her bed, still in her damp coat and hat. When she'd seen the advertisement in *The Mayfair Lady* it had seemed like the answer to a prayer. Her situation was impossible; it had no feasible solution; and yet it would inevitably be resolved one way or the other. She had no one to turn to. And then the advertisement. The service had to be offered by women; no man would advertise in *The Mayfair Lady*. For the first time she saw a smidgeon of hope on the bleak horizon. And now, as she read the response a second time and her eyes dwelled on each feminine stroke of the pen, she felt a strange but sure comfort. The only women friends she had known had been in her school in Bath. When she left there, sufficiently educated for a life as a governess, she had known only her employers, and there were no cozy female relationships to be developed there. Letitia Graham was about the worst Amelia had encountered.

"Miss Westcott? Your lunch is getting cold."

"I'm coming right away," she called back to the nursemaid, who'd accompanied her call with an imperative rap at the door. She discarded coat and hat, combed her hair, and returned to the day nursery to eat macaroni pudding with her charge.

Three o'clock came at last. Pamela went off with her mother and Amelia left the house. She walked quickly to Marble Arch. Gusty showers swept leaves from the trees and dampened the pavements and pedestrians scurried under umbrellas, sheltering in doorways or under awnings whenever they became particularly threatening. Amelia was unperturbed.

The Lyons Corner House was on the corner of Marble Arch, its glass windows steamed up with the rain outside and the warmth within. She went in, glancing at her watch. She was half an hour early. She selected a table in the window and took a seat facing the door so that she would have a clear view. She set her copy of *The Mayfair*

Lady on the table in plain view and ordered tea. The letter had said that the Go-Between would be carrying a copy of the newspaper; it made sense to Amelia that she should do the same.

Her tea arrived, with a hot buttered crumpet. She took her time, enjoying every bite. Apart from her late-night supper, which was always cold meat of some description and sliced tomato or beetroot, she ate every meal with her charge, and Pamela's tastes were monotonous. She kept her eye on the door and precisely at four o'clock, three women walked in. They wore hats with delicate little veils that covered only their eyes—neat hats—and subdued clothes that nevertheless shouted both money and elegance. Amelia felt her optimism fade. Then she saw the distinctive badge—purple, white, and green—that the tallest of the women wore; and she saw the copy of *The Mayfair Lady* that she carried. Her spirits lifted. This woman was a member of the WSPU.

The three women paused, looked around the restaurant, and Amelia hesitantly lifted her copy of the newspaper. They came towards her, putting back their veils as they did so.

"Miss Westcott." The woman wearing the WSPU badge held out her hand. "I'm Constance. Let me introduce my sisters. This is Prudence... and Chastity." She indicated her companions, who shook Amelia's hand and sat down.

"So how can we help you, Miss Westcott?"

Chapter 7

I need to find a husband," Amelia Westcott stated.

"Well, that's to the point," Constance observed, taking off her gloves and putting them in her handbag.

"It is what your service offers?" Amelia said, her heart fluttering, her gray eyes expressing uncertainty and anxiety.

"Certainly it is," Prudence said. "Let us order tea."

"Those crumpets look delicious," Chastity declared. "We shall have a plate of those and four cream slices." She smiled at the elderly waitress in her starched cap and apron.

The waitress made a note on her pad and went away with the weary flat-footed tread of one who spent far too many hours on her feet.

"So what kind of husband did you have in mind?" Constance asked.

"Well, I don't know exactly. I assumed you'd have a list ... a register or something ... of men looking for wives."

The sisters glanced at one another and Amelia's anxiety

increased. The return of the waitress with tea prevented further discussion but once she had gone and the thick china cups were filled, crumpets passed, Prudence took off her glasses, rubbed them with her handkerchief, and carefully replaced them on her nose.

"That is what we hope to achieve, Miss Westcott," she said. "But as of this moment we don't exactly have a register." She blinked once behind her glasses. "You see, you happen to be our first client."

"Oh." Amelia looked as confused as she felt. "How . . . how could that be?"

"Well, there has to be a first," Chastity pointed out, spooning sugar into her tea.

"Yes, we've . . . or rather, *The Mayfair Lady* has just started offering the Go-Between service," Constance explained, cutting a crumpet into neat quarters. "But I'm certain we can help you. You said something about a delicate situation. If you could tell us something about yourself and your position, we could make a start."

Amelia regarded the three sisters doubtfully. She had nerved herself to confide her wretched situation with a businesslike and efficient agency. She had not expected to take tea with three society ladies and discuss the matter as if it were mere social chitchat.

Constance saw her hesitation and said, "Miss Westcott, we understand something of your situation. It can't be pleasant to be subject to Lady Graham."

Amelia flushed. "How could you possibly know . . . ?"

"This is awkward," Prudence said. "We know Letitia. And we happened to discover that her daughter's governess was a Miss Westcott." She shrugged a little defensively. "It's inevitable in our position." She shrugged again.

Amelia reached for her gloves on the table beside her. "I cannot see how you could help me. I had assumed this would be a businesslike arrangement; I could not possibly confide my situation to people who would be in a position to betray my trust." Her hands shook as she struggled with her buttoned gloves.

There was a moment of silence, then Chastity leaned forward and laid a hand over Amelia's quivering fingers. "Listen for a minute, Amelia. We would not under any circumstances betray your confidence to *anyone*. We have a pledge of utter discretion. What we know of Letitia simply makes us all the more anxious to help you. You need a husband to escape her service. Is that the situation?"

There was such sincerity and sympathy in her voice that Amelia felt some of her earlier hope trickle back. She looked at the three women and read the compassion in their eyes. There was compassion but there was also strength and determination in all three faces that somehow imparted confidence.

Amelia made up her mind. *What did she have to lose, after all?*

"It's not as simple as that," she said, a dull flush creeping over her cheeks. "If it were, I would simply find another situation."

She had their complete attention. Tea cooled in cups, butter pooled beneath crumpets. "Two months ago I was in the country with Pamela. Lord and Lady Graham wanted her to spend the summer out of London in their country house in Kent."

The three sisters nodded. Amelia toyed with the spoon in her saucer, her eyes on the white linen tablecloth. "There were to be no formal lessons since it was a holiday, but I was to take her for instructional walks, supervise her riding lessons..." She paused and the flush on her cheeks deepened. "And supervise her music lessons. Pamela is always very reluctant to practice on the pianoforte. She is, I'm afraid, an impatient pupil in most areas."

"Her mother is not an advocate of education for women," Constance said.

Amelia gave a short laugh. "Indeed not. But it's hard to blame Lady Graham since her own education was so sadly lacking. Indeed, I believe she considers it to be a disadvantage in a woman."

"I'm sure she does," Prudence said, pushing her glasses up the bridge of her nose with a forefinger. Her eyes were shrewd as they rested upon Amelia Westcott. "The music teacher..." she prompted.

Amelia took a deep breath. "Henry Franklin," she stated on a swift exhalation. "The youngest son of Justice Franklin, the local magistrate and owner of the local brickworks. Henry's a musician; his father does not approve. He wants him to do the accounting at the brickworks. His two brothers work there and Mr. Franklin expects Henry to join them."

"And Henry refuses." Chastity took a cream slice from the plate and thoughtfully licked a dab of raspberry jam from her finger.

"Not exactly...he..." Amelia shrugged helplessly. "He goes into the office and tries to do what his father wants but it's killing his soul. His father said that if he could make a living at teaching music then he would cease his objections, but Mr. Franklin knows perfectly well that Henry couldn't survive as a musician without his support, and in exchange for that support he must do as his father says."

Constance thought that this Henry Franklin lacked strength of character if not conviction but she kept her mouth shut. She had the sense that this was only the beginning of Amelia Westcott's problem.

"I'm getting the impression that you and Henry Franklin developed an understanding while you were in Kent," Chastity said delicately, breaking off a piece of flaky pastry from her cake.

Amelia finally raised her eyes from the tablecloth. "Yes," she said bluntly. "Rather more than an understanding." She met their gaze without flinching. "As a result I now find myself in a delicate situation."

"Oh," Prudence said. "That's very awkward."

"A husband is the only solution," Amelia said. "Once my condition is known to Lady Graham she'll cast me out without a reference, and I'll never be able to find another situation. No self-respecting house would employ a fallen woman." She met their eyes again. "Would they?"

"No," Constance agreed. "You'd be blackballed."

"And besides, you'll have a baby to care for," Chastity said, frowning. "Even if you boarded the baby—"

"Which I would never do!"

"No, of course not," Chastity said quickly. "I wasn't really suggesting it as a possibility."

"So I need a compliant husband," Amelia stated. "I was hoping you might have one on your books. A widower, perhaps... someone who'd be willing to give me the protection of his name in exchange for everything else. Child care, housekeeping... whatever was necessary."

"That seems like exchanging one form of servitude for another," Constance said.

"What choice do I have?" Amelia laid her hands palms open on the tablecloth. "I am not a woman of independent means." There was a bitter note in her voice that drew the comparison between an impoverished governess and her present companions.

"Oddly, neither are we," Prudence said. "We're trying to keep our father out of debtors' prison and ourselves off the streets."

"Hence our venture with *The Mayfair Lady* and the Go-Between," Chastity said.

Amelia was silent for a minute. Then she said in a flat voice, "But none of you is pregnant."

"That is certainly true," Constance agreed. "So let's look at your options here. Have one of these before Chas eats them all." She offered the plate of cakes to Amelia.

"I've developed the most dreadful passion for sugary food," Amelia confided, taking one of the creamy confections. "Fortunately Pammy is kept well supplied with such things." She took a healthy bite, aware that she was feeling stronger, almost lighthearted. These three women had somehow managed to take the desperation out of her situation. She had no idea how, since they didn't appear to offer the salvation she had hoped for.

"It seems to me that Henry would be the best candidate," Chastity suggested somewhat tentatively. It was such an obvious solution she assumed there was a problem that Amelia had not divulged.

"Unless he's already married?" Prudence ventured.

Amelia shook her head and dabbed pastry crumbs from the corner of her mouth. "No, he's not. He can't afford to marry without his father's consent, and Justice

Franklin would not consent to his marrying an impoverished governess. Even though my family is every bit as good as the Franklins," she added with a flash of fire.

"But what if Henry earned his living independently of his father," Constance mused. "Could he get a job in a school as a music teacher? I believe some of the better prep schools even provide housing for their teaching staff."

"I could suggest it if I could get in touch with him," Amelia said, and now her voice lost its vibrancy. "I've written to him several times, although I couldn't tell him the situation. I couldn't risk writing something like that. Lady Graham probably reads my blotter in a mirror."

"I doubt she's clever enough," Constance said acidly.

A wryly appreciative smile touched Amelia's lips but her expression instantly returned to gloom. "I haven't heard a word from Henry. He's not answered a single one of my letters. He must have received them; the post is perfectly reliable. I can only assume he doesn't want to hear from me."

"There could be other explanations," Chastity said. "Perhaps he's not at the address anymore."

"In that case why wouldn't he write and give me his new address?"

"There you have me." Constance drummed her fingers on the table. "I suggest we find out."

"How?"

"Pay him a visit."

"But I could never get even a day's free time."

"Not you, Amelia, us."

"Yes, we'll go and make a reconnaissance," Prudence said. "We won't necessarily tell him anything specific; we'll just see what the situation is."

"It's a start, at any rate." Chastity touched Amelia's hand again. "Don't worry. We have plenty of time to sort this out. When do you think the baby's due?"

"Oh, not for another seven months." Amelia smiled, clearly making an effort to respond to Chastity's optimism.

"Then you won't start to show for another two or three months," Prudence stated. "And you can always loosen your gowns. You'll be able to cover it for quite a while."

Amelia nodded. "But I must make provision. I can't wait until the last minute."

"No, and we won't," Constance said firmly. "We'll start with Henry, and if that proves a dead end, then we'll find another solution."

Amelia glanced at the clock on the wall and gave a little cry of alarm. "I must get back, it's almost five-thirty. I must be back by six when Pammy gets back with her mother." She began to fumble in her handbag. "What do I owe you for the consultation?"

"Nothing," the sisters said in unison.

"And you won't owe us anything ever," Chastity declared, ignoring a slight twitch from Prudence.

"Oh, but I must pay you. You're providing a service for hire. It says so." Amelia tapped the copy of the newspaper on the table.

"It's all right," Constance said with blithe exaggeration. "We have the possibility of paying clients already. They can afford to pay a little extra."

Amelia couldn't help a wan smile. She laid a shilling on the table. "At least let me pay for my tea."

"If you insist." Prudence laid their own share on the

table beside Amelia's. Her sisters' reckless generosity was all very well, but a shilling was a shilling.

"I see you're a member of the WSPU." Amelia gestured to the badge Constance wore on her lapel.

"Yes, but I don't make it public." Constance unpinned the badge. "Because of *The Mayfair Lady*. I write a lot of political articles and we're lobbying for women's suffrage. I don't want people to guess that I might have anything to do with the newspaper. I wore the badge this afternoon to reassure you, since I'm guessing you sympathize with the Union."

"It did reassure me," Amelia declared, getting to her feet. "I have to keep my affiliation a secret too. I can rarely get to meetings."

"That will change," Constance stated. "One of these days that will change."

"Yes, Con's working on a Member of Parliament," Chastity said mischievously. "We have high hopes that the Right Honorable—" She broke off in confusion as Prudence trod hard on her foot and she realized what she had been about to reveal.

Fortunately, Amelia was too anxious to be on her way to pay much attention. She scribbled the address she had for Henry Franklin in the margin of *The Mayfair Lady* and Constance promised that they would pay their visit to Kent at the beginning of the following week.

"Meet us here next Thursday afternoon at the same time," Prudence said, giving Amelia her hand. "We'll have some news for you then."

Amelia nodded, seemed about to say something, then shook her head in a brief hurried gesture and left the Corner House.

"I'm sorry." Chastity said as soon as the door had shut

with a definitive ring of its bell on the departing client. "I can't think what made me forget she would know Max Ensor. She lives under the same roof as the man, for heaven's sake." She shook her head in self-disgust.

"Have another cake," Prudence said. "There was no harm done."

Chastity gave Constance a contrite smile. "Forgive me?"

"Sweetheart, there's nothing to forgive." Constance returned the smile. "Besides, it's true. You know I intend to work on him."

"I shouldn't have gabbed about your personal life," Chastity said.

"Forget it, Chas. My personal life in this instance is entirely bound up with my political life, and as such is hardly personal at all."

Prudence gathered up her belongings. "Either way, it should enliven the weekend somewhat. More than tennis anyway."

Constance was more than happy to take her sister's cue and let the subject drop. "I'm not sure I'm going to approve of this Henry Franklin," she said as they went out. She clapped her hand to her hat as a particularly energetic gust of wind whistled around the corner of Marylebone Street.

"We don't have to approve of him," Prudence pointed out. "Just bring him up to the mark. Shall we take a cab?"

"Only if we can afford it, Prue dear," Constance teased.

"Well, I'm not sure that we can," Prudence retorted. "With you and Chas insisting on forgoing our fees. How are we to make ends meet when we don't charge the clients?"

"We have to haul in the rich ones," Constance said. "I

couldn't bring myself to take that poor woman's money, and neither could you."

"No," Prudence agreed. "We'll call the experience payment enough."

"A happy solution." Constance hailed a hackney. "I have a feeling we're going to need all the experience we can get to make Go-Between a success. How on earth are we to compile a list of eligible bachelors? And we have to find a suitable country mouse for Anonymous. At least he's prepared to pay."

"Oh, that's simple." Chas climbed into the hackney. "Just take a look around at our next At Home. We'll find eligible bachelors and eligible maidens aplenty."

"And we compile our own registry," Constance said. "So simple, and yet so brilliant." She applauded her sister.

"I can think of a country mouse or two already. How about Millicent Hardcastle? I know she's no spring chicken but she's definitely on the market and she hates London, she always says so." Prudence leaned out of the window. "Ten Manchester Square, cabby."

Max Ensor stood beneath the clock in the center of Waterloo Station, a calm of presence amid the chattering, rushing throng beneath the cavernous vaulted roof of the concourse. On the platforms behind him trains puffed and blew shrill steam. Max stepped aside as a sweating porter raced past him pushing a trolley laden with baggage. A woman on very high heels that threatened to trip her at any moment clung to the arm of a red-faced man as they half ran behind the porter.

It was eleven-thirty on Friday morning and Max assumed the Duncan party would arrive with time to spare. He couldn't imagine any of the sisters in panicked haste. His valet had taken his valise and tennis rackets to the platform and was already stationed at the point where the first-class compartments would stop when the train came in.

He saw the sisters arriving through the central doors—as he expected, strolling in leisurely fashion, two porters carrying their bags. Lord Duncan was not with them, which surprised Max. It had seemed clear that the sisters were expecting their father to join them for the house party.

Constance greeted him with a wave and extended her hand as she came up with him. "Ah, Max, you're here nice and early."

He took the hand and lightly kissed her cheek as if they were old friends, before turning to shake hands with Chastity and Prudence.

"Where's your bag, Mr. Ensor . . . oh, no, that's ridiculous. If Con calls you Max, we can hardly persist in this formality. Max it shall be. Where's your bag, Max?" Chastity asked from beneath the floppy brim of a most fetching bonnet with tulle ribbons. Little did Max suspect that the bonnet was in its fourth reincarnation.

"Marcel has it on the platform. I hope it's all right if my manservant accompanies me. I can perfectly well do without him, if space is a problem."

"Oh, no, it's perfectly all right. David Lucan never goes anywhere without his valet. He's his mother's spy, you see. Poor David can't take a step without him," Chastity told him with her sweet smile.

"Platform Twelve, madam," one of the porters stated pointedly, shifting the weight of the bags from one hand to another. "Train'll be in by now."

"Oh, yes, of course. Let's go." Constance followed the porters across the concourse, her stride long and easy. Max kept pace beside her.

"Your father's not accompanying you?"

"Oh, yes...no...it's so vexing," she said. "I'll tell you when we're installed. And you have every right to be annoyed."

He looked askance but said nothing until the four of them were ensconced in a first-class carriage, their luggage safely stowed, the porters tipped, and Marcel sent off to his seat in third class.

"It's all the earl of Barclay's fault," Chastity said, unpinning her bonnet. She stood up to set it on the luggage rack. "He's an old friend of Father's and he's just acquired a motor. And, of course, he had to offer to drive Father down to Romsey in it."

"And, of course, Father had to accept," Constance said. "It puts me in such an awkward position, Max. You were so understanding about our little problem and it was all for naught."

"Oh, quite the opposite," he said with a gallant bow. "Now I have the company of all three Duncan sisters."

"Instead of just me," Constance said with a mock sigh. "I'm sure I would have been sad company."

She was poking fun at him, at the suave and automatic little compliment he'd paid them, just as she had accused him of being insincere during their dinner the previous evening. It exasperated him that she would object to a formal courtesy, even if it was an empty compliment.

"Yes," he agreed. "People who don't know how to accept a compliment with grace do tend to be poor company."

Constance's eyes widened. She had not expected a comeback and she had never been accused of gracelessness before. For the moment she was silenced.

She inclined her head in acknowledgment and offered a half smile that held a hint of rueful apology. Her mother had often warned her about the dangers of her too-smart tongue, of how it could come back to bite her. And she remembered how Douglas too in his quiet way would offer a smiling reproach when she hadn't been able to resist the pointed witticism that had a sting in its tail. He had told her that she shouldn't make a habit of employing her wit to put others at a disadvantage. Not a very attractive quality, he had said once. She could hear his voice now, so gently and earnestly reproachful, and suddenly bit her lip, turning to gaze out of the window at the passing countryside until the lump in her throat had dissolved. Maybe she would have been a much nicer person if Douglas had lived. But he hadn't. So she would just have to watch herself and her tongue a little more carefully. And certainly with Max Ensor. She was developing a healthy respect for him as an opponent.

Max rose to pull down the window. He looked along the platform. "Are you expecting any of your other guests on this train?"

It was Prudence who responded. "I hope not. We usually take the early one so that we're there ahead of people. Most people take the two o'clock and arrive in time for tea."

The compartment door opened and a gentleman in the frock-coated uniform of a headwaiter bowed to them. "Will you be taking luncheon with us today, ladies ... sir?"

"Oh, yes," Constance said, recovering her poise.

"The dining car will open at twelve-thirty. Will it be a table for four?"

"Certainly," Max said.

The dining-car attendant bowed and withdrew, drawing the compartment door closed behind him, and Constance turned back to the carriage.

"A train journey wouldn't be the same without brown Windsor soup in one's lap," Prudence observed, unfolding a copy of the *Times* and adjusting her spectacles.

"Oh, I love eating on the train," Chastity declared. "Particularly tea. Those delicious scones and clotted cream, and those lovely little chocolate sponge cakes. Although," she added, "breakfast runs it a close second. Kippers and brown bread and butter."

"Pork sausages," Constance said. "Sausages and tomatoes."

"I get the impression you ladies are hungry," Max observed with amusement.

"Well, we were up very early and it's been a long time since breakfast," Prudence said. None of them mentioned that since Lord Duncan had not graced the breakfast table the usual delicacies had not appeared. The sisters made do with toast and marmalade.

"Do you do crosswords, Mr.... uh ... Max?" Prudence took a sharpened pencil from her handbag.

"Not habitually, but I'm willing to help." He rested his head against the starched white antimacassar and prepared to relax.

Constance was sitting opposite him and he was enjoying the view. She had unfastened the top buttons of her blue linen jacket, which nipped her waist in the most satisfactory fashion. He could see the pulse at the base of her throat, the slender rise of her neck, the slight glisten of moisture on her skin in the stuffy warmth of the compartment. Her legs were crossed at the ankles, very slender ankles, he noticed, and very long and slender feet encased in navy blue kid shoes. He wondered lazily about the rest of her leg, the calves and knees and thighs running up beneath the thin material of her skirt. Her legs were long, that fact required little detective work. And they would be as slender as the rest of her. Her wrists were slim, her fingers long, but her hands nevertheless had a strength to them. They were competent hands. Miss Duncan was a competent woman. Combative, however. But he'd always liked a challenge and this one promised to be more than ordinarily enticing.

She was leaning now to look at the newspaper her sister held, a frown on her brow as she puzzled over a clue. He could see the faint blue veins in her temple. Suddenly she raised her eyes and looked at him. Her eyes were dark green, the green of moss beneath the trunk of an ancient oak. They held a question, a hint of speculation, and he knew she had been aware of his observation. He had a feeling she was sizing him up in her turn.

Max smiled and she dropped her eyes to the crossword again, but not before he'd seen the tiny twitch of her mouth. The weekend, he reflected, could take some interesting turns.

Chapter 8

"here are you going to put him?" Prudence asked in a low voice as they stood on the platform of Romsey station. Max was out of earshot, supervising the unloading of their bags.

"The South Turret," Constance replied in the same conspiratorial undertone.

Chastity chuckled, adjusting the wide brim on her beribboned straw boater. The South Turret had one rather special attribute. "Just what do you have in mind, Con?"

A speculative glint sparked in her sister's eyes. "I'm thinking I'd like to show Mr. Ensor what can happen when a woman takes the initiative. I don't actually think he believes that women *can* take the initiative. I'm certain he believes they *shouldn't*," she added. "It might open his eyes a little to the idea of women playing on an even field. What do you think?"

"Not to pour cold water or anything, Con, but you might be a little overconfident," Prudence observed with a frown. "I don't think the Right Honorable Gentleman is that easy a target. He certainly gave you your own on the train." She took off her glasses and blinked myopically at her sister in the bright sunshine.

Constance grimaced. Practical Prudence, as usual, had put her finger on the flaw in her plan. "I hate to admit it but he had a point," she said ruefully. "But that just makes it more of a challenge." She thought about Max's speculative and almost hungry scrutiny in the railway carriage. If she could exploit that, it would be a weapon in her arsenal more than powerful enough to meet the challenge.

"So you're going to try to seduce him?" Chastity asked, with a hint of alarm. Her hazel eyes beneath the brim of her hat were filled with doubt.

"Not entirely," Constance denied. "Just play with him a little, make him feel a little less sure of himself. He'll be more fertile soil for planting if he loses some of that utterly masculine conviction of superiority."

"I hope you know what you're doing," Chastity said.

"I'm not sure that I do," her sister confessed. "But the idea's appealing. I'll just see where it leads."

A man in the leather waistcoat, apron, and britches of a groom emerged from the tiny station house. "Bags are all loaded, Miss Con. The gentleman's waiting with the trap."

"Thank you, George." The sisters followed him through the station, calling a greeting to the stationmaster, who touched his forelock in salute. The Duncan family had owned Romsey village and most of the outlying countryside since feudal times. In these more enlightened days the tenant farmers and villagers worked independently of the Manor House, but social tradition died hard.

Outside, on a sunny square of daisy-studded grass, a dun-colored pony in the harness of a trap nibbled the grass. Max stood at its head, idly scratching between the animal's pointed ears. Marcel was adjusting the straps that held the bags securely on a shelf at the rear of the trap.

"Is it far to walk to the house?" Max asked as the sisters came over.

"About a mile. Why? Who wants to walk?" Prudence asked.

Max gestured to the trap. "I doubt there's room for us all in the trap. I'm happy to walk; I could do with stretching my legs after the train."

"Oh, two of us can stay here and George will come back," Chastity said. "It'll only take half an hour."

"Actually, I wouldn't mind the walk myself," Constance said casually.

"Then that's settled." Max waved a hand towards the lane in invitation. " 'Lead on, Macduff.' "

"It's actually 'Lay on, Macduff,' " Constance corrected him. "People always get it wrong." She declaimed with a theatrical air, " 'Lay on, Macduff; and damned be him that first cries.' " She paused and her sisters joined in with a rousing chorus, " 'Hold, enough!' "

"I can see I'll have to be a little more careful with my quotations," Max observed wryly.

"Oh, yes, around us you will," Prudence agreed, climbing into the trap. "We are the daughters of Emily Duncan, whose knowledge of Shakespeare was quite awe-inspiring. She could pluck a quote out of midair to suit any occasion."

"How intimidating," Max murmured.

"It was, rather," Chastity agreed, settling on the

bench beside her sister. "And it wasn't only Shakespeare Mother had at her fingertips. She could quote freely from all of the major poets and most of the minor. We'll see you back at the house." She waved gaily as George cracked his whip in a halfhearted fashion and the pony with an equal lack of enthusiasm raised its head from the grass and sauntered off down the lane.

"Your mother was a scholar, it seems," Max observed as he and Constance followed the trap.

"She was very erudite," Constance agreed. "Let's go over the stile; we don't want to swallow their dust, and anyway, it's prettier across the fields." She gathered up her skirt and waded through knee-high yarrow and ragged robin to a crooked and very rickety stile half buried in the overgrown hedge.

Max surveyed the stile doubtfully. "That doesn't look very safe."

"Oh, it's perfectly safe. I just have to be careful not to tear my skirt on a loose nail." She examined the obstacle in her turn. "Actually, I'll have to hitch my skirt up fairly high."

"I'll close my eyes," he offered.

"That's very gallant but quite unnecessary," she said. "I won't show you my knickers." With which she raised her skirts above her knees and hopped with agility if without elegance over the stile, giving Max all the empirical evidence he needed to confirm his guess about the length and shapeliness of her legs.

"There." She shook down her skirt and gave him a grin that was pure seductive mischief and completely took his breath away. "Now you. Watch out for the nail on the top bar. It's right where you have to swing your leg over." She pointed helpfully to the sharp piece of rusty nail. "It could catch you in the most awkward spot."

Max pulled on his right earlobe. It was an automatic gesture going back to his childhood whenever he was at a loss for words or confused by a situation. At present he was suffering from both conditions. Either this woman was teasing him shamelessly or she was issuing an equally shameless invitation. There were two questions: Which was it? And what in either case should he do about it?

Constance stood with her head to one side, watching him. "If you're afraid you'll tear your clothes I'll come back over and we'll go on the lane."

He made no answer, merely stepped onto the crosspiece, swung his leg over the top bar, and jumped down into the clover-strewn field beside her. She nodded her approval and turned to head across the field.

Max decided that whatever the answer to the first question, he knew what he was going to do about it. "Just a minute," he said. He caught her arm and swung her back towards him, turning her into his body. Her look of surprise was very gratifying. "I think I can take a hint," he said, clasping her face between both hands.

It was a hard kiss, nothing exploratory about it, and Constance, after a startled instant, let it happen. Her head fell back and she opened her mouth beneath the insistent pressure of his lips and tongue. He moved a hand behind her head and held her firmly for the utter possession of his mouth and tongue. He drove deep within the moist softness of her mouth, his tongue probing every corner of her cheeks, the roof of her mouth, the even lines of her teeth; their tongues joined in a dancing duel until Constance was breathless, her head held so firmly she couldn't move it aside if she wanted to.

She could feel his body hardening against her, the insistent nudge of his penis into her lower belly, and her loins tightened, then seemed to swell and open in response. She caught herself thinking that this was not the way she had intended to play this, but nevertheless she was clasping his buttocks, pressing her fingers deeply into the rock-hard muscles, squeezing and kneading, holding him tightly against her so that he could feel the knobbly bones of her hips beneath the fine linen of her skirt.

And then he let his hand fall from her head and lifted his mouth from hers. He stepped back from her, drawing a ragged breath. She saw the rigid bulge in his trousers and could guess at his discomfort. Her own disjointed sense of interruption, of abrupt deprivation, so disoriented her for a moment that she could only stand there, taking quick shallow breaths through her mouth.

Finally she closed her mouth, put her hands to her face, feeling its heat. She touched her lips; they felt twice their normal size. "Yes," she said. "You could say that."

"Say what?"

"That you can take a hint." Her eyes involuntarily darted down his body again. He was still hard.

He followed her eyes and gave a rueful sigh. "An inevitable consequence."

"Yes, I realize. If it's any consolation, I'm not exactly comfortable myself."

"One should not begin something one's not prepared to finish," Max said dryly. "But you were extremely provoking."

And she had been right that he needed to have the

upper hand, Constance reflected. It was a pity she'd been so sure of herself she hadn't anticipated such a response to provocation. She began to wonder if Prue was right and perhaps she had bitten off more than she could chew. Seduction was a dangerous game if it got out of hand, and she'd certainly lost the initiative in this round.

Max seemed unaware of her cogitation. He was much more interested in the field around them. "We appear to have entertained the cows at least."

Constance saw that they were surrounded by a circle of interested bovines, placidly chewing the cud and gazing at them with soulful brown eyes. She advanced a few steps, stamped her foot, and clapped her hands. They ignored her.

"I actually don't like cows," Max confided, regarding their audience dubiously. "I'm not a country boy, I'm afraid."

"They won't hurt us. We'll just walk through them." Constance stepped forward with a purposeful air, still clapping her hands. To Max's relief the cows turned aside as if the curtain had come down on a theatrical performance.

They continued their walk in a reflective silence. Uneasily, Constance tried to sort out what had just happened. It was clearly the opening volley in a game, one she had started, but now she wasn't so sure that she wanted to continue it. It was one thing to control the moves, quite another to have them controlled. Maybe seduction was not the way to go about converting Max to her cause. He had proved himself a dominating man— not domineering necessarily, but definitely dominating. She had thought she could handle him, manipulate him to her own ends, but she had not reckoned with her own responses. That kiss had shaken her out of her complacency. It had happened so quickly, taken her off guard, but whatever excuses she made she could not deny that it had rocked her to her core. She had kissed many men with varying degrees of enthusiasm. Only Douglas had aroused her deepest responses. The last few minutes had opened something inside she had almost forgotten. A very dangerous hunger. But was it a danger to be avoided or to be embraced?

Max walked just ahead of her, swishing at the overgrown hedgerows with a stick he'd snapped from the hedge. The repetitive motion quietened the turmoil in his head. He was startled at the ease with which Constance had returned his kiss. Did she habitually yield to casual sexual encounters? In general he avoided them himself but he was deeply disconcerted by the power of his own suddenly revealed lust for the woman walking nonchalantly behind him across the field. He hadn't expected it at all. He had known, or thought he had, exactly where he was going with this lightly flirtatious pursuit. He merely wanted to get some insight from this exasperating woman into the workings of the WSPU.

And then she'd provoked a response and he'd intended to teach her a little lesson by giving her more than she'd bargained for. Instead of which, the shoe had been on the other foot. So much for the best-laid plans of mice and men.

Romsey Manor was at its core a lime-washed, half-timbered Tudor house that had been added to by successive generations of Duncans, so that it now had a mix-and-match style of architecture that gave it a charmingly untidy and informal air. They walked up from the river that ran at the bottom of a sweep of lawn leading to a long terrace at the side of the house.

Prudence and Chastity were standing on the terrace, leaning over the low parapet as Max and Constance came up. "We guessed you'd come across the fields," Chastity said.

"It's quicker," Constance responded, hoping that all signs of that lust-filled embrace had diminished. "I'll show Max to his room."

"Jenkins is organizing tea, and George has gone back to the station to meet the next train. William's gone with him in the gig, so they should be able to bring most people back in one trip."

"Is Father here yet?"

"Not yet."

"Let's hope they haven't overturned in a ditch," Prudence said. "I don't trust Lord Barclay any farther than I can throw him. He's probably pickled in brandy by this time in the afternoon and won't be able to see straight."

Constance grimaced. "In that case Father will be driving, and that's not going to advance our cause. You know what he's like once he gets the bit between his teeth." She shrugged. "Come, Max, I'll show you upstairs. I expect your valet will be waiting for you."

Max had the sense that the Duncan sisters found their father, as affable as he seemed to be, something of a trial. He followed Constance into the cool house. The smell of last winter's wood smoke from the fireplace, potpourri, and beeswax mingled pleasantly in the air. A bevy of young girls, brought in from the village to help for the weekend, he guessed, were setting out tea in the long, beamed-ceiling drawing room under the watchful eye of Jenkins, who had presumably come down from London on an earlier train.

"Is Mr. Ensor's valet in his room, Jenkins?"

"Yes, Miss Con. Miss Prue said the South Turret, so I sent him there with the bags."

Constance nodded and led Max across a dark hall, with the same Tudor beams and a massive fireplace and inglenook at one end, and up a curved Elizabethan staircase. "The South Turret is in the Queen Anne part of the house," she said, turning aside down a long corridor. At the end there was a narrow flight of stairs spiraling upwards and around a corner.

He followed her up. At the very top was a thick oak door. Constance opened it and entered the round chamber lit by four round mullioned windows. Marcel was hanging evening clothes in a Jacobean armoire.

"It has its own bathroom." Constance gestured to a door in the far wall. "Small but adequate. The water's heated with a gas geyser and it takes ages to run a bath."

"I'm duly warned." He looked around the room. It was immediately obvious that it was totally private. Anything could go on up here and no one in the rest of the house would be any the wiser. He glanced speculatively at Constance. She smiled blandly.

What was she up to now? Before the encounter in the field among the cows he would have assumed it meant nothing. Someone had to have this bedroom. And it was a very pleasant room. But now he wasn't so sure. He returned the bland smile without comment.

"It's one of my favorite rooms in the house," Constance said. "I usually give it to first-time guests."

She turned back to the door. "Well, I'll leave you to refresh yourself and see you downstairs for tea."

The door closed behind her. Max, whistling softly to himself, went to one of the open windows and looked out over the surrounding Hampshire countryside. From his aerie the gorse and bracken-covered heaths and hillocks of the New Forest stretched in a golden sea to a line of wind-battered pine trees on the horizon. Beyond them would lie the sea itself. He could smell the salt in the air. It was as powerful as the rich scents of lust.

He wondered what the next steps in this dance would be, as he turned back to the bedroom, to what could so easily become a cozy little love nest, to respond to Marcel's inquiry about his dress for the evening.

"I've had an idea," Constance said, swinging her croquet mallet as she watched the play on the green. It was early evening and the sinking sun slanted through the summer dry leaves of the copper beech tree that shaded the croquet lawn. Max was in the process of knocking Lord Duncan's ball out of play.

"You're full of them," Prudence said. "Oh, well played." She applauded as Max's ball cracked neatly against his opponent's, sending it shooting to the far side of the lawn. "That's going to give Father a challenge."

"He'll enjoy it," Constance said. "Anyway, I think we have to find David Lucan a wife."

"That won't be easy. He only wants Chas," Prudence pointed out.

"Well, he can't have me," Chastity stated. "And I have to admit, I'm beginning to get just a little fed up with the doe eyes that follow me everywhere. I might even have to be rude."

"All the more reason for us to find him another goddess." Constance shielded her eyes against the sun and looked across to where Lord Lucan stood with a group of nonplayers holding cocktail glasses as they watched the game.

"But what about Mama-darling?" Prudence asked. "I don't think she wants him to be independent."

"True enough. We have to find a wife for him who will be the perfectly submissive daughter-in-law so that she can bully both of them in her benevolent fashion and cluck over their children and tell them exactly how to bring them up. And," Constance added on a note of triumph, "I have just the lady in mind."

"Sounds like a pretty grim fate," Prudence pointed out. "Are you sure you want to condemn some poor innocent maiden to such a life?"

"It won't be so bad if the poor innocent maiden is unenlightened," Constance said. "We can't expect to liberate the entire female sex from ordinary domestic oppression in one fell swoop. We have to recognize that there are some who genuinely don't want freedom. Even Mother said that."

"So which innocent maiden did you have in mind?" Chastity inquired, leaning her mallet against a wrought-iron bench.

"Hester Winthrop."

"Hester?" Both sisters stared at her, then looked across the croquet lawn to the very young lady, dressed in a modestly styled evening dress of a pastel pink and standing demurely beside her mother.

"She's very pretty. She's very docile. She comes from

an excellent family and there's no shortage of money there. How could the dowager Lady Lucan object to such a match?"

"But she's so shy. She'd never put herself forward to attract his attention," Prudence objected.

"Isn't that a task for the Go-Between?"

"Girls . . . girls . . . surely you should be mingling with our guests."

The sisters sighed in unison and turned with almost identical polite smiles to greet their aunt, Lord Duncan's sister, who assumed the role of official hostess at her brother's social events since it was considered an unsuitable function for a young unmarried daughter. And the Duncan sisters had not yet reached the age where the sobriquet of spinster would be automatically attached to them. The boring organizational details of social events their aunt cheerfully ceded to her nieces, but the social obligations she performed with the utmost aplomb.

"I didn't know you'd arrived, Aunt Edith." Constance bent to kiss her. "We were just waiting our turn."

"Well, mingle with the guests." Edith shooed at them even as she accepted dutiful kisses from Prudence and Chastity. "What will people think to see you standing like wallflowers talking among yourselves?"

"We *are* playing croquet, Aunt," Constance pointed out. "We're just waiting our turn."

"Go and talk to that nice Lord Lucan, Chastity. And Prudence, Lady Anne needs someone to talk to."

Rescue came as Lord Duncan, finally in possession of the ball, missed his next shot and it was Constance's turn to play for the Duncans against the so far invincible team headed by Max Ensor.

"You'll have to excuse us, Aunt," she said with a

smile. "It's time for us to play. Chas, I'm going to take your ball right the way round." She pointed to the hoops. "You'll come in for the final shot against the marker."

"You think you can?"

"What do you think?"

"Go to it." Chastity waved her on. She was a fairly weak player and Constance was as competitive a player as her father, and now had the edge that age had taken from him.

Lord Duncan came forward as his oldest daughter stepped onto the immaculate lawn. "Now, Constance, you have to get my ball back in play."

"Yes, Father," she said. "But I have something else to do first." She gave Max a sweet smile as he stood to one side with his mallet resting lightly on the grass. "A little revenge."

"Don't waste your shots," Lord Duncan boomed irritably. "Just keep your ball in play and get mine close to the sixth hoop."

"Good advice," Max said as she took up her position, legs apart, mallet held with both hands between her feet, ready for her swing. "Why go after me? I'm not presenting any threat to you lying over there."

"Oh, yes, you are," she said, clipping her bottom lip between her teeth. "Believe it or not, Mr. Ensor, I can play this game rather well. And I have my own strategy."

"I'm certain you do," he murmured. "I've noticed how skillfully you play your games, Miss Duncan."

She paused, her mallet halfway in position for the swing. It was pure gamesmanship, of course, but it seemed a trifle underhanded to confuse croquet with the other game they were playing. But then, in croquet all was fair. It was a no-holds-barred competition and she was as cunning and ruthless as anyone when it came to trickery. She swung the mallet back between her feet and tapped the ball through the first hoop.

She walked to her ball, took up her position, and once again tapped it with just sufficient force to touch Chastity's ball, which lay in a direct line with the second hoop. She lined them up and this time hit hers smartly so that it pushed Chastity's ball through the hoop and rolled merrily after it.

Max leaned against the beech tree and watched with both amusement and admiration as Constance took her own and her sister's ball through every hoop, tapped the finish post with her own ball, and handed the mallet to her sister so she could perform the final service with her own ball.

"Oh, well played, Chastity. Well played." David Lucan applauded loudly.

"David, I didn't do anything, except for the last shot," Chastity protested, setting aside her mallet. "Constance played my ball as well as her own. Didn't you see?"

The young man looked discomfited, and Chastity immediately smiled and went over to him. "Doesn't she play well?"

"Oh, yes," he said, "but not as well as you."

Chastity decided that it was time Hester Winthrop entered the scene.

"Now, do you have the seating plan, Prudence?" Edith asked, fussing with her fan. "Where have you put Mr.

Ensor? He should be at your father's end of the table, I believe. He and Lord Barclay. They can talk politics."

"It's possible they don't want to, Aunt," Prudence said. "They have enough of politics in London. We put him between Constance and Lady Winthrop." She understood now why Constance had put Hester and Lord Lucan together, as far from Lady Winthrop as it was possible to get.

"Oh, well, if you think that will please everyone, dear, I'll leave it to you." Edith smiled vaguely and went off to chat with her own cronies.

Prudence, waiting for her turn, thought about Hester Winthrop and David Lucan. It was an inspired match. But how on earth were they to levy some kind of fee when they set up the happy couple if the happy couple didn't know they'd been set up? It was all very well Constance having these inspired matchmaking ideas, but how were they to make any money out of them?

She picked up her mallet and went onto the lawn as her father knocked the finish post with his ball.

"Such delightful young women . . . such a pity they can't find husbands," Lady Winthrop confided to her bridge table after dinner. "I wonder why Chastity doesn't take Lucan?" She raised her pince-nez and looked across the drawing room to where the subject in question was talking with Hester. David Lucan stood behind the sofa gazing at Chastity like an anxious puppy.

"He would be a good catch . . . four spades," her partner said. "But Emily brought them up with some strange ideas . . . most unsuitable. Of course, poor dear Constance would have been married years ago if—" She placed a finger over her lips as Edith Duncan approached the table.

On the other side of the room Chastity smiled over her shoulder at David Lucan and said, "Do sit here and keep Hester company, David. I have to make sure everyone has what they need."

She patted the sofa invitingly as she rose to her feet. "Don't look alarmed, Hester. David doesn't bite. Besides, you two have something in common. You both love dogs."

Of course, Hester loved King Charles spaniels, and David bred Staffordshire bull terriers, but that was a mere detail, she thought as she went off, leaving them sitting awkwardly beside each other on the sofa. A few moments later she was gratified to see that they were at least talking.

"See," she said to Prudence. "I think Con has the right idea. We go out and find our clients."

"Yes, and just how do we tell them that although they didn't know it, an organization called the Go-Between set them up together and now it wants to charge them a fee?" Prudence demanded.

"Awkward," agreed Chastity. "But we can't talk about it now. Aunt Edith is convinced we're not doing our hostly duty. Every time she sees us talking together she does that wave of hers."

"We'll discuss it tonight. But what do you think's going on with Con?" She looked across the drawing room to where her elder sister was playing at a second bridge table, partnered by Max Ensor.

Chastity followed her gaze. "I don't know, but something. Whatever it is between them you can almost feel it from here. They're radiating some kind of electricity."

Prudence nodded. "I've never seen Con lose her detachment with a man before . . . at least not since Douglas died. I just wonder if she knows she has."

"Perhaps she hasn't," Chastity said. "She's always the one in charge, and we know she's playing her own game with Max."

"Somehow I don't think she's playing anything but bridge right now," Prudence said.

"No," Chastity agreed thoughtfully. "Do you think she's forgotten how much he annoyed her at the beginning? Surely he hasn't changed over night. A person doesn't just lose those opinions at will."

"Maybe he hasn't lost them," her sister said. "Maybe he's just playing them down because he knows they annoy her, and he doesn't want her annoyed . . . at least not until he's had his wicked way with her," she added with a grin.

She expected her sister to laugh but Chastity's expression remained solemn. "If he has an ulterior motive in pursuing Con, I hope it's not one that's going to hurt her."

"Oh, Lord!" Prudence sighed. "What should we do?"

"I don't think we can do anything. You know how Con is. Once she's decided upon something, nothing will distract her."

"What do you think of Max Ensor? Do you like him?"

Chastity shrugged. "I don't know. Sometimes I do, and sometimes I have a feeling that he's a bit too glib for comfort. He's ambitious, that's for sure."

"Mmm," murmured Prudence, reflecting that in her own way so was Constance.

Chapter 9

Constance would not have been surprised at her sisters' observations. They knew her almost as well as she knew herself. As the evening had progressed she had had to force herself to concentrate on her cards. Once or twice she had been in danger of unforgivably trumping her partner's ace when she lost track of trumps. Her gaze kept drifting disconcertingly to her partner's hands, which were constantly in play as he shuffled cards, riffled through his hand, made his discard. While she'd admired them before, she hadn't noticed how strong and flexible his fingers seemed to be...and in the next moment she caught herself thinking of those hands on her body, the fingers playing upon her skin.

This was not going according to plan. Goose bumps prickled on her bare arms and her stomach kept doing a nosedive. One minute she was cold, drawing her richly hued shawl of Indian silk up over her shoulders, and the next plying her fan vigorously. She could only hope that her distraction was not obvious to her fellow players, though Max Ensor seemed aware of it. Although he played with steady concentration, once or twice he raised his eyes from the cards and glanced at her across the table. It was a glance that contained the speculative hunger she had noticed on the train and that had emboldened her to play her little game at the stile.

They were fighting some battle here, fighting for control of whatever was to happen next. Lascivious anticipation flooded her, ran swift and hot in her veins. She wanted his body, wanted to touch every inch of him, bury her mouth and nose in his skin, taste him from the pulse in his throat to his big toes. She wanted to look at his sex, hold it, stroke it, lick it. She wondered if he had hair on his back and if it ran down his spine to his backside. Were his thighs hairy? His toes even? And what of his chest? Were his nipples small and almost invisible, or would they be prominent and dark, and harden quickly beneath the flick of her tongue?

Dear God, she thought in sudden desperation, aware of the moistening in her loins, the sudden pulsing of her sex. She had never been able to do that to herself just by thinking. Her only hope lay in the possibility that Max was suffering the same agonies of frustrated lust. But when she looked at him she saw nothing but the calm, neutral expression of a skillful bridge player.

"Constance, it's your bid." Her father's impatient voice crashed into her lubricious reverie with the icy force of an avalanche.

"Oh, yes, I'm sorry. What's the bidding? I didn't hear."

"I bid one heart, your father bid two spades, and Lord Barclay passed." Max regarded her with a curious little smile and she had the uncomfortable impression that he'd been listening in on her thoughts. Which of course was absurd, when she couldn't read his at all.

"We need forty points for the rubber," Max reminded her.

Constance couldn't imagine how they'd found themselves in a winning position with the way she'd been playing. Max was obviously skilled enough to compensate for her own absentmindedness.

She looked again at her cards. "Three no trumps."

"What?" Max stared at her in disbelief. For forty points that was sheer overkill and Constance would have to play it. He didn't have much faith in her play this evening.

Constance shrugged her shoulders but said nothing. She had a three no trump hand and if Max had enough points to bid a heart, so long as she kept her wits about her and counted carefully, they would make it. It went against the grain to play for less than they could get. Adrenaline surged through her as her competitive spirit finally vanquished all distraction. She no longer needed to force herself to concentrate, and steadily gathered tricks with her high cards. At the end, she looked up triumphantly. "There," she said, laying down her last card. "We made it."

"So I should hope," her father said. "With a hand like that, how could you lose?"

"I have a feeling Max thought I could lose very easily," she said, looking at him across the table.

He raised his hands palms up in disclaimer. "Not at all. I had every faith."

"Oh, yes?" She gathered up the cards. "I think that's as much as I can play tonight. Shall I find someone to make a fourth?"

"No, I too have played enough," Max said, rising from the table. "Gentlemen, I thank you." He smiled amiably at their opponents.

Lord Duncan set two guineas on the table and the earl of Barclay did the same. The baron pushed them across the table. "Your winnings, Ensor. I'll leave it to you to divvy it up with my daughter." He got to his feet. "Let's find that single malt I've been keeping, Barclay. You care to join us, Ensor?"

Max shook his head. "No, thank you, sir. I'd like to take a stroll in the garden with my partner, if you would permit it?"

Lord Duncan gave a low rumble of laughter. "You jest, sir. My daughters have all been beyond my control since they gained their majority . . . and probably before it," he added. "Come, Barclay." He flung an arm around his crony's shoulders and ushered him off.

"Does the lady permit it?" Max inquired, handing Constance her share of the night's winnings. Her green eyes had an unusual glitter in them as she took the money.

She tucked the winnings into her evening bag. "I think there must be a full moon. Perhaps that explains why I was so absentminded during the rubber."

"You gained it back for the last hand," he observed.

"Perhaps the clouds obscured the moon."

"Perhaps." He gave her his arm and she laid her hand on the silky black sleeve. A little current ran through her hand and up her arm. She tried to ignore it.

They walked out onto the terrace and Constance was relieved to find that they were not alone. It was a warm night and indeed a full moon and most of the house party had come outside. She couldn't see her sisters anywhere, but she did spy David Lucan and Hester Winthrop standing in awkward silence against the parapet. Maybe easing that match along a little would help her to ignore these ridiculous twitches.

"I just want to talk to Lord Lucan," she said. "He looks as if he needs a helping hand with Hester."

Max regarded the couple. "He looks old enough to conduct a conversation with a young woman without guidance," he objected.

"Yes, but Hester is so very shy and David's not very forthcoming at the best of times. I'll just go over and smooth the path for them." She took her hand from his arm. "You really don't have to come."

"I do if I want your company," he stated.

Prudence came out of the house at this juncture and Constance beckoned her over. "Prue, I thought we might encourage David and Hester a little."

Prudence looked in their direction. "They need more than a little."

"Are you matchmaking?" Max demanded.

"No . . . of course not," Constance denied. "But we do have a responsibility to ensure that our guests are enjoying themselves in congenial company."

"And you've decided that those two are congenial company for each other? Sounds like matchmaking to me . . . arrant interference." He shook his head. "Typical female nonsense. I shall go and join your father and Lord Barclay over the single malt."

Constance watched him return to the house with his long rangy stride. "Typical female nonsense, indeed!" she said indignantly.

"The leopard doesn't appear to have changed his

spots." Prudence gave her a sister a shrewd look. "Or do you think he has?"

Constance shook her head. "Oh, no. Not in the least."

"So you're still intent on taking him down a peg or two?"

Constance glanced at the moon, then confessed, "Yes, absolutely. The problem, Prue, is that my body's not as much in my control as my mind. For some reason lust is on a rampage. I've never felt anything like it before. It's so perverse. I'm determined to use him; I dislike everything he stands for; but my body doesn't seem to give a damn." She shook her head. "It must be the moon."

"What are you going to do about it?" Prudence regarded her sister with fascination and a degree of alarm.

"I have no idea." Constance opened her hands in a gesture of hapless resignation. "Part of me says, sit back and enjoy the ride, but the rational side of me says, run like hell. Oh, well . . ." She shook her head again, reached into her handbag, and took out her bridge winnings. "By the way, this was my share of the game against Father and Lord Barclay, might as well put it back into the family coffers."

Prudence took it. "Circulation," she said. "Now, that's an idea. Maybe if you could keep winning against Father we could keep his money circulating within the family and out of the clutches of the outside world."

"Nice idea," her sister responded with a sardonic smile. "If you ask me, I think we'd do better to wean him off Lord Barclay. The man gives me the shivers. I know he and Father have been friends for years, but it seems to me he's always got some scheme that he wants Father to get involved in. Either that or he's gambling and carousing with him."

Prudence nodded. "I feel the same way. Mother didn't like him either. On a more hopeful note . . . what shall we do with those two would-be lovebirds?"

"Tennis," her sister said. "Tomorrow afternoon. We'll partner them together and Hester will see how masterful he is on the court, and David will be able to protect her and make her plays for her."

Prudence laughed, although she couldn't fault her sister's reasoning. They crossed the terrace to where the pair stood half facing each other, half facing away, their awkward uncertainty palpable.

"David, Hester, isn't it a beautiful night?" Constance said cheerfully. "Have you looked at the moon?"

"It's lovely, Miss Duncan," Hester responded in subdued tones.

"Hester, do call me Constance. 'Miss Duncan' makes me feel so old."

Hester blushed and stammered that she'd had no intention of implying any such thing.

Constance merely laughed. "David, I think you should take Hester across the lawn to the ha-ha and look at the moon on the river. It's always spectacular on the night of the full moon."

Lord Lucan was too well-bred to voice the objections that sprang to mind. His mother would not approve of his walking in the moonlight in such a secluded spot with a young lady, and besides, he didn't know what to say to her.

Hester murmured that she should ask her mama but Constance said bracingly, "I'll tell your mama if she asks for you. But she's playing cards and I'm sure she won't notice your absence for at least ten minutes. Do go and look at the moon on the water."

Lord Lucan offered his arm and Hester took it with proper maidenly hesitation and they walked off across the lawn.

"There," Constance said, dusting off her hands. "That's done. And I'll lay any odds that Lady Winthrop won't object to the match."

"There's still the dowager to consider."

"Oh, she'll be easier than you think. We'll visit her when we're back in town and sing Hester's praises discreetly. We can hint that David seemed to find her congenial and then we can take Hester to visit her ourselves. She'll charm the old biddy with that sweet shyness. And the two mamas will get on perfectly well and have a wonderful time planning the wedding and arguing and competing over the arrangements. The lovebirds won't need to worry about a thing."

"How are we going to profit from this particular piece of Go-Between business?" asked Prudence. "Even assuming we pull it off."

"Well, I was thinking...if the mothers did decide that it was a good match, they might be grateful enough to make a contribution to a charity we support, one that helps indigent gentlewomen...poor spinster ladies down on their luck?" She raised her eyebrows at her sister.

Prudence stared at her in astonishment. "Con! That is so...so *devious*!"

Constance shrugged. "Needs must, Prue. And I don't really see that it matters in what guise we get paid. We'll still have performed the service."

"You're shameless," her sister declared.

"You may well be right," Constance said, glancing once more up at the moon. "I have a feeling the rational side of me is going to yield the fight tonight. What have I got to lose, Prue?"

"Your objectivity," her sister responded promptly. "If you fall for him he'll be of no use to you. You won't even want to influence him."

"I'm not going to fall for him," Constance declared. "I'm just going to get lust out of my system. I couldn't fall for someone who believes women should be kept pregnant, barefoot, and in the kitchen."

"He's not quite that bad," Prudence remonstrated.

"Perhaps not," Constance conceded. "He believes we should devote ourselves to the nursery and the household and in exchange be kept plied with chocolates on silken sofas with pleasant little amusements like shopping and gossip." She smiled. "What do you think it's going to do to his preconceptions when I grab the tiger by the tail?"

"God knows!" Prudence threw up her hands.

"I'm going to have a bath," Constance said. "I'll tell Aunt Edith on my way upstairs."

"Since you can't be good, be careful," Prue advised.

Constance laughed, kissed her sister's cheek, and went back into the house. In the bathroom she shared with her sister she ran a bath and undressed as the water ran. She took out the pins from the chignon at the nape of her neck and removed the pads that had supported the mass of her hair piled elaborately on top of her head. She brushed it to loosen the tightness of the back-combing and then twisted it into a simple knot on top of her head and pinned it securely.

She sprinkled lavender-scented bath salts into the hot water. The geyser labored and wheezed and complained but the hot water came out nevertheless. The soft glow of the gas lamp threw shadows across the vast space that was a converted bedroom. In winter the wind found its way under the door, through every chink in the window frames, and seemed to search out cracks in the plaster ceiling to chill every inch of a bather's skin exposed above the water, but on a warm summer night the bathroom with its huge wide-edged claw-footed tub was inviting.

She stepped into the gently steaming water and with a sigh of pleasure lay back, resting her neck on the edge of the bath. The full moon was a great golden round filling the open window that faced the bath. She could hear the soft murmur of voices from the terrace below as the late-retiring guests continued to chat, and the sweet strains of a piano drifted upwards. Chastity was playing; she recognized her touch with the Mozart sonata. When would Max decide to retire, she wondered, closing her eyes.

She reviewed the contents of her wardrobe, considering what to wear when she climbed the stairs to the South Turret. There was a robe of Chinese silk that had belonged to her mother. It was a wonderful emerald green that did very nice things to her eyes. A fiery orange dragon twisted and twined down the back, and it had lovely wide mandarin sleeves. But then there was the filmy muslin negligée over the white silk shift. Did she want demure or sexy; bold or artlessly seductive?

There was a discreet knock at the door and she turned her head lazily against the rim of the bath. Prue or Chas would have an answer. "Come in."

The door opened and Max Ensor stepped into the soft glow of the bathroom.

Constance was too surprised to move. She simply stared at him.

He closed the door and turned the heavy key that the sisters always ignored. The bathroom was their private domain and no one but themselves would enter it except a maid in the morning to clean it.

"Your sister told me I would find you here." He leaned his back against the door and surveyed her through hooded eyes.

That would be Prudence, Constance thought. It would never have occurred to her that Max would act on that information in such a breathtakingly brazen fashion. It hadn't occurred to Constance either. But once again he had whipped the initiative out of her hands.

She didn't move as she considered what to do, aware that every moment she kept silent would make dismissing him that much harder. Pride warred with desire. She felt her nipples peaking below the level of the water as his gaze roamed over her. Her body beneath the lavender-scented water was clearly visible. Still she said nothing.

Max pushed himself away from the door and slowly took off his coat. He hung it over the top rung of the towel rail and unfastened his diamond cuff links. He placed them on the top of the wooden chest, where they glinted in the glow of the gas lamp on the wall above.

Deliberately he rolled up his sleeves. Constance watched him, mesmerized by the slow neat movements of his long fingers. His forearms were dusted with curly dark hair. He came over to the bath and sat on the edge, a half smile playing over his mouth as he looked down at her. He dipped a forefinger in the water then reached forward and touched her forehead where her hair grew back in a widow's peak. He drew the finger down over the bridge of her nose, over her lips, beneath her chin to the rapidly beating pulse in her throat.

Ah well, Constance thought, closing her eyes. So much for pride. She waited, barely breathing. The finger continued its progress down between her breasts, dipped into her navel, slipped over her belly, to come to rest at the line of curly water-dark hair at the apex of her thighs.

His hand slid beneath the water to cup the soft mound of her sex without pressure or demand, and he leaned forward, bracing himself with his free hand on the edge of the bath, to kiss her. A light, brushing kiss this time, his tongue sliding over her lips, not demanding entrance, dipping into the corners of her mouth. Then he straightened, kissed the tip of her nose, and withdrew his hand from between her thighs, but she could still feel the warmth of his palm, the light touch of his fingers.

He reached for the large round sponge on the edge of the bath and soaped it. He didn't take his eyes off her and the golden silence enwrapped them. He drew the soapy sponge over her neck, then held one breast clear of the water and soaped it, watching the nipple stand up from the white bubbles, hard and pink against the dark brown circle of the areola. Her breast was firm and round in his hand, neither large nor small. He paid the same attention to its fellow, then dipped the sponge in the water, rinsed it, and reapplied the soap.

"Shall I do your back?" The sound of his voice, soft though it was, was startling in the suspended silence of the bathroom.

Constance sat up and leaned forward. Max moved behind her. She had an elegant back, long, narrow, curving gently at her waist and then flaring at the hip. Tendrils of damp hair escaping from the knot wisped on the back of her neck. He soaped her pointed shoulder blades and down her backbone to the base of her spine, where the cleft of her buttocks began. His breath caught in his throat and the deliberate composure that had accompanied him into the bathroom abruptly left him. He dropped the sponge into the water and stood up.

"Don't be long," he said, taking a towel from the rail and dropping it onto the stool by the bath where she could reach it easily. He picked up his coat and cuff links and left the bathroom, closing the door softly behind him.

Constance exhaled slowly. Every inch of her body was sensitized from the tips of her toes to her prickling scalp. She traced the path of his finger down her body and between her legs. The slight brush of her fingertip against her sex sent a rush of sensation that almost engulfed her. She stood up in a shower of drops and reached for the towel, stepping carefully onto the thick, fluffy bath mat. She looked at herself in the mirror on the wooden chest and saw that her cheeks were flushed, loose tendrils of hair clinging to her damp forehead. Her eyes glowed with expectation.

"God in heaven!" she muttered, leaning over to pull the plug from the bath. She was way out of her depth here. She had had the advantage of surprise for the briefest of time at the very beginning of this embryonic relationship, but now she was the one with the ground cut from beneath her feet. It didn't seem to matter what she wore up the stairs to the South Turret. Any message she might have intended to give had already been read and answered.

She wrapped herself in a fresh towel and went into

her bedroom next door. She smoothed a body oil scented with sandalwood into her skin, took the pins from her hair, and brushed it again until it fell in a gleaming russet cascade down her back. It occurred to her that she was preparing herself like some seraglio inhabitant for a night with the pasha. The thought brought her a flash of much-needed amusement and perspective.

She chose the Chinese robe anyway. It had little mother-of-pearl buttons all the way down the front, but she stopped fastening them when they reached her knees. It would take far too long to undo them all. She turned the gas down low and left her room.

The stairs to the South Turret were in shadow, the only illumination moonlight pouring through a window at the top, sending a narrow silver path down the middle of the stairs. Constance didn't knock on the door but lifted the latch and pushed it open.

The round chamber was flooded with moonlight. The gas lamps had not been lit. Max lay in a dressing gown on the bed, propped against the carved headboard, his hands linked behind his head.

"Welcome," he said, swinging off the bed. He came towards her, hands outstretched. She put her hands in his and he drew her against him. "You smell delicious."

"Rather like a love slave in a harem, I was thinking."

He laughed against her mouth. "You do realize that laughter is the antithesis of an aphrodisiac."

She drew her head back and looked into his eyes. "Is it?"

For answer, he unfastened the top six buttons of the robe. With remarkable dexterity, Constance thought. He slid his hands beneath to cup her shoulders, then brought his hands to her breasts, holding them as he had

done in the bath. He flicked the nipples with his fingertips until once again they were hard and erect.

"I don't know how slowly I can do this," he murmured, lifting her breasts free of the robe that was now
slipping off her shoulders. He bent his head to her
breasts and she shrugged her shoulders slightly so that
the partially unbuttoned robe fell down her arms to slide
from her body in a silky rush.

She stood naked in the warm light of the summer's
full moon. And now it became imperative that Max too
should show himself. She unfastened the girdle of his
robe and without finesse pushed it off his shoulders.
Then they stood face-to-face, her breasts touching his
chest, the slight roundness of her stomach curving into
the hollow of his. Her arms were around his waist, her
hands on his backside. His penis flickered against her
belly. She stepped closer and stood on his bare feet with
her own. Now they were so close their thighs were
pressed together, their faces barely an inch apart.

"We'll go slowly another time," Constance said, flat-
tening her palms on his backside and pressing him hard
against her loins.

He could feel the heat of her body like a forest fire.
The scent of her arousal mingled with the scent of sandalwood. He put his hands to her waist and lifted her off
his feet. She was no featherweight and he dismissed
quickly any romantic notions of carrying her to the bed.
He set her down and it was she who led him to the high
poster bed.

He fell down onto the bed and pulled her on top of
him, having a vague notion that this might prolong matters a little. But he was mistaken. Constance swung
astride him, and the minute the heated core of her body

touched his belly, she bit her lip hard. She rose up on her knees, took his penis between her hands, and guided him in.

For a moment they lay still, conjoined, neither daring to breathe as they learned the feel of each other. He was so big inside her, he seemed to fill her. He moved once, just the slightest lift of his hips, and the rush of the orgasm that had been waiting to explode for hours ripped through Constance, and as she felt the deep pulsing throb of his flesh within her it happened again. Another wave of intense orgasmic delight, smaller this time but just as blissful, brought a cry of pleasure to her lips and she fell forward, burying her face in his chest as his hand weakly stroked her hair.

After a long and insensible time Max lifted her off him. She rolled to her side as they disengaged and lay inert, watching as he slid the protective shield from his now flaccid flesh.

"I didn't think of that," she said almost apologetically. She had been aware of the sheath when she'd held him but in the heat of the moment it had barely registered.

He shrugged. "It only takes one of us."

"I suppose it does." The image of Amelia Westcott swam across her internal vision. Henry Franklin hadn't thought of precautions, and if Amelia had had an experience that in any way resembled Constance's in the last minutes, she couldn't blame Amelia for not having the foresight. It was a humbling reflection.

"Thank you for thinking of it. I'm embarrassed I didn't." She touched his cheek as he lay down beside her, then closed her eyes. "I think I have to sleep a little."

He slipped an arm beneath her, rolling her into his embrace.

They awoke together an hour later. The moon had dropped below the level of the window and the round chamber was now in darkness. The utter stillness of a sleeping house lay below them. Constance rolled onto her back, shivering in the cold night air.

She nudged Max, who was stirring beside her. "It's cold, Max. Can you move for a minute so that I can pull the covers over us?"

He muttered sleepily, then sat up and swung his legs over the bed, struggling into a sitting position. He stood up and stretched, then lit the gas lamp on the bedside table. "Someone thoughtfully provided a decanter of cognac. Would you like a glass?"

"Not a whole one. I'll have a sip of yours." She pulled back the sheet and coverlet and plumped up the squashed pillows, setting them against the headboard. "I'm not at all sleepy now."

He filled a glass from the decanter on the dresser and came back to the bed, climbing under the covers beside her. He handed her the glass and she took a sip. He turned his head to look at her as she lay back on the propped pillows. "Somehow I get the impression that wasn't your first time."

Constance shot him a puzzled and wary look. "Does that shock you?"

"I'll admit to surprise," he said, taking a sip of brandy. "This afternoon in the field, I was surprised. But not since."

"And not shocked?" she pressed.

"It's unusual."

"For unmarried women not to be virgins," she stated flatly.

"Yes," he agreed. "Would you deny it?"

"I wouldn't know," Constance said. "It's not a question I go around asking the unmarried women of my acquaintance."

He laughed and held the brandy goblet to her lips. "Come, don't get on your high horse, Constance. I'm not criticizing, how could I possibly after such a night? I was merely stating a fact."

"Are you sure you're not going to say that you couldn't respect a woman of easy virtue?" Constance took the glass from him and drank.

"I've told you before not to put words into my mouth." He swung off the bed and filled another glass, since it seemed he'd lost possession of the first one. "You were engaged, were you not?"

Constance stiffened. "What's that got to do with it?"

He shrugged and turned back to the bed. "Obvious, I would have thought. Did you anticipate the wedding night?"

Constance closed her eyes for minute, thinking about Douglas. "No," she said flatly. "Douglas had a finely honed sense of right and wrong, honor and dishonor." She smiled slightly. "It could be quite exasperating sometimes."

"Did you love him?" He watched her closely, seeing how her mouth had softened.

"Oh, yes," she said quietly. "He was my life. I was twenty-two when he was killed, and I thought my life was over. I knew absolutely that no other man could ever match up to Douglas." She opened her eyes. "And I was right."

He winced slightly, although he knew he had no reason to feel insulted. One brief and passionate tumble didn't entitle him to compliments, let alone favorable comparisons with a dead fiancé. They didn't even know each other in any real sense.

"And yet you've spent time with other men," he said neutrally. "You'll forgive me if I say you seem to enjoy the pleasures of sex."

"I do," she said. "When it suits me. After Mother died the three of us decided that virginity was a burden we'd rather lose. Marriage isn't exactly a top priority for any of us, but we didn't want to die wondering, if you see what I mean."

Max looked at her with fascination. He'd never met any woman whose ideas remotely resembled those of Constance and her sisters. He wasn't sure whether their attitudes repelled him or attracted him.

Constance took another sip of cognac and continued, "So we gave ourselves a year, and by the following New Year's Eve we were all three no longer in possession of our virginities."

"Did you choose your . . . your . . ." Max gave up and waved a hand helplessly.

"Our deflowerers?" Constance said. "Oh, yes, of course we did. They were all decent men for whom we felt both attraction and liking. And they had to be willing and in our confidence. It was all very straightforward and pleasant and we all still like each other very much."

"Do I know any of them?"

"I don't think you'd want to know names," Constance responded, turning her head on the pillow. "Why on earth would you?" She made a move to get up.

"Don't go," he said softly. "It doesn't seem right to end the evening on this fractured note. If I've offended you, I apologize. We don't really know each other very well yet."

Constance hesitated. He was right. It seemed both ungracious and silly to spoil what had been a glorious few moments. She flipped aside the covers in invitation and he set down his glass and slid in beside her again.

"Shall we take our time this time," he murmured, kissing her ear.

For answer, her fingers tiptoed delicately down his body.

Chapter 10

"L ord Lucan is a wonderful partner for Hester," Chastity observed to Lady Winthrop as they sat beneath an umbrella outside the tennis court watching the game of mixed doubles in progress. "He seems to be able to anticipate her every move across the court."

"Hester is not in general overly fond of any kind of sporting activity," Lady Winthrop declared. "Indeed, I advised her most strongly not to take part this afternoon. It's far too hot to be running around like that. If she's not careful she'll start to perspire, and that's so unattractive in a woman."

"I think David is doing most of the running around, Lady Winthrop," Prudence pointed out, refilling glasses from the tall jug of lemonade. "That's why he makes such a perfect partner."

"He's a very personable young man," Lady Winthrop conceded, taking a delicate sip from her glass. "I'm slightly acquainted with his mother, although she doesn't go about much. Rather frail, I understand."

There was very little that was frail about the Dowager

Lady Lucan, Prudence reflected even as she murmured agreement. "David is a wonderful son," she said. "So caring and supportive of his mother."

"Excellent qualities in a son," Lady Winthrop muttered, fanning herself vigorously. "And a goodly fortune, I understand." This was a mere reflective murmur, to which her companions made no response.

"Con seems to be doing her best to give Hester and David a win," Chastity said quietly to her sister as they moved away from the group under the umbrella. "But I get the impression Max is not too happy about it."

Prudence chuckled. "He looks mad as fire. He's playing his heart out and every time the serve comes to Con she just pats it across the net to fall at Hester's feet so that she can't possibly miss it."

"And dear sweet David can't see what she's doing and just assumes that Hester's playing like a goddess," Chastity said on a bubble of laughter. "Con's so devious."

"I told you about her plan to collect donations from the satisfied mamas for a charity for indigent spinsters," Prudence reminded her. "She's utterly shameless. I don't know where she gets it from."

"Mother was not exactly straightforward in all her dealings," Chastity replied. "Look how she pulled the wool over Father's eyes."

"I don't think Con's pulling the wool over Max Ensor's eyes," Prudence observed, shading her eyes against the afternoon sun as she watched the court. "He looks ready to whack her with his tennis racket."

"They certainly don't look like lovers who spent a night of unbridled passion," Chastity agreed. "Has she said anything to you about it?"

"Not a word. But there hasn't been much opportunity

today for a sisterly tête-à-tête." They fell silent, listening to the summery twang of tennis balls on rackets, the rhythmic thud as the ball hit the well-manicured grass.

On the court, Constance served to Hester. Her ball hit the net and Max muttered savagely from his position close to the net. He picked up the ball and slammed it back at her. She caught it on her racket, smiled sweetly at him, and delivered her second serve. It rolled across the net to land at Hester's feet. Hester hit it with the air of surprise she'd been wearing since the game started and laughed delightedly when it went over the net. Max returned it easily but he was so out of temper that he sent it over the back line.

"Game, David and Hester!" Constance called cheerfully. "Change ends."

"What the hell are you playing at?" Max demanded in a fierce undertone as they walked to the other end of the court.

"Tennis," she said with the same sweet smile. "Of course, my arm is nowhere near as powerful as yours. I am a mere woman, after all. But I'm doing my best."

"Don't give me that!" he exclaimed. "You're playing pat ball to Hester."

"Oh, but look how happy it's making her . . . and see how David is glowing with pride in her. He's looking at her in just the way he looks at Chastity . . . or, I hope, *did* look at Chastity."

He spoke through thinned lips. "I tell you straight, Constance, you had better play this next game competitively or I shall walk off the court."

"Oh, how unsportsmanlike," she protested. "There's more to a game than just winning."

"Not in my book," he retorted, moving to the back of

the court to accept David's serve. "And mark me well, I mean what I say."

Constance pursed her lips. She hadn't expected him to like what she was doing, but she hadn't expected quite such a furious reaction. He obviously had a very finely honed competitive streak. She understood it, since she was fiercely competitive herself, except in certain circumstances, like the present. However, she decided she'd better give this game her best shot in the interests of keeping the peace.

Max nodded grimly when she began to play with more verve and the game picked up speed. They were still a set down but at least Constance was finally giving their opponents a game, and if she played properly they might win this one and have a chance for the match. It didn't take him long, however, to see that every time they pulled ahead she would subtly drop a point. It annoyed him so much, it put his own game off and they lost the set and the match by an infuriatingly narrow margin. He controlled his irritation sufficiently to congratulate the winners, shaking hands warmly with the beaming David and the rosily delighted Hester, but then he stalked off the court without a word to Constance and headed for the house.

Constance swung her racket thoughtfully, then she hurried after him, catching up with him as he reached the terrace. "Max?"

He stopped without turning around. "Well?"

She put a hand on his arm, laughing up at him. "Oh, don't be cross. It was all for a good cause."

"I don't consider arrant meddling in other people's affairs a good cause," he declared, glowering at her. "It's just blatant matchmaking."

"But it's not doing any harm." Constance wiped her damp brow with the back of her hand.

Max's annoyance vanished into the humid air. There was something overpoweringly sensual about her flushed cheeks and the beads of perspiration gathered on her brow and in the hollow of her neck just above the open collar of her white silk blouse. He pictured her breasts as he'd seen them that morning when she'd finally left his bed, and he imagined the little trickle of sweat that would be gathering in the deep cleft between them.

"Just leave me out of such nonsense in future," he demanded, taking her elbow and moving decisively with her behind a screen of box trees planted in big tubs along one side of the terrace.

Constance offered no objection to their abrupt seclusion in the narrow space. She rested her hands on the parapet behind her and leaned back, tilting her head to look up at him with an inquiring air.

"Suddenly I find myself with an overpowering need to kiss you," he said, running a finger over her slightly parted lips. "There's something incredibly sensual about a woman all flushed and bedewed with exertion, although, given the way you were playing, I'm astonished you managed to break a sweat at all."

"Not in the last game," she protested, as her heartbeat quickened and a thrill of anticipatory desire prickled over her scalp and down her spine, setting her nerve endings on edge.

"Yes," he conceded, "you worked very hard at losing that one." He laid a fingertip on the moist skin of her throat, feeling the pulse run swift beneath his touch. Her tongue touched her lips, and her eyes in the greenish shade of the trees glowed deepest emerald. Little sparks of light flickered in their depths as she tilted her head farther back, offering her throat for his mouth.

His lips followed the fingertip and he pressed his mouth into the hollow, licking the sweat from her skin, up beneath her chin, as if it were an ice cream. She laughed softly, running her hands over his back, feeling the heat of his skin beneath the thin fabric of his white linen shirt.

He moved his mouth to hers, lightly brushing at first, then with more force, pressing her lips open even as she pretended to resist. His tongue played with hers, touching the tip, curling around, stroking the underside. Desire shimmered, flashed between them.

His hands were on the buttons of her blouse, flipping them open with deft haste. He unbuttoned the camisole she wore beneath and she felt the air on her bare skin. He took his mouth from hers and bent to kiss her breasts, running his tongue up the cleft between them to her throat, savoring the salty sweetness of her skin. He held her waist between his hands as he devoured the creamy blue-veined roundness of her breasts, the erect rose-pink nipples, his breath a warm, swift rustle across her sensitized flesh. She bit her lip to keep from crying out as desire grew, spreading a honeyed warmth through her loins and belly. She caught his head between her hands, curling her fingers into the luxuriantly thick silver of his hair, tracing the shape of his ears, pinching his earlobes in an effort to contain the surging power of her need.

They didn't speak. Their breathing fast, they fumbled with her white linen skirt and lacy knickers, with the buttons on his trousers. He lifted her against him and she clung to his neck as he slid within her. She kissed him, sucking on his mouth, his tongue, nipping at his lips, holding herself still as he thrust deep to her core. She threw back her head as he drove once more hard and fierce inside her and left her body the instant the wave broke over them.

Only as the violent beating of her pulse slowed in her ears did Constance hear the voices on the terrace beyond the screen of box trees. She put her hand over her mouth, laughing silently. Max shook his head at her and hastily rearranged his clothes before tucking her breasts back into her camisole and rapidly rebuttoning her blouse while she pulled up her knickers and dropped her skirt over the general muddle beneath.

"How shocking of us," she whispered in a voice that didn't sound as if she was in the least shocked. "What are we going to do? They're all having tea. We can't just walk out of here as if it's the most normal thing in the world for a couple to skulk behind a hedge."

The level of voices beyond the trees rose slightly and under cover of the buzz Max hissed, "Over the parapet." He swung himself onto the ledge and then dropped to the flower bed beneath behind the shelter of a luxuriant buddleia bush. "Come on." He held up his hands.

Constance grinned and sat on the edge, swinging her legs over. She dropped to the ground beside him, pressing backwards against the wall. She whispered, "You go first. I'll have to go upstairs before I can show myself in public."

He nodded, turned to go, then turned back and kissed her with something akin to savagery. "You are a very wicked woman," he murmured, sounding almost angry, then he sauntered away, hands in his pockets, around the side of the house.

Constance waited a few minutes, then keeping close to
the wall, hidden by the bushes in the flower bed, hastened away to the back of the house. In the bathroom she
stripped to her skin, tossed her tennis clothes into the
hamper, and sponged herself down. In her bedroom she
changed into an afternoon dress of dark green muslin
and tidied the tangled mess of her hair. Laughter bubbled continuously inside her like a mountain spring. She
would never have expected such a flagrant indiscretion
from Max Ensor. Perhaps the man was not completely
beyond redemption after all. If he could forget his principles and hidebound attitudes in such spectacular fashion, surely he could be persuaded to broaden his mind in
other areas too.

Humming to herself she returned to the terrace, im-
maculately tidy, only the darting sparkle in her eyes an
indication that anything out of the ordinary had happened.

Prudence shot her a speculative glance and Constance
gave her a sunny smile. Prudence abandoned her teapot
and the platter of sandwiches she was offering and came
over to her sister. "You look very smug," she accused.

"Well, with reason. Look how David and Hester are
getting along. My little tennis ploy seems to have
worked a treat."

"I notice your partner didn't think much of it. Where
is he?" She looked around the terrace. "I haven't seen
him since he left the court looking like thunder."

Constance shrugged. "Probably licking his wounds in
private. Have you been working on Lady Winthrop?"

"Chastity and I have dropped a few well-placed comments, which she seemed to take to heart."

"Good. Then we'll go to work on Lady Lucan as soon as we're back in town."

"Don't forget we have to see Anonymous on Wednesday morning and we need to go in search of Henry Franklin on Tuesday, before we meet again with Amelia on Thursday. When are we going to have time to visit Lady Lucan?"

Constance gave a wry smile. "The Go-Between seems to be up and running. And we have to put together the next issue of *The Mayfair Lady* too. An edition every two weeks is a lot of pressure."

"No peace for the wicked," Prudence said with a shrug. "Where are you intending to spend tonight?"

"Why?"

"Well, we could work on the paper if you didn't have other plans."

"I think I will have," Constance said. "But we could do some work first."

"You can't do without sleep altogether," her sister protested.

"Oh, for the moment I can," Constance said. "Just for two more nights. Once we're back in town it'll be different. Look, there's Father in that wretched motorcar of Barclay's." She gestured to the driveway, where a motorcar was chugging up to the house, Lord Duncan in driving goggles behind the wheel.

"We're never going to keep him from buying one of those," Prudence said with a sigh.

"He can't buy it if there's no money," Chastity pointed out. Her sisters hadn't heard her soft-footed approach.

"He'll borrow it at some outrageous rate of interest," Prudence stated, her mouth tight.

"Perhaps we can pawn the silver," Constance suggested. "And Mother's diamonds. They must be worth the price of a motor."

"You're not serious!" Her sisters stared at her.

She shrugged. "I can see it coming to that. Either that or we prepare to have a major confrontation and force him to acknowledge the truth."

Her sisters gazed out over the garden in bleak-faced silence. Constance was right. They could manage the ordinary expenses of daily life and some of the luxuries their father considered necessaries, but any expense as extreme as a motorcar was beyond their ingenuity.

"Perhaps we could put him off the idea," Chastity said thoughtfully. "Supposing he had a miserable experience with one. You know how he can make up his mind one minute and change it the next without so much as a blink of an eye. Maybe we could just put him off the whole idea."

"Chas, you are very clever," Constance said, patting her sister's shoulder. "I'm sure we can come up with a plan."

"Oh, yes, easy," Prudence scoffed. "In our copious free time."

"Don't be gloomy, Prue." Constance leaned over and kissed her sister. "We haven't been defeated yet."

"Satisfied passion seems to have made you overly optimistic," Prudence declared.

Constance smiled.

"Oh, I think I'm too scared, Lord Lucan. The lake's so deep and cold." Hester stood on the little jetty at the side of the ornamental lake clutching her parasol. "What if the boat overturns? I can't swim." She gazed up at him, her eyes round and large as platters beneath an enchanting straw bonnet festooned with flowers.

"There's nothing to be afraid of," he said, patting her shoulder. "I'll row you safely across to the island, I promise you." He offered her a smile that managed to be both protective and slightly patronizing as he held the little rowboat against the side of the jetty. "It's very pretty over there," he added in a cajoling tone.

Hester looked doubtfully across the expanse of smooth green water to the little island adorned with a Grecian temple. Two other rowboats with a full complement of passengers were already approaching the island, and no one so far had managed to get their feet wet.

"Come, Hester, David will take care of you," Chastity said from her position in the rowboat. "He's a very good oarsman, I can vouch for it, and we'll have the most beautiful view of the sunset from the temple."

"Oh, I do so wish to see it, but . . . oh, dear." Hester bit her lip and fixed her eyes once more upon Lord Lucan, who unconsciously straightened his shoulders.

"I rowed for Harrow, Hester," he offered, and it seemed to Chastity that his voice had somehow become deeper as his posture became more commanding. Her lips twitched. Little Hester certainly seemed to arouse the man in David Lucan.

Chastity exchanged a glance with Constance, whose own eyes were alight with amusement as she stood on the jetty with Max, who was tapping his foot with ill-concealed impatience at this shilly-shallying.

Max stepped around Constance and twitched the painter out of David's hand, murmuring into his ear, "For

God's sake, man. Just pick her up and put her in the boat while I hold it steady."

The tips of David's ears burned crimson. He stared at Max, then cleared his throat, and without further ado took the advice. Hester gave a little scream as he lifted her off the jetty and deposited her rather unceremoniously into the rowboat. She sat on the thwart with a gasp, clutching her parasol, and gazed at David in awe as he jumped down into the boat beside her.

He was still blushing as he stammered, "F-forgive me, Hester. I thought it best to help you make up your mind."

"Oh, yes, David," she breathed, her eyes shining. "I won't be at all frightened now. I know it's quite safe."

Max tossed the painter down to David. "Give me strength!" he muttered to Constance. "How the hell deep is this damn lake?"

"No more than three feet," Constance returned with a chuckle. "Don't be such a curmudgeon. It's young love we're promoting here."

He gave her a look to curdle milk and declared, "We'll take that other boat." He gestured to a skiff, the last remaining craft at the jetty.

"There's room for us all in David's boat," Constance murmured.

"We'll take the other one," Max repeated. "My patience won't stand another second of that simpering."

"Oh, you are so unromantic," Constance declared. She called out to her sister, "Max wants to take the skiff, so we'll see you over there."

"You want me to be romantic?" Max demanded in clear surprise as the rowboat pulled away. "That's rich, coming from someone who doesn't have a romantic bone in her body."

Constance laughed. "Unfair and ungallant." She untied the skiff's painter. "Are you rowing or am I?"

"I am." He rolled up the sleeves of his shirt and Constance caught herself watching his hands again, the deft movements of his long fingers. She had noticed already that his forearms and angular wrists were very strong, and she wondered not for the first time what he'd done with his life before he'd gone into politics. There was something very physical about him. Not the kind of man to have spent time in dusty offices or the halls of academe. How strange that she'd had no real interest in his past. It had seemed sufficient to know that he was Letitia's brother and an MP who could be put to good use. Now, however, she wasn't so sure. She still didn't even know his age, let alone whether he'd ever been married.

She jumped unaided into the skiff. "How old are you, Max?"

He gave her a quizzical look as he stepped in beside her. "That's rather sudden."

"Not really. I've just never thought to ask before. I'm twenty-eight, if you want an exchange of information."

He shook his head as he sat down on the mid thwart. "It never occurred to me to wonder." He took up the oars. "I'll be forty in two months' time."

"Ah." She nodded. "I guessed around there."

He laughed and pulled away from the jetty. "Any other questions?"

She let her hand dangle in the cool water as he rowed. "Ever been married?"

"No."

It was her turn to look quizzical now. "Ever been in love?"

"That's a different matter."

"What happened?"

He shipped his oars and the little skiff bobbed gently as two stately swans glided by. "I met her in India. She was the wife of the commander of the garrison at Jodhpur. She was lonely, bored, rather older than I was." He shrugged. "To cut a long story short, we had a very passionate liaison. She was going to leave her husband, ask him for a divorce, and we were going to come back to England and live, social outcasts of course, but happily ever after."

His mouth twisted in an expression of self-mockery and his blue eyes had an ironic gleam in them that Constance didn't like very much. "But you didn't," she said.

"No, we didn't. She decided she couldn't bear the disgrace, that it would damage her family's reputation. There was a child, a son, and she was afraid that her husband wouldn't permit her to see the child if she left him."

He took up his oars again and resumed course towards the island. Constance felt that she should be satisfied with his answers, but she knew he'd left a lot unsaid. She took her hand from the water and shook silvery drops from her fingers, watching as they caught the light from the sinking sun that was turning the surface of the lake a soft pink.

"What were you doing in India?"

"After Oxford I joined the East India Company's cavalry." He gave a short laugh. "I didn't get on with my father and putting an ocean between us seemed like a good idea. I resigned my commission when..." He shrugged and let the sentence hang. "So there you have my history, Miss Duncan."

"And now you're a politician." She dipped her fingers in the water again, making little circles on the smooth surface.

"It seemed a suitable career for a man of my age and gravitas." He glanced at her and she saw he was smiling now, the laugh lines creasing around his brilliant blue eyes as he squinted against the sun.

"And what political issues interest you the most?" she inquired, drying her fingers on her handkerchief.

"That's far too big a question to answer now." He pulled strongly on the oars and the skiff darted up to the jetty on the island, where the guests were beginning to climb the hill to the temple.

"Jenkins is opening the champagne on the terrace," Prudence said, giving her sister a hand out of the skiff. "If we don't hurry, though, we'll miss the sunset. You took ages getting across."

"Ah, well, Max is not too expert with a pair of oars," Constance said with a devilish smile. "He caught at least three crabs."

"Calumny!" he exclaimed.

She laughed and began to stride up the little hill in the wake of their guests, who were already crowding onto the paved terrace outside the little white structure. Jenkins and a manservant moved among them with trays of champagne flutes.

"You seem to be getting along remarkably well with our Right Honorable Gentleman," Prudence said in an undertone, taking a glass from the tray. "Are you sure you haven't lost your objectivity, Con?"

Constance hesitated. She glanced to where Max stood

at the edge of the terrace, glass in hand. She always thought he looked very striking in ordinary formal dress, but he was undeniably attractive with his tall lean frame clad in white flannels and open-collared shirt, the sleeves rolled up to his elbows, revealing bronzed fore-arms. His hair glistened in the sun. "Just to look at him makes my knees go weak," she said. "Whether that's the same as losing my objectivity, I don't know. Don't you think he's the most handsome man?"

Prudence laughed. "He's good-looking, I'll give you that. You don't think he's pompous and arrogant any-more?"

"Oh, yes, he's both of those things," Constance de-clared. "It's just that there are some physical compen-sations that at the moment seem to outweigh the disadvantages."

"That won't last," Prudence said. "Lust has a time limit."

"Then my objectivity, if it is temporarily lost, will soon return," her sister responded.

Prudence raised an eyebrow but made no comment.

Chapter 11

M ax was striding up the steps of the house in Manchester Square early on Tuesday morning when the door opened before he could reach it and the three sisters emerged, dressed for the street.

"We'll be back late this afternoon, Jenkins," Constance was saying over her shoulder as she stepped out, drawing on her gloves. "Oh, Max. What are you doing here?"

It was a less than ecstatic welcome, he thought. "I should have thought that was obvious," he said with a wry smile. "I was coming to call upon you. What are you doing out so early? It's barely nine o'clock."

"I'm afraid that we have to go out."

"Anywhere special?"

"We're taking a train," Chastity said.

"Yes, an early train and we must hurry, or we'll miss it," Constance said. "I'm so sorry, Max. Can you call another time?"

"Where are you going by train?" he inquired, intrigued but also a little put out by her casual demeanor.

They had parted company at Waterloo the previous day on their return from Romsey. It had been a decorous farewell, taking place as it did in public, but he had rather expected a hint of special warmth in her manner towards him when they met next. He had actually tried to resist the urge to rush around to Manchester Square at the earliest possible opportunity, but the impulse had been irresistible. Now he was beginning to regret it.

"Oh, just an errand we have to run in the country," she said with a vague gesture, starting down the steps. "But you could call tomorrow. We'll be out in the morning, but tomorrow afternoon we have our At Home."

"Unfortunately I must be in the House of Commons tomorrow afternoon for Prime Minister's Question Time," he said a little stiffly. "I was hoping to invite you for lunch today. I was going to leave an invitation with Jenkins since I assumed you would not yet be up and about."

"I'm so sorry." Constance had already begun to walk quickly along the pavement. "That would have been lovely, but we have this other engagement, you see. Prudence, can you hail that cab coming around the corner?"

"Well, I won't keep you." He bowed and waited as the three sisters climbed into the hackney. Constance waved to him as the hackney moved off, and he could read only distraction in her gaze, not a hint of intimacy or even regret at her abrupt departure.

He frowned. He was far too experienced to be put out by a woman's seeming indifference, let alone to suffer from piqued pride. It was an old feminine trick to blow hot and cold. For some reason women thought it made a man more eager. But he'd learned to ignore it before he was out of adolescence. It was strange, though. Constance was the last person he would have expected to employ such a hackneyed girlish trick.

Constance sat back in the corner of the cab, hanging on to the leather strap as the hackney swung around the corner into Marble Arch. "Well, that was a little awkward."

"You were a little brusque," Prudence observed.

"It's just that I know where we're going," Constance said. "We're in cahoots with his sister's governess, on an underhanded mission to liberate her from Letitia's tyranny. I couldn't think what to say to him."

"You could have invited him for dinner this evening. Or even suggested he take you out," Chastity pointed out. "He did look rather hurt," she added sympathetically.

"I suppose so." Constance fixed her gaze on the street beyond the window. Chastity's sensitivity was having its usual chastening effect. She said slowly, "But in truth I don't want things to move too fast. It was one thing while we were at Romsey, but back in London it seems, well, too precipitate."

"You certainly didn't hesitate about jumping into his bed," Prudence observed in a rather dry tone. "I would call that more than a little precipitate."

"Maybe I got a little more than I bargained for," Constance said frankly. "I seem to be paying for it with doubts now." She turned back from the window and gave her sisters a rather helpless little smile. "Some kind of lover's remorse."

"So, you did lose your objectivity." Prudence looked at her sharply.

"I must have done." Constance shrugged. "But it's coming back now. I have to take control of things again. And the only way to do that is to go slowly."

Her sisters merely nodded. They didn't disagree with her, but they had watched her spectacular loss of control with some trepidation and both rather doubted her ability to get it back again as easily as she seemed to think.

"So, how are we going to proceed with Henry Franklin?" Prudence asked.

"First we have to find him. Then we have to get him alone," Constance said, happy to have the subject changed. "We'll try his father's office first."

"Are we going to cajole him or bully him?" Chastity asked.

Constance considered. "Maybe both," she said. "Of course, it depends what he's like. How resistant he is. But maybe you should be nice and I should be nasty. Then when he doesn't know which way is up, Prue can chip in with some practical suggestions."

"That might work," Prudence agreed. "But if he's really weak and already bullied by his father, we're going to have to give him courage... build him up, not knock him down."

"Let's decide when we meet him."

The hackney drew up outside Waterloo station and they hurried onto the concourse. The train for Ashford was already steaming at the platform. "We'll buy tickets on the train," Constance said. "There's no time to stand at the ticket window."

They settled into a compartment, bought their tickets from an elderly and avuncular ticket collector, and

Constance unscrewed the lid of the thermos flask she carried in a capacious straw handbag. She filled three dainty cups and passed them around as the train's whistle blew and the train jerked forward.

"Did you bring sandwiches?" Chastity leaned forward to peer in the basket.

"Cheese scones and cold sausages," her sister told her. "But we should save them until later. I've no idea whether we'll get any lunch."

"Oh, but there's Bakewell tart too," Chastity declared happily, ignoring her sister's suggestion and taking a slice of the almond and jam tart. "Mrs. Hudson's specialty. We can have that now. It goes so well with coffee."

The journey took an hour and a half and the train chugged into Ashford station just before noon. The sisters descended to the platform and looked around for a pony and trap to hire to take them into the town.

"Franklin Construction," Prudence said, reading off the paper that Amelia Westcott had given them. "West Street."

"Let's ask the stationmaster."

Constance went into the small station house. A grizzled man gave her a nod and told her that while there were no traps for hire she could walk into the center of town in fifteen minutes and would find West Street running off the market square. Franklin Construction was the gray building halfway down on the left.

Constance thanked him and returned to her sisters. "Looks like it's shank's pony."

Prudence glanced up at the overcast sky. "Let's hope it doesn't rain."

Franklin Construction turned out to be a substantial building occupying the center block of West Street.

Constance looked up at the sign over the door. "I get the impression that Franklin Senior has a thriving concern here."

"More than enough to support a musically talented son," Chastity agreed.

"Mmm." Prudence nodded thoughtfully. "Well, let's see what we can discover." She walked boldly to the door and turned the knob. A bell jangled as it opened onto a neat office, with three desks and a wall of filing cabinets.

A man with a drooping moustache and pale sad eyes behind wire-rimmed spectacles looked up from a stack of inventories as they entered. He offered a hesitant and somewhat puzzled smile and rose to his feet. "What can I do for you, ladies?"

"We're looking for Henry Franklin," Constance said, deciding that the direct approach was the best. "Do you happen to know where we could find him?"

"Well, right here, madam. I am Henry Franklin." He gazed at them in frank bewilderment. There were ink stains on the white cuffs of his shirt showing beneath the slightly short sleeves of his coat. His appearance was untidy, careless, as if it mattered not a whit to him, and his hair was too long. But his hands were long and white, the nails meticulously manicured. A pianist's hands, Constance thought. It was hard to guess at his age but he looked so worn and dispirited that she thought he was probably younger than he appeared.

"What can I do for you?" he asked again.

Constance looked around the office. She could hear voices from behind a door in the far wall. "Are you in a position to leave here for a few minutes and talk privately with us?"

"But what is it about?" He glanced nervously to the door as the voices rose; one in particular was loud and peremptory.

Papa Franklin. The sisters exchanged a quick glance.

"Amelia." Chastity spoke in a soft and gentle whisper, coming over to him, regarding him intently from beneath the upturned brim of her crushed-velvet hat as she laid a hand on his arm. "Where can we go to talk?"

He looked at her like a panic-stricken deer. "Has something happened to her? Is she all right?"

Constance glanced at Prudence and received a faint nod of agreement. "Yes to the first, and no to the second," Constance stated, her voice as low as Chastity's but nowhere near as sympathetic. "You need to talk with us, Mr. Franklin." She glanced to the door behind him. "We would not wish to involve anyone else."

His complexion was now ashen. "In the Copper Kettle, on Market Street. I sometimes take my lunch there. I will meet you in fifteen minutes."

"Then we will see you in fifteen minutes," Chastity said in the same gentle tones. "Please don't worry, Mr. Franklin. We mean you no harm." She followed her sisters outside, casting him a further encouraging glance as she went through the door. He did not look encouraged.

"Will he come, d'you think?" Prudence asked.

"Oh, yes," Constance declared. "He'll come. Out of fear. He probably thinks we're going to blackmail him."

"Well, we are, after a fashion," Prudence said.

Constance regarded her in surprise for a second and then laughed. "If it comes down to it, Prue, of course we are. We're discovering any number of dubious talents that we never knew we possessed."

The Copper Kettle was a small chintzy tea shop. The sisters examined the menu.

"The Welsh rarebit is very good, madam," the waitress told them, pointing with her pen to the item. "We gets lots of compliments on the rarebit."

"What about the veal and ham pie?" Prudence asked.

The woman shook her head. "Wouldn't go for it myself, madam. That jelly stuff's not so fresh . . . Cod 'n' chips is good, though."

Prudence grimaced. "I have enough cod in my life. What do you think, Con?"

"Welsh rarebit," Constance replied. "And a pot of tea." She added sotto voce to Prudence, "I don't trust the coffee here."

"Three rarebits it is, then, and a pot of tea for three." The woman scribbled on her pad.

"We are expecting someone else to join us," Chastity said. "Mr. Henry Franklin."

"Oh, Mr. Henry always has sardines on toast," the waitress said cheerfully. "Every day . . . rain or shine, it's sardines on toast." She gave them a curious look. "New to town, aren't you? Friends of Mr. Henry, are you?"

"Yes," Prudence agreed with a smile.

The waitress hesitated, her expression hungry for more information, but something about the calmly smiling impassivity of the three women before her shut off her curiosity like a closed tap. "Well, I'll put in Mr. Henry's sardines on toast, then, and bring another cup." She took her pad and went off.

Henry Franklin came into the café a few minutes later. He looked around with an air of anxious suspicion, then approached the table, unwinding his muffler. An unnecessary garment given the humidity of the overcast day, the sisters reflected as they smiled and gestured to the fourth chair at the table. But perhaps he had a throat condition.

"The waitress says you always eat sardines on toast, so we ordered them for you," Chastity said with a reassuring smile. "We're all having the Welsh rarebit."

"I hear it's excellent." He sat down, his eyes darting from side to side. "I only have half an hour. Please tell me what you want." He took off his glasses and polished them on a less than pristine handkerchief. His eyes without their protection were weak and watery.

"We don't want anything," Chastity said, leaning across the table towards him. "We're here for Amelia because she cannot be here for herself."

"I don't understand. She . . . Amelia and I . . . we agreed not to see each other again. It's impossible." He returned his glasses to his nose. "My father would never permit such a match. What has *happened* to Amelia?"

"What often happens when two people make love," Constance said calmly, pitching her voice low so that no one but her immediate audience could hear her.

Henry sagged in his chair. He wrung his hands convulsively and gazed helplessly at them. "I d-don't understand."

"What don't you understand?" It was Prudence's turn now. She sat next to him, turning sideways to face him. "It's a simple fact of life, Henry. These things happen. But when they do, then decisions have to be made."

"You would not expect Amelia to carry this burden alone." Chastity rested a hand on his. "You are far too good a man to do that, Henry. I know you are."

The waitress appeared behind them with a laden tray, and Constance said, "It's so nice to see you again, Mr.

Franklin. We were passing through Ashford on our way to Dover and thought how delightful it would be to catch up with you. We had such a delightful time at the musicale in Dover. Do you still play?"

Henry mumbled something. His grayish pallor was waxen and beads of perspiration stood out on his brow. He stared down at the table until the waitress had set down their plates and left, her backward glance brimming with speculation.

"Why didn't she write and tell me?" he said, poking at his sardines with his fork. "I don't understand why she didn't write to me."

"But she did," Prudence said. "She told us she had written several times, although she didn't mention her present situation. But you never wrote back."

"I didn't receive her letters. We'd agreed not to see each other again, so I just assumed that she was holding to that."

"Well, what could have happened to her letters?" Constance asked, taking her fork to the crisp bubbly cheese topping of her rarebit.

Henry looked up and stated bitterly, "My father sees all the post that comes into the house before anyone else does. He distributes it at the breakfast table."

"And he knew about your understanding with Amelia?" Constance took a mouthful of her lunch. It was surprisingly good, with just the right mustardy bite to the cheese.

"Someone told him they'd seen us out walking in the evenings. He was very unpleasant about it." He shuddered at the memory. "I couldn't bear to listen to him . . . to the things he said about Amelia. He said she wasn't good enough for a Franklin, that she was a woman of loose morals . . . oh, dreadful things."

"Why didn't you stand up to him?" Prudence asked, pouring tea from the big brown pot.

"That's easy for you to say," he responded as bitterly as before, cutting his sardines into minute fussy little pieces. "You don't stand up to my father. No one does. He threatened to throw me out on the street if I ever saw or spoke with her again. It was no idle threat, I can promise you."

"Then what are you going to do?" Chastity's voice was still soft and sympathetic.

He made a helpless gesture with his hands. "What *can* I do? He'll throw me out without a penny and I can't support a wife and child without money."

"You could always earn it," Prudence pointed out dryly.

"Doing what?" he exclaimed in an undertone. "I'm good for nothing but playing the piano."

"You work as a clerk in your father's office," Constance pointed out. "You could find such a job elsewhere."

"It's killing my soul," he said with a mournful sigh, echoing Amelia's observation.

"And what do you think carrying an illegitimate child is doing to Amelia's soul?" Constance demanded, her patience all but exhausted.

Henry looked as if he was about to cry. He covered his face with his hands.

"Do you love Amelia?" Chastity asked.

"We can't live on love!" He looked up and the hopelessness in his eyes stirred even the impatient Constance to sympathy. She glanced at Prudence.

Prudence took off her glasses and then replaced them, pushing them up the bridge of her nose with a firm, decisive forefinger. "This is what you must do."

Henry gazed at her with the soulful hopeful eyes of a dog unsure whether he was about to receive a stroke or a kick.

"You have to declare your independence from your father before you do anything else. You will come to London, where you will marry Amelia in a civil ceremony at the registrar's office in the borough where Amelia lives. You will find a job as a clerk. We shall help you do that— in fact, we shall hold your hand throughout. Once you've sorted that out, then you will take Amelia to visit your father. It will be a fait accompli and I'm willing to bet that the prospect of a grandchild will soften him. You will present him with your own plan. Amelia is a clever woman, good with figures, with writing letters...she has any number of the skills essential for running an office. She'll take over the office instead of you, and you will start building a private practice teaching piano. If he refuses to be reconciled, and he won't, then you simply return to your job in London. If he knows that he can't bully you, he'll think twice. I promise you."

"Oh, masterly, Prue," Constance said. "So what do you say, Henry?"

He looked winded. He could no more imagine withstanding the incredible force of this trio of women than he would an avalanche. "How will I get his permission to go to London? He'll never give me the time off."

"You weren't listening, Henry." Constance leaned across the table towards him. "Prue said that you have first to declare your independence from your father. You won't ask his permission. You will simply leave here and commit yourself to a new life. If you can't face him in person, then write him a letter. Take the night train if it'll be easier. You can stay with us for a few days until you can find somewhere for both of you to live. I would think Amelia could hide her marriage and go on working at the Grahams for another month or so, if necessary. It would give you more time to get established. But first you *must* get married."

He rubbed his eyes with the heel of his palms. "But a registry-office wedding. Surely Amelia would not want that. She'll want a proper wedding."

"Amelia wants a wedding...*any* wedding...just as long as it comes with a marriage certificate and a ring on her finger," Constance declared. "Now, if you write her a letter telling her what you've decided we'll take it to her when we see her on Thursday."

"I have pencil and paper." Prudence rummaged in her handbag and produced a small notebook and a pencil. "There."

Henry took them. He looked down at his now cold sardines, then back at the three women who were regarding him steadily. They were an irresistible force, and perhaps, just perhaps, they were a match for his father. He felt a faint stirring of energy. With them at his back, there was no telling what he could do. "When shall I come to London?" he asked.

They all smiled at him and he felt their approval like a warm bath.

"The sooner the better," Prudence said. "This coming weekend, if you like. We'll expect you on Sunday."

He took a deep breath, then said in a rush, "Yes...all right. On Sunday."

"We'll arrange with Amelia for the marriage license,

and next Thursday, on her afternoon off, you can be married."

"Oh, dear," he said, shaking his head. "It's...it's quite overwhelming." He began to write in the notebook. The sisters returned to their cooling lunch.

Half an hour later they were on their way back to the station, Henry's letter to Amelia tucked into Constance's bag.

"Do you think he'll come?" Prudence asked with a slightly worried frown.

"Yes. I don't think he'll let Amelia down once he's made a promise," Chastity responded. "Besides, he's not going to risk our coming back here and talking to his father. Con implied, in no uncertain terms, that we would if he didn't show up on Sunday."

"It was a bit heavy-handed," Constance admitted of her parting shot as they had left the café. "But I thought fear might give him more backbone." She added with a rueful grimace, "I just hope we're doing the right thing for Amelia by forcing this. Henry's such a broken reed."

"I don't think you need worry about that," Prudence said stoutly. "Amelia's strong enough for both of them. It isn't as if she doesn't know his weaknesses. She'll run their marriage and he'll do as he's told. If she can manage the kind of brat that young Pamela Graham seems to be, I'm sure managing Henry will be a walk in the park."

Constance nodded with a chuckle. "I'm sure you're right. I wonder if Max has a secretary."

"Why?"

"Well, if he doesn't, I'm sure he needs one. I would have said we have the perfect candidate in Henry Franklin."

"Is there no limit to your deviousness, Con?" Prudence demanded as they reached the station.

"I don't know. I haven't found one yet," her sister responded with a grin. "I'll just have to see if I can persuade him."

"So the husband works for Max, and the wife for his sister, and neither of their employers knows they're married?" Chastity shook her head.

"It'll only be like that until Amelia has to leave the Grahams because of her pregnancy," Constance said piously. "It's hardly a deception at all."

"Tell that to the marines!" scoffed Prudence.

Constance laughed. "Well, I can talk to him anyway."

They sat down on the station platform to wait for the train and Chastity sighed. "It's very tiring work, this Go-Between business. And tomorrow we have to take care of Anonymous and his requirements."

"No peace for the wicked," Constance agreed.

"No peace for those in straitened circumstances," Prudence amended.

"We'll wait behind the curtain at the back of the shop, Chas," Prudence said the following morning, glancing quickly behind the counter. "Mrs. Beedle says we'll hear everything that goes on from there if you and Anonymous conduct your business over by the biscuits." She gestured to a dusty corner where packets of biscuits lined the shelves amid jars of liquorice sticks and farthing candies.

"You've time for a nice cuppa, Miss Con. If the gentleman's not coming until eleven o'clock." A round woman with her white hair in a neat bun, her starched apron rustling with her step, emerged from behind the curtain of heavy drugget, the brass rings rattling on the rod as she pulled it aside. "I always have a cuppa about now. And a nice bite of lardy cake, just made this morning. We'll hear the bell if anyone comes in." She gestured to the bell over the shop door.

"Oh, I love lardy cake," Chastity said. "It'll give me heart for my lonely task."

"Chas, I'll do it if you're really uncomfortable," Prudence said quickly.

"No, of course I'm not. I was only joking." Chastity followed her sisters behind the counter and through the curtain into a small neat kitchen where a kettle whistled merrily on the range.

"Sit you down now." Mrs. Beedle gestured to the round table on which reposed a very sticky currant-studded sugary concoction. She set out cups, warmed the teapot, measured tea, and filled the pot. "There now." She set it on the table with a milk jug and sugar bowl. "You'll have a piece of lardy cake, Miss Con."

Constance hated lardy cake. It was far too greasy for her taste, but she asked for a tiny slice for politeness' sake. She could always slip it onto Chastity's plate when their hostess wasn't looking.

The bell rang in the shop and Mrs. Beedle twitched aside the curtains. "Oh, it's just Mr. Holbrook, come for his newspaper and his cigarettes." She bustled out, greeting the customer cheerily.

Chastity took a large bite of her cake and licked her fingers. "This is so sinful."

"It's terrible," Constance said, pouring tea. "I don't know how you can eat it."

"It's a very fine lardy cake," Prudence declared, licking her own fingers.

"Have mine." Constance put her slice on Chastity's plate and glanced at the clock. "It's nearly eleven. I wonder if he'll be early."

The doorbell jangled again. They all looked towards the curtain. A man's voice, lowered to a bare murmur, reached them from the shop. "It's him." Chastity wiped her fingers on her napkin, took a quick gulp of tea, and stood up, adjusting her thick black veil. "Can you see my face?"

"Barely."

"I'll try my French accent."

Mrs. Beedle emerged from the shop. "Gentleman's here for you, miss."

"Thank you." Chastity nodded at her sisters, braced her shoulders, and went into the shop. Her sisters moved as one away from the table to the curtain. Constance tweaked it aside a fraction so that the corner of the shop where the biscuits were arrayed was visible.

"You are looking for me, m'sieur." Chastity's exaggerated French accent caused her sisters momentary disarray as they struggled with involuntary laughter. She sounded like a French maid in a Feydeau farce, Constance thought.

"You are the Go-Between from *The Mayfair Lady*?" The man was in morning dress, carrying a top hat and a silver-knobbed cane. His hair was gray and rather sparse on top and he wore pince-nez perched on the end of a long, thin nose. A neat little moustache graced his upper lip. He looked undistinguished but perfectly respectable.

"I am its representative," Chastity said.

He took off his gloves and offered his hand with a bow. She gave him her own gloved hand and gestured to the corner of the shop. "Let us talk there, if you please. We will be quite private."

He looked around. "I had expected an office."

"We have our own reasons for wishing to remain anonymous also, m'sieur."

The sisters behind the curtain exchanged approving nods.

"But you can help me?"

"I will know that better, m'sieur, when you have answered some questions." They moved into full view of the watchers behind the curtain. "You must understand that the ladies who are interested in our service request only the most impeccable referrals."

"Yes . . . yes . . . of course. I would not expect otherwise," he said hastily. "Please do not misunderstand me, madam. I meant to cast no aspersions—"

Chastity held up a hand, cutting him off. "That is all right, m'sieur. We understand each other. Let us review your circumstances and the qualities you desire in a wife. You say that you prefer to live in the country?"

"Yes . . . yes. I have a small estate in Lincolnshire. Not a grand mansion, you understand, but more than comfortable. I am possessed of a comfortable fortune." The words seemed to be tumbling over themselves in his haste to get them out. Constance and Prudence knew what was happening. Chastity frequently had this effect on people. Her very posture and the softness of her voice, even in its present disguise, always implied sympathy and an empathetic ear.

"And you are looking for a wife." Chastity nodded her veiled head. "Someone with quiet tastes, no doubt."

"There is little excitement in our village, madam. Of course, my . . ." He coughed behind his hand. "My wife would entertain the vicar and his wife, the squire and his lady from the next village. We have little card parties, and occasional musical evenings. But in general we lead a quiet life."

"And as I understand it, you require neither beauty nor fortune?" Chastity managed to sound slightly incredulous.

"I require a companion, madam. From what I have read, beauty makes a poor companion. It is too much interested in itself. I abhor vanity in a woman."

"And just what have you been reading, my friend?" Constance inquired sotto voce behind the curtain. Prudence kicked her ankle.

"That does not concern the Go-Between, m'sieur," Chastity said with a neutrality that neither of her sisters could have managed. "We are only in the business of making introductions. It is for our clients to decide if they will suit."

"Quite so . . . quite so." He coughed again. "As for fortune, I believe I have more than sufficient to support a wife." He turned his hat around between his hands, brushing nervously at the brim. "I would not care for an extravagant wife, madam. My fortune is sufficient for a quiet and comfortable life, but we do not indulge in excessive luxury in Lincolnshire."

Chastity nodded, her expression hidden behind the muslin folds of her veil. "And do you have any other requirements, m'sieur?"

"I must have a wife of good family . . . who can hold her head up in our little society." He reddened, then continued hesitantly, "A lady not beyond the age of . . ." He cleared his throat. "... of child bearing would be an advantage. An heir, you understand?" He gave an embarrassed smile.

"I understand perfectly," Chastity said. "And it is possible that I have a recommendation for you, m'sieur. I can effect an introduction if you so desire."

"I would be most grateful, madam." He clasped his hands together in a fervent gesture.

"Next Wednesday you should come to the address on this card at three o'clock." Chastity handed him a visiting card. "It will be a simple At Home. The lady I would recommend to you will be wearing a white rose in her buttonhole. You will ask your hostess to make the introduction if you decide you wish to meet the lady."

He looked down at the engraved card and said doubtfully, "Manchester Square. This is Mayfair. Would a lady of retiring tastes frequent such an elegant address?"

"M'sieur, you want a lady of impeccable lineage. Where else would you expect to find such a one? Everyone's tastes vary, regardless of their position in society."

"Oh, bravo, Chas!" Prudence applauded silently.

"Of course ... of course." Anonymous nodded vigorously, still examining the visiting card. "The ladies at this address ... the Honorable Misses Duncan ... they will know why I'm there? How should I introduce myself?"

"With your name, m'sieur. I assume if you decide to pursue this further you would see no difficulty in making your identity known at that point."

"No," he agreed. "No, it would not serve a useful purpose to remain anonymous if I'm to court a lady. But what of my hostesses? Are they associated with the Go-Between?"

"The Go-Between has nothing whatsoever to do with Ten Manchester Square," Chastity lied smoothly. "The At Home is merely a convenient way for you to meet a possible wife in secure and respectable circumstances. You will present your card to the butler in the usual way and when you are announced to your hostesses, you'll simply say that you are an acquaintance of Lord Jersey's who happened to mention that he would be at Manchester Square that afternoon and you wish to talk with him. Needless to say, he will not be there, so there will be no awkwardness, and since many people attend the ladies' weekly gatherings, no one will think anything of your dropping by. How you choose to pursue the introduction once it's made is no concern of the Go-Between."

"I see. It seems very complicated."

"It is simply in the interests of discretion, m'sieur. For both you and the lady." Chastity managed to sound rather stern.

He nodded hastily. "Yes . . . yes, of course. Most necessary." He turned the card over in his hands. "Is there a fee for this consultation, madam?"

"You have paid the fee for this morning's consultation, m'sieur," Chastity said. "However, if you wish to take up the recommendation and present yourself at Manchester Square, then there is an additional five guineas owing now. If you choose not to, then, of course, we have no outstanding charges."

"May I know something more of the lady before I decide?" He asked the question with all the hesitation of a schoolboy afraid of making a fool of himself.

It seemed to Chastity that for the extra five guineas he was entitled to some more information. "She is a lady of good family . . . her father is a clergyman. I believe her to be this side of thirty-five. Of pleasant appearance and demeanor but no fortune, and she has a devout temperament. I would imagine she would enjoy the company of the wives of squires and vicars."

"It seems you have understood my needs very well, madam. I assume that the lady is interested in acquiring a husband."

"I believe so. But the Go-Between can make no guarantees as to her response."

"I understand." He extracted five guineas from his coat pocket. "I will attend the At Home at Manchester Square on Wednesday, precisely at three o'clock."

"Perhaps you should make it closer to half past," Chastity said, tucking the note into her handbag. "People don't always arrive on the dot of three."

"Oh, no. Quite . . . quite. Ladies are often unpunctual." He stroked his neat, waxed moustache, an enthusiastic gleam now in his eye.

Chastity said, "I trust you will find that this recommendation suits your requirements, m'sieur." She extended her hand. "I bid you good morning."

He shook it eagerly. "Good morning, madam." He bowed and left the shop, something of the cock in his walk.

Chastity threw back her veil and breathed deeply, fanning her hot face with her hand.

"You were amazing, Chas." Prudence pulled back the curtain with a clanking of the brass rings.

"That accent is straight out of Feydeau," Constance said. "I can't think Anonymous believed in it for a minute."

"I don't think he cared," Chastity said. "Anyway, all

we have to do now is ensure Millicent Hardcastle comes on Wednesday, and we have to contrive to put a white rose in her buttonhole. But I don't think I should be there, just in case he recognizes me."

"No," Prudence agreed. "Even without the veil and the phony French accent his suspicions might be aroused if he talks to you."

"I'll make myself scarce. But now I need more lardy cake."

"As much as you want, duckie." Constance held the curtain aside for her. "That was an astonishing performance. I don't know any Lord Jersey. Is there one?"

Chastity grinned and sat down at the kitchen table. "Not to my knowledge. That's why he won't be there on Wednesday. I was quite proud of myself. And actually I think Anonymous will really suit Millicent." She bit into the cake. "Mrs. Beedle, this is the best I've ever had."

Jenkins's sister beamed. "Eat it up, m'dear. Eat it up. It doesn't keep. I'll be back to minding the shop now. Take your time." She headed for the curtain, then said, "Oh, quite slipped my mind. There's another letter for you. I put it up behind the tea caddy." She pointed to the shelf and the brightly painted tin tea caddy.

Constance took down the letter. "Aunt Mabel or the Go-Between...any guesses?"

Her sisters shook their heads and waited expectantly. Constance slit the envelope and opened it. She read in silence, her expression rapt.

"Well?" Prudence demanded finally.

"It's a letter from a reader in Hampstead asking if we would publish the schedule of meetings for the WSPU," Constance said slowly. "She writes that it would be a great service for people who can't attend regularly or declare their affiliation openly." She looked up, eyes shining. "We're getting through! Finally we're reaching these women."

Her sisters rose and hugged her. It was Constance's triumph but it was also their mother's, and as such belonged to them all. They stood close together for a minute, silent with their own memories. Such moments still happened often between them and they had learned to live with the knowledge of loss and take comfort from the shared memories.

When they moved apart, Chastity dashed a hand across her eyes and asked, "So, what now? These five guineas are burning a hole in my pocket. How about we treat ourselves to lunch?"

"Something modest," Prudence said. "If we spend it as soon as we get it we're never going to be solvent."

"Modest, it is," declared Constance. "And afterwards we'll have time before the At Home to scoop up little Hester and take her to visit her future mother-in-law, then bring her to the At Home, where David is bound to be in attendance. That should be good eventually for a substantial donation to the fund for indigent spinsters."

Chapter 12

A secretary could only add to your consequence," Constance said from her supine position on a blanket on the lush green riverbank just below Windsor Castle.

"And why would my consequence need such an addition?" Max inquired, looking down at her with a quizzical gleam in his eye. "I'm quite satisfied with it as it is."

"Oh, but you're bound to be a Cabinet Minister soon," she said. "And there must be so many details of your life that need to be arranged. Appointments, topics for speeches. Why, you might even want someone to write speeches for you. And I'm sure you could use the help of someone to look things up for you . . . references, legal and parliamentary precedents. Those sorts of things."

"What are you up to?" he demanded, reaching to refill their glasses from the champagne bottle on the grass beside him.

"Why would you think I was up to anything?"

"Oh, Constance! Don't treat me like an idiot."

She sat up. One really couldn't play games with Max

Ensor. She said with an air of open frankness, "There's a man I'd like to help. He wants to marry an acquaintance of mine but he needs to get regular employment if he's to support a wife and family. He's very able at office work, although his passion is music. He's a very talented pianist but he can't make enough teaching piano. So I thought perhaps you might try him out."

"Very well. Send him to see me."

"You'll see him...just like that?" She couldn't help her astonishment.

"Why not? Isn't that what you wanted?"

"Well, yes, but I thought I'd have to work on you a lot harder."

"Oh, so that's what lies behind the charming, compliant, sweet-tempered façade I've been treated to all morning," he declared. "I should have known. You were just buttering me up. I would never have expected it of you...you of all women!"

Constance felt her cheeks warm at this well-justified accusation. "I have to use what tactics are available to me," she said defensively. "I wasn't to know you would be so compliant yourself. You haven't exactly demonstrated that tendency in the past."

"Neither, my dear, have you."

The arid observation brought a rueful smile to her lips. "True enough. We're not the most peaceable pair, are we? I admit I had a reason for trying to make sure we didn't have any differences of opinion to spoil the mood. But it was a lovely picnic lunch and I enjoyed both it and your company regardless of ulterior motive."

He was silent for a minute, then said, "You didn't seem too pleased to see me the other morning."

"You took me by surprise," she said. "I had things on my mind and you took me by surprise."

"I'll know better another time," he said as dryly as before. He was quite certain that there was more to it.

She hesitated, wondering if this was the right moment to move things onto a more confiding level. If she was to influence his opinions they needed to be a lot more intimate and trusting with each other. Lust alone wouldn't do it. She had no idea whether they could move their affair into something meaningful, let alone what would happen if they did, but the possibility intrigued her. Of course, if he had no intention of taking things to a deeper level, and he had given no indication that he did, then if she pushed now it might drive him away.

The silence had gone on too long and she made up her mind. Do or die. "I was...am...afraid that things are moving too fast. I know I was responsible for what happened at Romsey Manor, but when we got back to London I started to think that we don't really know each other at all. I enjoy your company." She gave a tiny little laugh that almost sounded embarrassed. "I'm in lust with you. But in the cold light of day that's not enough."

Max was taken aback. He had not expected such a frank invitation, or was it a challenge, to explore the possibilities of a deeper relationship. At least not so soon. In truth, he hadn't thought her interested in anything more than a passionate, lighthearted affair, and it hadn't occurred to him to consider whether he was interested in more than that either. Was she saying now that if he turned down this invitation—or challenge—then their present involvement was at an end? He certainly wasn't ready for that to happen.

"Then perhaps we should start to get to know each

other," he said in a considering tone. "Perhaps we have been putting the cart before the horse." He turned sideways on the grass to look at her, his blue eyes resting intently on her face. "Tell me about the most important thing in your life. Apart from your family, I mean. What stirs you, Constance? What makes your blood run hot?"

She gave another little laugh. "You mean apart from having sex with you?"

"Be serious," he chided. "You were the one who started this conversation."

"Women's suffrage," she said, her fingers tightening around the stem of her glass at the familiar surge of energetic fervor the topic always brought her. "I am passionate about women's suffrage. About equal rights for women. It is the driving force of my existence."

"I knew your views on the subject," he said. "You don't hide them. But is it really *that* important to you? The driving force of your existence?"

"Absolutely," she said, returning his intent gaze. "Without exaggeration."

He was once more taken aback. How could anyone describe a single political issue as the driving force of her existence? It was the description of a fanatic. "Then you're a member of the WSPU?"

"Of course," she said. "But I don't broadcast it. It would upset my father. The time will come to be open about my affiliation, but not yet."

"I see."

She continued to look at him with the same intensity, as if she would read behind the seemingly placid façade of his countenance. "You think a member of the Union makes an uncomfortable bedfellow, Max?" There was a hint of mockery in her voice. "Better to know that now rather than later."

"You are always putting words into my mouth, Constance," he snapped. "Give me a chance to respond in my own way."

"I'm sorry," she said swiftly. "It's a terrible habit I have, I know."

He almost laughed. "Do you really know it?"

"Yes. I jump too quickly. I've been told it many times."

"By whom?" He watched her now, his gaze slightly softened as he saw the flash of distress cross her eyes.

"My mother...Douglas...my sisters. All people I love...loved." She shrugged. "I don't seem to have learned the lesson, though."

"No," he agreed. "But I think that's enough self-flagellation for one day. And to answer your question, if that's what it was, I don't see the point of women's suffrage, as I've said before. But I'm perfectly happy to tolerate an opposing viewpoint."

"Tolerate!" Constance exclaimed. "That is so patronizing, Max."

He thought for a minute, then said, "My turn to apologize."

Constance accepted this in silence. Then she said, "If you would come to a meeting, you might see the point. You could meet Emmeline Pankhurst. At least open your mind."

It would also give him the opportunity to see the organization from the inside, he reflected. The closer he got to its inner workings, the more he would discover.

"You could also tell us what the government is doing, or thinking," she continued into his silence. "You wouldn't be betraying any secrets. You told me that they were at least looking into the issue of whether women tax and ratepayers should qualify. I don't suppose that's a government secret."

What a conniving creature she is, he thought with a flicker of amusement. She had every intention of milking him for useful information. Which put them both squarely on the court on opposing sides of the net. One of them was going to be useful to the other. It would be interesting to see which one served first.

"I can tell you nothing that the newspapers don't report every day," he said with an easy shrug. "But I will come to a meeting with you."

"There's a meeting at Kensington Town Hall at seven o'clock the day after tomorrow. Could you make that?"

"Possibly." He cast her another sidelong glance. "Are there any demonstrations planned?"

Constance shook her head. "It's just a meeting," she said. "I'll meet you on the steps, if you like."

"I assume I'll need someone to vouch for me."

"Not necessarily, but we do keep an eye on who attends. We can't be too careful, there's so much hostility to the cause."

"Ah." He nodded, and she frowned slightly, wondering why she felt a sudden stir of unease, as if something wasn't quite right. She looked over at him, but he seemed his usual perfectly relaxed self.

"And after the meeting you may dine with me," he said.

It was a statement, not an invitation. "If that's the bargain," she responded without expression.

"Oh, dear." He shook his head. "Let me try that again. Miss Duncan, porcupine though you are, will you do me the honor of dining with me after the meeting?"

"I should be delighted, Mr. Ensor, thank you. It will give us the opportunity to discuss your reactions and deepen your understanding of the issues." She offered him a bland smile, but beneath he could detect a hint of triumph. She was convinced she had had the last word. And she was right, he concluded. For the moment anyway.

"The pleasure will be all mine, ma'am."

Time to back off, Constance decided. She was sufficiently wary of Max's ability to bite back not to belabor the victory. "I should get back," she said, stretching languidly. "That was such a clever picnic. Those lobster sandwiches were wonderful. And those baby veal and ham pies...I adore them. Did Letitia's cook prepare it for you?"

"Actually, the dining room at the House of Commons," he said, tipping the remains of the champagne into their glasses. "The chef is very good. I hope you'll dine there with me one evening."

"I should love to," Constance said with a gracious smile. She drained her champagne and gave him her glass as he packed the remains of their picnic away in the hamper.

She got to her feet and shook out her cream muslin skirt. "I shouldn't have worn this, it's so pale it shows every stain." She peered over her shoulder to check the back. "Are there any grass stains?"

Max examined her back view with considerable interest. He smoothed out the folds, patted them back into place. "Not that I can see."

"And you certainly took a good look."

"What did you expect?"

She made no reply, concentrating instead on tying the

wide green ribbons of her straw boater in a bow beneath her chin.

Max hoisted the picnic basket over one arm and gave her his other and they walked up the bank to where his motorcar was parked on the narrow lane.

"What kind of motorcar is this?" Constance asked as she walked around the shiny dark green vehicle while Max stowed the wicker hamper in the space beneath the front passenger seat.

"A Darracq. They make them in Paris."

"Is it very expensive?" She ran a hand over the gleaming bulbs of the two massive headlights. It looked enormously expensive.

"Yes," he said succinctly.

"How reliable are they in general?" She continued her tactile exploration of the vehicle. It was a beautiful thing.

"Not very," he said, struggling to fit the hamper in the tiny space. "But it's the price you pay. It adds to the excitement."

"So they often break down in inconvenient places?"

"Oh, they always choose the most inconvenient places to break down." He straightened and brushed off his hands. "As I say, it's the price you pay for vanity."

"For showing off," she accused with a grin.

"If you insist."

"Actually, I can't say I blame you. It's very beautiful." Constance stepped onto the running board and looked at the chrome-and-brass interior, inhaling the rich smell of leather. "So, what makes them break down? That lever over there?" She pointed to the gear shift.

"No, the gears are generally reliable enough, so long

as you treat them properly. It's the engine and the fuel feed usually. Are you getting in?"

"Oh, yes, of course. Sorry." She jumped off the running board so that he could open the door for her. "I could have climbed over that. It's barely a door at all."

"True enough." He closed the door after her and went around the front to crank the engine. It fired on the third turn, he stowed the crank and then swung a long leg over the door on the driver's side and slid into his seat behind the wheel.

"So, what could cause a problem in the engine or the fuel feed?" Constance asked as the car jumped forward on the dirt lane.

"The wrong fuel mixture. A loose wire. Any number of things." He turned the car in the narrow lane.

"Could one make that happen?" she inquired.

Max finally realized that there was some significance to this apparently artless interest in the workings of the motorcar. He looked over at her. "Be more specific."

"Well, if for instance one wanted a car to break down at a certain point a long way from convenient assistance, is there any way to do that?"

"Am I being involved in some nefarious scheme here?"

"It's my father. He tells us he's taking delivery of a new Cadillac tomorrow afternoon. But we can't let him keep it," she said simply. "He has very little patience and if it causes him the slightest inconvenience he'll give up on it in disgust. We have to find a way to fix the engine so that happens."

"Dear God!" he exclaimed, hooting his horn at a cow that was wandering slowly across his path. The animal kicked up its heels at the strident sound and ran for the open field across the lane. "You and your sisters are planning to sabotage your father's new car?"

"In the interest of his safety, yes," Constance said with a sweetly innocent smile. "Better a damaged car and a live parent than the reverse."

"And you want me to help you?" He was incredulous, and yet it seemed entirely in keeping with what he had learned about the Honorable Misses Duncan since they'd first swum into his ken.

"If you wouldn't mind. It is in a very good cause. Life and death, really. We'd do it ourselves but we don't know much about engines. As yet," she added.

"As yet," he muttered. "Perhaps you'd like to drive us home."

"Oh, I'd love to. May I?" Constance turned sideways in her seat, her eyes shining. "I've been watching you, and it doesn't look that difficult."

It wasn't once you'd mastered the gears, Max admitted to himself. But he wasn't about to admit that to Constance. "I don't think it's something that would come easily to women," he stated. "They're not mechanically minded and the gear changes are quite complex."

Constance gave a crow of laughter. "Why did I expect you to say anything different? Just wait and see, Mr. Ensor. Women will be driving these things before you know it."

"And in the meantime, on your own admission, you don't know much about engines," he reminded her. He wasn't prepared to contest her statement, since he was beginning to get the suspicion that if society was peopled by women like Constance Duncan and her sisters, there would be women behind every steering wheel in the country.

"No," she agreed. "Which is why I am so humbly asking for your help."

"And how am I supposed to help?" He kicked himself for asking the question. It was only going to lead him into trouble.

"We thought that after Father takes delivery and after his first run, then when he stables it, or whatever it is you do with motorcars in the mews, we could fiddle with it so that when he next took it out it would be unreliable."

"And when is this operation to take place?"

"Tomorrow night." She looked across at him. "Are you free tomorrow night?"

"For sabotage?"

"That's harsh."

"But true."

"Yes," she agreed. "He'll be so thrilled with the motor after his first run that he'll want to take it out the next day, and we'd like it to break down on him just far enough from the city for it to be incredibly inconvenient. He won't want to drive it after dark the first day, so once he's stabled it tomorrow evening we could do what's necessary. In fact," she added with growing enthusiasm, "you don't need to do anything yourself. Just tell us what to do. You won't be involved in any way."

"No, just an accessory after the fact."

"Don't worry, we won't hand you over to the authorities."

"And I won't worry about tarnishing my spotless reputation as a Member of Parliament." He raised his eyebrows in sardonic punctuation.

"Will you help?" Her voice was suddenly serious. "Just tell us what to do."

"For God's sake, Constance, isn't there a simpler way to achieve your object?" he demanded, fighting the unnerving sensation of slipping fast down an icy slope. "Why do you have to come up with such a devious scheme?"

"Believe it or not, it is the simplest way," she said. "Father has to decide for himself to give up the idea, he won't listen to anyone else." She turned sideways on her seat and laid a hand on his arm. "We really need you to help. There's no one else we can ask."

"Oh, God help me," he muttered. "All right, I'll come round and I'll tell you what to do." Even as the words emerged, Max couldn't believe what he was saying. How could he possibly be agreeing to help in such an addled scheme? He should surely be showing male solidarity with Lord Duncan rather than with the man's eccentric daughters. He looked at Constance in exasperation and found something in the glow of her dark green eyes that answered his question. When she wanted to be, Constance Duncan was irresistibly bewitching. No man stood a chance.

"Thank you," she said with a radiant smile. "Will you come round at about ten o'clock tomorrow night, then? Father will be at his club."

"I can't promise a time," he said. "It depends how late the House sits."

"Yes, of course," she said amenably. "Whenever it's convenient...we'll just wait up for you." She busied herself retying the ribbons of her hat more securely against the rush of wind as Max increased his speed.

"By the way, what's the name of this potential secretary you're sending me?"

"Henry Franklin. Should he come to the House of Commons next Monday morning?"

He adroitly swung the wheel to avoid a stray dog that had run barking into the road at the sight of the motorcar, and then said, "It would be simpler to send him to my house. I meant to tell you ... I've found a suitable house in Westminster. I signed the lease yesterday."

"Oh, that's splendid. Does that mean we might—" She bit off the rest of the sentence in some confusion. Here she'd been telling herself to pedal slowly and now suddenly she was back in the Tour de France.

"It certainly means we could," he said solemnly. "Should you decide to speed things up a little again."

Constance bit her lip. "I haven't. It just slipped out. I told you I'm in lust with you. But I'm serious about learning things about each other."

Max took his eyes from the road for a minute to look at her. There was nothing playful about her at the moment; in fact, he thought she looked somewhat confused. "Let me return the compliment," he said, and she gave him a quick and rather grateful smile.

"I don't see why we can't gratify lust and a thirst for knowledge at the same time," he suggested. His windtossed hair shone in the sun, and the blue of his eyes seemed even more intense than usual as they rested on her countenance. The sight of him made her knees go weak again.

She cleared her throat. "About this house ... ?"

"It's furnished. I have the key." He patted his breast pocket.

"That's convenient. I should be interested in looking at it."

"That could be arranged."

* * *

"Where were you all day?" Prudence asked as Constance came into her bedroom dressed for dinner.

"Having a picnic along the river at Windsor," her sister replied. "I came to borrow your topaz earrings. They go so well with this dress."

"In the box." Prudence gestured to the jewel box on her dresser. "What about the rest of the day?"

"Max has taken a lease on a house in Westminster."

"Oh. Objectivity went by the board again, did it?"

"Maybe." Constance sifted through the box and selected the earrings. "Honestly, I don't know, Prue. I don't know whether I'm on my head or my heels. I've never felt like this before."

"Not even with Douglas?" Prue turned on the dresser stool to give her sister her full attention. It was unlike Constance to express this kind of confusion.

Constance shook her head, tossing the earrings from hand to hand. "No, it was very straightforward with Douglas. I knew I loved him and he loved me. There was nothing . . . nothing oppositional about our relationship. I didn't feel the need to best him all the time. And yet with Max it's as if there's an edge to almost everything we say. I feel I can't let myself be vulnerable . . . let my guard down. And yet he's never done anything to justify that feeling. Only his Neanderthal attitudes about women."

She shrugged, and fastened the topaz earrings. "Normally I just despise men who hold those views, but it's not possible to despise Max."

"No," agreed Prudence with conviction. "One could loathe him, but one certainly couldn't despise him."

"And I don't loathe him," Constance said with a resigned smile. "Quite the opposite. It's very confusing, Prue."

"I can believe it."

"But on a more positive note," Constance continued, "I did get Max to agree to see Henry. On Monday at his house."

"Oh, wonderful." Prudence turned back to the mirror and took up her comb again. "Amelia sent a note to say that she's arranged for the license, and the wedding is scheduled for next Thursday afternoon at four o'clock at the registry office in Caxton Hall. We're to be witnesses."

"Always assuming Henry plucks up the courage to get himself here," Constance said a touch gloomily. "The farther I'm away from him, the more pessimistic I get."

"Don't be. Chas is confident he'll come. She's never wrong."

"You have a point. Where is she tonight?"

"Dining with David and Hester at Lady Winthrop's."

"Ah." Constance raised an eyebrow. "Matters move along, then."

"So it would seem," her sister agreed.

"I also persuaded Max to help us with the motor business," Constance said, a gleam now in her eye. "Tomorrow night."

"I don't believe it," her sister declared. "He's so straitlaced, how did you ever persuade him to lend himself to such a trick?"

"It was surprisingly easy, actually. He tried to resist, but somehow..." She gave a blasé shrug. "He just couldn't."

"You are so wicked!"

"I'm in good company, sister dear. As I recall, this was Chas's idea."

Prudence acknowledged this with a resigned chuckle and rose from the dresser stool. "Are you ready to go down? Lord Barclay is dining with us."

"Oh, God help us!" Constance exclaimed. "And I was having such a satisfactory day."

Chapter 13

I s that the doorbell?" Chastity sprang to her feet the following evening and ran to the parlor door.

Constance glanced at the clock. It was just ten-thirty. "It must be Max." She followed her sister out onto the landing, Prudence at her heels. "Jenkins, is it Mr. Ensor?"

"It is indeed." Max appeared in the dim light of the hall and put one foot on the bottom stair, looking up at them as they clustered at the top of the stairs. "Did I keep you up?"

"No, no, of course not," Constance said. "Come upstairs to the parlor. Jenkins will bring you a whisky if you'd like. Otherwise we have cognac up here."

"Or hot chocolate," Chastity called cheerfully.

"Whisky, thank you, Jenkins," Max said, and came up the stairs. "Your father's out of the way?"

"Yes. He's been gone all evening. Jenkins has the keys to the motorcar."

Max's eyebrows lifted. "Your butler knows about this?"

"Oh, yes, Jenkins knows everything about this family. Every dirty little secret we have," Prudence declared. "He would help us himself but he doesn't know anything about motors."

Max's eyebrows remained uplifted.

"You look very clandestine," Constance said approvingly. "Very secretive with that long black cloak. You'll just blend into the shadows."

"I thought I had better dress the part." He assumed she had no secrets from her sisters and gave her an unceremonious kiss. Their lovemaking the previous afternoon had been of a rough-and-ready nature, a wild tumble in the deserted house, and he was somehow still in the same frame of mind. She was dressed simply but with customary elegance, in an evening gown of lavender crepe, and he had an urge to rumple her, to pull the pins from her hair, to roll her on the carpet and kiss her senseless. It was not his usual style at all and he found this strange aberration amusing, although puzzling. He put it down to the disreputable if not downright illegal character of the evening's activity.

After an instant of surprise at the salute, Constance offered no resistance to the kiss, and a gleam showed in her eyes, as if she could read his mind and was indulging her own memories.

Her sisters exchanged a glance and moved farther into the room, turning their backs to the doorway. Jenkins came up the stairs with a tray bearing the decanter of whisky and a glass. Without haste, Max raised his head and straightened, moving away from Constance into the parlor. The smile lingered on his mouth and in his eyes, however.

"Did you bring anything to do this with?" Chastity asked, noting his empty hands and clearly empty pockets.

"I don't need anything. Constance said the motor was a Cadillac... Oh, thank you, Jenkins." He took the proffered glass.

"It is, but what's the significance of that?" Constance asked.

"I'll show you when we look at the motor. You need to understand that while I hate to disappoint you, I have no intention of doing damage to that motorcar. It's far too valuable a machine."

"I quite agree with you, sir." Jenkins paused on his way to the door.

"Oh, Jenkins, how could you?" Prudence said. "You know how things stand."

"Yes, I do, Miss Prue, but if there's a way to persuade his lordship to give up the motor without vandalizing the vehicle, then I think we should consider it."

"Well, of course we don't want to do wanton damage," Constance said. "What *are* we going to do, then, Max?"

"A little trick with the fuel tank," he said, taking a sip of whisky and nodding his appreciation. "Lord Duncan knows his single malts."

"Our father's tastes are as perfect as they are expensive," Prudence declared. "Only the best of anything comes into this house."

Max wondered at the caustic undertone to the comment, but he didn't pursue it. He'd already noticed that something was amiss between Lord Duncan and his daughters, but he didn't feel inclined to pry. Maybe as he got to know them better it would come out. Not that he wasn't already well on the way to getting to know them all far too closely for comfort, he reflected dryly. Engaging with them in an act of sabotage at dead of night was as intimate a deed of friendship as he could imagine. It was certainly as close as he wanted to get to the nefarious heart of the Duncan trio. He had the feeling there was very little they wouldn't do if they saw a need, and he doubted they'd have any scruples as to the tools they used to go about it. He had certainly been shamelessly co-opted.

He glanced across the room to where Constance sat perched on the wide arm of a sofa, so casual, so elegant, yet so wonderfully, wildly sensual when the mood took her, and he understood with absolute clarity why he had allowed himself to be so co-opted.

He set down his empty glass. "This is a rather messy operation, and since I have no intention of dirtying my own hands, I'm wondering if you three shouldn't change into something a little less delicate."

"Oh, we can do that." Chastity was already heading for the door. "We'll only be a few minutes."

"How messy?" asked Constance warily. She had the feeling that Max was rather relishing the prospect of standing aside in pristine elegance while they got themselves covered in whatever grease and mess went into a motorcar's engine.

"Very," he said with a glimmer in his eye that told her she had been right. "And smelly too." And now he couldn't help a grin of satisfaction.

Reprisal time, Constance thought with reluctant acceptance. She followed her sisters to the door. "We'll be back in a minute."

Max poured himself another drink and idly glanced around the room. It was a pleasant, informal parlor, with an endearing shabbiness. He wandered over to the secretaire and his eye fell on a copy of *The Mayfair Lady*. It was hardly surprising to find the broadsheet here since he knew they read it. He turned aside, and then spun back. Something had caught his eye. Something very odd. He picked up the sheet and stared at the date. *Monday, July 31st*. But that was two weeks hence. What were they doing with an advance edition?

But of course it was obvious. They were responsible for it. His earlier hunch had been right.

He heard voices in the corridor and dropped the sheet on the desk and walked swiftly to the window. When the door opened he was innocently looking down onto the dark garden, his recharged glass in his hand.

Constance immediately sensed something different about him. A sudden tension between his shoulders, the set of his head. He turned from the window and said, "What a pleasant room this is."

"Yes, it was our mother's favorite room, very much her own. We haven't changed anything since her death." Constance's eyes darted around the room, fell upon the secretaire and the broadsheet lying in full view. How could they have been so damnably careless? *Had he seen it? Should she ask him, mention it casually, and see how he responded?*

It was a ridiculous dilemma. She didn't want to draw his attention to something he might not have remarked. Even if he had seen it he might not have noticed the significance of the date. Current issues were to be found everywhere, so finding one here was not remarkable. But if he had seen it and noticed that it was not the current issue, then their secret could be broadcast throughout Mayfair by tomorrow evening if he chose to betray it. He wouldn't do that, of course. At least not without talking to her first. She was sure of it. *Wasn't she?*

She walked casually to the secretaire and as casually tidied up the papers on the top. Her gaze flicked across to him but he didn't seem to be aware of what she was doing. Inconclusive, she decided, but there was no time to worry about it at the moment.

"So, are we suitably protected for this dirty work?" Chastity asked cheerfully. "We're wearing our oldest clothes."

Max regarded them with his head cocked as he considered this. They were swathed so completely in heavy cotton aprons that he couldn't see what they wore beneath.

"We have gloves too." Prudence showed him the thick cotton gloves. "They're what the housemaid uses to clean the grates."

"You'll do," he said. "Let's get on with it."

Constance led the way downstairs. They took another flight of stairs down into the vast basement kitchen. Three oil lamps stood on the massive deal table.

"There's no gas light in the mews, so we'll have to take oil lamps. Jenkins filled them and trimmed the wicks for us," Constance explained. She asked doubtfully, "Are you sure we don't need anything? A knife or something?"

"I already told you, you're not going to do any damage...not so much as a scratch on the paintwork," he said, following them out into the small courtyard behind the kitchen. He thought it was like following a trio of Florence Nightingales as they rustled along in their aprons, holding their lamps high. Three very subversive ladies with lamps. How had he possibly found himself in this absurd position?

They crossed the courtyard and went through a gate into the mews. It was in darkness, no lights showing from the coachman's accommodation above the stable block. The smell of hay, horseflesh, and manure was strong in the air and a horse whinnied from the stable as they crossed the cobbles.

"It's in here," Prudence whispered, turning a key in a double door in the building next to the stable. The doors creaked open and they went in, holding their lamps high. The light fell on a gleaming vehicle, all chrome and brass, and the smell of new leather was stronger even than the stable smell.

"Beautiful," Max said involuntarily. He ran a hand over the motor's shining hood. "These Cadillacs are magnificent . . . an ideal model for our purposes," he added.

"Give me a horse anyday," Chastity declared, setting her lamp on an upturned barrel. "Do we need the keys? Con has them."

Max shook his head. "We don't need to start it." He walked around to the back of the car and bent to look underneath. "Good, just as I thought. Cadillacs usually have a tap, so we don't need to siphon." He stood up. "Now, one of you find a bucket. Constance, feel under here." Constance knelt on the stone floor and reached a hand under the car. "Just to your left, there's a tap. Can you find it?"

"Yes, it's here." Her fingers closed over the tap.

"All right. Keep your hand there. Prudence, bring the bucket and position it beneath the tap. That's right. Now, Constance, open the tap. Let the spirit trickle out slowly . . . very slowly, so you can control the flow. No . . . that's too fast. Close it off again."

"It would be so much easier if you would do this," she said, gritting her teeth with concentration. Her voice was muffled, her fingers cramping from the strain, her shoulders tight with the awkward position. "You know what you're doing."

"Oh, no. This is your show. My hands are going to stay clean." As if in emphasis, he drove them into his coat pockets. "Chastity, you'll need several more buckets."

"I'll get them from the tack room."

"What is this stuff, anyway?" Prudence asked, wrinkling her nose as she straightened. She took off her glasses, which had misted over, and peered at him myopically in the shadowed garage.

"Fuel. Motors have to run on something, or didn't you know that?"

"There's no need to sound so patronizing," Prudence said, replacing her glasses. "As it happens, I'm with Chastity when it comes to a preferred method of travel." She bent again to the bucket. "Can you manage, Con?"

"I think so. I think I've mastered the flow now . . . if I keep the tap at half cock."

"All right, that's enough. You don't want to drain it," Max instructed.

Constance swiftly closed the tap. She stood up, wiping her reeking hands on her apron with a grimace of distaste. "I think I get the point of all this. How much have we left in?"

"Enough for about two miles, I would guess. A motor-car as big and heavy as this won't do more than ten miles to the gallon. But there'll be spare cans stowed at the back for refueling. Probably in a little compartment behind the jump seat."

Constance found the compartment. "There are three in here."

"Take 'em out."

She lifted them out with a grunt of effort. They seemed to weigh a ton. She shot Max a resentful glare, which he either didn't notice or chose to ignore.

"Now pour about half of each one into the spare buckets. But be very careful. It's dangerous stuff, very volatile . . . it doesn't take much to ignite it."

"How comforting," Constance murmured. "I suppose you wouldn't consider lifting this damned can yourself?" She heaved the first one up onto her hip.

"Absolutely not. Aren't women supposed to be a match for men in everything?"

"There are some physical facts you can't get around," she said with a distinct snap. "And being sardonic isn't helping matters."

"My apologies." He tried to hide a grin but failed.

"Let me help." Prudence came to her sister's aid, supporting the can as Constance tilted it into the bucket.

"Chastity, can you find some lamp oil from somewhere?" Max inquired.

"How much?"

"As much as you can."

"I'll look in the scullery. I believe there's a barrel of it stored there." Chastity started for the door, then paused, her hand on the latch. "I'm sure I can manage to roll it across the kitchen courtyard without assistance."

There was an instant's expectant pause but Max remained silent, nonchalantly leaning against the stone wall, hands still firmly inactive in his pockets.

"I'll help you, Chas." Prudence released her supporting hand on the fuel can as Constance took its now reduced weight, and went off with her sister.

Constance set down the half-empty can, unscrewed the top on the second one, and hefted it onto her hip. She didn't look at Max.

He couldn't maintain the charade as he watched her struggles in the flickering lamplight. "Here, let me do it."

"I can manage, thank you," she said with icy dignity. "You wouldn't want to spoil your clothes. Or dirty those so-perfect hands. Why, you might even break a fingernail."

"Give that to me." He stepped forward and laid hold of the can. For a moment she resisted, then realized that they were both going to end up drenched in this foul-smelling spirit if they wrestled over its possession. She relinquished it, controlling a sigh of relief, and stepped back, wiping her hands again on her apron.

"So, the idea is for my father to run out of fuel so that the car will strand him somewhere?"

"That is the idea." He set down the half-emptied can and unscrewed the top on the third one.

"But won't he notice that these are only half-empty?" Constance was fascinated now.

"They won't be. We're going to mix the spirit with lamp oil." He set down the third can and casually wiped his hands on Constance's apron. "Is there a tap in the yard?"

"By the horse trough."

She followed him out into the moonlit yard and stood back while he rinsed his hands at the tap and dried them on his handkerchief. She followed suit at the tap. "What will happen then?"

"You have to get the mix of spirit and lamp oil exactly right for the engine to run smoothly. We're not going to worry about the correct proportions, so the motor will run for a little once the tank's been replenished from the spare cans and then sputter and die. It won't come to any harm, but it will be very inconvenient for the driver."

"You mean that every time he thinks he's got it going again, it'll stop?" she said with an awed nod. "Oh, that is very clever. It will drive him mad. I think I may have underestimated you, Mr. Ensor."

"Now, that would be unwise." He looked at her as she stood in the shadowy silver light of the moon, apron-wrapped, disheveled, her hair coming loose from its pins, a streak of dirt smeared across her cheek, a film of sweat on her forehead. "I ceased to underestimate *you*, Miss Duncan, somewhere around the time you were climbing over stiles."

She smiled slowly, brushing a loose strand of hair from her forehead with the back of a damp hand. "And has anything else occurred to confirm that opinion, Max?"

Would he say anything about The Mayfair Lady? *Drop just a hint that would tell her whether he'd seen the edition in the parlor?*

The sound of a barrel rolling across the cobbles stilled any response he might have made. Chastity and Prudence rolled the wooden barrel of lamp oil towards the open garage doors. Max licked the corner of his handkerchief and wiped the smear of dirt from Constance's cheek before following her sisters into the garage.

Thoughtfully, Constance followed. Tomorrow there was the WSPU meeting, and afterwards they were to have dinner. There would be opportunities to probe a little then. But she decided she wouldn't mention the matter to her sisters, not until she had some idea of whether they had cause for concern.

"I hope we didn't go too far," Chastity said in Fortnum and Mason the following afternoon. "He went out in that motor at eleven o'clock this morning and he wasn't home when we left." She took a forkful of the meringue on her plate, neatly scooping up escaping crème chantilly as she bore the morsel to her lips.

"In the company of the earl of Barclay," Prudence reminded her, refilling her teacup. "I'd worry more if he was alone."

"I think the company of Barclay is worse than no company at all," Constance stated, setting down her pen and raising her head from the sheet of paper on the table in front of her. "I was having a rather interesting conversation with Dolly Hennesy this morning. I bumped into her at the hairdresser's."

"Gossip, Con?" Prudence took an almond slice from the plate on the table. She raised her eyebrows, her light green eyes teasing. "I thought you didn't have time for it."

"I don't," her sister replied, sipping her tea, unperturbed by the teasing. "But this is germane gossip. Barclay, it seems, is suspected of philandering."

Prudence no longer looked amused. "That's hardly unusual," she said grimly, driving her fork into the cake. "Father's not exactly pure as the driven snow."

"But I don't believe our father goes around fathering offspring on women in his employ."

Prudence set down her fork and pursed her mouth in a silent whistle. "No," she agreed. "That he would not do. What are you saying?"

"That the earl of Barclay is well known for dabbling in such brooks," Constance declared. "At least two women, from what I heard." She leaned forward, her voice dropping. "I also hear that he has something of a reputation in his clubs for not being . . . how shall I put it? Not being exactly prompt about settling his gambling debts."

"I know he's loathsome," Chastity said, her own eyes wide at this revelation. "But surely not even Barclay would do something so . . . so ungentlemanly," she finished for want of a better description. A failure to settle gambling debts in a timely fashion was probably the most heinous social crime.

"If it's true why hasn't he been blackballed?" Prudence asked, going straight to the heart of the matter.

Constance shrugged. "It seems that no one is prepared to come out and accuse him to his face."

"But why ever not?" Chastity picked up a neglected hazelnut with delicate fingers. She gazed intently at Constance as she popped the nut between her lips.

"I was thinking a discreetly anonymous hint at the possibility of a scandal in the pages of *The Mayfair Lady* might elicit an answer," Constance said with a distinctly evil smile. "I don't really care a fig about the gambling debts but I cannot abide men who won't honor their responsibilities to women. We brought Henry Franklin up to the mark, why not Barclay? Mother would approve."

Prudence nodded with a degree of satisfaction. "That is certainly true." She wiped her mouth on her napkin and frowned for a moment in thought. "And he couldn't possibly get back at us," she said slowly. "We're anonymous. It's just an anonymous broadsheet."

Constance hesitated, wondering whether perhaps she should confide her anxieties about what Max might have seen the previous evening.

"Something bothering you, Con?" Chastity, as usual, caught the flicker of uncertainty on her sister's face.

"No," Constance said definitely. "I'm trying to think how to write an obliquely accusatory piece. Have another meringue . . . those coffee ones look delicious."

"Not that you would sully your delicate taste buds to try one," Chastity observed, helping herself to the pale golden meringue.

"My pleasure is of the vicarious variety." Constance glanced at the clock at the end of the tearoom. "I have to get to Kensington Town Hall by six o'clock, to meet with Emmeline before the meeting itself starts."

"And you have to dress for dinner with Max afterwards," Prudence said. "We should get going."

"Well, take a look at this." Constance passed across the paper she'd been writing on. "I was roughing out the piece on Barclay. It's crude at the moment, but we have time to refine it." She gestured to the waitress for the bill.

Prudence glanced at the sheet, shook her head doubtfully, and passed it to Chastity. "However you refine it, Con, it's incendiary."

Constance shrugged. "Men who do what he does have to bear the consequences."

"I hope to God he never discovers who wrote it."

"Father will be mad as fire if his friend's attacked like this," Chastity observed, rather anxiously, as she perused the paper. "You know how devoted he is to Barclay. And he always stands by his friends regardless of the rights and wrongs of an issue."

"We won't publish it yet. I need to check some of the facts and gather more ammunition. It may take a couple of months to get it all together." Constance took back the paper. "Dolly had the name of one of the women. She's in some Home for Fallen Women in Battersea. I'll go and talk to her first."

"How does Dolly know these things?" Chastity asked.

"Her housekeeper happens to be the cousin of Barclay's housekeeper." Constance folded the paper and slipped it into her handbag. "Dolly has tentacles that reach everywhere when it comes to gossip."

"I hope they *don't* reach everywhere," Prudence said with feeling. "At least not as far as Ten Manchester Square." She gathered up her gloves and bag. "Let's go. Maybe Father will have made it home by now."

They caught an omnibus outside Fortnum and Mason and arrived home to find Lord Duncan, red-faced and bursting with frustration and fury, pacing around the hall.

"Damned machine!" he exploded as they walked through the door. "Had to leave it in Hampstead. Right in the middle of the heath!"

"Why, what happened?" Constance asked, drawing off her gloves, her expression all sympathetic interest.

"Broke down! Not once but four times, would you believe! Damnable things, they are. Horses don't break down on a man." His lordship wiped his sweating brow with the jaunty checkered cravat he'd worn for his drive.

"Oh, dear," said Chastity, laying a soothing hand on his arm. "How disappointing for you. Jenkins, bring his lordship a whisky." She kissed her father's cheek. "Tell us exactly what happened."

"No, don't," Prudence murmured sotto voce to Constance, as Chastity urged her father into the calming atmosphere of the drawing room. "I don't think we need to know."

Constance shot her a warning look and followed her sister and parent, unwinding her chiffon scarf as she did so.

"Wouldn't have been so bad if Barclay hadn't been there," her father declared, his voice still brimming with fury. "There I was, boasting of this damned Cadillac, supposed to be more reliable than that Panhard of Barclay's, and what does it do but strand us in the middle of the heath. First hill we come to, it gives up, rolls back to the bottom." He took the full glass of whisky offered to him by a studiously impassive Jenkins.

"'Run out of fuel,' Barclay says, 'must have used more than you thought yesterday,' so we refill it and it starts . . ." He paused to drain the glass. Jenkins, at his elbow, took it from him without instruction. "Starts up sweet as a nut. We get to the top of the hill, go a quarter of a mile, and it stops again. Just stops dead." He took the refilled glass. "Three times . . . we refilled it three times, would you believe?"

Oh, yes, we would. Constance carefully avoided her sisters' eyes.

"Drained all three damned cans, then we had to walk all the way to the Bull and Bush. Just leave the bally motor right in the middle of the heath and walk. Miles, it was. Hot as hell. If it hadn't been for that Ensor fellow, it would still be sitting in the middle of the heath and we'd be twiddlin' our thumbs in the pub."

"Max Ensor?" Constance stared at her father. "How did he come into this?"

"Turned up at the Bull and Bush in a Darracq. Damned fine-looking motor. Drove us back to the Cadillac and towed the damned car back to the mews. And that's where it's going to stay until they come and take it away. Give me a damned horse anyday." He drained the second glass.

"How convenient that he appeared so fortuitously," Constance said. "As it happens, I'm having dinner with him tonight." She kissed her father. "I'm glad you're back safely. It must have been very frustrating, but Cobham won't be sorry to see the back of the motor."

Her father gave a reluctant crack of laughter. "No, damn his eyes. If his legs weren't so stiff he'd have danced a jig when he saw it towed in . . . well, I approve of Ensor. You have my blessing. Not that that would make any difference to you one way or the other," he added gruffly.

"Yes, it would," Constance said. "I wouldn't want to disoblige you, Father, in anything. None of us would."

He regarded her closely, then smiled. He seemed to have recovered his equilibrium. "No, I don't believe you would. Just like your mother . . . all of you. But you'd oblige me by getting a husband or two. Take a closer look at this Ensor, Constance. I like the fellow."

"Oh, I think I'll wait to be asked before I start planning my wedding," Constance said lightly. "Now, I must go and dress."

Chapter 14

Kensington Town Hall was deserted at six o'clock when Constance arrived. She hurried across the foyer and into a small cramped office at the rear. Emmeline Pankhurst and her daughter Christobel were talking in low tones with several other women.

"Constance, there you are," Emmeline greeted her with a warm smile. "There's coffee, if you'd like." She gestured to the coffeepot, but Constance, who knew how thin and ungrateful a beverage it contained, declined.

"We were just talking about a petition," Emmeline said. "One we would present at Westminster. If we could get together a large group of women prepared to march together to present it, we might get some favorable publicity. We thought we'd bring it up at the meeting tonight."

"We'd certainly get publicity," Constance said. "I wouldn't want to bet on whether it would be favorable."

"Well, it doesn't matter. Publicity is what we want if we're to raise the consciousness of women," Christobel declared with a militant air. Her mother, who took a rather more patient, long-term view of their movement, frowned a little, but knew better than to antagonize her daughter.

"I've invited a guest tonight," Constance said, brushing crumbs off the corner of the metal table before perching on it. "A Member of Parliament."

"A supporter?" Emmeline leaned forward with interest.

"Not yet. In fact, he says he doesn't see the point of women's suffrage, but he goes so far as to say that he's willing to tolerate an opposing point of view." She couldn't help a slightly ironic lift of her eyebrows.

"Pompous ass!" declared Christobel.

"He can be," Constance conceded, wondering why her hackles prickled at Christobel's declaration when she'd almost invited it. It was one she had been known to make herself. "However, isn't part of our mission to educate?"

"Is he educable?" demanded the younger Pankhurst with the same scorn.

"He's not a simple primate, Christobel," Constance said sharply. The other woman flushed slightly and fell silent.

"We might learn something from him ourselves," Constance continued in a milder tone. "He already mentioned that the government was considering the issue of women taxpayers. Maybe he can tell us more."

"Who is he?"

"Max Ensor. His constituency is Southwold. He won a fairly recent by-election, but from what I can gather he has the ear of the Prime Minister."

"Well, let's meet him this evening. Any interest shown in the movement by an MP is promising, even if he's not yet a supporter." Emmeline gathered up a sheaf of leaflets from the table. "Will you hand these out at the door, Constance? It's just a notice about the petition."

Constance took them. "Who's taking names tonight?"

"Geraldine, would you?" Emmeline turned to a thin, tall, elegantly dressed lady standing by the window.

"Yes, of course," she said in a soft voice.

"Then I think we're ready for the fray. Christobel is going to speak tonight and we'll invite questions from the floor." Emmeline rose from her chair. "Let's open the doors."

Constance took up her post at the door, handing out her leaflets to the women who hurried up the steps. They were women from every social stratum, some well dressed, some shabbily, some worn down with manual labor, some with hands that had never touched a washing-up bowl. But they all bore a similar expression, eyes bright with excitement and hope, energy and commitment radiating from them. They took the leaflets, some greeting Constance by name. She kept her eyes on the steps, watching for Max. There were a few men present, some alone, some with women. Constance was relieved to see that it was going to be a sizable crowd. It would have been embarrassing, not to mention unhelpful to the cause, for Max to have witnessed a sparsely attended meeting.

As it happened, she was in deep discussion with a woman she knew very well and missed his arrival.

"Do I get one of those?"

She jumped at the sound of the rich voice behind her and spun around. "Oh, I was looking out for you and then I got distracted." She held out a leaflet. "If you want one, then of course you may have one."

"Thank you." He took it, glancing at it as he did so. "A march on Westminster?"

"The presentation of a petition," she said. "You'll hear more if you come in. We're about ready to start."

He nodded and followed her into the hall. Constance stopped at a small table where her colleague sat with the sign-in book. "Geraldine, this is the Right Honorable Max Ensor. Max, may I introduce the Honorable Mrs. George Brand."

Geraldine offered her hand. "Good evening, Mr. Ensor. Welcome."

"Will you sign your name, or would you prefer not to make your attendance a matter of record?" Constance asked, trying not to make a challenge of the question. "We don't insist."

"I have no objection," he said, and signed his name in the book. "Why should I?"

"No reason that I can see," Constance said. "I'll sit with you. Normally I sit on the platform, but I won't this evening."

He smiled. "I am honored, ma'am."

"Don't be," she responded. "I merely intend to ensure that you sit it out to the end."

He shook his head in mock admonition and followed her to the front of the hall.

It was a lively meeting. Christobel had the ability to fire an audience in a way that her mother lacked. She spoke with a militant fervor that had the audience cheering, and questions came thick and fast when her speech was over. Constance contributed nothing, but sat quietly, vibrantly aware of Max beside her. He said nothing either, but he had evinced no restlessness, no impatience, no hostility to the speech. She cast him several sideways glances but could read nothing from his expression. The meeting ended promptly at eight-fifteen; there were many women in the audience who had to be back under their employers' roofs when the two hours between tea and supper that constituted their evening out were over.

As Constance rose to her feet she glanced behind her and saw Amelia standing at the rear of the hall. She must have arrived late. She had said how rarely she could make a meeting. Max had stood up now and he seemed to Constance suddenly to stand out like a sore thumb, head and shoulders above everyone else in the hall, exuding male power and privilege. She pushed past him with unseemly haste and as she reached the aisle managed to catch Amelia's eye. But Amelia had already seen her employer's brother. For a second she shot a startled, questioning glance at Constance, then she turned and hurried from the hall into the gathering dusk on the street.

One other complication that would have to be explained, Constance thought. They had decided not to tell Amelia in advance that they had designated Max as Henry's prospective employer. It had seemed a bridge best crossed if the plan worked out.

"Why the hurry?" Max asked when he'd finally managed to ease his way out of the row and into the aisle.

"Sorry, I didn't mean to push past you, but I thought I saw someone I wanted to speak to. I wanted to catch her before she left, but it wasn't her." She smiled up at him. "What did you think?"

"I don't know," he said. "I need time to digest."

"Would you like to meet Emmeline and Christobel? I told them you would be here."

"In what capacity?"

"A neutral observer," she replied.

"That seems accurate enough. 'Lay on, Macduff.' "

"A most educable primate," Constance murmured.

"I beg your pardon?"

"Oh, nothing . . . nothing at all." She gave him her radiant smile and took his arm. "Come, let's meet the Pankhursts."

They went up to the platform where the speaker and the women who'd accompanied her on the dais were surrounded by a group of voluble questioners.

"Constance, this must be Mr. Ensor." Emmeline, with impeccable courtesy, moved through the throng as soon as she saw them. A curious silence suddenly fell as they all realized there was a man among them.

Max felt like a circus animal. He smiled with what he hoped was a pacifying benignity and shook Mrs. Pankhurst's hand. "Thank you for allowing me to listen in, ma'am," he said. "A most interesting meeting."

"Interesting or merely amusing, sir?" The sharp question came from Christobel before her mother had had a chance to respond. She stepped forward, regarding him with sardonic hostility.

"I do not find this issue amusing, madam," Max said in a voice that would cut steel. His eyes, as cold and blue as glacier ice, stared at her with undisguised contempt. "You would do well to consider that if you wish to make friends of those in a position to help you, it's sensible not to make enemies of them first."

Constance drew in a sharp breath. She knew he could bite, but she hadn't realized quite how hard. She was torn between loyalty to Christobel and the reluctant acceptance that the woman had been unpardonably rude without provocation.

"We're all a little wary, Max," she said. "We've made friends with influence before and they've let us down. You have to understand that we don't trust easily." Her voice was quiet and reasonable.

Christobel's angry flush died down and she extended her hand to Max. "Constance is right, Mr. Ensor. It's a case of once bitten twice shy. But I apologize if my comment was gratuitous."

He smiled without resentment and took the proffered hand. "I understand, Miss Pankhurst."

"I hope you'll come to another meeting," Emmeline said. "We're quite shameless in our desire to recruit supporters in the government."

Max tapped the leaflet he held in the palm of his other hand. "You're planning a march on Westminster."

"It would help us greatly if a Member of Parliament would be willing to accept the petition," Emmeline said.

Constance felt Max stiffen and stepped in quickly. "Let's not make assumptions, Emmeline. We're not the press gang. This is not conscription."

Emmeline nodded. "You're right. Your mother would have cautioned in exactly the same way." She smiled at Max. "You never met Lady Duncan. She was a remarkable woman."

"I can imagine. I've met her daughters," he replied.

Constance decided she'd had enough of this. "You'll have to excuse us, Emmeline... Christobel. Max has another engagement."

They made their farewells, and once out on the street, where a few gas lamps now glimmered, Constance exhaled in a soft whistle.

"Awkward," Max agreed. "I hadn't expected to be ambushed."

"No," she agreed. "But desperation can cause generally intelligent people to sabotage their own interests." She tucked her hand into his arm as they began to walk down Kensington Church Street. "On the subject of sabotage, how did it happen that you turned up in the right place at exactly the right time in order to rescue my father?" She looked up at him, raising a quizzical eyebrow.

"Mere coincidence," he said.

"Liar. There was nothing coincidental about your arrival at the Bull and Bush on Hampstead Heath at the same time as my furious parent."

"He was certainly not a happy man," Max said. "I rather got the impression that your little device had succeeded. He was swearing he'd never touch a motorcar again."

"Yes, it succeeded, all right. But I still want to know how you happened to be there at the same time."

"I didn't see any virtue in making him any more uncomfortable than was necessary to achieve your object," he said. "So I followed them out of London. You have no objections, I trust."

"No . . . no, of course not. The poor darling was at the end of his tether by the time he got home as it was."

Max puzzled over the warm, affectionate tone she had used. It didn't seem to jibe with the exasperation he had noticed usually accompanied references to Lord Duncan. "Is your father a difficult parent?" he asked, stopping under a street lamp outside a small restaurant. He hadn't meant to probe this subject but somehow couldn't help himself.

Constance laughed, but it was a slightly self-conscious laugh, he thought. "No, he's incredibly indulgent. He never interferes with us at all."

"Then why does he annoy you?"

"Annoy me?" she exclaimed. "How could you say such a thing?"

"Give me some credit, Constance. I'd have to be blind and deaf not to notice how exasperated you and your sisters often seem when his name's mentioned."

Constance sighed. She could see no alternative to offering him a partial truth. "He's very stubborn," she said. "He gets ideas in his head that he won't let go. And they're not always very good or sensible ideas. Our mother managed him very well, so well that he never noticed he was being managed. When she died there was no one to put the brakes on. He lost a lot of money at one point on a foolish venture and we decided we'd have to learn to do what our mother did if we weren't going to end up in the poor house. We don't succeed all the time, and we do get frustrated."

"I see. I didn't mean to pry. Shall we go in . . ." He gestured to the restaurant behind them. "I made a reservation here. It's pleasant and very quiet. Unless, of course, you'd rather go somewhere more distinguished."

"No, this will be lovely." She was surprised at his choice of such an unpretentious, out-of-the-way spot, but also charmed by it. It was very small, the six tables basking in the soft glow of candles. They were shown to a table in the window by a cheerful woman, who greeted Max by name and shook his hand warmly.

"I've a wonderful pot-au-feu tonight, Mr. Ensor. I know how much you like that."

"We're in your hands, Mrs. Baker," Max said, holding Constance's chair out for her. "Or at least," he added, taking the seat opposite her, "I am, as always. I'm not sure

about Miss Duncan, she likes to make up her own mind."
His tone was teasing.

Constance unfolded her napkin and accepted the gibe
with good grace. "Tonight I'll follow your lead, Max."
She smiled up at Mrs. Baker. "I too am in your hands."

"Very good, madam." The woman returned the smile
and hurried away. Within a couple of minutes a waiter
appeared with a bottle of claret, which he opened, tasted
himself, and poured for them.

Max nodded his thanks. He said to Constance, "The
Bakers used to work for my family. Mr. Baker was my father's steward and his wife was our housekeeper. They
came into a little money and decided they wanted to run
their own business." He gestured to the small room.
"This is the result. They're doing very well, and I come
as often as I can."

"It's charming," she said. She took up her glass and
surveyed him thoughtfully over the lip. She'd said they
needed to learn more about each other, to deepen their
relationship beyond its undeniably wonderful sexual
component, and there was something about the intimacy
of their surroundings that seemed to encourage confidences. She wondered if he'd chosen it for that very
reason.

"So, when is this march to Westminster supposed to
take place?" he asked. "It doesn't say on the leaflet and I
didn't hear a date mentioned at the meeting."

"I don't think it's fixed yet," she said. "Why? Are you
thinking of joining us?"

"I hardly think so." He sat back as the waiter set
bowls of onion soup in front of them, with a basket of
crusty bread. Max took up his spoon and inhaled the

aroma hungrily. "This is wonderful stuff. It cures whatever ails you."

Constance dipped her spoon into the rich brown liquid. Cheese bubbled in its depths. "If I eat this I'll never eat anything else."

"Oh, yes, you will," he said with confidence. "You won't be able to resist the pot-au-feu."

"It's very wintery food," she observed, twisting strands of cheese around her spoon. She took a mouthful. "Oh, but it is *very* good. Doesn't make for elegant eating, though," she mumbled through strands of cheese.

He laughed and leaned over to break the recalcitrant tangle with his fork as it dripped from her mouth. It was an intimate gesture, yet so natural that she barely noticed it.

She sipped her wine and wondered where this amazing ease had come from so suddenly. Exactly what kind of man was he? He was an expert and considerate lover; in bed he could be tender one minute and powerfully dominating the next. It made for wonderfully exciting love play. And in everyday life it was the same thing. He could be considerate, charming, entertaining one minute, and then arrogant, sarcastic, even pompous the next. She supposed that everyone had contradictions in their personalities, but Max's seemed more extreme than most.

"Why don't you just ask it?" he said into the silence that had gone on longer than she'd realized.

"Ask what?" She dipped her spoon in the soup again.

"Whatever question is burning on your lips," he said. "I can see you're dying to ask me something. So go ahead. I won't snap your head off."

"I was just wondering why, after your affair in India,

you never found another woman. It's unusual for a man to be approaching forty wifeless."

"Perhaps I just never found a woman I wanted to marry," he said. He set his spoon down and refilled their wineglasses. "Perhaps I feel that women aren't really to be trusted."

"That's a bit sweeping," Constance said. "Just because one woman broke a promise doesn't mean they all do."

"No, intellectually I know that. Let's just leave it that after the debacle in India I've never found another woman I wanted to get really close to."

"And you're not lonely?"

He shook his head. "Far from it. I don't have any difficulty finding congenial companions, my dear."

"Like me?" She could have bitten her tongue on the question but it came out anyway.

"Now, how am I supposed to answer that?" he demanded. "Either answer would be an insult."

"Answer it anyway." In for a penny, in for a pound, she thought.

He regarded her thoughtfully. "All right, I will. As it happens, you don't fall into the category of congenial companion. Partly because much of the time you're not in the least congenial, you're argumentative, and challenging, and very opinionated."

"Oh!" Constance gave a crow of laughter. "You only like women who agree with you and hang on to your every word, is that it?"

"No, it's not." He was smiling himself now. "This is an absurd conversation, Constance. But now I've started, I might as well finish. Those characteristics aside, I also find you exciting, somewhat puzzling a lot of the time, and when you choose to be, utterly captivating. There. Satisfied?"

She found she was blushing slightly. "I'm sorry I asked."

"Answer a question of mine now."

She nodded. It was only fair, although she was a little nervous as to what he would ask.

"You're a very passionate woman, both physically and intellectually. Don't *you* get lonely sometimes?"

Constance traced a pattern on the tablecloth with the tines of her fork. "I have my sisters. I'm not lonely in that respect at all."

"And in others?"

She looked up then and said frankly, "I never give it much thought, or at least, I didn't, until I met you."

"Should I take that as a compliment?"

"It's a fact. One I hadn't acknowledged until just now."

They fell silent as the waiter took away their soup bowls. Max wondered if the moment was ripe to ask her point-blank about *The Mayfair Lady*. But then he decided he would rather she told him herself. At some point he would try to tease a confession out of her, but he didn't want to spoil the present atmosphere.

The pot-au-feu was as delicious as Max had said it would be and Constance had no difficulty at all in finishing the plate. They followed it with a richly aromatic cheese from the Pyrenees, and Max ate a large slice of apple pie, which Constance regretfully declined.

He took a forkful of the flaky pastry with the thick slices of golden apple and plump raisins and held it to her lips. "You have at least to try it. Mrs. Baker makes the lightest, fluffiest pastry. Open up."

Constance opened her mouth and closed her eyes. It

was divine. She took up her own fork and helped herself to another mouthful from Max's plate.

"Are you sure you wouldn't like a slice of your own?" he inquired.

"Oh, no," she said. "I couldn't possibly eat another morsel." She reached across and dug in again.

"I give up." He pushed the plate across to her. "Eat that and I'll get another for myself."

"But I don't want any more," she protested. "I don't have a sweet tooth...except," she added with a rueful grin, "that this isn't at all sweet. It's just heavenly."

It was past midnight when they left the restaurant and walked into the warm darkness. Constance felt strangely light-headed, the wine perhaps, but it might be due more, she thought, to the sensation that she had never passed a more delightful and companionable evening. And she hadn't even missed their usual sparring. It had been remarkably relaxing and peaceable.

"Home?" he asked, hailing a hackney carriage that was clopping slowly towards them.

"Yours or mine?" She climbed in.

"That's a question whose answer I'm inclined to leave to the lady," he said, still standing on the pavement, waiting to tell the cabby where to go.

"Yours, then," Constance said, still feeling slightly and delightfully dizzy. "You can drive me home later."

"At your service, ma'am. Canon Row, cabbie."

"Right y'are, guv." The horse clopped on.

Constance turned her head lazily on the cracked leather squabs and watched Max's face in the alternating light and shadow as the carriage passed beneath street lamps. He reached out and touched her cheek, caressing the curve in the palm of his hand. The air was suddenly charged. Constance caught her breath as almost without warning lust engulfed her. She turned into his body, pressing her mouth to his. Her mouth opened beneath his, eager for the deep penetration of his tongue. She moved a hand to the bulge of his penis, pressing and rubbing the hard shaft through the fine material of his trousers. He groaned against her mouth. Heat swept up her body, setting her skin afire.

Max reached a hand beneath her skirt, sliding up the silk-clad length of her leg. His fingers insinuated themselves into the wide lace-edged legs of her drawers, crept upwards as she squirmed on the seat, found what they were looking for. She gasped, her thighs falling open in wanton abandon to give him easier access. Her belly clenched, her loins tightened, then she bit her lip hard to keep silent as the wave of pleasure peaked and receded.

"Dear God," she whispered. "We're in a hackney cab."

He laughed softly, although his breathing was ragged and his own eyes glowed, luminous with his own urgent desire. "I wasn't expecting that," he said, withdrawing his hand slowly. The scent of her was on his fingertips. "Of all the incontinent urges." He laughed softly again.

Constance straightened her skirts, smoothing them over her knees with fussy little pats that occupied her until her heart had slowed, although the languid afterglow of that brief but intense climax still infused her. "I feel guilty," she said. "We didn't share it."

"Oh, yes, we did," he murmured, his eyes still glowing as they held her gaze. "Touching you drives me wild. You feel so lush and open, so hot and eager. I want to bury my mouth in you, lick every drop of your arousal, drive my tongue to your core. And I shall."

He smiled a smile of pure sensual promise. "Just as soon as we get behind a closed door. I shall take every one of those elegant garments from you, one by one, and when you're naked I shall possess every inch of your body with my mouth and my hands. I intend to make you sob with pleasure, Constance. I intend to take you to heights you've never reached before. And when I'm finished, I promise you you will not be able to move a muscle."

Constance swallowed, the sound loud in the darkness. Her body was once again surging, her belly in a tumult. She shifted on the seat, trying to quiet the lusting clamor of her loins that were filled with liquid fire. "No more," she begged. "Don't say anything else until we get there. I can't bear it."

His smile now was both satisfied and wicked. "I love watching you like this," he murmured. "I love the idea that I can bring you almost to orgasm just by talking."

"It's sadistic," she said. "Pure sadism."

"Oh, come now. I'm only bringing you pleasure."

"Some pleasure is very close to pain," she said. The conversation was giving her much-needed distraction, enough at least to enable her to get out of the cab with some composure.

"And by the same token, some pain is very close to pleasure," he observed. "As the marquis describes so eloquently."

"You've read de Sade?" This was much better, she told herself desperately. Concentrate on a topic that, if not exactly far removed from sex, did at least have an intellectual component. "He's banned, isn't he?"

"One can buy underground copies in Paris. Would you like to borrow *Justine*? It's probably the best."

"Cannon Row, guvnor." The cabbie called from the box as the carriage came to a halt.

"We'll finish this fascinating discussion some other time," Max said, with that same wicked smile. "I have other things on my mind at present." He swung open the door and jumped down, giving Constance his hand to alight.

She stood on the pavement looking up at the tall terraced house while Max paid the driver. The house was in darkness, Max had hired no domestic staff as yet except for a daily cleaner. Marcel, his valet, had the night off and would not make an appearance until early morning.

"Would you really lend me *Justine*?" she asked as he inserted his key in the lock. "I would have thought you'd consider it unsuitable material for a woman."

"Don't try to distract me, sweetheart." The door swung open.

"I'm trying to distract myself," she said, stepping into the dark hall. She turned into his arms. It was a kiss that would devour her, an embrace that would swallow her whole like Jonah in the whale. She reached against him, standing on tiptoe to match her length with his. His hands spanned her narrow back, gripped her bottom fiercely, pressing her loins against his so that she could feel the pulse of his constricted penis. Her breasts were crushed against the starched white of his shirtfront. She wanted her clothes off, to feel the air on her skin, her body bared for his touch as he had promised.

As if he had divined her need, he stepped back, pausing to draw breath. It was dark in the hall, only a dim illumination from the lamp outside the door. He took her hand and pulled her behind him into the drawing room.

The curtains were drawn back and again the street lamp offered a faint glow.

"I need to see you," he said softly. He struck a match and lit the candles on the console table against the wall. The light was gentle and softening.

"We should draw the curtains," she said.

"No one can see in." He came up to her, took her hands, drew her over to the fireplace. He undressed her as he had promised, garment by garment, without haste, lingering over buttons and hooks, touching her skin as he revealed it inch by inch, kissing her shoulders, the pulse in her throat, the cleft between her breasts. Then she was naked and he was no longer leisurely. She writhed in his hands and beneath the mouth that explored and possessed her, opened her and probed her, branding her with a piercing pleasure that left her trembling, insensate, in thrall to the magic of this possession.

When he could bear his own need no longer Max pulled off his own clothes, maintaining contact with her body even as he did so, a stroking finger, a brush of his lips, the quick dart of his tongue while she stood as if robbed of all will. Then when he too was naked, she slid down his body, her hands running down his length, and took his penis in her mouth, giving back the pleasure he had given her and taking her own in the giving.

Finally he came down to the floor with her, kneeling in front of her, kissing her mouth, where he could taste his own arousal that mingled on his lips with the taste of Constance. He eased her to the floor, their mouths still joined, then he drew her beneath him, her thighs opening for him, the tender, now acutely sensitive entrance to her body closing around him as he thrust within. He pressed deep inside her. She held her breath as the spiral of pleasure tightened and she could sense the moment of explosive joy coming closer and closer. She tightened her inner muscles around him the instant before the coil flew apart and she screamed in the deserted house as the climactic finale ripped through her so that for a moment the only reality was sensation. She felt his body jarring, shuddering, the clenched, corded muscles in his upper arms as he held himself above her, then he too shouted out with the same wild abandon and then collapsed on her.

They lay together, breathing fast, their sweat-slick skin sticking together, until at last some sense of time and place returned to them. Constance weakly stroked his back and shifted her body in mute appeal. He rolled off her and lay on his back, his hand resting on her stomach.

"God's good grace," he said.

"God's good grace," she said. This was a man who knew how to keep his promises.

Chapter 15

The doorbell rang early on Sunday evening. The sisters were gathered in the drawing room, where they'd been all afternoon, trying to distract themselves from the agony of expectation. There was no guarantee that he would come, indeed even Chastity had begun to be plagued by doubts.

At the sound of the bell they looked at one another in silence. Chastity put her steepled hands to her mouth and they waited. Jenkins opened the door. "Mr. Henry Franklin, ladies."

Henry stepped hesitantly into the room. He carried a small valise and looked as harried and worn as he had done in the Copper Kettle. He set down his valise by the door and solemnly shook their hands.

"Jenkins, could you bring the sherry?" Constance asked. "I think Mr. Franklin looks as if he could do with something heartening."

"Certainly, Miss Con." Jenkins left the drawing room.

"I just walked away," Henry said, sounding bemused. "I wrote a letter and left it on the mantelpiece and I walked away. I caught the afternoon train." He shook his head in some kind of wonder. "He'll never forgive me."

"Don't be too sure of that," Prudence said, drawing him to the sofa. "We'll follow through with our plan and I'm sure he'll come round in the end."

Henry sat on the sofa, turning his hat between his hands. "How is Amelia?"

"Desperate to see you," Constance said. "Oh, thank you, Jenkins. I'll pour." She nodded to the butler as he set the tray with decanter and glasses on a side table. "Lord Duncan isn't dining in tonight, is he?"

"No, Miss Con. He's dining with Lord Barclay as I understand it."

"Then we'll dine with Mr. Franklin at eight as usual."

"Very well, miss. I'll take the gentleman's valise to the blue room."

Constance poured sherry and gave Henry a glass. He sipped it cautiously then with an air of sudden abandon gulped it down. Constance refilled his glass.

"Dutch courage," he said with an embarrassed smile.

"You don't need it now," Chastity said warmly. "You're here and it's done. Tomorrow afternoon I'll walk with you in the park when Amelia is walking her charge. We've arranged to meet, accidentally of course, in the rose garden. The child won't think anything of it if you and Amelia talk for a few minutes while I walk a little way with Pamela."

"And you have an interview with the Right Honorable Max Ensor tomorrow morning," Constance told him. "He's looking for a secretary. I told him you would make an excellent one. The work might even interest you. It's got to be more challenging than slaving in the office of a construction company."

Henry downed his second sherry. "I can't take it all in," he said.

"You don't have to all at once," Chastity told him. "The wedding is arranged for Thursday afternoon at Caxton Hall. It'll be a very simple ceremony and you and Amelia can have an hour to yourselves afterwards before she has to return to the Grahams."

"And as soon as you have employment and can find suitable lodgings, then Amelia can leave her employers and you'll set up house together," Prudence stated.

Henry looked dazed. "I don't know anything about London. I've never been here before. It's so noisy, even on a Sunday. I think I feel a headache coming on."

"I'll show you to your room and you can rest a little." Chastity rose from her chair. "Poor Henry," she said sympathetically. "We must seem such a managing group of females."

"You are," he said frankly.

"We only manage people for their own good," Chastity reassured him, taking his hand in a warm clasp. "We won't do you any harm, I promise."

He shook his head. "No," he said. "No, I don't suppose you would. Not intentionally." He allowed himself to be led from the drawing room.

"Oh, dear," Constance said when the door had closed behind them. "Do you really think he's what Amelia wants?"

"She said so," Prudence stated, pouring more sherry. "I don't think it's our place to veto her choice."

"No," Constance agreed. "But I foresee a very tedious evening."

"Do you think Max will try him out?"

Constance smiled involuntarily, reflecting that every

time she thought of Max these days this fatuous smile came to her lips. She just couldn't help it. "I think he'll do his best to see promise in him," she said.

Prudence was very aware of her sister's recurring smile. "I think you're in love," she stated.

Constance shook her head vigorously. "No, of course I'm not. I'm just in lust."

Prudence shook her own head as vigorously. "Don't fool yourself, Con. You certainly can't fool Chas and me. We've never seen you like this. Not even with Douglas."

"It'll pass," Constance declared.

"Do you want it to?"

Constance blew out her breath in a sound of pure frustration. "I don't know, Prue. I don't want to be in love with someone who's not in love with me."

"And he's not?"

"I don't think so."

"And would you know?" Prudence asked shrewdly.

"I would think so," Constance said. "Wouldn't you?"

"I don't know. Sometimes the last person to know something is the person closest to it." They turned as one to the door as Chastity returned.

"Is he all right?"

"He's just so befuddled, poor soul. I don't think he can believe what he's done." She looked closely at her sisters. "What were you two talking about?"

"Max," Prudence said. "Whether he's in love with Con. What do you think, Chas?"

"I think it's quite likely, but it's possible he doesn't know it," Chastity said after a moment's consideration. "Just think how he's changed since he met you. And he helped with the motorcar. He would never have done anything so unconventional before."

"And he went to a WSPU meeting with you," Prudence reminded Constance.

As if she needed reminding, Constance thought. That evening was indelibly etched in her memory. "I'll agree he's more open-minded than I had originally thought," she said cautiously. Then she shrugged. "Let's get back to Henry. If Max does employ him, then he'll need somewhere to live. I don't see him doing that alone, do you?"

"Maybe we should start up a housing rental agency," Prudence suggested. "In addition to the Go-Between, Mabel, and the Agony Aunt and all the rest of it."

"I trust you jest, sister," Constance said. "Our plates are so full we can barely keep the balls we have in the air. Did anyone invite Millicent to the At Home yet?"

"Yes, I did. I called round yesterday, just for an informal visit. I pressed her a little and she said she would definitely be here." Chastity took up her sherry glass again. "How are we going to put a white rose in her buttonhole?"

"We have to give different colored ones to every woman," Prudence said. "It doesn't matter how many reds and pinks and yellows we have, we just make sure there's only one white. And white will go with whatever color she's wearing."

"That'll serve," Constance agreed. "I should take Henry to visit Max, don't you think? He might never get there on his own."

"We should probably warn him to keep the name of his intended to himself," Prudence pointed out. "Just in case it comes up in conversation and he lets it slip to Max."

"Oh, what a tangled web we weave," Constance muttered. "I shall be so glad when we've got these two lovebirds safely joined in legal matrimony."

Henry was a quiet dinner companion, eating steadily, drinking very moderately, but he seemed to be a little less dazed by his present circumstances, and when the sisters rose from the table, suggesting he'd like to enjoy a glass of port, he said he never partook of anything stronger than wine or sherry and would accompany them to the drawing room, where, if they would like it, he would be delighted to play for them. He had noticed a particularly fine pianoforte in the room.

"How lovely," Constance said. "Thank you."

He smiled then and it was a very sweet smile and the sisters began to get some inkling as to what had appealed to Amelia. They understood completely when Henry began to play. It was as if he was transformed. The shy, weak bumbler was gone; in its place a man supremely confident in his talent. And it was a considerable talent. His execution was flawless, his interpretation both creative and sensitive.

They sat transfixed for close to two hours as he played tirelessly, and frequently from memory. Once or twice he paused between pieces to flex his long fingers, but they had the feeling that he wasn't really in the room with them. His expression was transfixed, abstracted. He was lost in the world of his music.

When at last he stopped, after a spirited rendition of a group of Chopin waltzes, the sisters applauded spontaneously. "That was wonderful, Henry," Chastity said. "No wonder you hate clerical work. If I had such a gift I wouldn't want to do anything else with my life."

He beamed, flushing with pleasure. "That's so kind of you."

"No," Constance said. "Not kind, just utterly truthful. We'll have to find a way for you to use your gift, but

I think we have to stick with the original plan for the moment."

"As long as I have access to a piano I'm willing to do other work. Now, if you'll excuse me, I've had a very long day." He offered a jerky little bow and left them.

"That was something of a revelation, although I don't suppose it should have been," Prudence observed through a yawn. "But I feel happier about Amelia's choice now."

Henry was visibly relieved to have an escort to Westminster. He nodded when Constance said he should not mention Amelia's name in the upcoming interview. "I wouldn't see the need," he said. "My private life is no business of a prospective employer."

They took the omnibus to Westminster and Constance rang the bell of the house on Canon Row. Max himself opened the door. "Good morning, Constance. I didn't expect to see you." He shook her hand with solemn formality.

"Mr. Franklin is new to London and I thought it would be nice if I made the introduction personally," Constance said. "Mr. Henry Franklin, the Right Honorable Max Ensor."

The two men shook hands, Henry regarding the taller man rather warily. He exuded London sophistication in a morning coat that bore all the marks of impeccable and expensive tailoring. Henry felt distinctly provincial in his Ashford tailored frock coat.

"I'll leave you to it, then," Constance said. "You can find your own way back, Henry?"

"I hardly think Mr. Ensor would consider employing

me if I was that incompetent," Henry said with a surprising touch of acerbity.

"No," Constance responded swiftly. "I was just being a mother hen. Forgive me."

Max's eyebrows crawled into his scalp at this description. He stared at her in open amusement. "Mother hen?"

"Good morning, Mr. Ensor," Constance said, and turned away, hiding her own laughter.

She walked over Westminster Bridge then hailed a hackney to take her to Battersea. The driver gave her a curious look when she alighted outside the drab building that housed the Battersea Home for Fallen Women. "I think you'd better wait for me," she said, looking around the mean streets. "There don't seem to be too many hackneys plying their trade around here."

"Not much trade to be 'ad, miss," he observed, unwinding his muffler. "'Ow long you'll be, then?"

"Not above a half hour," she said. "I'll pay for the wait."

He nodded, took out his newspaper, and began to study the racing pages.

Constance rang the bell of a door scarred and scuffed with peeling paint. It was opened by a rather fierce-looking woman in black with a stiffly starched apron. She looked like some kind of warder, Constance thought. Either that or a matron. And she was scrutinizing Constance in a less-than-friendly fashion.

"I wonder if I might talk to Gertrude Collins." Constance tried to strike a happy medium between haughtiness and supplication, although she deeply resented the harsh stare.

"Why would you want to do that?"

"I might have some helpful information for her."

Somewhere in the cabbage- and disinfectant-smelling depths of the house came the wail of a baby. "I mean her no harm, I assure you." She hesitated for a second then said boldly, "I am no friend to Lord Barclay."

The woman stared at her even more closely but now Constance could detect a slight crack in the harsh demeanor. "Are you a relative?" the woman demanded.

"No. Just someone who wishes her well."

"There's few enough of those around," the woman said. She opened the door a little wider. "She's maybe no better than she ought to be, but to be taken advantage of when she had little enough choice in the matter and then abandoned is sheer cruelty. I'd shoot 'em all."

Constance believed her. She accepted the implicit invitation to enter the house and followed a gesturing hand into a dank little sitting room with hard-backed chairs ranged along the walls and black and white oilcloth on the floor. A minute or so later a woman entered carrying a baby on her hip.

"What do you want with me?"

Constance left the dreary house half an hour later fired with righteous indignation and a soaring triumph. She had enough facts to make her story credible. The gutter press would pick it up with relish and Gertrude would reap the financial rewards while Lord Barclay was crucified on the cross of society's opinion. Such opinion would turn a blind eye to discreet peccadilloes with members of the underclasses, but it wouldn't turn a blind eye to scandal. And Constance in the pages of *The Mayfair Lady* was going to make a stink that would reek to the heavens. Barclay wouldn't be able to show his face in Town.

She arrived home in the middle of lunch, to be told that Henry had returned from his interview flush with success. He had liked Max Ensor and the feeling had apparently been mutual. He was prepared to start work the following Monday. He'd eaten some bread and cheese and gone out to buy an engagement ring for his beloved.

"It's astonishing how he's blossomed," Prudence said. "He even walks differently."

"We'd better find him another roof soon, though," Chastity put in, pouring lemonade into her glass. "Father's bound to terrify him at dinner. So, where have you been, Con?"

She told them as she helped herself to a dish of cauliflower cheese. When her recital was finished, Prudence said thoughtfully, "I just hope this crusading zeal isn't going to cause trouble, Con. It's not that I don't agree with you. The man's despicable. But we're playing with fire."

"How could he possibly associate the piece with the Duncan sisters, Prue?"

Prudence shrugged. "I don't know. But it makes me uneasy."

"Well, I'm going to meet Henry in the park for our stroll to the rose garden." Chastity rose from the table. "I can't wait to see them meet. It's so romantic."

"Henry . . ." Prudence exclaimed.

"Romantic," Constance exclaimed.

"Well, the idea is," Chastity said. "And I'm going to wear my best bonnet in honor of the occasion."

She dressed with great care as she'd promised and set out for the park twirling a sunshade. Henry was waiting for her as instructed just inside the Stanhope Gate. "Do you think she will like this?" he blurted as Chastity came up to him. He held out the small box. "It's an engagement ring. I know she can't wear it, but I felt it was the right thing to do."

"It's lovely," Chastity said, taking the ring and holding it to the sun. "Any woman would love it. It's so delicate."

"It's all I could afford."

"It's lovely," she reiterated firmly. "The rose garden is this way."

In the quiet fragrance of the garden they sat on a bench in the sun to wait. Henry kept getting up and pacing the narrow gravel paths between the vibrant rose beds. Every so often he seemed inclined to chew his fingernails but resolutely thrust his hands into his pockets.

Chastity heard the shrill tones of Pamela Graham from quite some distance away. She stood up, nodding to Henry. "Take my arm, Henry, and we'll stroll towards the gate over there. Try to act as if it's just a pleasant surprise to meet Amelia and her charge here."

"I'll try," he whispered.

Amelia opened the little iron gate, ignoring the protestations of her charge.

"I don't want to go in there, Miss Westcott. I don't like flowers. You promised we would find the swings."

"And so we will, Pammy," Amelia said calmly. "But I want to show you the birdbath in the middle of the garden. It's a dolphin." Her quick glance darted towards the two approaching her and her color ebbed for a second, her step faltered. Then she picked up her pace again.

"Miss Westcott, how nice to meet you here. Isn't it a

beautiful afternoon." Chastity smiled and extended her hand. "May I introduce Mr. Franklin?"

"Mr. Franklin and I are already acquainted," Amelia said softly, offering her hand to Chastity and then to Henry.

"He used to teach me the piano," Pamela pronounced. "Why are you in London, Mr. Franklin? You're not going to teach me piano again, are you?" She sounded horrified at the prospect.

"No, I don't believe so, Pamela," he said, his nervousness dissipating at the child's artless question. He realized he was still holding Amelia's hand and dropped it rather hastily.

Chastity bent down to the child. "Pamela, you probably don't remember me. I'm a friend of your mother's. And your uncle's," she added calmly.

"Uncle Max?"

"Yes, he comes to our house sometimes."

"I thought I saw Mr. Ensor with Miss Duncan the other day," Amelia said, her voice amazingly steady.

"Yes, they're old acquaintances," Chastity said. Chastity's romantic inclinations had been immediately satisfied by the look that had passed between the two as their hands had touched.

"I want to go to the pond," Pammy stated, dancing agitatedly on the path.

"I'll come with you," Chastity said. "I love to sail twigs on the pond. We'll play a game." She took the child's hand and led her off, studiously avoiding a backward glance at the reunited lovers.

After a decent interval that would not seem remarkable to Pamela they returned to the rose garden. Amelia was there alone. "I was about to come in search of you," she said. Her cheeks were slightly flushed, her eyes very bright with what Chastity was sure were tears. "Such a charming gentleman, Mr. Franklin."

"Yes, how curious that we should both know him," Chastity said. "Pamela, do you see that beautiful butterfly over there. On the yellow rose." She pointed towards a Red Admiral butterfly resting on the flower some ten paces away. Pamela ran over. Chastity turned back to Amelia. "Is everything all right?"

"Oh, yes. Wonderful. But . . . but, Chastity, I own I'm uncomfortable with the involvement of Mr. Ensor."

"Don't be. Constance has him well in hand," Chastity said, aware that she was probably promising a great deal more than the truth. "He doesn't know anything about you and Henry, and once you're married it's none of his business anyway."

"I suppose that's so," Amelia said with a little sigh. Then her expression brightened. "He gave me a ring, Chastity. Such a pretty engagement ring."

"And on Thursday you'll have the gold band to go with it," Chastity said, giving her a quick hug. "We just have to find Henry a place to live."

"I think," Amelia said quietly, "that Henry can do that for himself. You and your sisters have done enough."

"If you think so," Chastity said. "We don't wish to interfere."

Amelia laid a hand on her arm. "Once we're married, Henry will take on the responsibilities of a husband. I assure you."

"Oh, I believe you," Chastity returned. "He played for us last evening. It was sublime."

Amelia smiled. "Yes," she said. "Sublime." She stood

in reflective silence for a minute, then called, "Come, Pammy, it's time to go."

On Wednesday afternoon, a large display of cut roses stood on the hall table, their thorns clipped, the stems neatly wrapped in tissue paper. Chastity fussed over them, rearranging them in order of color, then mixing them up again. "It's a very eccentric thing to do," she said, setting the single white rose just a little apart. "To give out roses."

"It's a charming gesture," Prudence said stoutly. "People will be enchanted. My only worry is that Millicent will fail us. We know Anonymous will come because he paid to do so, but supposing Millicent changed her mind, or had a headache or a more pressing engagement?"

"Let's cross that bridge when we come to it," Constance said in a somewhat distracted tone. She was reading a letter that had just been delivered. "Max makes his apologies, he can't call this afternoon, but he's inviting me to dine with him in the House of Commons this evening."

"Will you go?"

Constance gave her sister a look that declared an answer was hardly necessary.

"Wear the green and black silk," Prudence said with a laugh. "It's so striking."

"And Mother's diamonds," Chastity said. "With that gorgeous emerald green shawl."

"Whatever you say," Constance agreed. "I wouldn't argue with either of you." She moved towards the drawing room as the doorbell rang. "Don't forget, Jenkins. The white rose for Miss Hardcastle."

"I have not forgotten, Miss Con," the long-suffering butler declared as he crossed to the front door.

The sisters exchanged a quick grin. "I'll make myself scarce," Chastity said. "Good luck." She crossed her fingers and went upstairs to await the outcome. Her sisters hastened to position themselves in the drawing room to receive their guests.

Anonymous arrived punctually at half past three. He handed his card to Jenkins, offered his excuse for being there, and was ushered into the drawing room. A buzz of conversation rose and fell from the small group gathered there. The women all wore roses pinned to their corsages, but a quick glance revealed no white rose.

Jenkins announced him: "Arthur Melvin, Esquire."

Constance came forward, just the right questioning note in her voice as she said, "I don't believe we've had the pleasure, Mr. Melvin. I'm Constance Duncan."

"Forgive the intrusion," he said. "I was given to understand Lord Jersey would be calling upon you this afternoon, and I have an urgent need to meet with him."

Constance made a show of looking around the drawing room. "I'm so sorry, he hasn't appeared as yet. Perhaps later. Do come and meet my sister, and you'll take tea, I hope."

She exchanged a speaking glance with Prudence as she introduced him. There was still no sign of Millicent. The no-longer-anonymous client was looking around rather restlessly, but he managed to comport himself graciously when introduced to the other guests.

"Miss Hardcastle, Miss Duncan," Jenkins intoned

from the doorway, and Millicent, sporting the white rose, came in.

"Constance, Prudence, I'm sorry to be so late," she said, coming towards them, hands outstretched. "One of our housemaids had the most dreadful toothache and I had to take her to have it pulled. She was too terrified to go alone."

Millicent was neither plain nor attractive, but she had a certain sweetness of countenance that bespoke her nature. She was approaching her mid-thirties and beginning to accept society's opinion that she would never catch a husband. Or at least she gave the impression of such acceptance for the sake of dignity, nothing was worse than being pitied, but in private she yearned for a home of her own away from the constant attendance upon her invalid mother, who was a past mistress at the art of manipulating her ailments to control her daughter. Millicent dreamed sometimes of a child, a house in the country, and a quiet, undemanding husband. But she kept her dreams to herself.

The sisters greeted her warmly and she turned from them to acknowledge other acquaintances. Arthur Melvin was balancing his teacup in one hand and a plate of cake in the other. He stood on the outskirts of the group as Millicent chatted, inquiring about health and families with an air of genuine concern.

Arthur noted her costume: a neat and very plain coat and skirt of brown serge, with a matching hat adorned with a pheasant's feather. It was serviceable rather than elegant. He liked the softness of her voice and her general demeanor that bespoke a rather retiring nature. All in all, he thought, on first acquaintance Miss Hardcastle exactly matched his specifications. He moved around the group to where Miss Duncan stood by the piano talking to a very young girl.

"Ah, Mr. Melvin." Constance smiled at him as he approached. "May I get you more tea?"

"No, I thank you." He set his cup and saucer and plate on the top of the piano. "I was wondering if I might have an introduction to Miss Hardcastle."

"Why, certainly," Constance said. "She's such a charming woman." She led him across to Millicent and performed her first true client introduction, then she stepped back and left them to it.

"How do you think it's going?" Prudence murmured half an hour later.

"I don't know. But they're still talking," Constance murmured back. "I think we've earned our fee."

Chapter 16

Constance draped the emerald green silk shawl over her bare shoulders and fingered the diamond necklace nestled around her throat. "You don't think the diamonds are a little too much?"

"Absolutely not," Prudence declared. "But the tiara might be since it's only dinner."

"That's a relief," her sister said. "I was afraid you were going to insist on it."

"If you were going to a ball, I would." Prudence clasped a diamond bracelet high up on her sister's forearm where it wouldn't be hidden by her long gloves. "Let Chas put the finishing touches to your hair."

Constance sat down in front of the mirror watching critically as Chastity tied a black velvet ribbon around the elaborate braided chignon at the nape of her neck. "This style suits you so well," Chastity said, teasing a few strands onto Constance's forehead to soften the line. "And the simplicity sets off the gown and the diamonds."

Constance rose from the stool and examined her reflection in the long mirror. Her gown was of pale green silk interwoven with a delicate black filigree pattern. Black silk gloves, an ivory fan, and a tiny diamond-studded evening purse completed the ensemble. "I think I look rather untouchable," she said.

"Tantalizingly so," Prudence said with a laugh. "What more could a man want?"

"In the august halls of the Houses of Parliament a man's mind should be on serious matters," Constance said with a righteous air. "I wouldn't wish to distract him."

"Well, if you're to arrive punctually you should go now." Chastity went to the bedroom door. "Cobham will be waiting for you."

Constance followed her, as Prudence adjusted the set of the shawl. "I hope this evening goes all right. I feel bad about abandoning you to Henry and Father."

"Oh, it'll be fine, don't give it a second thought," Prudence said, giving her a little push through the door. "Father's never discourteous with strangers even if they annoy him. And once Henry starts to play after dinner, you can lay odds he'll be heading for his club."

Constance couldn't argue with this, and wasn't inclined to. Her sisters accompanied her to the street, where Cobham waited with the carriage. "If you decide on another night on the tiles," Prudence said with a knowing smile, "make sure you're back in plenty of time for the wedding tomorrow."

Constance didn't deign to reply. She climbed into the carriage and sat back in the dim interior as the carriage moved at Cobham's stately pace along Whitehall to the Houses of Parliament. She alighted at St. Stephen's Gate and the police inspector who had charge of the gate came forward to greet her.

"Miss Duncan, Mr. Ensor told us to expect you. He's awaiting you on the terrace. One of my men will escort you."

A policeman offered a deferential bow and she followed him through the long stone corridors and out onto the terrace that overlooked the Thames.

Max was standing with a group of people beside the balustrade, his eyes on the doors. As soon as he saw her, he came across with swift step. "Constance." He took her hand and raised it to his lips. An unusual salute but one that seemed in keeping with their setting and the exquisite formality of her costume.

"You take my breath away," he murmured into her ear as he tucked her gloved hand into the crook of his arm. "We aren't dining alone since unchaperoned ladies are rather frowned upon here, but I trust you'll find our companions congenial."

Constance had expected this. It was one thing to dine alone with a man who was neither relative nor fiancé in the Café Royal or an out-of-the-way restaurant on Kensington Church Street, quite another in this bastion of male power and privilege.

She was, however, surprised to find herself dining with the Prime Minister and three of the most influential members of his Cabinet, all accompanied by their wives. The startling thought occurred to her that she was being vetted as a suitable wife for an up-and-coming politician. In these circles, a man's wife was a vital asset. She could make or break a parliamentary career.

She gave Max a speculative glance as they were seated at a prominent, large round table in the Members' dining room. He gave her a bland smile and turned to address a remark to the lady on his right. Constance picked up her own conversational ball with the ease of habit and training, ensuring that nothing revealing, nothing of any importance was said by herself or either of her table neighbors.

Her fork faltered when the Chancellor's wife declared in a voice that carried into one of those moments of silence that sometimes fall on a group, "As Asquith always says, man is man, and woman is woman. Parliament cannot make them the same." She plied her fan, a tiny pink patch of indignation blooming on her cheeks.

Constance caught a sudden warning in Max's eyes. She picked up her fork again and poked at her roast beef. So she was to be muzzled. Her opinions would embarrass him. Well, so be it. This dinner table was hardly the forum for an impassioned diatribe on the manifest injustice of the disenfranchisement of women. It would win ncither her nor her cause any friends.

But Max's warning rankled. He'd accompanied her to a WSPU meeting. He'd met the Pankhursts. He knew how passionately she felt about this. Surely if he had any respect for her views he wouldn't prevent her from presenting them for informed and respectful discussion.

The ladies rose when the Prime Minister's wife gave the signal, and repaired to the retiring room, leaving the gentlemen to enjoy port and cigars, while the women gossiped companionably, made what repairs were necessary to appearances, and sipped coffee in the adjoining lounge.

Constance was prepared for the inquisition. "How long have you known Mr. Ensor, Miss Duncan?" Lady Campbell-Bannerman inquired, settling back on the sofa with her coffee.

"A few weeks," Constance responded. "I know his sister, Lady Graham."

"Oh, yes, of course. A charming woman. Her husband takes his seat regularly in the Lords, I understand."

"So I believe." Constance sipped her coffee. She appeared perfectly relaxed, no hint of the coiled spring of tension as she waited for the test that was bound to come.

"Lord Duncan too, I understand, is most assiduous in his parliamentary duties."

"My father takes his seat regularly," she said. "He always has done."

"And you, Miss Duncan? Are you interested in politics?"

"Very." She smiled the smile of the tiger.

"It's a little unseemly for a woman to be interested in politics. Even those of us whose domestic lives are governed by our husbands' political work," Lady Asquith said. "Our role is to provide him with the atmosphere in which to do that work . . . nothing contentious, perfect harmony at home."

"Oh, yes, we must make certain that he's never aware of the little domestic trials and tribulations that beset us," one of the other women confided, leaning across to Constance, patting her hand. "Our men do the vital work of the country. We're so privileged to assist them."

Constance smiled faintly.

"It's the least we can do, after all, when we're so fortunate to have such men to decide all these matters for us, to come to decisions for our own good. Don't you think, Miss Duncan?"

"No," Constance said, setting down her coffee. "No, ma'am, I don't think so at all. I find nothing fortunate or privileged about having decisions made for me by men, who make them simply by virtue of being men. I consider myself perfectly capable of making decisions for my own good."

There was a shocked silence. Only Constance, it seemed, was unmoved by her speech. She waited a few moments, then, when it seemed no response was to be forthcoming, rose with a murmured excuse and made her way out to the terrace again.

She heard Max's voice as she passed an anteroom to the dining room. She paused, unwilling to enter in case it was one of the areas restricted to women. It was a fair assumption that it was, since women were allowed in very few areas of the Houses of Parliament. And not even Constance would break such a rule.

He was speaking clearly, as were his companions, the Prime Minister and Asquith. And she listened unabashed once she heard the first sentence.

"There's to be a deputation to the House with a petition," Max said. "I don't know when, the date hasn't been decided as yet."

"We must refuse it," Asquith said. "If we accept a petition we're giving legitimacy to the question."

"That's certainly a point," Max replied. "But it will also enrage them." He gave a short laugh. "I've seen these women in action, Prime Minister, and they're very passionate about their cause. I see our best course of action as appeasement. We take the petition, we just don't act on it."

I've seen these women in action. Constance could barely swallow her rage. Her nails bit into her gloved palms as she held herself still and quiet. How could he sound so dismissive? How *dare* he make light of the confession she had made to him of her own driving commitment? She had been trying to change his mind about women's suffrage, but she had also been willing to share confidences with him because she thought something good for both of them might come of it. And what did he do with those confidences? Make light of them, and use them to work against the Union.

"I have an ear to the ground," Max was saying. "I can probably get details of their next move before it goes public. It'll give us time to plan a strategy."

"Good man. Forewarned, as they say."

Constance left her post. She wanted to leave the House altogether but caution held her back. Until she had decided what to do, she didn't want Max to know what she'd overheard. The cold voice of reason told her that acting in haste and fury was always unwise. This betrayal required an altogether subtler response. For the moment her anger masked her hurt, and for the moment she welcomed that distance. When it came it was going to be wretched. She had allowed herself to get close to him, to conjure with the idea of love, and therefore of a future. Instead she had invited betrayal.

The cooler air of the terrace fanned her cheeks, cleared her head a little, and when Max came up behind her she was able to turn and greet him with a smile.

"I didn't realize you were out here alone," he said, leaning beside her on the parapet, resting his arms along the ledge. Below them the tide was high and the river was still busy with laden barges heading for the docks despite the late hour.

"I found my companions' conversation rather irritating," she said flatly.

"Oh." He shook his head. "I was afraid of that."

"Then why did you invite me? Weren't you also afraid I might embarrass you?"

"No," he said, sounding surprised. "Far from it. Why would you think such a thing?"

She shrugged. "I don't know. I'm tired, Max. I've had a rather busy day."

"Then I'll take you home." He gave her a searching look. Constance was rarely tired. She always seemed to have boundless energy. And yet she certainly seemed to be drooping a little tonight. He thought perhaps it had something to do with her woman's cycle. He had noticed often enough how at certain times of the month perfectly rational, even-tempered females became emotional and distracted.

Constance wondered how he could stand there, talking to her, behaving exactly as usual when he had just come from a conversation where he had talked so matter-of-factly of deceiving her, as if it was the only course of action, the obvious course of action. It was almost impossible to believe. But she had heard what she had heard. Her first impression of Max Ensor had been the correct one, and she had allowed her emotions, her self-indulgent impulses, to rule her. Typical female, she thought in disgust.

She couldn't bear his company another minute and said abruptly, "Would you make my excuses. I don't feel at all well. I'll take a cab home."

"No, I'll take you home. Did you have a cloak?"

"No." She drew the shawl tighter around her. There was no graceful way to refuse his escort home, and she was not ready to confront him yet.

Max made no attempt at conversation. He put an arm around her in the cab but when she twitched aside he let his arm drop immediately. He couldn't imagine what could be wrong between them, therefore there wasn't anything wrong. She was tired. It was the wrong time of the month. It could be no more than that.

He walked her to her door and bent to kiss her. She turned her face aside so his lips made contact with her cheek not her lips. "I expect you have a headache," he said sympathetically. "I understand about these things."

Constance stared at him. *Understand?* Understood what things? How could he possibly understand? And then it dawned on her as she looked at him, saw the warmly concerned but nevertheless slightly patronizing smile in his eyes. Of all the typical male conclusions to draw. He could think of only one explanation for why she suddenly seemed less accessible to him.

Max hesitated, wondering whether to say something else in the sudden silence, then while he was still wondering, she had bidden him good night and disappeared inside, using her own key in the door.

Max stood on the pavement, frowning. Then he shook his head and walked away, unaware of Constance at the landing window watching him go.

Constance went into the parlor where, as she'd known, her sisters were waiting up for her.

"What in the devil's name has happened?" Prudence demanded the instant Constance walked in.

"Con, you look as if you've seen a ghost," Chastity said in concern. "Are you ill, love?"

"Sick at heart," Constance said with a bitter smile. "I am so stupid! Here am I priding myself on how clever I am and how I can outwit anyone, particularly any man, and I fall for the oldest trick in the book. What a dupe!"

She poured herself a glass of cognac and stood by the empty grate, one elegantly shod foot on the fender.

"I think you'd better tell us the whole," Prudence said. "I'm assuming this has to do with Max?"

"Everything to do with Max."

She told them and they listened in stunned silence. "And do you know what?" Constance asked with a short laugh as she finished her recital. "He decided that my sudden reticence was because I have the curse. Of all the insulting . . ." She gave another bitter laugh and drank her cognac.

"What are you going to do?" asked Prudence, deciding to leave the sympathy to Chastity, who, tearful herself, was already hugging her sister. Constance needed practical help as well as sympathy.

Constance disengaged from Chastity's embrace and dug into her purse for her handkerchief. She wiped her damp eyes with a decisive movement, as if putting all pointless emotion behind her. "I am going on the attack," she declared. "In the pages of *The Mayfair Lady*. If we get it to the printer in the morning, will it make Saturday's edition, Chas?"

"I would think so," her sister replied. "Sam's usually pretty flexible. If necessary he can just add another page."

"Good," Constance stated. "Max Ensor isn't going to know what hit him."

"It seems appropriate," Prudence agreed. "But shouldn't you talk to him first about what you heard?"

"No." Constance shook her head firmly. "I shall avoid him, or perhaps *evade* is the better word, until after the article is published. If I have to meet him, he'll have nothing but smiles. I want him to be completely off his guard, and then ambushed. Totally blindsided." Her mouth was set in a grim smile. "For the next day or two I can be in seclusion with my *womanly troubles*."

The grim smile took a suddenly wicked turn. "You two can have some fun with that. If he comes a-calling, you can offer some delicate little evasions and hints. It'll feed right into his insulting assumptions. I might even hide behind the curtains while you do it."

"You won't, not if you expect us to be convincing," Prudence declared, but she too had a wicked gleam in her eye. "But I own it might be amusing. Don't you, Chas?"

Chastity looked less entertained by the prospect than her sisters. She wore a preoccupied frown. "Will you name him in the article, Con?"

"Oh, no, Chas." The smile grew grimmer. "I'll just make sure that there are enough details to identify a certain Right Honorable Gentleman . . . *right honorable, indeed!*" She shook her head again in disgust and refilled her glass. "You two go on to bed. I'm too worked up to sleep, so I'll get started on my article." She moved energetically to the secretaire, glass in hand.

"If you're sure," Chastity said doubtfully.

"Quite sure. I'll not be good company right now. I need to do this if it's to get to the printer's in time for next week's edition." She sat down and drew a pad of paper towards her. "Oh, by the way, how was Henry?"

"Nervous as a stray kitten," Prudence said. "He barely managed a word at dinner despite Father's best efforts to draw him out, and then he played the piano for over an hour afterwards. Father listened politely for about half an hour, then beat a retreat to his club. We sent Henry to bed at eleven. Chas would have tucked him in if I'd let her."

Constance smiled, but it was a distracted one. "We'll get him to Caxton Hall tomorrow, then?"

"Oh, yes, no doubt," Prudence stated. "And Amelia will manage him from then on." She paused, her hand on the door. "Quite sure you're all right, Con?"

"Quite sure." Constance had already begun to write.

Her sisters exchanged a glance and then with a murmured good night left her to it.

It was close to three o'clock before Constance finally set down her pen, satisfied at last with what she'd written. If Max Ensor's ears weren't on fire at this minute they certainly should be. A wave of tiredness washed over her. She stood up, yawning. She felt purged of her hurt, or was it only masked by her anger? By the satisfaction of venting that anger?

In her heart she knew she hadn't begun to touch the wound. It was easier for the moment to blame herself for failing to trust her instincts and to rage at Max for his treachery. The pain would come later. She went up to bed, and to her surprise slept like a log until mid-morning.

She was awoken by Chastity, who came in softly carrying a tea tray. She set the tray on the dresser and drew back the curtains at the long windows. Gray light entered the room. "Oh, dear," Constance said. "Not a pretty day for a wedding."

"No, but it's not raining." Chastity poured tea and brought it over to the bed. "You slept late."

"I worked late." Constance sat up and took the tea with a grateful smile. "Just what I need, Chas."

Chastity sat on the edge of the bed with her own cup.

"Prue's taken your article to the printer, then she's going to the florist to choose the flowers. We thought a red rose for Henry's buttonhole and we'll all wear white ones. Then we thought a small bouquet of pink roses and maybe lilies of the valley for Amelia. Whatever looks fresh and pretty. Prue is good at flowers."

"Do we know what Amelia's wearing?"

"It has to be black."

"Black?" Constance raised her eyebrows. "Why, pray tell?"

Chastity grinned. "Amelia wrote to say that she'd managed to get an extra hour off this evening... nice of Letitia, wasn't it?"

"Charming," Constance agreed. "What convinced her to be so generous? A dying mother?"

"Almost," Chastity said. "The funeral of a dearly beloved aunt."

"Hence the black." Constance laughed but without much humor. "At least any color flower will go with that." She held out her cup for a refill. "The ceremony's at four?"

"Four-thirty, to give Amelia time to get there, since she can't leave the Grahams until four. Prue and I will bring Henry. We thought you should escort Amelia, since you're sisters under the suffrage flag." Chastity's smile was a little teasing. "You'd be the most suitable maid of honor. We'll play groomsmen."

Constance frowned slightly. "I feel bad that you're doing all the heavy lifting with Henry."

"Oh, don't give it a second thought." Chastity stood up. "Prue and I have Henry down to a fine art. You'll wait for Amelia outside the Grahams' when she gets off at four and escort her to Caxton Hall. Then we'll go to

Claridges for a celebration tea afterwards. We booked a private room, so there'll be no danger of running into anyone. It would be a little awkward if we bumped into Letitia, or Max, wouldn't it?"

"Extremely," Constance agreed dryly.

Chastity continued, "After that they'll have a couple of hours to . . . to . . ."

"Consummate their union," Constance finished for her. "Where are they going to do that?"

"Henry found a little residential hotel on the Bayswater Road. Quite cheap, but he says it's clean and respectable. He's going to move there until he can find lodgings. Apparently Max gave him an advance on his salary to help him get set up."

At the mention of Max's name Constance's expression grew somber. "Well, at least he can be generous," she conceded.

Chastity said only, "I'll leave you to get up, then."

Constance tossed aside the covers. "I'll be down in half an hour." Chastity nodded and left with the tea tray.

Constance examined the contents of her wardrobe, her expression abstracted. She needed something suitable for a registry-office wedding and a subdued celebration. Finally she chose a suit of pale gray shantung with a deep green silk blouse. She plaited her hair and looped it into a chignon at the nape of her neck, then went downstairs. She was midway down the stairs when she heard Max's voice coming from the open doors of the drawing room.

She stopped dead, her hand on the banister, one foot raised for the next step down. Prue was saying in conspiratorial tones, "Oh, I'm so sorry, Max, but Con's not feeling too well this morning. A touch of stomach ache, you know."

"Yes, and a headache," Chastity chimed in. "It's so trying," she added with a heavy sigh. "And poor Con seems to suffer more than any of us."

"I see." He coughed and Constance grinned to herself. He sounded distinctly discomfited at this confidence.

"She was not too well last night," he continued with another little cough. "I thought perhaps it was... well... I do understand." Despite her delight in his obvious embarrassment, his voice, rich and mellow, sent the usual prickles up her spine. Lust, it seemed, was invincible, resistant even to treachery.

"Do give her my best regards," Max said, his voice coming closer as he moved to the door. Constance hastily stepped up the stairs, out of sight of the hall. "I'll call tomorrow, when I hope she'll be feeling better."

"Oh, I would leave it for several days," Chastity advised. "At these times, Con's often not comfortable leaving the house for a while."

Constance choked on her laughter. Chastity was rarely outrageous but when she chose to be, no one could better her. She could almost feel sorry for Max, whose footsteps receded rapidly across the hall and out of the door opened by an impassive Jenkins.

"Chas!" Constance exclaimed, hurrying down the stairs. "That was not in the least subtle."

"It wasn't intended to be," her sister said with a touch of defiance. "He deserved it."

"At least it ensured he won't be ringing the doorbell for a couple of days," Prudence said. "Are you going to have a late breakfast, or wait for an early lunch?"

"Oh, I'll wait. I'm not particularly hungry. I want to

show you my article and we'll decide where to run it. It'll mean rearranging the layout since it's rather a long piece."

"In that case, I'll bring coffee to the parlor, Miss Con," Jenkins announced from the middle of the hall, where he'd been listening and drawing his own conclusions.

"Oh, yes, please, Jenkins. And if Mrs. Hudson has made some of those little coconut cakes, could we have some of those too?" Chastity said over her shoulder as she ran up the stairs.

"I'll see what there is, Miss Chas." Jenkins hesitated, then said, "Am I to assume that Mr. Ensor is no longer welcome, Miss Con?"

Constance paused, then said, "No, Jenkins, for the moment he's perfectly welcome. In a few days I guarantee he won't darken our doors again."

Jenkins allowed himself the merest lift of an eyebrow. "I see." He went off into the back regions of the house.

At three-thirty Constance left the house and took the omnibus to Park Lane. She walked to the Grahams' house on Albermarle Street and strolled casually along the opposite side of the street, hoping that Amelia would emerge before someone in a neighboring house noticed the lady carrying a bridal bouquet who seemed to have nothing better to do on an overcast afternoon than walk up and down the street.

Punctually at four o'clock Amelia, clad in black and heavily veiled, appeared from the side entrance to the house. She paused for a moment, looked up and down the street, saw Constance, and without acknowledgment hurried towards Park Lane. Constance followed.

On the relative anonymity of Park Lane, Amelia stopped and Constance came up beside her. Again they didn't acknowledge each other. Constance hailed a hackney. "Caxton Hall," she said as she climbed in. Amelia followed her.

Once in the seclusion of the cab's dim interior Amelia put back her veil. "My heart's fluttering like a bird's," she said. "I can't quite believe it's really going to happen."

"Believe it." Constance took her hand and squeezed tightly. "Henry will not fail and neither will my sisters."

At that, Amelia gave a weak smile. "Poor Henry. Subject to this monstrous regimen of women."

"Better that than his tyrannical father."

"True enough." Amelia leaned back against the squabs. "I never imagined going to my wedding in funereal black . . . but then," she added with a tiny laugh, "I never imagined going to my wedding at all."

Constance handed her the bouquet. "Maybe this will put you in a bridal frame of mind."

Amelia took the flowers and inhaled their delicate scent. "You and your sisters seem to think of everything. I can't tell you how grateful I am."

"There's no need for gratitude," Constance said easily. "Just think that in an hour you will be a married woman." She smiled encouragingly at Amelia, who was very pale. "And in about seven months you'll give birth to a perfectly legitimate seven-month child. Henry will be a successful private secretary to a Member of Parliament, and you'll take the babe to visit his grandfather, and Justice Franklin will embrace his grandchild and accept his daughter-in-law and take his son back into the fold."

Amelia turned her head against the squabs to look at Constance. "Are you the optimist you make yourself out to be?"

"Where men are concerned?" Constance asked after an instant's deliberation. "No, Amelia."

"That's rather what I thought," Amelia said. "Neither am I."

"But this will turn out all right," Constance stated.

Amelia smiled again. "Yes," she said. "I know it will. I don't place much faith in Henry's father, but Henry will stand true."

"With you behind him."

"Yes," she said with a laugh. "With me behind him."

The hackney drew up outside the imposing edifice of Caxton Hall. Constance paid the hackney and took Amelia's arm. "Ready?"

Amelia nodded and dropped her veil. "I suppose they're used to this hole-in-the-corner business in a registry office."

"Don't think like that," Constance chided. "This is perfectly legal and it doesn't matter what anyone thinks. Let's go inside." She strode towards the double doors, her arm firmly tucked into the bride's.

Henry was waiting in the foyer with Prudence and Chastity. If anything, he looked paler than Amelia. He kept one hand in his breast pocket, clasping both the marriage license and the wedding ring. His free hand he gave to his bride as she reached him.

"Is all well, dearest?" he asked in a low voice in which a distinct tremor could be heard.

"Yes, perfectly well." Amelia put back her veil and smiled at him. "You're very brave, Henry."

He shook his head vigorously. "No, dearest, you are the brave one."

"I think you're both very brave," Prudence declared before this exchange of denials could continue into the evening. "Now that we're all here we can go into the anteroom." She led the way across the galleried foyer, towards a door at the rear. Henry and Amelia followed, with Chastity and Constance close behind.

The registrar's clerk greeted their arrival with a pointed look at the clock. It said four twenty-five. He made elaborate play of looking into an appointment book. "Mr. Franklin and Miss Westcott?"

"Yes," Henry said. He cleared his throat. "I am Mr. Franklin and this is my . . . my . . . Miss Westcott." He stepped forward, holding Amelia's hand tightly in his.

The clerk looked askance at Amelia's funereal garb then looked again at the clock. He neither spoke nor moved until the hands touched the half hour, then he rose, gathered up a file folder, and disappeared through another door.

"Friendly fellow," Prudence observed.

"He just likes the power," Constance responded acidly. "Petty bureaucrats are all the same."

"Both sexes," Prudence said with a half smile.

Constance shrugged. "Probably, but there aren't that many women in positions of power, however petty."

"Yes, Con," Chastity agreed with an exaggerated sigh that made them all laugh. Henry and Amelia hadn't taken their eyes off the door through which the clerk had disappeared, and when he returned still clutching his book they simultaneously straightened their shoulders.

"The registrar is ready for you," the clerk intoned. "If you would give me the license." He held out his hand.

Henry relinquished the paper and they followed the clerk into a pleasant paneled room that was nowhere near as institutional as Constance and her sisters had feared it would be. There was even a vase of daisies on the marble mantlepiece. The registrar nodded at the little party and took the license from his clerk. He showed little expression in either voice or countenance as he went through the simple businesslike ceremony.

Henry and Amelia made their responses with conviction; indeed, it seemed to Constance that Henry grew taller and more assured with each declaration. When he slipped the ring on Amelia's finger his hands were perfectly steady; the bride's trembled. The registrar stamped the document with his official seal and Mr. and Mrs. Franklin exchanged a kiss.

"Congratulations." The registrar shook both their hands and smiled a courteous dismissal. The Duncan sisters exchanged smiles of relief.

"And now," Chastity said when they were all once more in the street, "we eat cake. I ordered a beautiful gâteau at Claridges."

"And champagne," Constance said. "Tea seems a little pedestrian for a wedding feast."

The newlyweds didn't appear to be taking much in. They both seemed stunned as they stood hand in hand on the pavement.

"Two cabs, I think," Prudence said with a significant glance at her sisters. Constance nodded and stepped to the curb. She put two fingers to her mouth and produced a most unladylike whistle that had instant success. They urged Amelia and Henry into one cab and Constance told the cabby to deposit them at Claridges. She closed the door on them and brushed off her hands with a gesture of satisfaction. "That'll give them ten minutes of privacy."

It was a privacy they clearly put to good use. Amelia emerged from the seclusion of the cab looking rather flushed and rumpled, her hair escaping its pins. Henry had an air of complacent satisfaction and he kept a possessive arm around Amelia's shoulders.

Prudence slipped into the hotel ahead of the rest of the party, and when they joined her in the foyer, a footman stood ready to escort them to a small private room.

"You're such a sentimental Scrooge, sister dearest," Constance murmured affectionately, taking in the table set with cake and champagne. "I wish I'd thought of this."

"It only takes one of us to do this," Prudence said in the same low tone. "You've fixed up Henry with a job. They can take it from here."

Constance nodded, reflecting that that minor deception would have meant very little if she and Max still had the possibility of remaining friends. It felt rather different now.

Chapter 17

Henry was sorting the mail when Max entered his office at home early one morning several days later. "Anything of interest, Henry?" He tossed his newspaper onto the windowsill.

"Mostly bills, sir. A couple of letters from constituents." Henry indicated the neat pile of opened mail on the desk.

"You're here bright and early," Max remarked, standing at the window looking out onto the street, where a few pedestrians battled heads-down against a strong gusty wind that was sending hats tumbling into the road.

"I was wondering, sir, if I could start an hour early every morning and leave at half-past three on Thursdays," Henry asked timidly, a flush blooming on his cheeks.

Max turned from the window. "Do you have something special to do on Thursday afternoons?" he inquired in a friendly fashion.

"Well, yes, sir, as it happens."

Max smiled. "Why do I think it must have something to do with a young lady?"

Henry's blush deepened. "As it happens, sir . . ."

Max laughed. "I see no difficulties, Henry."

"Thank you, Mr. Ensor." Henry went back to work with his paper knife.

Max picked up the already opened mail and flicked through it. He was feeling restless, dissatisfied in some way, although he couldn't put his finger on the cause. Unless, of course, it was because he hadn't seen hide nor hair of Constance for days.

"You did make sure those flowers were delivered to Miss Duncan at Manchester Square yesterday?" he asked.

"Yes, of course, Mr. Ensor. The florist promised they would be delivered by four o'clock. In fact, I believe this is a letter from Miss Duncan." Henry proffered a slim white envelope emblazoned with the Duncan crest.

Max took it, trying not to betray his eagerness. He recognized her writing, a bold but elegant flowing script that matched the writer. He slit the envelope and unfolded the thick sheet of vellum. The message was disappointingly short.

> *Dear Max,*
>
> *What lovely flowers. Thank you so much for the kind thought. I had wanted to thank you in person for such a lovely evening at the House of Commons but I was a little under the weather when you called the next morning. Please forgive my negligence and accept my thanks now.*
>
> > *In haste,*
> > *Constance.*

Max read and reread the short note. It had no perceptible warmth in it and contained not even a hint of a future meeting. It didn't make any sense. And why the haste? He crumpled the vellum and tossed it into the wastepaper basket. Of course, it was always possible she was rather busy. Putting out that broadsheet every fortnight must take up a lot of her time. He frowned in thought, trying to remember the date on the mockup that he'd seen in the parlor. He couldn't remember it exactly but it had to be around now. Maybe the Duncan sisters had been taken up with their editorial activities.

"Henry, I'd like you to go in search of the latest edition of a publication called *The Mayfair Lady.*"

"I don't believe I've heard of it, sir." Henry raised inquiring eyebrows.

"No, it has a relatively small circulation, I believe. You might have to try several newsagents. I would think you might find a copy around Parliament Square somewhere. It has a certain political thrust to it and I would imagine its editors would try to place it prominently with Westminster vendors."

"Very well, sir. I'll go right away." Henry took up his hat.

Max sat down at his desk to begin tackling his constituency mail but after a minute his hands fell idle and he stared frowning at the window. A light scatter of raindrops hit the glass. Perhaps he should simply pay a morning call at Manchester Square. He realized that a few days ago he wouldn't have thought twice about such a visit. It was perfectly natural, a perfectly acceptable thing to do on a Saturday morning. She would either be there or she wouldn't. And yet something indefinable held him back. Unease, a nameless unidentifiable sense of trouble, kept him sitting at his desk staring out at the stormy morning.

What could possibly be wrong? Had something happened to her? Some family trouble? With her father perhaps? Or one of her sisters? If so, then he must go to her. But she hadn't asked for his help, or his comfort, or anything else that he might usefully have to offer if something was wrong. And surely they were close enough for her to turn to him. When it came to making mischief with her father's car she hadn't hesitated to co-opt him. Perhaps, he thought, she was so taken up with the WSPU at the moment that she had no time for anything else. That would not be surprising. She had described her involvement there as the driving force of her existence.

He stood up abruptly. It was a ridiculous business. She had to be exaggerating the passion of her involvement. She was an intelligent, reasonable woman, not some wild fanatic. Somehow he would have to get her to see reason, to step back from the whole enterprise. She was entitled to her opinions, he would never dispute that, but he couldn't possibly have a wife who was an active suffragist. God knows what it would do to his career.

Max dropped his pen to the desk and ink spattered across the blotter. He had just silently given words to something he hadn't realized he had been contemplating. But, of course, in the deepest recesses of his mind it had been there for weeks now. She had fascinated him from the very first moment he had met her. And little by little that fascination had become the all-powerful need to have and to hold her, to claim her for his own, now and forever.

He was not given to fanciful turns of phrase and he found himself absurdly trying to hide an embarrassed smile from the deserted room. He told himself that she would make him the most unrestful wife. But then there was the reverse side of the coin. Excitement. She exhilarated him and excited him, even as she challenged him. But she was an impossible wife for a career politician.

Which left him precisely where?

He heard the front door close, the sound of Henry shaking an umbrella in the hall, his quick step. "Just started raining cats and dogs, Mr. Ensor," Henry observed as he came in. "But I found the paper. Yesterday's date, so it's the latest edition." He took the folded broadsheet from inside his coat. "I don't think it's wet." He handed it to his employer. "The newsagent said it was selling like hotcakes."

Max nodded absently as he scanned the headlines. He noticed that the list of contents now included information on upcoming WSPU meetings, to be found on the back page. There was the usual black box: **Will the government give votes to women taxpayers?** Then his gaze was riveted by the headline to the article immediately underneath.

The Government resorts to spying

Shame on Sir Henry Campbell-Bannerman and his Cabinet. It has come to our notice that a certain Right Honorable Gentleman has undertaken to supply the government with information about the plans of the WSPU by posing as a friend to the Union. A secret informer. Is the Union so threatening to the entrenched ranks of our government that

they must resort to such underhanded trickery to get the better of it? Are women so threatening? Can they not be faced in the open? What does this say about the moral courage of our government? Must we conclude that women frighten them so much they can't possibly face giving them even the simple power of the vote? The Right Honorable Gentleman, who, one has to say hardly deserves the title, has weaseled his way into the confidence of members of the Union with false statements of interest and friendship, only to betray them. One wonders how his constituency, the urban center of S——wold, will view such behavior in the man they have so recently elected to represent their interests in Parliament. It is hardly the behavior of an honorable man. Or an honest man. Or a courageous man. The Right Honorable Gentleman, eagerly embracing the dishonorable trade of a spy, is no more than the Prime Minister's cat's paw.

There was more of the same but Max barely took it in, although his eyes followed the print. His anger surged in a great crimson wave and he was unaware that he had lost all color, his complexion ghastly, a gray shade around his mouth that had thinned so as to be almost invisible.

"Is everything all right, Mr. Ensor?" Henry stared at him, unable to conceal his shock at this abrupt transformation. "You don't look well."

Max looked up from the paper. His blue eyes pierced Henry like sharpened icicles and the secretary took an involuntary step back. "I am quite well, thank you, Henry." Max folded the broadsheet and tucked it in the inside pocket of his waistcoat. His voice sounded unfamiliar to Henry. It was curiously clipped and had quite lost its mellow tones. "I am going out. I don't know when I shall be back. I would be glad if you would answer this correspondence for me. I'm sure you'll know exactly what to write. Leave the letters on the desk for my signature."

"Certainly, sir," Henry said to Max's fast-disappearing back. The door closed with a soft click that was somehow more menacing than a slam. Henry scratched his head, wondering what it was in *The Mayfair Lady* that had so incensed his employer.

Max went upstairs for his waterproof driving coat, his vizored cap, and goggles. He moved like an automaton along the current of his fury. It was all clear to him now. Her sudden withdrawal that evening, her avoidance of him since. Constance must have overheard his conversation with the Prime Minister in the House of Commons after dinner last Wednesday. He couldn't recollect the exact words that had been spoken but he could imagine how the gist would have sounded to that particular eavesdropper. And she'd been preparing her revenge ever since.

Below the level of his rage ran the acknowledgment that she was entitled to her own anger at what she would have perceived as deception. But why didn't she simply come out with it, confront him? Any man would have done so. Instead she chose to attack him in such a fashion . . . to hold him up to the scorn and mockery of his friends and colleagues. Such an embarrassment could ruin him. It was unendurable. *And by God, she was going to pay for it.*

He was halfway down the stairs, buttoning his coat,

when the doorbell pealed. The male half of the couple he'd recently employed to run the house for him emerged from the back regions and went to the door.

"Is Mr. Ensor in?"

It was Asquith's voice. Max felt his jaw clench, his nostrils flare. So it had begun already. He stepped into the hall. "Thank you, Billings, I'll look after Mr. Asquith."

The manservant moved away from the door. "Very well, sir."

The Chancellor entered the hall, shaking rain off his tall beaver hat. "Ah, Ensor, do you have a minute?"

Max nodded and gestured to the morning room. "You've seen *The Mayfair Lady,* I assume?"

"It arrived with my breakfast. My secretary found it in the newsagent's on his way in. What's to be done about it? Scurrilous rag!" Asquith declared as he entered the room. "Who's responsible, that's what I'd like to know. I'll have 'em jailed for libel."

"Except that it's not," Max observed dryly. "Coffee, or something stronger?"

"Nothing, thank you. What d'you mean it's not libel?" Asquith brushed the brim of his hat with a rough sweep, sending raindrops flying across the room.

"I certainly had the intention of using any inside knowledge I gained to keep the government informed." Distantly Max wondered whether he was losing his mind. He was going to wring her neck...tear her limb from limb...boil her in oil. And yet it sounded as if he was defending her.

"But this!" Asquith pulled the broadsheet from his pocket and waved it disgustedly at Max. "What kind of cowardly attack is this?"

Max merely raised an eyebrow. He forced himself to put his anger aside for the moment. He would only survive Society's malicious gossip and the inevitable—if veiled—pleasure his peers would naturally take in his discomfiture by appearing detached and relatively indifferent. He had to treat the matter in public as one not deserving of attention or even a hint of annoyance.

In private it would be a different matter. "It'll blow over," he said.

Asquith gave him a shrewd look. "It implicates the government in something shady. The Prime Minister's not too happy."

"No, I don't suppose he is." Max perched on the arm of the sofa. He shrugged. "It's a scurrilous piece with no proof offered. No one really takes any notice of these termagants. They just don't realize it yet." Even as he said this he felt a pang of conscience. Constance and her friends were too intelligent, too passionate, too committed to a basically selfless cause to be dismissed with such contempt. But she deserved it, he told himself. She had thrown down the gauntlet and had no right to object to the manner in which he chose to pick it up. He would meet public mockery with its like.

Asquith was still regarding him closely. "I suppose you have no idea who's behind it? Seems likely it's someone who knows you."

"Someone with a grudge," Max said. "Politics is a world that harbors grudges, Asquith. And whoever's responsible for this broadsheet clearly enjoys exploiting them."

"I suppose so." Asquith looked at the broadsheet in his hand with a puzzled frown. "Not the first time you've been mentioned in it."

"No," Max agreed without expansion.

Asquith gave him another look. "Not a case of hell hath no fury, is it?"

Max gave a short laugh. "No," he declared with finality. Constance could not complain of being scorned by her lover. The deception that had produced such a savage attack had had nothing to do with the glories of their shared lust . . . their deepening emotional intimacy. It wasn't directed at Constance personally . . . unlike the fiercely personal nature of her revenge.

His mouth tightened again. He stood up abruptly. "If you'll excuse me I've some business to attend to. I'll wait upon the Prime Minister this afternoon if he wishes it. But there's little I can offer in the way of explanation." *Or excuse*. But he kept the addendum to himself.

"Of course . . . of course. I'm sure the Prime Minister will understand. Such things happen in public life. We all know it." Asquith nodded with a vigor that was not quite convincing. "Best let it just blow over, as you say."

Max nodded and accompanied his visitor outside onto the wet street. "I'm going to the mews for my motor. Can I drop you somewhere?"

"No, thank you, I'll take a cab to Downing Street. It's no distance." Asquith extended his hand. "We have to deny this rumor, of course."

It seemed that the Chancellor had finally come to the point, Max reflected as they shook hands. He had been sent with the message that it was Max's responsibility to ensure that the rumor caused Downing Street no embarrassment.

"Of course," he said. "But I wonder whether by denying it we give it credence?"

The Chancellor coughed into the gloved hand now returned to him. "The PM thought that perhaps you could discredit it. Imply a personal grudge...that kind of thing, don't you know?"

Max felt his anger return in full flood. She had put him in the most impossible position. To attack the anonymous editors of *The Mayfair Lady* would make him look a fool, tilting at windmills. To expose Constance and her sisters as the editors, to so much as hint at his relationship with Constance, was out of the question. Unimaginable.

But the Honorable Misses Duncan were going to bear the full brunt of his outrage. And Constance was going to write a retraction.

"Assure the Prime Minister, if you will, that I have the situation in hand."

"Of course." Asquith was all acquiescent courtesy. A gentleman's word was his bond and a gentleman didn't question its ramifications.

They nodded, exchanged smiles, and parted company. Max strode to the mews, where his Darracq was garaged. He put up the canvas roof, reflecting that its open sides would give him little protection from the rain, but it was better than nothing. Within ten minutes he was driving to Manchester Square, swiping the rain off his goggles every few seconds.

He parked the car in the square and mounted the steps to the front door of the Duncan mansion, his urgency belied by his measured pace. He pressed the bell, resisting the impulse to keep his finger on it. It was opened in Jenkins's customarily stately fashion.

"Mr. Ensor, how nice to see you," the butler declared without cracking a smile. "Miss Duncan is not at home, I fear."

"I see." Max put a foot in the door. "Miss Prudence, or Miss Chastity, perhaps?"

"They are at home, sir. But I don't know if they're receiving visitors."

Max reflected. He didn't want a showdown with Constance's sisters. It would be a pointless waste of energy. "Do you happen to know where I might find Miss Duncan, Jenkins?" he inquired mildly.

"Not offhand, sir. I expect she will be home this afternoon."

Max felt the crackle of the broadsheet inside his waistcoat. It was Saturday. There was bound to be a meeting of the WSPU at lunchtime when shop workers would be beginning the half holiday that started the weekend. Constance was probably in attendance. What better place to confront her?

"Thank you, Jenkins. I'll call again later." He smiled a benign smile and ran lightly down the steps to his car as if he had not a care in the world. He cranked the engine, getting soaked in the process, and then under the inadequate shelter of the car's canopy he examined the back page of the broadsheet. There was a meeting at noon in a church hall on Brompton Road. He put the car in gear and headed for Knightsbridge.

Jenkins waited until the visitor had driven off before he closed the door. The sisters had not confided in him, which was in itself unusual, but he knew that something was amiss, and that it had everything to do with Miss Con and Mr. Ensor. He went upstairs to the parlor.

"Mr. Ensor was here inquiring after Miss Con," he declared from the doorway.

Prudence looked up from the ledgers she was balancing. "Did he say why, Jenkins?"

"No, Miss Prue."

"Did you tell him where she was?" Chastity asked from the depths of a sewing basket where she was selecting stockings that needed darning.

"No, Miss Chas."

"Well, that's all right, then." Chastity smiled at him.

"May I inquire as to the problem?" Jenkins asked.

Chastity wrinkled her brow. "I think Con had better tell you. It's not really our business."

Jenkins bowed. "I understand, Miss Chas." He left them to their darning and their bookkeeping, understanding perfectly.

"Are you sure you're ready to do this, Constance?" Emmeline asked as they stacked papers on the table beside the door to the church hall.

"Yes, it's time I was blooded," Constance said with a grim, tight smile. She was going to make her maiden speech at today's meeting.

"This resolution has nothing I suppose to do with that extraordinary revelation in *The Mayfair Lady*?" Emmeline inquired with a shrewd look. "I assume you've seen it. Everyone else seems to have done."

"I saw it," Constance said shortly. "And I blame myself. I introduced the man, after all. I don't know how I was so blind."

"But who *did* know what he was up to?" Emmeline wondered. "It's intriguing you must admit."

"Very," Constance agreed.

"We're blithely assuming it's true," the other woman mused. "There was no hard evidence presented, though."

Constance glanced at her. "I don't doubt it."

"No, well, you know him better than I do."

"I thought I did."

Emmeline nodded and left it at that. "There might be press here this morning to hear your speech," she warned. "Are you ready for the publicity?"

"I'm ready to stand up and be counted," Constance responded. "My father will be quite apoplectic, but he'll get over it."

"And your friends?"

"If they're my friends they'll stand by me. If they're not it's no loss." She sounded much more nonchalant than she felt. Her anxiety stemmed not from the prospect of speaking in public and making her affiliation known to the world, but at the possibility that someone might link her with *The Mayfair Lady*. But her sisters were resigned to that chance, accepting that it was time for Constance to declare herself. If there were rumors and whispers, then they would face them down with placid denial.

Constance went up to the platform to check her notes. People were beginning to trickle into the hall, shaking umbrellas, discarding wet hats and coats. The smell of damp wool was in the air. She wondered if the rain would keep people away. She wondered if Max had yet seen *The Mayfair Lady*. Apprehension niggled. What would he do? He would have to do something. Another man maybe would let it go, but not Max. And mingling with apprehension was the uncomfortable thought that perhaps she had gone too far. It was such a personal attack. Her sisters had said nothing about the piece, although she assumed they had read it before Prue took it to the printer. Their silence she felt was eloquent.

In all honesty Constance admitted to herself that the

virulently personal tone of her revenge stemmed from her own hurt and sense of betrayal. It was not a well-thought out response. There was nothing balanced about it. And even though she felt it was justified, she couldn't control her uneasy anticipation of his response. Or the recognition that he was entitled to come at her with the same teeth she had used on him.

She looked up from the notes in her hand as the other leaders joined her on the platform. The hall was two-thirds full, expectant faces raised to the dais. The door-keeper was just closing the door when Max Ensor walked in.

Constance froze.

Max looked straight at her as she stood behind the table on the dais. For a moment she was aware only of his eyes. They were like twinned blue sheets of fire and she had to resist the instinct to draw back from the scorching heat of his anger, the blistering power of his determination.

Clearly he *had* read the new edition of *The Mayfair Lady*. And clearly, as she had suspected, he had seen the mock-up of the broadsheet that evening of sabotage and put two and two together.

But then her own anger returned fresh and raw to banish the tremor of alarm at the sight of him. *How dare he come here now? What was he intending to learn this morning? Did he really imagine he would be permitted to stay now that his deceit had been exposed?*

She glanced down at her hands. To her surprise they were quite steady. She spoke, her voice carrying across the heads in the body of the hall, and the slight buzz of conversation died.

"This is a meeting for supporters of the WSPU, Mr.

Ensor. We do not welcome spies. I must ask you to leave."

Max had not expected this. The sheer brazen effrontery of her head-on attack took his breath away. He took a step towards the dais.

"I should warn you, sir, that if you do not leave of your own free will then there are plenty of people here to help you on your way. What as women we may lack in physical prowess we make up for in numbers." Stinging irony edged her voice. "I can imagine the national press would find it a most interesting story."

There was dead silence in the hall. No one seemed to breathe for a minute. All eyes swiveled to the man standing at the back of the hall, gloves in hand, driving goggles pushed up on top of his rain-soaked cap.

Max could barely credit what he was hearing, but he wasn't going to put her sincerity to the test. He had no choice but to accept an ignominious defeat and retreat.

"We will have an accounting, Miss Duncan. Make no mistake." He didn't raise his voice but every word was as clear as if he'd used a megaphone. He turned on his heel and walked from the hall, letting the door slam behind him.

And now Constance's hands shook so hard that the notes she was holding fell to the table. She concentrated on putting the scattered sheets together, keeping her eyes down, aware that she was the focus of everyone's attention both in the hall and on the dais.

"You didn't expect that, I gather," Emmeline murmured, helping to scoop up the papers as Christobel broke the momentary hush by reading the minutes of the last meeting.

"I didn't expect him to come here," Constance returned in a low voice. "He must have suspected that a lot of the people who would come to a WSPU meeting would have read the article. *The Mayfair Lady* is known as a pro-suffragist publication."

"Perhaps he wanted to defend himself," the other woman observed.

"This is not the forum for it," Constance said with a snap. She knew she had overreacted and her anger now was directed only at herself. "You wouldn't have tolerated his presence, surely?" She heard the defensive thrust to the question.

Emmeline shook her head. "I don't know." She hesitated, then said, "It doesn't do our cause much good to make enemies in high places, Constance."

"He was an enemy already," Constance said. She felt a flash of empathy for Christobel's impatience with her mother's softly-softly approach. She glanced at Christobel who raised her eyebrows interrogatively. Constance nodded. She was as ready as she would ever be. Christobel took her seat as Constance moved to the podium.

Chapter 18

Max sat behind the wheel of his motor as the rain drummed on the canvas roof. It took five minutes to clear his head. Of all the lunatic impulses! To put his head in the lion's mouth like that. It would simply feed straight into the rumor mill and add yet more titillating detail to the article in *The Mayfair Lady,* which would be on every tongue by the end of the day. It was bound to reach Fleet Street by some route or another, and if there had been any members of the press in the hall they were going to have a field day. He had been blinded by his own fury, his desire to exact vengeance on that arrogant, insulting, impossible woman. How had he ever thought he could make her his wife? Madness . . . sheer madness.

But he had to concentrate on damage control. Raging at Constance wasn't going to help at the moment. When he got his hands on her, then he would have an accounting, but for the moment he had to think clearly.

He cranked up the engine, climbed in, and drove back to Manchester Square, where he parked on the far side of the square garden from the Duncan house. A massive oak tree in full leaf offered sufficient cover if anyone cast a casual glance around the square, but he was perfectly positioned to observe any comings and goings at No. 10.

He saw Lord Duncan leave in the family carriage soon after one o'clock and it was close to two o'clock before a hackney cab delivered Constance to her door. By that time his already vile temper was incendiary. It had stopped raining finally but his waterproof driving coat was still soaked through, and rain dripped from the sodden canvas hood above his head, unerringly finding a path inside his collar and down his back.

He got out and walked across the garden, heedless of the effect of puddles and wet grass on his once-shiny shoes. He mounted the steps to the front door and pressed the bell, this time keeping his finger on it until the door was opened.

"Mr. Ensor." Jenkins looked at him askance, at the finger still resting on the bell.

"I saw Miss Duncan come in a few minutes ago," Max said brusquely, pushing past the butler into the hall. "Where is she?"

"She's at luncheon, sir." Jenkins's eyes darted involuntarily towards the door to the small family dining room, where the ladies ate when they were alone.

"Then she won't mind being disturbed." Max gave him a nod and strode to the door. Jenkins, for once disconcerted, scurried behind him murmuring protestations.

Max flung open the door and stood there in the doorway. The three sisters stared at him, for the moment too taken aback by the abrupt nature of his arrival to react. "Constance, I want to talk to you," he stated. "You two, leave us alone, if you please."

"We're having luncheon," Prudence protested. "You can't throw us out of our own dining room."

"Actually, Prudence, I both can and will. Now, you and Chastity, *out*, please." The " 'please' " did nothing to soften the command.

Constance stood up. "There's no need to disturb my sisters. We'll go into the drawing room. There's no one there." She swept past him without an upward glance. It seemed to her that he was radiating so much heat, he was too hot to touch. Her heart pounded uncomfortably and her palms were suddenly clammy. She didn't look at her sisters either, knowing that if they guessed at her sick turmoil they would insist on standing behind her.

Max followed her, leaving Jenkins to close the dining room door.

"Blood is going to flow." Prudence half rose from her chair and then sat down again. "But I think we'll be surplus to requirements."

"We'll mop up later," Chastity said with what her sister considered remarkable composure. She smiled at Prudence. "Don't worry, Prue. This has to happen if Max and Con are ever going to accept that they love each other."

"Last week I might have agreed with you," Prudence said. "But I can't help thinking things have gone too far. Con actually threatened to throw him physically out of a meeting. In *public*. It's all totally out of hand now."

"Oh, I wouldn't be so pessimistic." Chastity sliced lemon meringue pie. "They're both extreme, passionate people, they're going to loathe each other as much as they love each other. It'll always be like that. Let's just hope they don't break too many plates, at least not of the heirloom variety."

"You are so sanguine." Prudence shook her head and helped herself to pie.

There was silence in the drawing room as the two faced each other. Constance had walked swiftly and without thought to the spot where she felt most comfortable, with her back to the fireplace. Max remained by the door for the moment, his back against it, as if to hold it against intruders.

"If you'd like to start with an apology, I'm listening," he said after a minute, amazed at the mildness of his tone. It bore no relation to the state of his temper.

"Oh, live your fantasy," Constance exclaimed. "You want *me* to apologize. What for? I merely exposed you for what you are. A trickster, a spy, a dishonest—"

"Enough," he declared, his voice rising a notch as he came across the room towards her. "I have had enough of your insults, Miss Duncan. One more and I won't answer for the consequences."

"Oh, typical male response," Constance scoffed. "Threats of violence are always the answer." She sounded braver than she felt. He seemed to have grown somehow taller and broader in the last few minutes.

Max inhaled sharply. He was not going to play that game, but he was prepared to match her when it came to wrestling in the mud. He turned aside and sat down on the arm of the sofa, idly slapping his gloves into the palm of one hand. "You will apologize, Constance, and you will write a retraction for the next edition of that broadsheet," he stated. "If you do not, somehow it will become common knowledge that you and your sisters are behind *The Mayfair Lady.*"

"You would *do* that?" She stared at him.

"If you make it necessary. Just bear in mind that you fired the first salvo."

"Because you *used* me," she said, soft and fierce. "You pretended to like me . . . to share things with me, and all along you were merely interested in using me as a way into the secrets and plans of the Union. I *heard* you. I heard what you said to the Prime Minister. 'I've seen these women in action. I have an ear to the ground.'"

Max winced, remembering. But he wasn't going to allow her the high ground. "Just one minute, I did not pretend—"

"No, *you* wait just one minute," she interrupted. "Deny it if you can. Deny that you said those things."

"You're taking them out of context."

Constance laughed. "Oh, a typical politician's defense. Whenever you're caught, the old excuse is trotted out: *taken out of context.*" She mimicked his tone. "What was the context, Max? A quiet collegiate postprandial conversation in the bastion of male power. I heard what I heard."

Her voice rose as she saw that she had him on the run. "You deceived me, pretending to . . . Oh, I can't talk to you. I can't bear to be in the same room with you." She made a brusque, dismissive gesture, turning her head aside as she tried to control the choke in her voice, to force back the tears that were both angry and hurt. She would not show him any weakness.

But he heard it anyway and came back at her. "And weren't you intending to use me in the same way? To get me to use my political influence to advance your cause. Wasn't that behind your initial interest in me?"

"That's not the same thing at all."

"Isn't it? You mean I'm fair game and you are not?" He was incredulous. "Come on, Constance. You insist women are men's equals, so why do you demand special treatment?"

"I'm not," she declared. "That's a thoroughly spurious argument and you know it. I didn't attack you personally, manipulate you, pretend to feel something . . . anything . . . just to gain information that I could use against you."

"And what do you consider this?" He pulled the sodden paper that had once been the broadsheet from inside his coat. "This is the most blatant, underhanded, utterly personal attack . . . far far worse than anything I intended. It's designed to ruin my career. Can you live with that, Constance, while you prate your high principles and moral convictions?" He threw the paper to the carpet at his feet.

"How *dare* you deny what you intended? How *could* you lie? I heard you . . . I heard what you said to your Cabinet friends. You were going to use our . . ." She waved an all-encompassing hand. "Whatever you want to call what I stupidly thought was between us, simply to advance your career. You can't deny that."

"I can deny that I meant you any—" The rest of his sentence was drowned in a cascade of water as Constance, enraged beyond thought or reason, took advantage of his seated position, picked up a round bowl of sweet peas, and tipped it over his head. Water and fragrant, vividly colored flowers dripped from his head, clung to his shoulders, fell into his lap.

He jumped up with a violent execration, scattering sweet peas left, right, and center. Constance stared at him aghast, her fingers pressed to her lips. Laughter suddenly bubbled in her eyes, inappropriate but helpless laughter.

"What the *hell*!" He dashed at the water. "What the *hell* was that?"

"I'm so sorry," she said through the bubbling laughter. "But you provoked me to such an extent that I couldn't help it. Here, let me." She approached with her handkerchief and dabbed ineffectually at his shoulder. A flower was caught in his hair, another one behind his ear. Solicitously she reached up to dislodge them. He slapped her hand away.

"I'm so sorry," she said again. "But you were already very wet anyway. In fact," she added with her head on one side, "I think the floral touch is something of an improvement. I'll get a towel." She moved to the door but he caught her arm, swinging her back towards him.

"Oh, no, you don't. Not until I've wrung your neck. You *vixen*, Constance." Laughter still mingled with anger glittered now in his eyes and was matched with hers. His hands encircled her neck, the fingers pushing up her chin. "*Shrew*," he said.

"I think at this point in the play you're supposed to say, 'Come on and kiss me, Kate,' " she murmured.

"Will you ever stop putting words into my mouth?"

"I doubt it."

"Then, 'Come, kiss me, Kate, we will be married o' Sunday.' "

"Oh, nicely capped," she whispered. "Very nice, Mr. Ensor."

"Be quiet!" His mouth enforced the command. The passionate force of his kiss had little of the lover about it. He held her head in a vise; the pressure of his lips on hers was so fierce it was as if he would brand her with the imprint of his mouth. Constance couldn't resist even had she wanted to, and indeed matched force for force, as if the kiss was some kind of exorcism that finally blunted the blade of their mutual anger.

"I told you everything would work out," Chastity said from the doorway, surveying the couple, who seemed to be locked in some elemental struggle.

Constance drew away from Max and looked over his shoulder at her sisters. She touched her swollen lips with her fingertips and caught her breath. "You're not supposed to creep up on people."

"Well, we got worried when the shouting stopped," Prudence said, coming fully into the room with Chastity. "So we thought we'd better make sure you weren't both bleeding on the floor. Whatever happened to Max? He's growing sweet peas."

Max ran his hands through his hair, dislodging a bloom. Water dripped from his hair. "I trust Constance is the only virago in the family." He shrugged out of his driving coat and went to the door. "Jenkins?"

"Right here, sir." Jenkins stepped instantly out of the shadows beneath the staircase.

"Take this and see what you can do with it, please. And bring me a towel."

Jenkins took the coat, holding it at arm's length. "May I suggest your morning coat also, Mr. Ensor. A warm iron will have it good as new. And perhaps I could offer one of Lord Duncan's shirts."

"Just take care of these two." Max handed him his black coat. "I don't imagine the ladies will object to my shirtsleeves."

"Not in the least," Chastity said, ignoring the ironical note to his statement.

"Are you sure you wouldn't like a dry shirt?" Constance asked.

"Quite sure, thank you. Your solicitude overwhelms me. Bring me a large whisky, will you, Jenkins?"

"Very good, sir." Jenkins bore his sodden burden towards the kitchen.

"So you've patched things up," Prudence said, surveying the flower-littered carpet.

"Far from it," Max replied. "Matters couldn't be further from patched."

"Oh," Chastity said in surprise. "We rather thought, seeing you—"

"Never jump to conclusions," Max said. "Your sister and I still have a great deal to discuss . . . a small matter of reparations, for instance."

All eyes turned to Constance who was now standing with her back to the room, seemingly oblivious of her companions, gazing out at the dripping trees.

"Reparations, Con?" Prudence queried.

"Max and I do perhaps have things to discuss," Constance said without turning back to the room.

"Then we'll leave you to it." Chastity tapped Prudence's arm imperatively. "I think we're once again surplus to requirements, Prue."

"Oh . . . yes . . . yes, I suppose we are." Prudence followed her sister somewhat reluctantly to the door just as Jenkins entered with a tray and a large towel draped over one arm.

"I took the liberty of bringing you a glass of sherry, Miss Con, since you don't care for whisky." He set the tray on a console table and handed Max the towel. He cast an impassive glance around the room, his gaze coming to rest on the flower-strewn wet carpet. "Should I clear this up, Miss Con?"

"Not just for the minute, Jenkins. The carpet's seen worse."

Jenkins offered a half bow in acknowledgment and left the drawing room. In the hall he encountered Prudence and Chastity, who were hovering a few feet from the door. He coughed pointedly before making his stately progress to the kitchen regions.

"He's right, we shouldn't listen," Prudence said. "Con will tell us everything later."

"I read somewhere about a trick with a glass," Chastity said rather wistfully. "If you put it upside down against an adjoining wall you can hear what's going on on the other side."

"No," Prudence declared. "We're going upstairs to the parlor." She took her sister's arm and bore her off.

In the drawing room there was silence while Max rubbed his hair dry with the towel and blotted as much water as he could from his trousers. He rolled his sleeves up to his elbows, combed his now unruly hair with his fingers, and then filled a glass from the whisky decanter.

"Would you like sherry, Constance?"

"Yes, please." She turned finally from the window and drew in a quick breath.

"What is it?" The question was sharp.

She shook her head. "It's nothing . . . just that when you look like that . . . all disordered and casual and careless . . ." She stopped. She wanted to say, *as you look when you've been making love*, but now didn't seem quite the moment to invoke such an image.

He waited, eyebrows raised, but she shook her head

again. She wasn't going to tell him she found him irresistible, that he turned her knees to butter, and her loins to molten lava. He handed her a glass of sherry and she took it with a murmur of thanks.

The doorbell rang and they both paused, listening, both assuming it would be Lord Duncan. Jenkins's step crossed the hall, there was a soft murmur of voices, feet moving to the stairs. Constance breathed again. Her father would not be a welcome intrusion at this point.

"So, how are you going to put this right, Constance?" He gave the broadsheet at his feet a disdainful nudge with the toe of his shoe.

"If it's untrue, why don't you write a denial? We'll publish it in the next edition."

"No, I'm not going to dignify the accusation with a denial. I intend to ignore it. You will retract it."

Constance set down her sherry glass. She folded her arms and surveyed him. "I am willing to apologize to you for the personal nature of the attack, but I will not retract the statement that you intended to spy on us. I was not mistaken. I heard what I heard."

"Those meetings are public. Anyone, supporter or opponent, can gain entrance."

"But not anyone can listen to the private deliberations of the leaders of the Union. That was what you intended doing, and you intended to prepare the government for any action we decided to take."

Max sighed. "Maybe I did. But I never pretended to you that I was a supporter of your cause. Quite the opposite. I said I was willing to listen to your point of view, that was all. You had absolutely no excuse to go off the deep end like that." He held up a hand as her mouth opened in protest. "No, just hear me out. I did not lie to you about any of my feelings. I did not use you, or trick you, or pretend to feel something for you that I did . . . *do* . . . not. Is that clear?"

Constance still stood with her arms folded, frowning at him. "What did . . . *do* . . . you feel for me?" she asked slowly.

He tossed back the contents of his glass before speaking. Then he said, sounding more exasperated than anything, "Let me put it this way. I was perfectly serious about the statement when I capped your Shakespearean quote a few minutes ago."

"You mean *The Taming of the Shrew*?"

"Precisely."

"*Come, kiss me, Kate,*" she murmured, then her eyes opened wide as she recalled how the quote had finished.

"Married?" she demanded in utter bewilderment. "You want me to marry you?"

A look almost of pain crossed his face. "God knows why. I must have done something unspeakable in a past life to be condemned to such a fate in this one."

Constance did not take the declaration amiss in the least. Her heart seemed to be turning somersaults. "I won't stop putting words into your mouth," she said, wondering at the absurdity of such a response at such a moment.

"I don't doubt it. However, I have discovered a full-proof way of silencing you." A smile lingered now in the depths of his eyes, tugged at the corners of his mouth. "So, Miss Duncan, will you marry me?"

"I wonder what *I* did in a past life," she mused, tapping her mouth with her fingertips.

"Is that my answer?"

She nodded. There was no other response possible.

They were made for each other, on the battlefield or in the bedroom. She loved him, even when she was cursing at him for an arrogant, opinionated louse. And how perverse was that? But she knew it was the same for Max. That edge they shared was what made them perfect partners. She could never consider marrying anyone else. No one else could come close to Max. The younger Constance would have lived in loving harmony with Douglas, she knew that. But she also knew that the person who had been forged by his death and her mother's would not have suited the gentle Douglas at all. What strange twists fate took. Constance had known without articulating it to herself for weeks now that she could never be happy with anyone but Max. She hadn't believed it could happen, because the one issue on which they could not agree was totally divisive. There was no room for compromise.

She said with some difficulty, feeling as if she was killing a fledgling that had not felt its wings, "What about your career? I can't compromise my work with the suffragists."

"Can't or won't?" He watched her closely over his shoulder as he took his glass to the decanter on the console table.

"Both," she said simply. "You can't marry me, Max. It'll ruin you."

He had thought that himself once. Now it seemed merely something that had to be worked around. He filled his glass and turned back to her. "We'll just have to find a way to accommodate the driving force of your existence and the driving force of mine. In fact at this juncture marriage will repair what damage you've managed to do to my reputation in the pages of that paper of yours. It seems like a very elegant solution to me."

Puzzled, she frowned at him. "I don't understand how...Oh, yes I do." She laughed, shaking her head. "Of all the devious tricks, Max. Is that the only reason you want to marry me?"

"Absolutely," he said blithely. "I make it a habit to use you, if you recall, to manipulate you for my own ends."

The laughter died in her eyes. "I'm willing to bury that if you are."

He set down his glass again and opened his arms. "Come here, you."

She crossed the carpet and reached her own arms up to encircle his neck. Her head fell back, exposing the column of her throat as she looked into his eyes. She read there love, desire, hungry need, and she felt the surge of all three flowing swiftly in her blood.

"I love you," he said, holding her waist between his hands. "And I will stand by you always. Even when I don't agree with you in private I will support you in public. You will never have cause to doubt my loyalty to you...my wife. That is a promise I make to you now, every bit as binding and solemn as the promises I will make at the altar."

"I love you," Constance said. "And I will support you in public. You will always know what I am doing or am about to do if it will have an impact on your career. That is the promise I make to you now, as binding and solemn as the promises I will make at the altar."

He kissed her then, still holding her lightly, his lips tender this time, gently exploring the corners of her mouth, the tip of her nose, the edge of her chin in a playful caress. He kissed the fast-beating pulse in her throat, and Constance pressed herself against him, feeling light as air, thistledown in the wind, as if some massive burden had been lifted.

"So," he said softly, palming the curve of her cheek, "we have dealt with that little matter once and for all."

"Once and for all. And once the engagement is made public—Max Ensor to wed an outspoken suffragist—no one would dare give credence to that article."

"I'll get Henry to send the notice of the engagement to the *Times* for tomorrow's edition," he said. "The sooner it's public, the sooner this will die down." Then he frowned. "Of course, I must talk to your father first."

"Oh, there's no need for that. I'll tell him myself when he comes in," Constance said airily. "He already told me he'd find you a perfectly acceptable son-in-law, so he won't make any objections."

"You've had this conversation?"

"No, it wasn't a conversation," Constance corrected. "It was one of Father's little declarations that follow his laments. He makes them at frequent intervals in the hopes that one of us will make it to the altar."

Max decided not to pursue that line of discourse. "Be that as it may, I should talk to Lord Duncan."

"You're not marrying into a conventional family, Max."

He scratched his head and yielded the issue. "I suppose I knew that." He bent and picked up the discarded copy of *The Mayfair Lady*. "I imagine you'll be continuing with this." He sounded resigned.

"I must. It's our only means of support."

"What?" He stared at her. "I don't find that amusing."

"No," she agreed. "Neither do we. But it's the plain

truth nevertheless. And now you're going to be one of us, I suppose we should let you into all our shady secrets."

Dear God! Max thought. *Now he was going to be one of them.* Somehow her calmly matter-of-fact statement brought it home to him with vivid reality. He was marrying Constance, but she came in a trio. Take one, take all, when it came to the Duncan sisters. He would never have a minute's peace again.

Constance read his thoughts with remarkable accuracy, but then, they were fairly transparent. "It's not as bad as you think," she said, laying a comforting hand on his arm. "We're really quite harmless."

"You are not in the least harmless," he stated with some vehemence.

Constance laughed. "Come upstairs with me now. We have to tell Chas and Prue and then we'll try to put you in the picture about our finances. You ought to know I come with no fortune, merely a load of debt. But it won't concern you in the least. The three of us are working it off nicely now and I'm quite self-supporting." She took his hand and led him to the door. "Come and be welcomed to the family."

Max went willy-nilly, still trying to comprehend what she had said about being self-supporting. A man took a wife, he supported her. That was the way it was. The way it *had* to be. *Didn't it?* He decided not to pursue that line of discourse either for the moment.

As they entered the hall, voices came from beyond the curve of the staircase. Prudence, Chastity, and Amelia came into view, talking intently as they descended. Prudence saw Max and Constance first. Her step faltered as she wondered whether to bundle Amelia back upstairs before she encountered Max, but Amelia took the decision out of her hands. She came down to the hall.

"Constance, I was talking with your sisters," she said with a fair assumption of ease. "Good afternoon, Mr. Ensor."

Max was wondering what on earth his sister's governess was doing paying an afternoon call in Manchester Square when she was supposed to be in charge of his niece.

"Miss Westcott," he said politely, managing just a hint of question in the greeting.

"Not Miss Westcott," Constance said, wishing that this revelation could have come at a more suitable moment. There'd been all too many revelations thus far today. "This is Mrs. Henry Franklin, Max."

Max looked at her. He looked at her blandly smiling sisters. He looked at the serious yet determined countenance of Amelia Westcott. "Henry?" he inquired on a note of incredulity. "My secretary, Henry Franklin?"

"Well, yes, as it happens," Constance said, regarding him rather warily. "Secretaries are permitted to marry, I believe."

"It's hardly my business," he said, raising his hands in disclaimer. "My sister, however . . ."

"I have left Lady Graham's employ, Mr. Ensor," Amelia informed him. She was rather pale, but utterly determined.

"I see. Is this recent?"

"As of one hour ago," Prudence said. "Your sister, Max, saw fit to accuse Amelia of neglecting her duties by attending WSPU meetings during her hours of liberty."

"Which were few and far between," Chastity put in.

Amelia broke in softly, "Lady Graham leveled her

accusations when I happened to discover her going through my private correspondence. I felt I had no choice but to resign immediately."

"And how long have you and Mr. Franklin been married?"

"Just over a week, sir."

Constance had persuaded him to employ Henry. He had seen no need for a secretary, but she had said she wanted to do a favor for an acquaintance who wanted to get married and needed a situation so that he could support a wife. No wonder Henry wanted to take off early on Thursdays, Max reflected somewhat dourly. As he recalled that was the governess's afternoon off.

Max looked at the three sisters, who returned his look with a mixture of defiance, bravado, and confidence. He turned a somewhat sardonic gaze on his bride-to-be. "More matchmaking, Constance?"

"It *is* part of our business," she said with a tiny shrug. "I explained that we need to support ourselves."

"Yes," he said faintly. "Yes, so you did." He turned back to Amelia. "Pray accept my congratulations, Mrs. Franklin."

"Thank you, Mr. Ensor." Amelia hesitated, then said, "I hope this won't jeopardize my husband's—"

Max interrupted swiftly. "Hardly, ma'am. Your husband and I deal very well together. I wish you all the best in your future life. If I can do anything to ease matters between you and my sister over your resignation, then please don't hesitate to tell me."

"Well, actually you could," Chastity said before Amelia could refuse an offer that from experience she accepted as merely form kindness. "Letitia is refusing to allow Amelia to fetch her clothes or any of her belongings."

"I'll take care of that," Max responded. "Give me the address, Mrs. Franklin, and I will see that your possessions are delivered there in the morning."

"You are too kind, Mr. Ensor."

He bowed. "It's the least I can do, ma'am. My sister is frequently overhasty when matters don't go her way, but she is quickly brought to reason again."

The Duncan sisters exchanged glances at this nice brotherly apology. Amelia took her farewell and Chastity went to Max and kissed him soundly on both cheeks. "So, have you set the date?"

Max didn't trouble to question how or why Constance's sisters had come to that conclusion. He said merely, "I'm assuming your sister will do that."

"But we have to put you in the picture first," Prudence said. "It's not quite as simple as you might think around here, Max."

He raised his hands again in disclaimer. "Oh, no, Prudence, make no mistake. I am under no illusions. If you think it will do me good, then by all means put me in the picture. But if you think it wouldn't hurt to spare me the details, then I don't insist on full disclosure."

"In for a penny, in for a pound," Constance said, taking his hand once more and leading him to the stairs, following her sisters.

"Love one, love all," he murmured.

"Only up to a point," Constance whispered. She raised her voice. "Prue, we'll talk about this later."

Prudence glanced back. "Of course." She winked and followed Chastity into the parlor.

"We go this way." Constance turned down a side corridor and opened the door to her bedroom. "I think you need to get out of those wet clothes." Her fingers moved over the buttons on his shirt. "Shall I draw you a bath?" She touched her tongue to his nipples, smiling as they hardened beneath the caress. Her hand slid into the waistband of his trousers, slithering flat-palmed over his belly. Her fingers reached down. "A bath now or after?"

For answer he pulled the pins from her hair, untangling the russet cascade with his fingers. He unbuttoned her blouse, his fingers deft despite his haste. He pushed the thin white lawn from her shoulders and unbuttoned her chemise. He took her breasts in his hands and kissed the nipples, as she had done for him. His hands spanned her rib cage, then lifted her bodily and tumbled her onto the bed at her back.

"I—" she began.

"No words." He kissed her into silence. "Words only get us into trouble."

Constance smiled, a lazy languid smile of agreement, as she helped him push aside her skirt and petticoat and drawers. With fingers as deft and as urgent as his she unbuttoned his trousers, helping him to push them down his ankles. She took his penis between her hands, held it between her breasts, took it in her mouth. She inhaled the essence of this man who was to be her husband. She tasted his sea-salt taste. She gloried in her possession of him. Her fingernails raked his buttocks as she drew him deep into her mouth, watched with open eyes his face as he reared above her, his eyes glowing with passion, his wonderful mouth parted on an ecstatic breath.

Then slowly, infinitesimally, he withdrew from her

mouth. He moved down her body, laid his head on her belly, and smiled up at her. "Even stevens, sweetheart. Between the sheets or on the dueling field."

"Oh, yes," she breathed, as his mouth found her core. "Oh, yes."

Chapter 19

"More wedding presents, Con." Chastity staggered into the parlor under a pile of packages, kicking the door shut with her foot. "And Aunt Edith is arriving this evening." She set her burdens down on the floor.

"Dear Aunt Edith," Prudence said with a note of resignation. "Why does she think we need a mother figure for this wedding? She's a sweetheart but she'll only interfere with all the arrangements and then we'll have to rearrange them again."

"You know how she's always tried to take Mother's place," Constance said somewhat absently without raising her head from her writing. "She thinks it's the thing to do. We can live with it."

Prudence laughed. "You're becoming so mellow these days. Has Max told you yet where you're going to honeymoon?"

Constance set down her pen and turned to face the room. "No," she said, not sounding in the least mellow. "I can't get anything out of him. He says it's traditional for the groom to keep the bride in the dark about the honeymoon. I mean, really! Who gives a damn about tradition?"

"Max, clearly," Chastity said, sitting on the floor beside the newly arrived packages and attacking the bindings with a small knife. "But he's only teasing you."

"I am aware of that," Constance said. "And it doesn't make it any easier. How do I know what to pack in my so-called trousseau if I don't know what we're going to be doing? For all I know we could be climbing the Pyramids or rowing a boat down the Amazon."

"That doesn't sound like Max's kind of thing at all," Prudence observed, kneeling beside Chastity to help with the unpacking.

"I'm not sure *what* his kind of thing is," Constance said in some disgust.

"Well, come and help us unpack this stuff. Maybe it's a second set of cutlery."

"I just want to finish this." Constance turned back to the secretaire. "I want it ready for the next edition."

"That'll come out when you're on honeymoon," Chastity said. "You'll miss the fireworks...Oh, no it's not cutlery, it's silver candlesticks." She held them up. "They're lovely. From the Armitages. You can say what you like about Elizabeth, but she has impeccable taste."

Constance set down her pen again. "Let me see. Oh, yes, they are gorgeous." She shook her head slightly. "People are so amazingly generous. I can't help feeling rather guilty. I'm sure I don't deserve any of it."

"It's a wedding, Con. Everyone loves a wedding, particularly this one. Your maiden speech for the WSPU is splashed all over the newspapers, and then in the same breath in the same papers your engagement is announced to a politician who's been excoriated in that dreadful rag *The Mayfair Lady* for spying on the Union. It's the most delicious topic of gossip the town has had in many months."

Constance couldn't help a rueful laugh. "At least the engagement mollified Father. I really thought he was going to have an apoplexy when he discovered about me and the Union."

"Well, since Max can do no wrong in his eyes you're basking in vicarious approval now," Prudence commented.

"Long may it last." Constance took up her pen again. "He's not going to like this, though. I'm actually quite glad I won't be here when it comes out. I know it's cowardly of me, and he won't know I wrote it, but I'm still glad I'll be well away."

"You're really laying into Barclay?" Chastity stood up and came to read over her sister's shoulder. Her eyes widened. "I'm not sure I want to be around either."

"I have no choice," Constance said. "The deeper I dug the more dirt I came up with. The man's in league with the devil. Once this hits the streets, all the national press are going to take it up. I've identified three women he's basically raped, made pregnant, and then abandoned. They'll all get paid to give their stories, which is some consolation for them, and then I've——"

A brisk knock at the door gave her pause. Max entered on the knock. "Good afternoon," he said cheerfully. "Oh, those are lovely." He picked up one of the candlesticks. "Don't we have half a dozen of these already?"

"No," Constance said. "That's cake forks."

"Oh." He came over and kissed the back of her neck.

"So diligent...what are you doing, writing thank you letters?"

Constance hesitated. "Uh...yes," she said.

"*What* are you doing?" he demanded, not fooled for a moment.

"Oh, just something for the next edition of *The Mayfair Lady*," she said vaguely, blotting the paper and managing to leave the blotting paper covering the sheet. "Tell me where we're going, Max."

It was a safe distraction. He shook his head, laughing at her. "Wait and see. This time tomorrow you will know."

"Well, will it involve a boat journey?"

He laughed again.

"A train?...Your motor car?"

"I told you, wait and see. I am really relishing imposing good old-fashioned tradition on you for once, my dear, and I'm not about to give up the pleasure too soon."

"There are times," Constance declared, "when I can't imagine why I'm marrying you."

"Would you like a reminder?" His eyes narrowed.

"I think this is our cue to find something else to do," Chastity said, heading for the door. "When you're finished reminding and remembering we'll be in the drawing room waiting for Aunt Edith."

"Perhaps we should take these with us," Prudence said, swiftly removing the papers from the secretaire. "Wouldn't like the wind to blow them away." She whisked out of the parlor with the incriminating sheets. Max was still something of a tender flower growing in the soil of the Duncan sisters' activities and mustn't be given too many shocks at once.

"So?" Max said thoughtfully. "What should I remind you of first?"

"Better start at the beginning," Constance said, slowly rising to her feet. "I seem to be suffering from total amnesia."

About the Author

Jane Feather is the *New York Times* best-selling, award-winning author of *Kissed by Shadows, To Kiss a Spy, The Widow's Kiss, The Least Likely Bride, The Accidental Bride, The Hostage Bride, A Valentine Wedding, The Emerald Swan*, and many other historical romances. She was born in Cairo, Egypt, and grew up in the New Forest, in the south of England. She began her writing career after she and her family moved to Washington, D.C., in 1981. She now has over ten million copies of her books in print.

And look for the next two tales of the
delightful and vivacious Duncan sisters...

Jane Feather's

The Bride Hunt
Prue's story
March 2004

and

The Wedding Game
Chastity's story
April 2004

Read on for a preview...

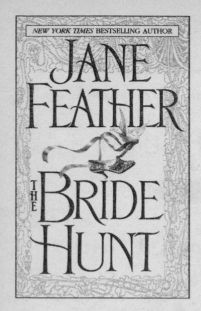

NEW YORK TIMES BESTSELLING AUTHOR

JANE FEATHER

THE BRIDE HUNT

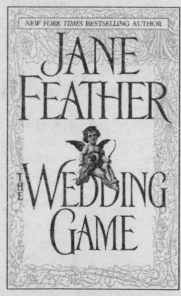

NEW YORK TIMES BESTSELLING AUTHOR

JANE FEATHER

THE WEDDING GAME

The Bride Hunt
On sale March 2004

Prudence sat back. Covent Garden was a strange choice of venue under the circumstances, she thought a little uneasily. The restaurants around the Opera House and the theaters of Drury Lane would be very public, and there were bound to be people she knew. If she was seen with Sir Gideon, there would inevitably be talk, and maybe later, when the trial started, someone would remember seeing them together and start to wonder. It was a little too risky for comfort. It seemed stupid now that she hadn't asked where he was taking her, but at the time the question hadn't occurred to her. When a man asked you for dinner you either accepted or you didn't. You didn't base your response on the kind of entertainment he was offering.

The chauffeur drove slowly and considerately through the puddle-strewn streets. When they turned into the thronged narrow streets around Covent Garden, Prudence drew farther back into the vehicle's interior and wished she'd thought to bring a veil.

The car drew up outside a discreet-looking house with

shuttered windows and a door that opened directly onto the street. The chauffeur helped Prudence out of the car and escorted her to the door. She glanced up at the house. It bore none of the telltale signs of a restaurant. In fact, she thought, it had the air of a private home.

The door opened a minute after the chauffeur had rung the bell. A gentleman in austere evening dress bowed a greeting. "Madam, Sir Gideon is awaiting you in the red room."

Red room? Prudence glanced at the chauffeur as if for enlightenment, but he had already stepped back to the street. She found herself in an elegant hall with a black and white marble floor and elaborately molded ceilings. A flight of stairs with gilded banisters rose from the rear.

"This way, madam." The man preceded her up the stairs and along a wide corridor. Voices, both male and female, came from behind closed doors, together with the chink of china and glass. Prudence was as intrigued as she was puzzled.

Her escort stopped outside a pair of double doors in the middle of the corridor, knocked once, then with an almost theatrical flourish opened both doors wide. "Your guest, Sir Gideon."

Prudence stepped into a large, square room, furnished as a drawing room except for a candlelit dining table set for two in a deep bow window overlooking a garden. It was immediately obvious why it was known as the red room. The curtains were red velvet, the furniture uphol- stered in red damask.

Gideon Malvern was standing beside the fireplace, where a small fire burned. He set down the whisky glass he held and came across the room. "Good evening, Miss Duncan. Let me take your coat."

His evening dress was impeccable, tiny diamond

studs in his white waistcoat. As she removed her head scarf, Prudence had a flash of regret at her own carefully chosen costume. In the interests of making absolutely certain the barrister understood that this meeting was not a social occasion, she had decided to preserve the image of the dowdy spinster she'd created in his chambers that afternoon. In fact, without exaggeration, she looked a fright in a hideous brown dress she'd unearthed from a cedar closet that hadn't been opened in ten years. She had no idea where the dress came from. It certainly wasn't something her mother would ever have worn. She unbuttoned her coat with some reluctance and allowed him to take it from her. He handed it to the man who had ushered her upstairs. The man bowed and withdrew, closing the doors gently behind him.

Gideon surveyed his guest, one eyebrow lifting a fraction. He was trying to imagine how any woman, let alone one as relatively young as this one, could deliberately choose to dress with such abominable lack of taste. One had to assume she had *chosen* the gown she was wearing, just as she had chosen her costume that afternoon. Perhaps, he thought, she was color-blind as well as short-sighted, or whatever problem she had with her eyesight that obliged her to wear those thick horn-rimmed spectacles. She was certainly fashion-blind. His nose twitched. Could that possibly be a whiff of mothballs emanating from the folds of her dreadful evening dress?

"Sherry," he said. "May I offer you a glass before dinner?"

"Thank you," Prudence responded, well aware of his reaction to her appearance. It was exactly what she had intended, but it still left her chagrined. She was far more used to admiring glances than the barrister's look of mingled pity and disdain.

"Please sit down." He gestured to one of the sofas and went to the sideboard, where decanters of sherry and whisky stood. He poured sherry and brought the glass over to her.

"Thank you," she said again, with a prim little smile that she thought would be appropriate to her appearance. "What is this house?"

"A private supper club," he said, taking a seat on the sofa opposite her. "I thought a restaurant might be a little too public." He sipped his whisky.

"It wouldn't do for us to be seen together," she agreed, smoothing down her skirts with a fussy little pat of her hand.

Gideon could only agree wholeheartedly. He wasn't sure his social reputation would survive being seen in public with such a wretchedly drab companion. He watched her covertly for a moment. She wore her hair twisted tightly onto her nape in an old-fashioned bun stuck with wooden pins. But the stuffy style couldn't do much to disguise the lustrous richness of the color. Somewhere between cinnamon and russet, he thought. No, something wasn't quite right. He couldn't put his finger on it, but there was something out of kilter about the Honorable Miss Prudence Duncan. He remembered that moment in his chambers when she'd taken off her glasses as she launched her attack. The image of that woman and the one in front of him somehow didn't gel. And after his late-afternoon's reading he was not about to jump to conclusions about any of the Duncan sisters.

"As I recall, Miss Duncan, you said you took care of the business side of the publication. I assume you're something of a mathematician."

"I wouldn't say that precisely," Prudence stated. "I would describe myself as a bookkeeper."

At that he laughed. "Oh, no, Miss Duncan, I am convinced that you are no more a bookkeeper than your sister is the writer of penny dreadfuls."

Prudence looked startled. "Have you been reading copies of *The Mayfair Lady* since this afternoon?"

"I discovered an unexpected source of back issues," he said dryly. "Curiously enough, under my own roof. My daughter and her governess appear to be avid readers."

"Ah," she said. "Your daughter. Yes."

"That appears to come as no particular surprise to you," he observed.

"*Who's Who*," she said. "We looked you up."

He raised an eyebrow. "So you know more about me than I do about you, Miss Duncan."

Prudence felt herself flush as if he was accusing her of prying. "*Who's Who* is a matter of public record," she stated. "Besides, if we hadn't looked you up we wouldn't have been able to find you."

"Ah," he said. "Sensible research, of course."

"Does your daughter live with you?" She couldn't hide her surprise.

"As it happens," he responded shortly. "She attends North London Collegiate for her formal schooling. Her governess takes care of the wider aspects of her education. It seems that women's suffrage is of particular interest to Miss Winston, hence her familiarity with your publication." He rose to take his glass to the sideboard to refill it after casting a glance towards Prudence's barely touched sherry glass.

This was a man of surprises, Prudence reflected, unable to deny that her interest was piqued. North London Collegiate School for Ladies, founded in 1850 by the redoubtable Frances Buss, one of Prudence's mother's female icons, was the first day school to offer a rigorous education to young women. Miss Buss, like the late Lady Duncan, had been a fervent supporter of women's rights as well as education.

Prudence took a healthy sip of her sherry. "You believe in women's education, then?"

"Of course." He sat down again, regarding her a little quizzically. "I imagine that surprises you."

"After your diatribe this afternoon about how women are not equipped—I believe I have that right—not *equipped* to enter the battleground of lawsuits and suchlike, I find it incredible. I think you advised me and my sisters to confine ourselves to the gossip of our own social circles and keep away from pen and ink." She smiled. "Do I have *that* right, Sir Gideon?" She leaned over to put her now empty glass on the sofa table.

"Yes, you do." He seemed completely untroubled by the apparent contradiction. "The fact that I support the education of women does not deny my assertion that the majority of women are uneducated and ill equipped to deal in my world. More sherry?"

He reached for her glass when she nodded, and went back to the sideboard. "Were that not the case, there would be little need of my support for the cause." He refilled her glass from the decanter and brought it back to her. He stood looking down at her with that same quizzical, appraising air. Prudence was distinctly uneasy. It felt as if he were looking right through her, through the façade she was presenting, to the real Prudence underneath.

"Your daughter . . ." she began, trying to divert his attention.

"My daughter is hardly relevant here," he responded.

"Suffice it to say that under the guidance of Miss Winston she's a passionate supporter of women's suffrage."

"And are you?" The question was quick and sharp. Without thinking, she took off her glasses, as she often did in moments of intensity, rubbing them on her sleeve as she looked up at him.

Gideon took a slow breath. Wonderful eyes. They did not belong to this spinsterly dowd. So, just what game was Miss Duncan playing here? He had every intention of discovering before the evening was done.

"I haven't made up my mind on that issue," he answered finally. "Perhaps you should try to convince me of its merits while you attempt to persuade me to take on your defense." A smile touched the corners of his mouth and his gray eyes were suddenly luminous as they locked with hers.

Prudence hastily returned her glasses to her nose. That gaze was too hot to hold. And there was a note in his voice that made her scalp prickle. Every instinct shrieked a warning, but a warning about what? Rationally, he couldn't possibly be attracted to her, yet his eyes and voice and smile said he was. Was he playing some cat-and-mouse game? Trying to fool her into a false position? She forced herself to concentrate. She had a job to do. She had to persuade him that he would find their case interesting and—

Her mind froze. Was this part of what would make it interesting for him? An elaborate, cruel game of mock seduction? Was there some kind of quid pro quo here to which she was not as yet a party?

Prudence thought of *The Mayfair Lady,* she thought of the mountain of debt that they were only just beginning to topple. She thought of her father, who so far had been protected from the truth, as their mother would have striven to protect him. With those stakes, she could play Gideon Malvern at his own game and enjoy the sport.

She gave her skirts another fussy pat and said with a schoolmistressy hint of severity, "On the subject of our defense: as we see it, Sir Gideon, our weakness lies in the fact that we do not as yet have concrete evidence of Lord Barclay's financial misdoing. However, we know how to find that. For the moment, we have ample evidence to bolster our accusations of his moral failures."

"Let's sit down to dinner," he said. "I'd rather not discuss this on an empty stomach."

Prudence stood up. "I'm impressed by your diligence, Sir Gideon. I'm sure you had a full day in your chambers and in court, and now you're prepared to work over dinner."

"No, Miss Duncan, *you* are going to be doing the work," he observed, moving to the table. "I am going to enjoy my dinner while you try to convince me of the merits of your case." He held out a chair for her.

Prudence closed her lips tightly. This was the man she had met that afternoon. Arrogant, self-possessed, completely in control. And much easier to deal with than the glimpses she'd had of the other side of his character. She sat down and shook out her napkin.

Her host rang a small bell beside his own place setting before sitting down. "The club has a considerable reputation for its kitchen," he said. "I chose the menu carefully. I hope it will meet with your approval."

"Since you've just told me I'm not going to have the opportunity to enjoy it, your solicitude seems somewhat hypocritical," Prudence said. "I would have been content with a boiled egg."

He ignored the comment and she was obliged to admit that he was entitled to do so. She took a roll from the basket he offered while two waiters moved discreetly around them, filling wineglasses and ladling delicate pale green soup into fine white bowls.

"Lettuce and lovage," Gideon said when she inhaled the aroma. "Exquisite, I think you'll find." He broke into a roll and spread butter lavishly. "Tell me something about your sisters. Let's start with Mrs. Ensor."

"Constance."

"Constance," he repeated. "And your younger sister is called . . . ?"

"Chastity."

He sipped his wine and seemed to savor this information. There was a distinct gleam in his gray eyes. "Constance, Prudence, and Chastity. Someone had a sense of humor. I'm guessing it was your mother."

Prudence managed not to laugh. She declared, "We are the perfect exemplars of our names, I should tell you, Sir Gideon."

"Are you, indeed?" He reached to refill her wineglass and once again shot her that quizzical look. "Prudence by name and prudence by nature?" He shook his head. "If they match their names as appropriately as I believe you match yours, Miss Prudence Duncan, I cannot wait to meet your sisters."

Prudence ate her soup. She wasn't going to step into that quicksand. If he was beginning to see through her pretense, she wasn't going to help him out.

"This soup is certainly exquisite," she said with one of her prim smiles.

He nodded. "It's one of my favorite combinations."

She looked at him, curiosity piqued once more despite her intentions to stick with business. "I get the impression you're something of a gourmand, Sir Gideon."

He put down his soup spoon. "We have to eat and drink. I see no reason to do either in a mediocre fashion."

"No," Prudence responded. "My father would agree with you."

"And you too, I suspect." He twirled the stem of his wineglass between his fingers. Her appreciation of the white burgundy in her glass had not gone unnoticed.

Prudence realized that her façade had slipped. She said with a careless shrug, "Actually, in general I'm indifferent to such things. We live very simply, my sisters and I."

"Really," he said, his voice flat as a river plain.

"Really," she said firmly, starting to reach for her glass, then putting her hand back into her lap instead.

The waiters returned, removed soup plates, set down the fish course, and left.

"Plaice," the barrister said, taking up his fish knife and fork. "A seriously underappreciated fish. Simply grilled with a touch of parsley butter, it's more delicate than the freshest Dover sole."

"In your opinion," Prudence murmured, slicing into the slightly browned flesh. The addendum passed unnoticed by her companion, who was savoring his first mouthful. She took her own and was forced to admit that he had a point.

"There is no way to fight Barclay's libel action without you and your sisters divulging your identities."

It was such a stunning change of subject, Prudence was for a moment confused. It was an attack rather than a continuation of their conversation. She blinked, swiftly marshaled her thoughts, and entered the fray. "We can't."

"I cannot put a newspaper on the stand." His voice had lost all trace of conversational intimacy. He pushed aside his plate. "I spent the better part of two hours reading back issues of your broadsheet, Miss Duncan, and I do not believe you and your sisters lack the intelligence to imagine for one minute that you could escape the stand."

Prudence wondered if this was an ambush. Part of the cat-and-mouse game. "We cannot take the witness stand, Sir Gideon. Our anonymity is essential to *The Mayfair Lady*."

"Why?" He took up his wine goblet and regarded her over the lip.

"I do not believe *you* lack the intelligence to answer that question yourself, Sir Gideon. My sisters and I cannot divulge our identities because we propound theories and opinions that, since we're women, would be automatically discounted if our readership knew who was responsible for them. The success of the broadsheet depends upon the mystery of its authorship, and its inside knowledge."

"Ah, yes, inside knowledge," he said. "I can quite understand that no one would speak freely to you if they knew they could be opening themselves to the ironical, if not malicious, pen of *The Mayfair Lady*."

"I would dispute *malicious*," Prudence said, a slight flush warming her cheeks. "*Ironical*, yes, and we don't suffer fools gladly, but I don't consider we're ever spiteful."

"There's a difference between malice and spite," he said.

"It's a little too subtle for me," she responded frostily.

He shrugged, raised his eyebrows, but made no attempt to amend his statement.

Prudence took a minute to recover her composure.

She knew that she and Constance had a tendency to indulge their own sharp and sardonic wit, but it was a private pleasure. Chastity was usually their only audience and even she, the gentler-natured sister, could be roused to blistering irony in the face of social pretension or arrant stupidity, particularly when someone was hurt by it. In the broadsheet they certainly made fun of such failings, but they never named names.

He spoke again while she was still collecting her thoughts. "Miss Duncan, if you cannot defeat this libel, your broadsheet will cease to exist. If, as I understand you to say, your identities are forced into the open, then your broadsheet will also cease to exist." He set down his glass. "So, now, tell me what legal help I can offer you."

So that was it. In his judgment they had no possibility of winning. Never had had. So it *was* cat and mouse. But why? Why this elaborate dinner just to watch her squirm like a butterfly on the end of a pin? Well, whatever the reasons, she was not about to accept his assessment meekly and go on her not-so-merry way.

Once again she took off her glasses and rubbed the lenses with her napkin. "Maybe, Sir Gideon, we're asking the impossible, but I was given to understand that you specialized in impossibilities. We are not prepared to lose *The Mayfair Lady*. It provides us with a necessary livelihood, both the broadsheet and the Go-Between. We would never get clients for that service from among our own social circle if they knew whom they were dealing with. That must be obvious to you."

"The Go-Between . . . that's some kind of matchmaking service that you advertise. I didn't realize you ran it yourselves." He sounded both amused and faintly incredulous.

Prudence said as coldly as before, "Believe it or not,

Sir Gideon, we're doing rather well with it. You'd be surprised at the unlikely matches we've managed to make." She said nothing further as the pair of waiters returned, did what they had to, and left them with veal scallopini on their plates and a very fine claret in their glasses.

Gideon sampled both wine and veal before he said, with a slight shake of his head, "You and your sisters are certainly an enterprising trio."

Prudence, still holding her glasses in her lap, directed her myopic gaze at him. Immediately she remembered that this was a mistake. Whenever she took off her glasses his expression changed unnervingly. She put them back on and now fixed him with a deep frown between her brows and a hard glare behind her lenses. Everything in her expression indicated conviction and the absolute determination to deal with the impossible. "Enterprising or not, we have to win this case. It's as simple as that."

"Simple as that," Gideon said, nodding slowly. "I am to put a sheet of newspaper on the witness stand. Just supposing we set that difficulty aside, there is another one. Would you mind telling me exactly how you propose defending the publication's accusations of fraud and cheating?"

"I told you earlier, Sir Gideon, that we have a fairly good idea where to find the evidence."

He touched a finger to his lips. "Forgive me, Miss Duncan, but I'm not sure that that assertion is sufficient."

"You will have to find it so. I cannot at this point be more specific." She sipped from her wineglass, clasped her hands on the table, and leaned towards him. "We need a barrister of your standing, Sir Gideon. We're offering a case that you should find challenging. My sisters and I are not hapless defendants. We're more than capable of acting vigorously in our defense."

"And are you capable of paying my fee, Miss Duncan?" He regarded her now with unmistakable amusement, his eyebrows lifted a fraction.

Prudence hadn't expected the question, but she didn't hesitate. "No," she said.

He nodded. "As I thought."

Her frown deepened. "How could you have known?"

He shrugged. "It's part of my business sense, Miss Duncan. I'm assuming that your brother-in-law, Max Ensor, is not offering to support you."

Prudence felt the heat again rise to her cheeks. "Constance—we—would never ask him to do so. And he would not expect it. This is our enterprise. Constance is financially independent of her husband."

His eyebrows lifted another notch. "Unusual."

"We are not usual women, Sir Gideon. Which is why we're offering you the case," Prudence declared with sublime indifference to the realities. "If we win—and we *will* win because our cause is just—then we'll happily divide the damages at whatever proportion you dictate. But we cannot broach our anonymity."

"You think you will win because your cause is just?" He laughed, and it was the derisive laugh she detested. "Just what makes you think the justice of your cause guarantees justice in the courts? Don't be naïve, Miss Duncan."

Prudence smiled at him without warmth. "That, Sir Gideon, KC, is precisely why you will take our case. You like to fight, and the best fights are those that are hardest to win. Our backs are against the wall, and if we lose, we lose our livelihood. Our father loses his illusions and we will have failed our mother."

She spread her hands in a gesture of offering. "Can you resist a battle with such stakes?"

He looked at her. "Were you designated spokeswoman because of your persuasive tongue, Prudence, or was there another reason?"

"We divide our duties according to circumstance," she responded tartly, noticing only belatedly that he had used her given name for the first time. "Either of my sisters would have willingly tackled you, but they had other things to do."

"Tackled me?" He laughed, and this time it was with pure enjoyment. "I have to tell you, Prudence, that you'd have done a better job of tackling me without the..." He waved an expressive hand. "Without the playacting... that prim smile and that ghastly dress." He shook his head. "I have to tell you, my dear, that it's simply not convincing. Either you improve your acting skills or you give up the pretense. I know perfectly well that you're a sophisticated woman. I also know that you're educated and that you don't suffer fools gladly. So I would ask that you stop treating me like one."

Prudence sighed. "It was not my intention to do so. I wanted to be certain you took me seriously. I didn't want to come across as some flighty Society flibbertigibbet."

"Oh, believe me, Miss Duncan, that you could never do." The disconcerting smile was in his eyes again, and she hadn't even taken off her glasses.

Prudence took the plunge. She had to at some point and it would at least banish that smile. "Very well," she said. "Will you take the case?"

And be sure to watch for the finale of the
Duncan sisters' escapades in . . .

Jane Feather's

The Wedding Game
Chastity's story
April 2004

Carnival Elation

7 Day Exotic Western Caribbean Itinerary

DAY	PORT	ARRIVE	DEPART
Sun	Galveston		4:00 P.M.
Mon	"Fun Day" at Sea		
Tue	Progreso/Merida	8:00 A.M.	4:00 P.M.
Wed	Cozumel	9:00 A.M.	5:00 P.M.
Thu	Belize	8:00 A.M.	6:00 P.M.
Fri	"Fun Day" at Sea		
Sat	"Fun Day" at Sea		
Sun	Galveston	8:00 A.M.	

TERMS AND CONDITIONS

PAYMENT SCHEDULE:
50% due upon booking
Full and final payment due by July 26, 2004

Acceptable forms of payment are Visa, MasterCard, American Express, Discover and checks. The cardholder must be one of the passengers traveling. A fee of $25 will apply for all returned checks. Check payments must be made payable to **Advantage International, LLC and sent to: Advantage International, LLC, 195 North Harbor Drive, Suite 4206, Chicago, IL 60601**

CHANGE/CANCELLATION:
Notice of change/cancellation must be made in writing to Advantage International, LLC.

Change:
Changes in cabin category may be requested and can result in increased rate and penalties. A name change is permitted 60 days or more prior to departure and will incur a penalty of $50 per name change. Deviation from the group schedule and package is a cancellation.

Cancellation:

181 days or more prior to departure	$250 per person
121 - 180 days or more prior to departure	50% of the package price
120 - 61 days prior to departure	75% of the package price
60 days or less prior to departure	100% of the package price (nonrefundable)

US and Canadian citizens are required to present a valid passport or the original birth certificate and state issued photo ID (drivers license). All other nationalities must contact the consulate of the various ports that are visited for verification of documentation.

We strongly recommend trip cancellation insurance!

For further details call 1-877-ADV-NTGE or visit www.GetCaughtReadingatSea.com

---

For booking form and complete information
go to **www.getcaughtreadingatsea.com** or call **1-877-ADV-NTGE**

Complete coupon and booking form and mail both to:
**Advantage International, LLC,
195 North Harbor Drive, Suite 4206, Chicago, IL 60601**